Praise for Jennifer Weiner

'Compulsive, engaging, well-written and surprisingly moving'
She

'Like Helen Fielding, Weiner balances romantic formula with fresh humour, deft characterizations and literary sensibility'
Guardian

'Immensely readable . . . Weiner's gift lies in her ability to create characters who both amuse us and make us care'
The Washington Post

'This incredibly funny book is so engrossing it should come with the warning: "Do not read on trains" – as you will miss your stop'
Now

'Jennifer Weiner has the knack of getting under her characters' skin . . . an immensely humane book'
Sunday Express

'Jennifer Weiner is a master of the modern-day fairytale . . . her heroines look just like us: self-deprecating, plagued by those few extra pounds – and ready for Prince Charming only once they've embraced their quirks. Weiner's latest effort is no exception'
Marie Claire

'Witty, moving, stupendously well written and deeply perceptive'
Jill Mansell

'Like real life, it's full of surprises – a far cry from your typical predictable girlie reads'
Heat Magazine

Jennifer
Weiner

Best Friends
Forever

POCKET
BOOKS

LONDON • SYDNEY • NEW YORK • TORONTO

First published in the USA by Atria Books, 2009
A division of Simon & Schuster Inc.
First published in Great Britain by Simon & Schuster UK Ltd, 2009
This edition published by Pocket Books, 2010
An imprint of Simon & Schuster UK Ltd
A CBS COMPANY

5 7 9 10 8 6

Simon & Schuster UK Ltd
1st Floor
222 Gray's Inn Road
London
WC1X 8HB

www.simonandschuster.co.uk

Simon & Schuster Australia
Sydney

A CIP catalogue record for this book
is available from the British Library

B Format ISBN 978-1-84983-748-4
A Format ISBN 978-1-84739-024-0

Printed and bound by CPI Group (UK) Ltd, Croydon, CR0 4YY

For Susan Abrams Krevsky—my BFF

"I can't say that I'm sorry for the things that we done
At least for a little while sir me and her we had us some fun"

—FROM "NEBRASKA" BY BRUCE SPRINGSTEEN

PART ONE

Reunion

ONE

*D*an Swansea came awake in the darkness, not knowing for a minute who he was or where. He lifted one hand to his head and groaned when it came away sticky with blood. Slowly (or at least it felt that way), things returned to him. His name. That he was outside in a parking lot, on his back in the gravel, and he was freezing. Also, except for his shoes and socks, he was naked.

He sat up, his stomach roiling as a wave of pain swept through him, and wiped his head again, flicking drops of blood onto the gravel. He'd followed a girl out here. A girl—her name was on the tip of his tongue, but he couldn't quite get it. A high school girl, an old classmate, with flashing white teeth and red soles on her shoes. Come to my car, she'd whispered. It's warm. They'd kissed for a while, with the girl backed against the driver's-side door, her mouth fiery underneath his, their breath steaming in the blackness, until she pushed him away. Take off your clothes, she'd said. I want to see you. It's freezing! he'd protested, but his hands were already working at the buttons of his shirt and the clasp of his belt, because it was cold but she was hot, and he wasn't passing this up. No way. He'd squirmed out of his clothes, kicking his pants off over his shoes, dropping each garment in a pile on the gravel, and when he looked up, naked and shivering in the cold, one hand cupping his cock, she was pointing something at him. His heart stopped—a gun?—but almost *before he'd thought the word, he saw that it wasn't a gun but a cell phone.*

The flash was brilliant, blinding him as she snapped a picture. Hey! *he shouted.* What the fuck?

See how you like it, *she'd snarled.* See how you like it when they're laughing at you.

He'd lunged for her, trying to snatch the phone. What is your problem?

What's my problem? *she'd answered, dancing backward on her red-soled shoes.* You're my problem. You ruined my life!

She dived into the car, slamming the door before he could grab the handle. The engine roared to life. He'd jumped in front of her, thinking she'd stop, but judging from the cuts on his side and the terrible sick throbbing in his head, maybe she hadn't.

He groaned again, pushed himself upright, and peered at the country club, which was empty and locked. Through the darkness, he could see the tennis courts off to one side, the golf course behind the building, the sheds and outbuildings underneath a stand of pine trees a discreet distance from the club proper. Clothes first, *he decided, and stumbled painfully toward the nearest building.* Clothes first . . . and then revenge.

TWO

Looking back, the knock on the door should have scared me. It should at least have come as a surprise. My house— the same one I grew up in—is set at the farthest curve of a cul-de-sac in Pleasant Ridge, Illinois, a Chicago suburb of fourteen thousand souls with quiet streets, neatly kept lawns, and well-regarded public schools. There are rarely pedestrians or passersby on Crescent Drive. Most weeks, the only signs of life after ten p.m. are the flash of headlights on my bedroom wall on the nights that my next-door neighbor Mrs. Bass has her Shakespeare Society meeting. I live alone, and I'm generally asleep by ten-thirty. But even so. When I heard the knock, my heartbeat didn't quicken; my palms did not sweat. At some level underneath conscious thought, a place down in my cells where, the scientists tell us, memories reside, I'd been waiting years for that knock, waiting for the feel of my feet moving across the floor and my hand on the cool brass knob.

I pulled open the door and felt my eyes get big and my breath catch in my chest. There was my old best friend, Valerie Adler, whom I hadn't spoken to since I was seventeen and hadn't seen in person since high school ended, standing underneath the porch light; Valerie with her heart-shaped face and Cupid's-bow lips and lashes heavy and dark as moth's wings. She stood with her hands clasped at her waist, as if in prayer. There was something dark staining the sleeve of her belted trench coat.

For a minute, we stood in the cold, in the cone of light, staring at each other, and the thought that rose to my mind had the warmth of sunshine and the sweet density of honey. *My friend,* I thought as I looked at Val. *My friend has come back to me.*

I opened my mouth—to say what, I wasn't sure—but it was Val who spoke first. "Addie," she said. Her teeth were gleaming, perfect and even; her voice was the same as I remembered from all those years ago, husky, confiding, an I've-got-a-secret kind of voice that she currently deployed to great effect, delivering the weather on the nightly newscasts on Chicago's third-rated TV station. She'd been hired six months ago, to great fanfare and a number of billboards along the interstate announcing her new gig. ("Look who just blew into town!" the billboards read, underneath a picture of Val, all windswept hair and crimson, smiling lips.) "Listen. Something . . . something really bad happened," she said. "Can you help me? Please?"

I kept my mouth shut. Val rocked back on high heels that seemed no thicker than pins, gulping as she raked both hands through her hair, then brought them to waist level and began twisting her belt. Had I known she had that haircut, that buttercup-yellow color, that shoulder-length style, with layers that curled into ringlets in the rain, when I'd given my hairdresser the go-ahead? I made a point of not watching her station, but maybe I'd caught a glimpse of her as I changed channels or the billboards had made an impression, because somehow here I was, in flannel pajamas and thick wool socks, with my ex-best-friend's hair on my head.

"Look at you," she said, her voice low and full of wonder. "Look at you," said Valerie. "You got *thin*."

"Come in, Val," I said. If time was a dimension, and not a straight line, if you could look down through it like you were looking through water and it could ripple and shift, I was already opening the door. This had all already happened, the way it always did; the way it always would.

THREE

I led Valerie into the kitchen, listening to the drumbeat of her heels on the hardwood floor behind me. She wriggled out of her coat and used her fingertips to hang it over the back of a chair, then looked me up and down. "You weren't at the reunion," she said.

"I had a date," I answered.

She raised her eyebrows. I turned away, filling the kettle at the sink, then setting it on the burner and flicking on the gas, unwilling to say more.

My night had not started out well. On the dating website's advice, I'd met the guy, my sixth blind date in as many weeks, at the restaurant ("Do NOT invite a stranger to your house!" the website had scolded. "Always meet in public, always carry a cell phone, car keys, and/or enough money for transportation, and always let a friend know where you are!") I'd gotten the first parts of it right, driving my own car, with my cell phone charged and enough money to cover the bill in my wallet, but I hadn't been able to fulfill the last part, on account of being, at the moment, friendless (friend-free?), so instead, I'd printed out a note in eighteen-point bold type and taped it to my fridge: I WENT TO MEET MATTHEW SHARP ON FRIDAY, NOVEMBER 23. IF ANYTHING HAPPENED TO ME, IT'S PROBABLY HIS FAULT. I'd added my date's telephone number, the name and address of the restaurant, and a photocopy of my insurance card. I'd thought for a minute, then added, P.S.: I WOULD LIKE A MILITARY FUNERAL . . . because, really, who wouldn't? Buglers playing taps equals guaranteed tears.

"Addie?" the man by the hostess stand said. "I'm Matthew Sharp." He was on time, and tall, as promised. This was a refreshing change: the five guys I'd previously met were not, in general, as promised. Matthew Sharp was neatly dressed in a tweed sports coat, a dark-blue button-down shirt, pressed pants, and loafers. His breath, as he leaned close to shake my hand, smelled like cinnamon, and a mustache bristled over his lip. *Okay,* I thought. *I can work with this.* True, the mustache was an unpleasant surprise, and his hairline had receded since he'd posed for his online picture, but who was I to complain?

"Nice to meet you," I said, and slipped my black wool coat off my shoulders.

"Thanks for coming." He looked me up and down, his eyes lingering briefly on my body before flicking back to my face. He didn't look appalled, nor did he appear to be edging toward the door. That was good. I'd dressed in what had become my date uniform: a black skirt that came to precisely the center of my knees (not short enough to be slutty, not long enough to be dowdy), a blouse of dark-red silk, black hose, black boots with low heels, in case he'd been lying about his height or, less likely but still possible, in case I needed to run. "Our table's ready. Would you like a drink at the bar first?"

"No thanks." The website recommended only a single glass of wine. I'd keep my wits about me and not give him any reason to think I had a drinking problem.

The hostess took our coats and handed Matthew a ticket. "After you," he said as I tucked my scarf and hat into my purse and shook out my hair. My calves had finally gotten skinny enough for me to zip my knee-high boots to the very top. I'd gone to my hairdresser that morning, planning on nothing more than a trim, but, buoyed by Paul's repeated use of the word "amazing!" and the way he'd actually gotten teary when he'd seen me, I'd allowed myself to be talked into six hours' and five hundred dollars' worth of cut, color, and chemicals, and left with a layered bob that Paul swore made me look sixteen from certain angles, honey-blond highlights, and conditioner with a French-sounding name, guaranteed to leave my hair frizz-free and shiny for the next four months.

I asked for a glass of Chardonnay, Caesar salad, and broiled sole, sauce on the side. Matthew ordered Cabernet, calamari to start with, then a steak.

"How was your holiday?" he asked.

"It was nice," I told him. "Very quiet. I spent the day with family." This was true. I'd taken the full Thanksgiving dinner—butternut squash soup, roast turkey, chestnut stuffing, sweet potatoes under a blanket of caramelized marshmallow, the obligatory pumpkin pie—to my brother, Jon, at his assisted-living facility on the South Side. We'd eaten sitting on the floor of his small, overheated room, our backs against his single bed, watching *Starship Troopers*, which was his favorite. I'd left by three and been back home by four. There, I'd made myself a cup of tea, added a slug of whiskey, and left a dish of chopped turkey and gravy out for the little black cat that frequents my back door. I'd spent the evening sitting in the living room, one hand on my belly, looking at the shifting grays and lavenders of the sky, until the moon came up.

"How about you?"

Matthew told me he'd had dinner with his parents, his sister, and her husband and kids. He'd cooked the turkey, rubbing butter and sage under the skin and slow-roasting it over a bed of onions. He said he loved to cook, and I said I did, too. I told him about my adventures in guacamole. He told me about the shows he watched on the Food Network and the hot new restaurant in Chicago he was dying to try.

The waiter slid our plates in front of us. Matthew tucked a tentacle into his mouth. "How's your salad?" he asked. A bit of fried breading was stuck in his mustache, and I had to fight an impulse to reach over and brush it away.

"It's great." It was overdressed, each leaf oily and dripping, but that was okay—a bad salad was a perfectly reasonable trade-off for, finally, thank you God, a decent date. I chewed a mouthful into lettuce-flavored paste, and we smiled at each other.

"Tell me about your job," Matthew said.

"I paint illustrations for greeting cards."

He actually seemed interested, which was a pleasant change from my previous dates. How had I gotten into that line of work? (Through my mother, who'd written copy for the same line of cards and had submitted one of my watercolors without telling me years ago.) Did I work from home? (Yes, I'd set up a studio in the dining room, with my easel by the window, where the light was best.) He asked about the hours, about my training, about whether I got lonely working all by myself, instead of in an office. I could have given him a soliloquy, an essay, could have sung an entire libretto on the topic of loneliness, but instead I'd just said, "I don't mind being by myself."

He told me about his job running a chain of self-storage warehouses in Illinois and Wisconsin. I asked about where he'd grown up and where he lived now, lifting a soggy crouton to my lips, then setting it back on the plate, untasted, waiting for the moment that had come during each of my other dates, when he'd start trashing his ex-wife. Of the five men I'd gone out with, four of them had proclaimed that their exes were crazy (one had upped his diagnosis to "certifiably insane"). The fifth was a widower. His wife had been a saint, which sounded even worse than crazy when you were the potential follow-up act.

He was nice, I thought, as Matthew expounded enthusiastically on the hike he'd taken just last weekend with the Sierra

Club. "I go out with them a few times a month," he volunteered. "Maybe you could join me?"

My first thought was that he was kidding—me, hike? Where, from the Cinnabon to the Ben & Jerry's? I still had to remind myself that I was now more or less normal-sized, and that Matthew had never seen me in my previous incarnation. "Sure. That sounds like fun." A hike in the woods. I let myself picture it: a red fleece pullover, a hat that matched my mittens, the thermos full of hot coffee that I'd bring. We'd sit side by side on a blanket in the leaves and watch as a stream burbled by.

Our entrees arrived. My fish was mealy at the edges, translucent in the center, tasting as dead as if it had never been alive. I managed two bites while Matthew told the story of how his colleague, a middle-aged middle manager named Fred, had suddenly taken it into his head to get his eyes done. "He came into the office and he looked— Well, one of the secretaries said he looked like a squirrel with something jammed up his . . ." He paused. A dimple flashed in his cheek. "Like a startled squirrel. Like his eyes were trying to jump right out of his head, and I heard that when his granddaughter saw him for the first time she started crying." He chuckled. I smiled. *Love me*, I thought, and sipped my wine and trailed one manicured thumbnail delicately along the edge of my blouse, beneath which my breasts swelled, clad in itchy lace, helped along by heavy-duty underwire.

Matthew leaned across the table, with his tie dangling dangerously close to the puddle of beef blood on his plate. "You're a really unique person," he said.

I smiled, shoving my doubts about the syntax of "really unique" to the back of my mind.

"I feel so comfortable with you. Like I could tell you anything," he continued.

I kept smiling as he gazed at me. He had nice eyes behind

the glasses. Kind eyes. Maybe I could talk him into shaving the mustache. I could see us together, on a slope covered with fallen leaves, my mittened hands around a cup, the coffee-scented steam curling in the air. *Please stop talking,* I begged him telepathically. *Every time you open your mouth, you are jeopardizing our beautiful life together.*

Sadly, Matthew didn't get the message. "Six months ago," he began, with his eyes locked on mine, "I woke up with a bright light shining through my bedroom windows. I looked up and saw an enormous green disc hovering above my home."

"Ha!" I laughed. "Ha ha ha!" I laughed until I realized he wasn't laughing . . . which meant that he wasn't kidding.

"I have reason to believe," he continued, and then paused, lips parted beneath his mustache, "that I was abducted by aliens that night." He was so close that I could feel his beefy breath on my face. "That I was *probed.*"

"Dessert?" asked the waiter, sliding menus in front of us.

I managed to shake my head no. I couldn't speak. I was single, true. I was desperate, also true. I had slept with only one man at the shamefully advanced age of thirty-three. I'd never heard the words "I love you" from someone who wasn't a parent. But still, I was not going home with a guy who claimed to have been violated by space aliens. A girl has her limits.

When the check came, Matthew slipped a credit card into the leather folder and looked at me ruefully. "I guess I shouldn't talk about the alien abduction on first dates."

I adjusted my neckline. "Probably not. I usually wait until the third date to talk about my tail."

"You have a tail?" Now he was the one who couldn't tell if I was kidding.

"A small one."

"You're funny," he'd said. There was a kind of drowning desperation in his voice, a tone I knew well. *Help me,* he was saying.

Throw me a rope, give me a smile, let me know it's okay. I got to my feet while Matthew searched his pockets for a few bucks to tip the coat-check girl, then followed him through the restaurant, waiting as he held the door. "You seem like a good person," Matthew said in the parking lot, reaching for my hand. I moved sideways, just enough so that I was out of his reach. *You're wrong,* I thought. *I'm not.*

Outside, the predinner mist had thickened into a chilly fog. Streetlamps glowed beneath golden halos of light. Matthew ran his hand through his hair. Even in the cold, he was sweating. I could see droplets glimmering through his mustache. "Can I call you?" he asked.

"Sure." Of course, I wouldn't answer, but that didn't seem smart to mention. "You've still got my number, right?"

"Still got it." He smiled, pathetically grateful, and leaned forward. It took me a second to realize that he intended to kiss me, and another second to realize that I was going to let him. His mustache brushed my upper lip and cheek. I felt absolutely nothing. He could have pressed a bottle brush or a Brillo pad against my face; I could have been kissing his lapel or the hood of my Honda.

By the time I got home, he'd already left a message, long, meandering, and apologetic. He was sorry if he'd freaked me out. He thought that I was great. He was looking forward to seeing me again, maybe on Sunday? There was a movie that had gotten a good write-up in the *Trib,* or a hot-air-balloon festival. We could drive out, pack a picnic . . . his voice trailed off hopefully. "Well," he said. "I'll talk to you soon." He recited his telephone number. I thumbed number three for "erase," kicked off my boots, twisted my bright new hair into a plastic clip, then sat on the edge of my bed with my face in my hands and allowed myself one brief, dry, spinsterish sob. *Don't get your hopes up.* The website didn't say that. It was what I told myself as inoculation against the fantasy, persistent as a weed, that one of these guys could be the one: that I could fall in love, get married, have babies, be normal. *Don't get your hopes up.* I'd chant it like a mantra on my drive to the Starbucks or the Applebee's or, with Date Number Four, the bowling alley, where, it turned out, the fellow had had the ingenious notion of combining a first date with a fifth birthday party for his son (his ex-wife had not been glad to meet me; neither, for that matter, had his five-year-old). *Don't get your hopes up* . . . but every time I did, and every time I got my stupid heart crushed.

"Oh, well," I said out loud. *Funny.* That had been nice to hear. But it was so unfair! To get a date on the Internet, a woman had to be many things, starting with *thin* and proceeding relentlessly to *attractive* and *pleasant* and *a good listener* and *good company.* Young, of course. Still fertile, still cute, with a good body and a decent job and a supportive (but not intrusive) family. The men didn't even have to be sane.

I looked at the clock, the antique pink-and-green enameled clock on chubby gold legs that I'd bought myself for my birthday. It was just after ten. The reunion would be in full swing. Merry Armbruster had called me that afternoon, making one more last-ditch plea for my attendance. "You look fantastic now! And I'm sure everyone's forgotten about . . . well, you know. We've all grown up. There's other things people will want to talk about."

Thanks but no thanks. I swallowed my vitamins with a glass of water and chased them with a shot of wheatgrass (I'd been drinking the stuff for two years, and it still tasted exactly like pureed lawnmower clippings). I hung up my date uniform, replaced the lace bra with a comfortable cotton one, pulled on my favorite flannel pajamas and a pair of socks, then sat back down on the edge of my bed, suddenly exhausted. Just lately, I'd been thinking a lot about the girl I'd been, and what she would have made of the woman I'd become. I imagined the little me standing at the doorway of my bedroom, once my parents', in a neat cotton sweater and a pleated skirt, dark-brown hair caught in a ponytail and tied with a ribbon that matched her kneesocks. At first she'd be pleased by the rich color of the paint on the bedroom walls, the oil painting that I'd done of a lighthouse casting its beam of gold over the water, hanging above the window. She would like the enameled vase on the bedside table, the crisp linen bedskirt and the trellised iron headboard, but then she'd realize that it was my parents' bedroom. *Still here?* she'd think, and I'd have to explain how I hadn't meant to stay, how I'd tried to go away to college, how I'd planned to live in a big city, to have boyfriends and an interesting job, to make friends and take trips and have an apartment that I'd decorate with souvenirs and statues and photographs I'd have taken on my travels around the world, how I'd planned on all of that, but somehow . . .

I rolled onto my side. My blood buzzed, and my thoughts were darting wildly, jumping from my date who'd looked so promising, to the website where I'd found him, to my exboyfriend Vijay, who'd been "ex" for four months, and who'd never exactly been a boyfriend. You couldn't call him a boyfriend, I guess, if we'd been out together in public only once, but I'd loved him with an intensity that I thought—or at least hoped—was reserved for the first man you'd wanted who'd broken your heart.

I squeezed my eyes shut and let my hand rest briefly on my belly, holding my breath as I pressed. Still there. The lump—it was actually more of a stiffness than a lump—was still there, between the ridge of my pubic bone and my belly button. I pushed at it, prodding with my fingertips. It didn't hurt, exactly, but it didn't feel normal, either. I didn't know how long it had been there—for years I'd been so fat I could have been gestating twins and probably not noticed—but I was sure that I knew what it was. Hadn't I watched my own mother die of the same thing? First her breasts, then her liver, then her lungs and her bones, then everything, everywhere.

I'd scheduled an appointment with my doctor for next week, the soonest they could take me. The receptionist's chirpy voice had cooled noticeably at my name, and I knew why. Last year I'd called in a panic after my fingers had found an odd-shaped protuberance on the side of my abdomen . . . which had turned out to be my hipbone. Well, how was I supposed to know? I thought, as sullen as I'd been when the nurse delivered the verdict, then stepped outside the exam room to laugh her stupid highlighted head off. You spend ten years in the neighborhood of three hundred and fifty pounds and see how well you recognize your own bones when you find them again.

Besides, this time it felt different. Big, strangely stiff, growing each day. I knew what it was, and deep down, I'd known that it was coming. Bad luck always found me. I was a bad-luck kind of girl. The cancer had eaten my mother and found her sweet, and now it had returned to Crescent Drive, hoping I'd taste the same. And maybe that wouldn't be so awful, I thought, as I lay on my fancy bedding, staring up at the crown moldings I'd hotglued in place with my birthday clock ticking quietly beside me. I could just give up on everything, starting with Internet dating. No more freaks and geeks and unexpected mustaches; no more regular-looking guys who turned out to be from the Twilight Zone. I could just read, stay in bed eating shortbread cookies and gelato, and wait for the end . . . and with that, I heard the knock at the door, and I went downstairs to find my best friend standing there, just like old times.

FOUR

By the time Jordan Novick, Pleasant Ridge police chief, arrived at the parking lot of the twenty-four-hour drugstore, the woman was almost in tears. "I can't figure out what's wrong," she said, brandishing her key fob and raising her voice as the infant in her arms howled. "It's a brand-new car. You're just supposed to walk up to it with your key fob, you don't even have to press anything, and I keep trying, but the door still won't open."

"Don't worry," he said, giving the woman a fast (and, he told himself, completely professional) once-over. Five-five, one-forty, Caucasian, brown and brown. Sweatpants, ponytail, crusted patch of either vomit or dried applesauce on her shirt, diaper bag on her shoulder, recycled-plastic shopping bag in her hand, panicked look in her eyes and dark circles underneath them. "Why don't you and the little one sit in the cruiser and stay warm?"

She nodded gratefully, babbling thank-yous as he walked her to his car and got her settled in the backseat. He took the woman's key fob, which held no actual keys, just a plastic rectangle, shut his car door, and stood for a moment, surveying the parking lot. The drugstore anchored one end of Pleasant Ridge's two-block downtown, which, Patti used to joke, had been zoned "cute." Next to the parking lot was the town hall, a stately brick building with Doric columns and a marble memorial to the World War II dead out front. Next to that was the organic grocery store, a coffee shop where you could obtain a four-dollar scone or a five-dollar cappuccino, the post office, a bookstore, and a handful of boutiques that sold things like potpourri and pottery. He scratched his stubble, thinking, then waved the key fob next to the driver's-side door of the Prius the lady had indicated. Nothing happened. He scanned the rows of cars and located three other Priuses (Prii? he wondered). The second one had an infant seat in the back, and its locks popped open obligingly when he approached. "Close the books on that one," Jordan said, then looked around to make sure no one had heard.

Back in the cruiser, the woman had pulled up her shirt, and the baby had stopped squealing and started nursing. Jordan caught a glimpse of the woman's bare white belly and the curve of her breast before hastily averting his eyes.

"I'm so sorry," she said, sounding wretched. "We ran out of Tylenol, and my husband's out of town, and I didn't know what else to do."

"It's fine," Jordan said. "I believe I've solved the mystery." He explained, without looking at her, that she'd been aiming her key fob at the wrong car.

The woman slumped back against the seat and pounded at her forehead with the heel of her free hand. "You must think I'm the biggest idiot in the world."

"No, ma'am," he said, and meant it. The biggest idiot in the world is the guy—the *detective*—whose wife is having an affair with her dentist and who fails to notice the new lingerie, or the gym membership, or that she's suddenly walking around with a mouthful of blinding-white teeth. "These things happen."

He waited until she'd burped the baby (its name was Spencer, and Jordan wasn't sure if that made it a boy or a girl), then walked her back to her car. "Drive safe," he said as she strapped

Spencer into the seat, fastened her own seat belt, and gave Jordan a weary wave.

He shoved his hands into the pockets of his parka and considered the night sky. *Something is coming,* he thought . . . but he couldn't say why he was thinking it, or what he imagined was approaching. Snow, probably—snow was usually coming toward the end of November in Chicago . . . but maybe something else was on its way, something better. Jordan took a deep breath, then climbed into his cruiser to head back to the station and type out a report on the Case of the Locked Prius, by far the biggest event of his shift. Something was coming, and he'd just have to hope that he was ready when it came.

FIVE

Valerie Adler's family moved into the green-and-tan ranch house across the street in June of 1983, when I was nine years old. They arrived on a Saturday morning. My brother and mother and I were sitting at the kitchen table as the moving van roared around the corner. Attracted by the noise, we went to the living room to look. I could hear the grumble of a lawnmower from the house next door (Mr. Bass would be pushing it, wearing a sleeveless undershirt and leather sandals that exposed his thick yellow toenails, while his wife watched from their screened-in porch, reading a paperback and pointing out the spots he'd missed).

"New neighbors," Jon called to my father, who was at his station at the stove, making his famous pancakes.

"Really?" My mother put her hands on Jon's shoulders, standing on her tiptoes to peek over his head. She watched the truck for a minute, then went back to the kitchen. That morning she was dressed in her blue cotton bathrobe, with her hair in a thick braid over one shoulder. Her breasts swung above the belt that barely made it around her midsection, and her broad feet pushed at the seams of her slippers.

This was the year I had begun to understand that most mothers weren't like my mother, that my family was different from other families in Pleasant Ridge. Some of my classmates' moms were skinny and some of them were plump, but none of the plump ones were near the size of my mom, who had to work hard every time she got up from a chair or out of our station wagon, who had to stand through my parent-teacher conferences because she couldn't fit behind the desks.

"Wow, look at her," I'd heard Lauren Felsey whisper to Kara Tait when my mom had come to school on Career Day. I'd felt furious at Lauren, but furious at my mother, too, for failing to be a normal mom, in jeans or khakis, with a neat haircut and a brisk manner. My mom was big, and soft, and dreamy, and until then I'd always thought she was beautiful. She had pale skin and rosy cheeks, like a painted doll, round blue eyes and light-brown hair that fell to the small of her back. At night, I loved to lie on her bed and watch her brush her hair, as light and fluffy as the stuff you'd pull out of milkweed pods. She had a beautiful voice, and even though she moved slowly, she was graceful and light on her feet, as if she were being moved by invisible gusts of wind. When I was in nursery school, I'd drawn pictures of her with a body made of clouds, outlined in blue crayon, big and puffy and insubstantial as air. I'd drawn myself on the ground, a squat flesh-colored stump with a scribble of brown loops for hair, holding on to her shoelace as a string, keeping her tethered to the world.

My parents had met in summer camp when they were seventeen. My mom had been in charge of the chorus and of writing the end-of-summer musical at Camp Wa-Na-Kee-Tah, and my father, tanned and broad-shouldered, had taught archery at the boys' camp across the lake. They'd never told me how they'd met. Sometimes I'd imagined that it had been in the water: that my mom had been swimming across the lake one bright summer afternoon with the shaft of a misfired arrow in her hand, and my father had swum out to meet her.

They'd both gone off to college, and then my dad had gone to

Vietnam, and they'd met again at a camp reunion the summer they were both twenty-five. My dad was doing odd jobs—he'd driven school buses for a while, and washed dishes in a restaurant. My mom was working at Marshall Field's, writing copy for the newspaper ads for hats and suits and dresses, and singing in community theater productions at night. She lived in an apartment downtown, with two roommates. "I walked right up to her and said, 'How's the prettiest girl in bunk eight?'" was how my father told it. "Oh, Ron," my mom would say, and swat at him with her hand or a dishtowel, but you could tell the story pleased her. They'd gotten married eight months after the reunion. My mother's roommates had been her bridesmaids.

My parents moved to Pleasant Ridge, and had a baby boy, my brother, Jon, and then me, eighteen months later. Fourteen Crescent Drive was a tranquil house, with no raised voices, not even a slammed door. As I got older, I learned that this was because of my father, of what had happened to him during the four months he never talked about, the months he'd spent in the war. He was as handsome as he'd been in the camp photographs I'd seen, but pale and thoughtful, twitchy and ill at ease unless he had a hammer or a screwdriver or some kind of tool in his hand. My father would flinch if the refrigerator door shut too fast or if one of us cracked open a can of soda unexpectedly. Once when we were sitting at the table, a car on Crescent Drive had backfired, the sound like a gunshot in the still summer air, and my father had jerked in his chair, as startled as if he'd been slapped. I remember how my mother had led him into the living room, how she'd wrapped her arms around him, murmuring things I couldn't hear, smoothing his hair from his forehead. "Mom?" I'd whispered, edging into the room.

"Addie, bring your dad a glass of water," she'd said without letting go of him or looking at me. I'd gone running to the kitchen, and by the time I came back they were sitting on the couch. Beads of sweat stood on my father's forehead, but he managed a smile for me, and the hand that took the glass trembled only slightly.

"Sorry, Pal," he said. "I just took a bad turn there."

When I was grown myself, I figured out that the war had been his bad turn. My father had been a good student in college, with law school or an MBA in his future, but whatever he'd done or seen overseas had ended that somehow. He couldn't manage a nine-to-five job, couldn't stand being inside all day, couldn't handle the pressures of deadlines or answering to a boss or dealing with the public. He worked as a handyman, doing small repairs, painting and shingling and plowing driveways in the winter. Every few months, I'd help him put up flyers in the grocery store and the post office—*Honey Do!* they would say. *I will do the things your honey don't!* I would decorate them with a drawing of my father on a ladder, painting a house one year, up changing a chandelier's lightbulbs the next, and he swore that the illustrated flyers got double the number of calls the plain ones had.

My mother worked full-time, first writing newspaper ads, and then copy for Happy Hearts greeting cards, contributing rhyming couplets for birthday and anniversary and get-well-soon and condolence cards. As the 1980s progressed, she wrote cards for Hanukkah and Kwanzaa and Secretary's Day. Eventually she worked exclusively on the Modern Moments line, which featured, for example, cards you could send to someone upon the occasion of entering rehab (*"I'm glad to know / You're taking this important step / Getting the help you need / For yourself and everyone who loves you"*).

Our house was a split-level ranch, brick on the bottom and pale yellow paint on top, with three bedrooms on the top floor (two of them tiny and one just small) and a kitchen and dining/living room downstairs, and a basement underneath that. The basement was my favorite part of the house. One side was a playroom—there was a piece of red-and-blue carpet left over from Jon's bedroom covering the concrete, a wooden toy chest with chipped green paint. On the other side of the basement was my father's workshop. He'd put a bright braided wool rug on the floor, an old black leather couch against one wall, and an ancient television set on a coffee table in front of it. His tools—the awls and hammers, the levels and chisels and saws—hung in neat rows on a pegboard, and he had a long work-table set on top of sawhorses next to a miter saw. There were plastic bins of fabric scraps, yarn, beads, tubes of paint, and coils of wire along the edge of the table, along with a record player, in a pebbly plastic carrying case with a bright orange handle, so my dad could listen to his comedy albums: Bill Cosby, George Carlin, Richard Pryor, Steve Martin, Bob Newhart, and Monty Python, while he built puppets, intricate marionettes with articulated joints and hinged jaws and painted faces.

Jon and I were the recipients of the bulk of his handiwork. My brother had a complete set of Viking puppets (they rowed a carved wooden boat), and a dozen wooden soldiers in miniature red felt coats, and a Superman that actually seemed to fly, suspended from fishing line above his bed. I had Flora, Fauna, and Merriweather, plus Aurora herself, from *Sleeping Beauty*, and a pair of puppets that looked like my parents (the mother's hair was fluff that I'd gotten from pulling apart and combing cotton balls, and the father wore a miniature cardigan, just like Mr. Rogers). For my birthday, my father was already working on a miniature me, with hair made from golden-brown thread, and a tiny copy of *Anne of Green Gables* glued to its hands. In addition to making puppets for Jon and me, my father made them for my mother's nieces and nephews, and dozens more that he'd pack into cardboard boxes and take to shelters in Chicago every December. "You could sell them," I'd suggested once, and he'd thought about it, then shaken his head. "They're not fancy enough for people to pay for," he'd told me. Maybe they weren't fancy, but I thought they were wonderful.

While my mother wrote on the sunporch, my father would straighten up around the house—"policing the area," he called it. He'd change the station wagon's oil, fix a leaky faucet or a squeaky hinge. He'd clean out the refrigerator, scrubbing the shelves, spraying them with Windex and wiping them down with paper towels before putting them all back. He would sweep and mop the garage floor, sift through our closets to pile up the clothes we'd outgrown, and pick up groceries twice a week. In the afternoons he'd return to the basement. The gooseneck lamp he'd picked up from someone's curb on trash day would be angled so that it shone a bright circle of light on whatever he was working on—cutting out a puppet-sized coat or a dress, or painting a pair of shoes on a puppet's wooden feet. One of his albums would be playing, and sometimes there'd be an open can of beer on the table. "Hey, Pal," he'd say, handing me the broom so that I could sweep wood shavings into a fragrant pile before he headed upstairs to join the family.

In the summer, Jon spent his afternoons at the swimming pool. In the winter, he'd go ice-skating in Kresse Park, dropping his backpack in the closet and dashing out of the house minutes after he'd entered it, with his skates laced together and slung over his shoulder. Jon played soccer in the fall and T-ball and, later, baseball in the spring. I wasn't on any teams—the combination of being shy and uncoordinated had proved fatal deterrents early on. My ankles wobbled when I skated, and when I swam, I stayed in the shallow end, where my feet could touch the bottom, one hand hovering by the pool's ledge, ready to grab on for support. Most afternoons I'd stay in my dad's workshop, sitting on the couch doing my homework, then sketching and painting while my father sawed and sanded and laughed along with Monty Python. "That, sir," we'd say together, "is an ex-parrot!" There was a half-sized refrigerator down where he kept his beer and grape soda for me and sometimes a candy bar that we'd share. On top of the fridge was a plug-in kettle where he'd heat water for instant coffee or hot chocolate in the winter.

I knew, from the other families on Crescent Drive and the kids at school, that nobody else's father stayed home while their mother worked. Most of the dads took the 7:44 train into Chicago. My school bus would roll past them every morning, lined up on the platform, wearing suits, carrying briefcases, reading newspapers folded into thirds. The truth was, I liked having my father around; I was never happier than when I was down in the basement, snug on the couch, working on long division or fractions or spelling words, and he'd call me by a private name, Pal. I loved that name. At school, I was nobody's pal. Even though I'd known most of my classmates since nursery school, it felt like they'd made a complex set of secret alliances when I wasn't looking; like every girl was paired off and spoken for by a best friend, and I was on my own, unless one of the teachers took pity and let me eat my lunch at my desk or work on my paintings during recess. Later, I would realize that my early exposure to all of that comedy hadn't helped. Word-for-word recitations of Bill Cosby's trip to the dentist or George Carlin's routine about there being no blue food were not the way to attract other little girls.

Jon and I watched as a faded red VW Bug pulled up behind the moving van. The woman who got out of the driver's seat was tall and tanned, with an ankle-length Indian-print skirt wrapped low around her hips, and blond hair piled on top of her head. She wore movie-star sunglasses, huge and opaque, leather thong sandals, and a stack of turquoise-and-silver bracelets piled on one wrist.

"Hippies," said my father. He'd tucked the pancake-batter

bowl under his arm and come to the window to see. He was freshly shaved. His hair was neatly combed back from his high white forehead. My guess was that he'd slept on the couch in the basement last night. *He has bad dreams,* my mother told me when I asked. Jon had another theory: he said that my father slept in the basement because they didn't love each other anymore. *Mom's a cow,* he'd said, and I'd punched him on the arm as hard as I could, then started crying. He'd stared at me for a minute, then hugged me roughly around my shoulders with his un-punched arm. *Don't cry,* he'd said. *It's not your fault.* Which was not the same as telling me that it wasn't true.

"Hippies on Crescent Drive?" my mother called from the kitchen. Jon pursed his lips in a soundless whistle as the woman with the bracelets stretched her arms over her head, exposing a sliver of midriff. Then the passenger's-side door of the Bug opened and a girl about my age got out. She wore droopy cutoff denim shorts and a dingy white T-shirt. There were ratty white high-top sneakers on her feet (*boy's* sneakers, I thought, and felt myself blushing on the girl's behalf). She was tall and gangly, with knobby elbows and narrow wrists.

"They've got a little girl, Pal," my father reported.

"Isn't that nice!" called my mom. "Addie, maybe you can go over and say hello."

I shook my head. There were people—my brother was one of them—for whom talking to strangers came easily. Then there were people like me, who had to plan out what they'd say in advance and rehearse the words in their heads, and still wound up dry-mouthed and stammering, or blurting out lengthy passages of Bill Cosby, when the moment arrived.

"Come on," my mother cajoled. "We can bake them cookies!"

The cookies were tempting, but not tempting enough. I shook my head again. My mom came back to the living room. She took my hand in hers and squeezed. I could smell her: Ivory

soap and vanilla mixed with hair spray and her perfume that
came in a white bottle with flowers painted on the sides and was
called Anaïs Anaïs. "Addie," she said, bending down to look at
me. "Imagine if you were that girl. You just moved to a new town,
you don't know a soul . . . wouldn't you like it if someone came
over to welcome you to the neighborhood?"

I didn't answer. I wasn't sure about this new girl, who seemed
utterly at ease, in a way I never was, like she had no idea that her
clothes and shoes and hair were all wrong. Jon peered out the
window again. "She's looking at us," he said. I held my breath,
watching, as the girl stood in the street with her hands in her
pockets, checking out our house. There was a hopscotch grid
chalked on our driveway, next to my bike, with a banana seat and
purple-and-silver streamers hanging from the handlebars, which
added up to the equivalent of a billboard stuck in our yard: *Nine-
year-old girl here!*

The girl squinted toward the window, and it seemed for a
minute that she was looking right at me. Then she crossed the
street, walking decisively across our lawn. We heard a knock, and
I turned to my mother. "Answer it!" I whispered.

She shook her head, bemused. "Adelaide, you can answer the
door by yourself."

I shook my head, wondering if I had time to dash back to the
kitchen and gobble a fast half pancake. Jon sighed, then got to
his feet. "Come on," he said. He took my hand, not unkindly,
marched me to the door, and pulled it open. The girl was standing there. "Hello," she said. Her voice was husky and low, a mem-
orable voice. "I'm Valerie Violet Adler. Who are you?"

"I'm Jon, and this is Addie. It's nice to meet you." My brother
gave me a pat on the back that was almost a shove and left me
there. For a minute, the girl and I just looked at each other. She
had freckles, big splotchy ones dotting her cheeks, and buck
teeth that were jagged along the bottom. Around one of her an-

kles was fastened a loop of colorful beads on blue thread, an item it had never occurred to me to want, a thing I was now certain I couldn't live another day without.

"We just moved here from California," she told me, pushing the hair that had escaped from the ponytail behind one ear.

"Hi," I said. My own voice was so soft I could barely hear it.

"I like your bike," said the girl.

"Do you want to ride it?" *Oh, no,* I thought as the tips of my ears got hot. That was wrong. I should have asked if she had a bike, should have said, *Maybe we can go for a ride together . . .*

The girl shook her head. "Mine's in there." She cocked her thumb toward the van. "Maybe we can go for a ride later. You can show me around."

I looked at the new girl, ready to offer her the most valuable thing I had, the secret that probably nobody else would tell her. "The lady who used to live in your house died there."

The other girl's eyes widened. "Really? She died in the house?"

"Uh-huh. It was the middle of the night, and the ambulance came and woke everyone up." I didn't tell her how Mr. DiMeo had walked outside alongside the body, holding his wife's hand, weeping, and how a week later he'd moved into the Presbyterian Home, where he'd eventually died. I'd save that for later.

"Huh," said Valerie. "That was my grandmother."

"Really?" I stared, wondering why I'd never seen her before.

The girl ran her tongue along the jagged ridges of her front teeth. "Do you know which room it happened in?"

"The big bedroom, probably," I said. I was already plotting when I'd ask her if she'd be my bosom friend, and whether "bosom" was a word I was prepared to say out loud. "Don't worry. Your parents will probably sleep there."

"My mom," she said. "It's just me and my mom. My parents are divorced."

"Oh." I didn't know anyone whose parents were divorced. It seemed both tragic and glamorous. Mostly tragic, I decided, thinking about my father singing in the basement, using his pocketknife to cut a Snickers bar in two pieces and offering me half.

"That's why we moved. My dad's a stuntman, so he had to stay in California. That's where the movies are."

"Oh," I said again. "Wow."

We stood there for a minute, Valerie on the threshold, all freckles and scabs and tangled hair, me with my hand on the doorknob, my starched skirt rustling around my knees. I can remember the dirt-edged Band-Aid on her elbow, the smell of syrup and bacon, the polleny, green-grass haze in the humid air. I can remember, even then, the feeling of my life balanced on top of a triangle—a fulcrum, it was called; my father had told me that—getting ready to tilt one way or the other.

Across the street, the beautiful woman raised her hand. Her silver bracelets clinked as they slid down her arm. I lifted my arm to wave back as Valerie looked unhappily over her shoulder. "Hey," she said, "can I come in? She probably wants to start unpacking." She yawned enormously. "We drove . . ." She paused, yawning again. ". . . all night." She flipped her ponytail over her shoulder. "Actually, not quite all night. We stopped at a rest stop. We camped out in the car. Did you ever do that?"

I shook my head. When my family went on car trips, we set out armed with an AAA TripTik and reservations at Days Inns along the way. My mother would pack picnic lunches: turkey sandwiches, hard-boiled eggs, carrot sticks, and a thermos full of milk.

"You can camp outside," Valerie said. "In your backyard. I'll show you how to make a tent. All you need is an old sheet." I nodded. I could picture it: a crisp white sheet forming a perfect triangle, Valerie and I, our faces lit by flashlights, side by side beneath it. Valerie lifted her head and sniffed. "Are you having breakfast?"

"Are you hungry?" I asked.

Her stomach growled before she could say anything. I swung the door open wide and made a little bow, a sweeping gesture with my arm, something I'd probably seen on TV. "Come in," I said, and she did.

SIX

In the kitchen, the kettle whistled. I turned the flame down and studied my old friend. Underneath her coat she wore a tight red dress that clung to her chest and hips and dipped low in the back. There was a belt of wide gold links around her waist and, on her feet, high-heeled pumps with pointed toes. Diamonds winked at her earlobes and on her right hand, and she carried a capacious handbag made of soft red leather over one shoulder. "Are you alone?" she asked.

No, I've got a bunch of Chippendale dancers back in the bedroom! Wearing nothing but baby oil and teeny little togas! "Yes, Valerie. I'm alone. What do you want?" I asked in a not entirely friendly tone of voice.

"I can't believe you're still here," she said, surveying the kitchen, which was much improved since she'd been there last. I'd taken up the linoleum and put in glazed terra-cotta tiles. I'd ripped out the mirrored backsplash, a living shrine to the 1970s, and banished the harvest-gold Formica and avocado-green appliances, replacing them with softer, richer shades: cream and butter and rich rusty red on the walls. A farmhouse sink with a gorgeously curved, ruinously expensive faucet sat beneath the window that looked out at the backyard. There was a round oak table, crisp cream-colored curtains framing the new windows, cabinets that I'd painted myself . . . but the liquor, that collection of dusty bottles of Chivas and Ronrico rum, some of them given to me as gifts and some dating from my parents' marriage, was still in the same place, in the cabinet over the refrigerator.

Val stood on her tiptoes and extracted a bottle of vodka. She rummaged in the freezer and came up with a handful of ice. "Drink?" she asked. I shook my head. She dumped the ice and a slug of vodka into a juice glass and gulped. Then she hoisted herself onto the counter next to the sink—her old familiar perch, the place I'd seen her a hundred, maybe a thousand times, with her long legs swinging, dirty white socks on her feet, and usually a scrape or a Band-Aid or two decorating each knee. "Where are Ron and Nancy?" I could hear the strain in her voice as she tried for her old familiar tone, that life's-a-lark buoyancy with which she'd formerly addressed, or discussed, my parents (how amused she'd been to learn that they had the exact same names as our president and first lady!).

I lifted the kettle from the stove. "They died."

"Both of them?"

"Yes."

Sadness flickered across Valerie's face. Her lips fluttered; her carefully tended eyebrows drew together. It was the same expression she probably used to convey her sorrow when telling the people of the Chicago metro area that there were thunderstorms on the way, and just in time to spoil the holiday weekend. "I'm sorry," she said. "I thought I'd heard something, but my mom moved away. When was this?"

"A while back." I pulled two mugs off the shelf, found spoons and tea bags and sugar. "Would you like some tea, or are we sticking with the hard stuff tonight?" Val shook her head. I put one of the mugs back and filled the other for myself as she rubbed her hands against her thighs, then wrapped her arms around herself.

"And Jon?" She hopped off the counter and circled the room,

stopping to check out a painting of a Granny Smith apple in a copper bowl. "Did you do this?"

I nodded. "Pretty," Val said, and wandered over to the refrigerator, where she read the note I'd taped there. "Military funeral?" she asked. "Did you join the army?"

"Valerie," I said. "We haven't spoken in years, and now you show up in the middle of the night, looking like you've seen a ghost, with blood on your coat . . ."

She cringed inside her red dress. "I can explain," she said. Instead of throaty, her voice sounded hoarse. "I'll tell you everything, but you have to promise to help me." *I'm not promising you anything*, I started to say. I'd gotten as far as opening my mouth when Val said, "It's about Dan Swansea."

My skin prickled with goose bumps. My mouth felt dry as salt. "What about him?"

"He was at the reunion."

I shrugged. No surprise there. Dan Swansea had been a star football player and the best-looking boy in our class. He'd also been a troublemaker, a snapper of bra straps, an instigator of food fights and Senior Skip Day, a creative and habitual cheater, the kind of guy who'd stuff the occasional nerd in a locker just to break up the boredom of the school week. For most of high school, he'd also been the object of my extremely secret crush. By senior year, he'd turned into something else altogether.

"He was there," she said, and shook her head. "I didn't think . . ."

"Why not?" My voice was flat. Dan Swansea and his friends had been barred from graduation, but I assumed that nobody back then had thought to keep them away from future reunions. As it was, they'd turned their ostensible punishment into a joke. Half the class, in solidarity with the boys, had also skipped the ceremony, and afterward I'd heard that Dan and his pals had made the rounds of all the choicest post-graduation bashes, the ones on the west side of town, where the parents had brought in kegs and paid for disc jockeys. They'd gone to the parties, wearing board shorts and PRHS T-shirts, playing water polo in backyard swimming pools, hoisting bikinied girls onto their shoulders for chicken fights. I'd collected my diploma to scattered boos from the audience and spent the afternoon helping my dad scrub the spray-painted words FAT WHORE off our driveway, while Dan and his friends were out drinking and dancing and probably fucking Val's fellow cheerleaders in the backseats of cars their fathers had bought for them.

"You know what? No." I pushed back my chair and got to my feet. "I think you should leave."

As if on cue, the big blue eyes that were more vivid than I'd remembered (colored contacts?) welled up. Valerie blinked, and tears coursed down her cheeks, cutting grooves in her makeup. And there were her freckles, underneath the foundation and the powder. Evidence of a simpler time. "Please." She stretched one fine-boned hand toward me. "Please help me."

"What if I don't want to?" I'd meant it to come out cool and removed. Instead, I just sounded petulant, like a three-year-old telling her parents that she wasn't ready to get off the merry-go-round.

"Addie, *please.*" More tears dripped down her cheeks. "Don't be so hard."

"Oh, please," I muttered . . . and that was as far as I got. *You broke my heart* were the words that had risen to my mouth, but I couldn't say them. That was what you said to a boyfriend, a lover, not your best friend. She'd laugh. And I'd had enough of being laughed at. I'd worked hard to get to a place where it didn't happen anymore, where I didn't move through life like a walking target, where it was just me and my paints and brushes and my big empty bed every night. "You weren't a good friend," I said instead.

"I know," she whispered. "I wasn't. You're right. But Addie ..." She looked at me, brushing tears from her cheeks, widening her eyes and aiming the full force of her beauty and vulnerability at me like a floodlight or a tractor beam, a thing you couldn't ignore and couldn't resist. "I'm in trouble. *Please.*"

I didn't say anything, but when I sat back down at the kitchen table, Valerie's face lit up. "You'll help me?"

"Tell me what happened."

She lifted herself back onto the counter. "It's a long story."

"How about the abridged version?" I let her see me glance at the clock above the stove. "I have to work tomorrow." This was true. There was no point telling Valerie that I worked at home, so it wasn't as if I had to punch a clock at nine in the morning. Painting greeting cards wasn't saving lives, although I liked to tell myself that I was making people's lives better in some tiny, transient way, bringing beauty and joy for less than three dollars a pop. My current project was a painting of a bouquet of flowers, yellow daffodils with one brilliant orangey-red tulip popping up from the center. *You're the best of the bunch,* the card would say inside.

Valerie wiped delicately beneath each eye with a fingertip sheathed in the dishtowel she'd grabbed.

"Dan Swansea," I prompted.

She drew a watery, wavering breath. "Well. You knew about the reunion, right?"

"I knew." For the past nine months, a steady stream of postcards in school colors had invaded my mailbox, addressed to Adelaide Downs '92, inviting me to dinner and dancing at the Lakeview Country Club, the same place that had hosted the class's senior prom, which, needless to say, I hadn't attended. *Bring pictures!* the postcards had urged. *Send news!* I'd pitched them all, not even bothering with the recycling bin, not wanting those red-and-cream rectangles hanging around where I could see them.

"Dan was there . . ." She started rubbing at her dress again.

"And?" My voice was calm.

"AndIthinkImayhavekilledhim."

I sat up straight in my chair. "What?"

She gave a shuddering sigh. "Killed him. I think maybe I killed him. Maybe. I'm not sure."

My mouth fell open. "You killed Dan Swansea?"

"Well, somebody should have!" Val hopped off the counter and started pacing, eyes blazing, high heels banging against the floor.

"Valerie . . ." I got to my feet, meaning to grab her by her shoulders, but she pushed past me. *Valerie.*

She turned and stared as if just remembering I was there. I took her hand and tugged her down into one of the chairs at the kitchen table. There was the sugar bowl, my teacup and spoon, her glass and the bottle of vodka, everything just as it had been, everything the same. I willed myself to be still, praying for my voice to be calm. If I wasn't panicking, she wouldn't panic, and she'd give me the whole story, a story that would make sense and have a beginning and an end and would not involve a corpse. "Tell me what happened. Start at the beginning, okay?" Another breath. "Start with Dan."

She looked down at her lap. "I saw him at the bar," she said. "Him and his friends." I waited. Valerie pressed her hands together. "I was just going to ignore him, but he walked right up to me, and it was okay at first. He said he'd seen me on TV, and how nice it was that someone from our class had gotten famous." She allowed herself to preen briefly at the word "famous." I didn't have the heart to tell her that reading the weather on the nightly news did not exactly make her a movie star. The truth was, anyway, she was right—if you considered the combined resumes of the 296 surviving members of our class, Valerie was the most famous ... unless you were inclined to count Gordon Perrault, who'd blown out his back raking leaves, developed an unfortunate addiction to fentanyl patches, and was currently serving five to seven for robbing a drugstore while wearing a Burger King mask.

"I was just having a good time, talking to people, and I had a few drinks, and things were winding down when I heard him at the bar. He was with Chip Mason and Kevin Oliphant, remember them?"

I nodded, vaguely recalling two hulking boys in football jerseys.

"And Kevin said something to Dan like, 'Hey, Valerie's here. You going back for seconds?' And Dan laughed. He *laughed.*"

I didn't answer. Of course he'd laughed. Laughing was what guys like Dan did.

"They didn't know I heard him," Val said. Her voice was climbing higher and higher. "So I went back to the bar, and I started flirting with him. You know. Touching his arm, asking lots of questions, acting like I was into him. I told him to meet me outside ... that I'd give him a ride. I waited for him, and he came outside, and we were fooling around and then ..." She gulped. "I made him take his clothes off."

I gaped at her. "Why?"

"Because it's humiliating," she said, as if this were obvious. "And it's cold out. *Major* shrinkage. I took a picture with my cell phone ..."

"As you do," I murmured.

Val ignored me. "I got in the car and I was going to drive away, you know, just leave him there, let him see how he likes being the one everyone's laughing at, and I turned the car on, and he was grabbing at the mirror, and I stepped on the gas, and I think he must have jumped in front of me and maybe I was in drive instead of reverse and then . . . he was . . ." She buried her face in her hands.

"You hit him?"

She bent her head, shoulders shaking, saying nothing.

I said it again, only this time not as a question. "You hit him."

"It was an accident," she breathed, and stared at me defiantly. "I think it was kind of the car's fault. I've got this new Jaguar. I didn't know my own power." She pushed her hair behind her ears, first one side, then the other, a gesture I remembered. "He deserved it," Valerie said. "He deserved it for what he did to me."

I couldn't speak. I could only look at her. Valerie twisted her hands in her lap. "I tried not to think about it . . . about what happened. About what . . ." She gathered herself. "What he did to me. And you . . . I'm so sorry, Addie," she whispered. "You were trying to do the right thing. I know that now."

"It doesn't matter," I said. My throat was thick with unshed tears; my eyes were burning. "It was a long time ago."

"But you were my *friend*." Val's voice cracked, and I made myself look away, knowing that if she cried, I'd cry, too, and if I cried, I would remember. I would remember, for example, a cardboard box filled with tangled marionette wires, or my brother's face, blank and bewildered, as the vice principal asked him, impatiently, which boys had thrown his backpack down the stairs, or Halloween night and the cop car parked outside my house, lights flashing, painting the walls red, then blue, red, then blue. I'd remember Mrs. Bass's voice on the telephone, telling me about my father. I'd remember covering my mother's body with a blanket that I'd knitted, telling her to rest.

"So then what happened?" I asked.

"He was by the Dumpster. He was lying there, bleeding. His . . . his . . ." She touched one hand to her temple. "He wasn't moving. I tried to get him to talk to me, but he was, like, passed out, and I was going to call 911, but I knew they'd trace the call and it would be in the papers, and I didn't know what else to do, so I grabbed up all his clothes and put them in the car and I came here." She looked up. "We have to go. You have to come with me. We have to go see if he's . . . if he's . . ."

"Dead?" I supplied. She made a mewling noise and reached past me, grabbing for the vodka bottle.

"Just so I'm clear here," I asked, "you never tried to get back into the country club? You didn't tell anyone?"

Val dumped more vodka into her glass. "I was so freaked out! I had blood on my hands, there was blood on my coat, and you know how I am with blood."

"Which you'd think would be a deterrent against hitting people with your Jaguar," I mused. My telephone—a new one, cordless and sleek—sat in the same spot on the counter where my parents' old rotary phone had been. I picked it up and pointed it at her. "Call the police."

"And say what?" she asked. "Hi, I think I just ran over this guy from high school, could you please go see if he's dead?"

"That sounds about right to me."

"We'll just go look!" she pleaded. "If he's alive, we'll call an ambulance and get him to a hospital! I promise!"

"And if he's not?"

She drained her glass, wiped her cheeks, and raised her chin. "Then I will call the police and turn myself in."

Ha. Valerie Adler was not the call-the-police-and-turn-yourself-in type. Valerie Adler was the steal-a-car-and-drive-across-the-border-to-Mexico type. She was also the type to stash her former best friend as a hostage-slash-accomplice in the passenger seat. She was brave and clever, ruthless and fearless. It was why I'd loved her so much when we'd been girls.

"We should call an ambulance. We shouldn't just be sitting here."

"Right," she said, and grabbed my hand. "Go get dressed. Let's go."

No, the rational part of my brain insisted, even as I walked upstairs to the bedroom that I still thought of as my parents' and pulled on jeans and a sweater and heavy black clogs. *You don't have to do what she tells you!*

I grabbed my purse, my keys, my wallet, watching my hands move as if they belonged to someone else, gathering my coat, my scarf, a hat I'd knitted. And then we were outside. The mist had turned into an icy drizzle, and Val's diamond earrings flashed in the moonlight, and somewhere in the stream of time, the waters were shifting, and all of this had happened already, only I didn't know it yet.

She handed me her keys. "Can you drive?" she asked.

"Better than you, evidently."

"Ha," she said, and followed me to the Jaguar. She got into the passenger's seat. I looked for signs of damage—a dent, a crumpled fender, a blood-washed headlight—but I couldn't see a thing. God bless British engineering. I got behind the wheel, backed carefully down the driveway, and aimed the car toward the highway.

SEVEN

The Adlers moved in during the last week of June, and by July, Valerie and I were inseparable. Every morning, I'd wake up and wave to her through the living room window, and she'd grin at me and wave back from hers. At noon, when Jon and I came home from day camp at the rec center, Valerie would be sitting on our front step, in her cutoff shorts and too-big flip-flops. Sometimes she'd be reading an Encyclopedia Brown book, or bouncing a red rubber ball that she kept in her pocket, but most of the time she'd just be waiting there, calm and patient in the sticky heat. My mom would make us lunch, and if he was home, my dad would join us for sandwiches, potato chips, pickles, and fruit, served with Country Time lemonade that we'd mix up and drink by the pitcher.

After the first week, we got used to setting an extra place at the table, and to making extra sandwiches. I usually ate one or one and a half of the ham and Swiss or peanut butter and jelly, and Jon always ate two, but Valerie could put away three sandwiches by herself, along with multiple helpings of chips, glasses of lemonade, a peach or a plum or sometimes both, and once, an entire quart of blueberries.

While we had lunch, my parents would ask us questions: What had we done that morning? What had we made in crafts?

Who had we played with? Jon, with his mouth full of whole wheat and lunch meat, would rattle off the names of a half-dozen boys, shoveling food into his mouth as fast as he could without my mother objecting. I'd keep quiet, letting Jon talk. There was one girl named Heather who would let me sit with her at snack time, but only if I gave her my graham crackers. When I told my mom about it, she got a sad look on her face and said it would probably be best if I just stayed with the counselors.

After lunch, my mother would return to the screened-in sunporch, taking along a notebook and a pitcher of iced tea. My father would return to the basement or the garage. Jon would dump his dishes in the sink, jump on his bike, and vanish until dinnertime. I'd pack snacks—cherries and pretzels, apples and granola bars—and wait for Valerie to determine our afternoon activity. She was full of ideas, and I was happy to go along with them. *Let's try to skateboard down Summit Drive,* she'd say, and off we'd go, to borrow a skateboard and give it a try. Or, *Let's ride our bikes to the mall and see a movie!* I was terrified of biking on busy roads, but even more terrified of telling Val that and having her find another friend, so I'd follow her, the taste of copper pennies in my mouth as I pedaled, my hands greased with sweat as I gripped the handlebars for the length of the two-mile trip.

Most days, though, we'd end up at the pool. Jon and I had summer passes to the Kresse Rec Center. Once Val's bike was unpacked, we'd ridden there together. While I'd carefully locked my bike to the bike rack, Val had squinted at the sign above the desk that said admission was fifty cents. "I don't have any money," she'd said.

"Oh." My face heated up. This was a complication that hadn't occurred to me. "We could go back home. I've got my allowance . . ."

"Let me think," said Val. She frowned at the sign. "Wait here," she said, then hopped back on her bike. A few minutes later she was back, flushed and sweaty and looking pleased. "Okay," she said. "Here's what we'll do." Her plan was for me to present my card to the bored, magazine-reading, gum-chomping teenage girl at the booth, then spread out my towel at the far edge of the deck, near the chain-link fence, and slip the card through the fence to Valerie, who'd use it to get herself in.

"But isn't that stealing?" I asked.

Val shook her head. "You're really just paying for the lifeguards, and I don't need a lifeguard. I'm a very good swimmer. In California, I swam in the ocean." I was meant to be impressed by this, and I was. I locked my bike to the rack, flashed my card at the girl behind the desk, who barely looked up from her *Cosmopolitan,* and made my way to the edge of the concrete. A minute later, Val was there waiting for me. I rolled my card into a tube, looked around to make sure no one was watching, and passed it through one of the chain-link diamonds. A minute later, Val was walking past the pool, a raggedy towel tucked under her arm, the knot of her bathing suit halter top sticking up from the back of her T-shirt. "See?" she said, spreading her towel out next to mine. "No big deal."

On rainy days we'd stay in the kitchen, making concoctions of peanut butter and coconut flakes and whatever else we could scrounge from the pantry, or we'd go to the basement and take turns doing laps with my old pair of roller skates while listening to Val's favorite (and as far as I could tell, only) record, a 45 of Kenny Rogers's "The Gambler." Sometimes my father would sing along.

One Saturday morning, Val gave her usual knock at our door, then, as had become her habit on the weekends, pushed it open and presented herself at the kitchen table. "Hey, Addie, can you come over? My mom and I are going to paint my room."

I looked at my parents. My father was scrambling eggs. My mother stood at the sink, rinsing juice glasses and humming to herself. "It's fine with me," she said. "Do you girls want some breakfast first?"

Valerie did. Perched on the edge of her seat at the kitchen table, all skinny legs and scabbed elbows, she polished off a plateful of eggs and French toast and bacon, then squirmed impatiently as my mother rejected the first two outfits I tried on, finally okaying an old pair of shorts and a ripped T-shirt previously destined for the rag pile. Val and I ran out the front door, dashed across my lawn, grabbed each other's hands, and sprinted across the street.

After her parents had died, Mrs. Adler had inherited the house on Crescent Drive. Her brother, Val's uncle who lived in Sheboygan, had gotten all of the furniture, and so far, Mrs. Adler hadn't bought anything new. There was a folding table and two metal chairs in the kitchen, a television set that stood on four orange milk crates in the living room, and in front of it, the DiMeos' old couch, a hulking antique made of red velvet and carved dark wood that I guessed the uncle either hadn't wanted or couldn't fit through the door.

When the DiMeos had lived there, the bedroom at the top of the stairs was crowded with a queen-size bed, two side tables, and a squat club chair covered in cabbage-rose print fabric. Now the room was almost empty, and the yellow carpet—pristine in spots where the bed and club chair had stood, sun-faded and stained everywhere else—was covered by a sheet of plastic. No, not a sheet. There were actually multiple sheets of Saran Wrap lining the carpet, and someone—either Valerie or Mrs. Adler—had Scotch-taped them together. Bare light switches jutted out of the walls, and strips of tape lined the edges where the wall met the ceiling and the floor. A third strip of tape split the wall in half. Two aluminum pie tins, one filled with pink paint, the other with green, sat on the Saran Wrap. Val's flimsy wooden dresser and single bed in its metal frame had been pushed into the center of the room. Lying on the bed, propped on one elbow, was Mrs. Adler.

"Good morning, Addie," she said, in her drawling voice. Her running shorts—navy-blue cotton with white piping—were as brief as the ones Daisy Duke wore on *The Dukes of Hazzard* reruns, and she didn't have a bra on underneath her white cotton T-shirt. She smelled like mentholated cigarettes and Breck shampoo, and looked more like a teenager than like a regular mother, barefoot with her hair pulled back in a blue bandanna and a thin gold chain around her neck.

"What does your mother do all day?" I'd asked Val once, when we were at the Kresse Park pool, treading water in the deep end (I stayed close enough to the wall to grab it if I had to). All of the mothers I knew were busy. They complained about it all the time—"I'm frantic," they'd say, or "I'm exhausted!" They drove carpools and led scout meetings and taught Sunday school; they shopped and gardened and cooked and cleaned. Some of them had part-time or full-time jobs in doctors' offices or banks or shops. Then there was poor Mrs. Shea at the corner of Crescent Drive, who had eleven children and spent all of her days doing laundry, or going to the grocery store to pick up her daily five gallons of milk. But Mrs. Adler didn't seem to do anything. She was always home, curled up on the couch watching soap operas, or lying on a towel in the backyard, wearing a white crocheted bikini, listening to the little boom box that she kept plugged in on the porch.

"She gets alimony," Val had told me, explaining that alimony was money her father paid her mother so that her mother could take care of herself and Valerie.

"But what does she do all day?" I'd asked again.

Val had shrugged under the water. "I guess she waits," she said. "She waits for it to be night."

In Val's room, I ducked my head shyly as I said hello. Mrs. Adler made me nervous. It wasn't just that she looked like a teenager. She behaved like one, too. She cursed, and smoked, and sat in the corner of the kitchen having long, tense conversations on the telephone with a boyfriend back in California. She did not believe in balanced meals, and thought that popcorn and Lipton's Cup-a-Soup was a decent dinner, even a decent breakfast in a pinch. Sometimes she'd let Val go days between showers—if she'd been swimming, she said, that was close enough. Val had no official bedtime. She got to watch whatever she wanted on TV, even movies and *Tales from the Crypt* on HBO, whereas Jon and I were always getting herded into the bathroom to wash our hands or upstairs to do our homework, and we didn't even have premium cable. Mrs. Adler, who was always saying *Call me Naomi,* seemed sometimes like an impatient babysitter, waiting for Valerie's real parents to come home and relieve her of her duties so that she could go live her actual life.

That morning she'd been lying on Val's bed with her torso curved around a clamshell that she'd been using for an ashtray. "My daughter"—she indicated Val with a cocked elbow—"wants a pink-and-green room."

"It's pretty," said Val.

"What should I do?" I couldn't wait to kick off my shoes and tie back my hair in a borrowed bandanna, to baptize myself in pink and green paint.

"Grab a roller." Mrs. Adler yawned, then fished a mother-of-pearl lighter and a box of Salem Lights from her pocket.

"Ugh. Ma!" Val coughed. "Remember? Lung cancer?"

Mrs. Adler flicked her fingers at her daughter cheerfully. "We're all gonna go sometime." I watched, entranced, as she extracted a cigarette from the crushed pack, tapped it against the crinkled plastic, lit it, and sucked in the smoke.

"She's disgusting," Val announced. I waited for the reprimand, for the *don't-you-talk-to-your-mother-that-way* that surely would have followed such a remark in my house. It never came. Mrs. Adler gave me a sly, pleased look—*That Valerie! Isn't she something?* She blew twin plumes of smoke out of her nostrils, then tapped the ash on the lip of the clamshell.

I crossed the room, my bare feet sticking to the Saran Wrap, and picked up a roller, aware that Mrs. Adler was watching me and looking amused. "Addie Downs," she said (talking about me like I wasn't even there was one of Mrs. Adler's favorite things). "The good influence."

I bobbed my head affirmatively and dabbed pink paint on the wall. Valerie, meanwhile, was slathering green on the bottom half of her section in speedy strokes, splashing droplets on the plastic, like she couldn't get the wallpaper to disappear quickly enough. I watched her, my forehead scrunched, as the paint pooled and beaded up on top of the wallpaper.

"Um," I said. Mrs. Adler raised her eyebrows. "Aren't you supposed to take the wallpaper off before you paint?"

Mrs. Adler looked at me, then at the wall. "Huh."

Valerie threw her roller onto the Saran-Wrapped floor, leaving a big blotch of mint. "MOM!" she yelled. I tensed, waiting for Mrs. Adler to tell Valerie not to raise her voice, but Mrs. Adler just shrugged.

"Honey, I never said I was an expert," she said, and ground out her cigarette in the clamshell.

"We could ask my dad," I volunteered. "He could help us. He did Jon's room last winter. I think that he rented a steamer from somewhere. You steam the paper first, and then you scrape it off, and then you paint the wall with white stuff. Primer, I think."

"Huh," said Mrs. Adler. "This is starting to sound complicated." Valerie, meanwhile, was staring at the half-painted wall with her chin trembling.

"You STINK," she said without looking at her mother.

"You are the WORST MOTHER EVER. We're doing this all wrong!"

Mrs. Adler uncoiled herself from the bed, planted her feet on the floor, placed her hands on her hips, and leaned backward. Her hair spilled out of the back of the bandanna, brushing the small of her back. "You're right," she said, not sounding especially concerned. "I have screwed this up completely. Then again, I never claimed to be a professional."

"You didn't have to be a professional!" Val yelled. "All you had to do was read a book or something!"

"You're right," Mrs. Adler said again.

"Read an *article*," Val said miserably. "You could've just read an *article*."

"Let me make it up to you," said Mrs. Adler. She put her hand on Val's shoulder.

Val shook it off, rattling her mother's silver bangles. "You can't. This is a disaster. All I wanted was a nice pretty room, with PINK and GREEN, a nice room like Addie has, and you said that I could . . ."

"My dad can help," I offered again, but no one was listening. I recognized that this was a bad situation, but I was still flushed with pleasure: Val wanted a room like I had.

"Disaster," Mrs. Adler agreed. "You're right. I vote we go clamming."

Valerie sniffled. "I don't want to go clamming. I just want to paint my room, and you promised that I could."

"It's one of the last nice weekends of the summer. We can paint your room anytime. But summer won't last forever."

Valerie frowned. "How are we supposed to get to Cape Cod?"

"We can drive."

I inched toward the bedroom door, unsure whether this was a private conversation, but reluctant to leave. Three years ago, my parents and Jon and I had driven to Lake Charlevoix and rented a cabin for a week. The cabin had been cobwebby and had smelled musty, and on the way up I'd shared the backseat with Jon, who'd spent hundreds of miles farting and then categorizing the smell of each of his farts ("This one smells like a McDonald's hamburger . . . ooh, here comes baby food"). I'd pinched my nose shut and kicked his legs, telling him to stay on his side of the seat. Jon had grabbed my seat belt and pulled it until I felt like I couldn't breathe. My father had snapped at us ("That's enough, you two!"), and my mother had tried to distract us with the license-plate game, which was hard to concentrate on when you were trapped in what smelled like a bowel movement on wheels.

"It'll take, like, two days," Val was saying. She'd gotten an atlas from between her mattress and her box spring and spread it open on the floor. "You see? This, right here?" She stabbed the state with her finger. "That's Illinois, and this . . ." She stabbed the map again. "Is Massachusetts. And this . . ." She whacked the page so hard that it rattled. "Is Cape Cod. All the way up here at the top."

Mrs. Adler adjusted her bandanna. "When does school start?" She looked at her daughter. Valerie looked at me. I swallowed.

"September third."

"That's not for another week!" Mrs. Adler said. "We've got plenty of time."

Val pouted. "We need a license."

"We'll use Poppy's."

"And a canoe . . ."

"We can borrow a canoe. Come on, come on, come on!" Mrs. Adler was saying. "It'll be an adventure! Go find your swimsuit!"

"We should call Poppy first."

"And a toothbrush! Pack your toothbrush!"

"Is there gas in the car? Do you have money for gas?"

"Don't be such a worrywart," Mrs. Adler said, and reached down to give Val a push. "Go throw some Tabs in the cooler. Oh, and Addie," she said as she walked out of the room, hips swaying, bangles chiming. "Ask your parents if you can come, too."

I exhaled, giddy with excitement and relief. Val's lips were tight as she bent down, dumped the paint out of the pie tins and into the cans, and tamped the metal lids back in place, but when she straightened, her eyes had their familiar spark. "Do you like clams?"

"I love clams!" I'd never eaten clams, but this didn't seem the time to say so.

"Okay." Val put one finger in the center of her chin. "You'll need a bathing suit and pajamas." She opened up her closet—my quick glimpse revealed that it was surprisingly empty—and pulled out a pink backpack and a sleeping bag that was ripped along one seam. Then she looked down the hallway and brought her lips so close to my ear that I could feel her breath, humid and maple-scented, against my cheek. "If you have any money, bring that, too."

Across the street, my parents had a brief, quiet discussion in the living room before deciding I could go (looking back, I think they were probably so relieved that I'd finally made a friend that they would have let me go to the moon with Valerie Adler). My mother gave me thirty dollars, which I folded carefully into my pocket before I raced off to grab my own backpack, clothes, money from my piggy bank, food from our cupboards ... and then we were in the car, with Mrs. Adler beeping the horn as we sped down Crescent Drive, on our way to the ocean.

I was only nine years old that summer, but I can still remember every detail of that trip: the sticky crosshatched vinyl of the

Bug's bucket seat branding the backs of my thighs, the salt and chemical taste of Tab in the back of my throat. I can remember the wind tangling my hair as we drove along I-90 through Indiana and Ohio, with the windows rolled down, Mrs. Adler's elbow cocked on the windowsill and Val sitting beside her with the atlas open in her lap, tracing our route with her finger.

At five o'clock, Val told her mother it was time to stop for dinner. Mrs. Adler seemed surprised to hear it, but she pulled into a McDonald's, where Val and I feasted on cheeseburgers and French fries while she sipped Diet Dr Pepper and smoked. By midnight we were in New York, between Buffalo and Albany, according to Val. Mrs. Adler pulled into a rest stop and parked the car way down the parking lot, as far away from the other cars and the glare of the lights as possible. I followed Val's example, carrying my backpack into the bathroom, where we used the facilities, washed our faces, brushed our teeth, and pulled on our pajamas. Then Val pulled out her sleeping bag, spread it on top of herself, and curled up in the Bug's backseat. Mrs. Adler got back in the driver's seat, reclining it as far as it would go. From the matter-of-fact way the two of them handled these arrangements, I figured this was something they'd done before.

"Are you okay, Addie?" Val whispered. Her eyes shone in the darkness as she popped her head between the seats to look at me.

"I'm fine," I said, pushing the passenger's seat backward until it was almost flat. I was actually thrilled. This, far and away, was the best adventure I'd ever been on.

"Goodnight to the back!" Mrs. Adler called.

"Goodnight to the front," Val muttered a little grudgingly. I wanted to tell her not to worry: that having a beautiful mother who would take her on trips like this was a hundred times better than a pink-and-green bedroom. I wanted to promise that I would paint her bedroom, and I'd get my father and brother to help; that I would do anything as long as we could be best friends forever.

"Goodnight, Addie," they said, and I said goodnight back. I was sure I'd never be able to sleep—the car was hot, and the seat was narrow, and the parking lot was brighter than any bedroom I'd ever been in. Worse, the half-open windows had allowed the car to fill with whirring, whining bugs. I slapped at a mosquito and shut my eyes . . . and when I opened them, the sun was up and I was stiff and dry-mouthed and in desperate need of a toilet. It was just after six in the morning. Mrs. Adler walked us back to the restrooms, moving with her usual lazy, rolling sashay. When we were scrubbed and brushed and combed and back in the car, she drove to a convenience store off the highway, where she bought doughnuts and milk and coffee and cigarettes. By noon on Sunday, twenty-four hours after we'd left Pleasant Ridge, we were whizzing past a red-and-white painted poster of a beach scene, with an umbrella stuck jauntily in the golden sand, and the words WELCOME TO CAPE COD written in red underneath it.

We spent the afternoon in a town called Eastham, on First Encounter Beach, where a river of salt water flowed through a marsh out to the bay. Mrs. Adler produced a bedsheet from the back of the Bug and snapped it open, bangles clinking as she spread it on the sand. She rubbed baby oil on her arms and legs and the belly her bikini left bare, then borrowed sunscreen from the plump, red-cheeked mother underneath the next umbrella and smeared it on our cheeks and underneath our swimsuit straps on our backs, where we couldn't reach. "Have fun, girls," she said, and stretched out on the sheet for a nap. Valerie showed me how to walk along the sand and lie on my back in the water so that the current could carry us around the bend of the beach out toward the open water. When the sun was high in the sky and other families were digging into their coolers, I shyly offered the bag of sandwiches I'd made back in Illinois. Peanut butter and raspberry jam on soft white bread tasted even more delicious if you ate it with salt-watery fingers and polished it off with warm Tab.

By five o'clock the other mothers were folding their umbrellas, shaking sand from their towels, and calling their kids out of the water. Mrs. Adler pulled on her faded pink tank top and a long white cotton skirt that fell almost to her ankles, and piled her hair into a loose knot on top of her head. She packed us back into the car and drove to a place Val identified as a "clam shack," a single-story gray-shingled square building with a yellow-and-white striped awning and the mouthwatering smell of deep-fried foods hanging over it like a fog. A line of vacationers snaked out the door and down toward the parking lot.

"Who wants lobster?" Mrs. Adler asked. Her nose and cheeks were pink from the sun, her blue eyes and blond hair vivid against them. She took her wallet out of her purse, reached inside, and frowned as she studied what she'd found in there: three crumpled dollar bills and a receipt from the gas we'd bought that morning.

"Oh, jeez," Val muttered, and kicked at the clamshells that made up the parking lot.

"Don't worry. Wait over here." Mrs. Adler tossed her wallet back into her purse and pointed to a bench across from the counter, where a row of sunburned men in baseball caps and shorts with tiny whales embroidered on them were sitting, waiting to pick up their food. Valerie groaned softly but sat, legs jiggling up and down, fingers scratching at a bug bite on her forearm. As I slid onto the bench beside Val, Mrs. Adler smoothed her hair, checked her reflection in the mirror, and joined the line. There were three workers behind the counter, two teenage girls and a teenage boy, all of them in white T-shirts with lobsters on the front. It took twenty minutes for Mrs. Adler to reach the front of the line, but when one of the girls called "Who's next?" Mrs. Adler waved a family in front of her, and waited until the boy was free. When he beckoned her to his register, I couldn't hear what she was saying, but I saw how her lips curved, how she bent close to him so that his nose was almost brushing her cheek.

"I hate when she does this," Val whispered. She'd scratched her arm so hard it was bleeding. I took a napkin from the dispenser on the counter and handed it over.

"Does what?" I wasn't sure what was happening. Mrs. Adler laughed, a high, glittery sound. One finger toyed with her gold necklace. The boy behind the counter said something. Mrs. Adler shook her head.

"She is trying," Valerie said coldly, "to get that boy to give us free lobsters."

My eyes went to the menu posted above the counter. Lobsters were $8.99 a pound. "I have some money," I said, pulling out the twelve dollars that were all that was left of the money my mother had given me (I'd paid at Burger King and for some of the tolls), plus the eight dollars and change I'd collected from my piggy bank. "Maybe we could get two pounds of lobsters?"

She shook her head. "It doesn't work that way. You have to pay for the whole lobster, even the parts you don't eat."

I looked at the lobsters scuttling around the bottom of the big green tank next to the cash registers. Their shells were greenish black; their claws were rubber-banded shut. I couldn't imagine eating one. "Don't worry," I said. "I've got a bunch more sandwiches. They're squished, but they're still okay. We don't need lobster . . ." I looked at the menu. "We could get hot dogs or fried clams . . ." But even as I was saying it, the boy behind the counter was setting two trays loaded with food in front of Mrs. Adler, who was making a show of searching her purse, then her pockets. She turned to Val. "Honey, have you seen my wallet?"

Val shook her head wordlessly. Her face was tight. I sucked in my breath. Mrs. Adler reached across the counter and put her hand on the boy's forearm. Valerie got to her feet. "Get ready."

"Is there a problem here?"

A man from farther down in the line stepped up to the counter. He wore a khaki uniform, pants and a matching shirt, with a dark-brown belt and a patch sewn on his chest. Mrs. Adler turned and gave him a dazzling smile, her hands clasped behind her back, like a shy little girl. "I was just telling this nice young man that I seem to have misplaced my wallet, and I've got two hungry girls here. We came all the way from Chicago. I promised them lobster, and I hate to disappoint them."

Valerie snorted. "Maybe I could call my parents," I whispered as Mrs. Adler kept talking to the man. Val shook her head.

The man in the uniform was laughing at something Valerie's mother had said. "Excuse me. Can we get some service, please?" one of the women in line behind them called. She had a toddler on her hip and another little boy tugging at the hem of her shirt. And then, miracle of miracles, the man in the uniform pulled out some bills folded into a silver money clip and handed a few of them to the boy behind the counter. "Allow me," he said.

Mrs. Adler beamed at him, patting her hands together in delighted applause. "Thank you," she said. Beside me, I felt Val's body uncoil, heard her breath gusting out as she exhaled.

Chris Jeffries, the shellfish constable—for that was what he was, not a policeman, as I'd first thought—had paid for a feast. There was corn on the cob and clam chowder and red plastic net bags filled with gray clams that Val and her mother called steamers. There was coleslaw and French fries and a tangled mound of thin, crispy onion rings, tall wax paper cups brimming with ice and soda, and little plastic dishes filled with melted butter. A dozen oysters lolled slick in their shells on a bed of crushed ice, and two giant lobsters sprawled over oval-shaped plates, leaking steaming pale-pink water. I watched as Mrs. Adler opened a plastic bag of oyster crackers and sprinkled them into her soup.

"Mmm," she sighed, swirling her spoon in the thick, creamy broth. She took a sip, closed her eyes, and sighed happily as the shellfish constable watched her. "You know what this tastes like? Summer. Doesn't it taste just like summer to you?"

Val didn't answer. Chris Jeffries spooned cocktail sauce and horseradish onto the oysters. He had thick features and close-set brown eyes and was tanned the color of leather. I wasn't very good at guessing grown-ups' ages, but I thought he was younger than Mrs. Adler, maybe just out of college. Maybe even still in college and doing this as a summer job, which made me wonder how he'd had the money to pay for our dinner. "I never thought of it like that," he said.

Valerie tucked her head down like a turtle, tore open one of the bags of steamers, and started nimbly plucking clams from their shells, dunking them in a dish of water to clean the grit off, then dipping them in butter and popping them into her mouth. "Want one?" she asked. "They're good." She speared a clam on a red plastic fork, dipped it, and handed it to me. "Just eat the belly, not the foot," she said, indicating the part of the clam that looked like a thick, wormy tail. I slipped the grayish clam gingerly into my mouth, bracing for the fishy taste and the slimy feel I was sure were coming. The only seafood I'd ever had was frozen fish sticks that my mother heated in the toaster oven. I closed my eyes and chewed, wincing at first at the slimy texture, then opening my eyes as the sweet, briny, buttery taste exploded over my tongue. "These are so good!"

Mrs. Adler laughed, and the shellfish constable actually clapped. "Enjoy," he said. I ate a whole bagful of steamers and an ear of corn drizzled with butter and sprinkled with grainy sea salt. I squeezed lemon onto a raw oyster and then, following Mrs. Adler's example, tipped the rough edge of the shell to my lips and slurped out the liquor and the meat. After my first few clumsy tries, I got the hang of the metal nutcrackers and the tiny three-tined fork, prying chunks of pink-and-white flesh out of the lobster claws and dousing them with butter, too, amazed at the taste of the meat, light and rich and sweet.

The shellfish constable told us how he and his brother had taken his brother's girlfriend, visiting from Minnesota, on a whale watch in Provincetown. The seas had gotten rough, the passengers had gotten sick, and the whale-watch workers had spent the whole trip running up and down the length of the boat, handing out Dramamine and then plastic bags. "I'd never seen so much vomit," he said, and Val and I laughed at the way he said the word—*vahhhw-mit.* "It was awesome."

"Awesome," I repeated. My fingertips and face were shiny with butter and clam juice. I wiped them until the napkin turned translucent, then added it to the pile that was growing in the center of the table, as Mrs. Adler and Chris Jeffries talked about their favorite beaches and the best places in Provincetown to watch the sunset. Valerie and I had sodas, and the grown-ups drank beer from green glass bottles, setting the empties down next to the trays littered with clam shells, straw wrappers, shreds of cole slaw, and puddles of lobster juice. Finally, Mrs. Adler turned sideways on the bench. She pulled up her skirt, crossed her long, tanned legs, and slipped a cigarette between her lips. Chris the shellfish constable hurried to pull out a book of matches and light it.

"I'm stuffed," she pronounced. The breeze was picking up, raising goose bumps on my bare arms and legs, bringing fall to mind. I thought of how it would feel to hurry home from school in October, with the sky getting dark and the wind at my back and Val at my side, talking about the Thanksgiving feast the sixth-graders prepared, and what we wanted for Christmas . . . what it would be like, for the first time in my life, to move through the school year and the concerts and the holidays with a friend at my side.

"Anyone for coffee?" the constable asked. He carried two cups back to the table, then handed Valerie a five-dollar bill. "Why don't you girls get some ice cream?" We bought cones from a window on the other side of the restaurant—vanilla for me, something called Moose Tracks for Val—and we ate them leaning against the sun-warmed curve of the Bug's hood while Mrs. Adler and the shellfish constable drank their coffee. She'd moved so that she was sitting next to him instead of across from him. Her hands fluttered in the air, lighting on his forearms, then his shoulders. I watched her rest her head on his chest as he slung his arm around her and pulled her close.

"We should leave soon," said Valerie. "Poppy goes to bed early."

"Who's Poppy?" I asked.

"My grandfather. My father's father. We used to come here every summer and stay with him." She licked her ice cream, catching a brown dribble as it slid down the side of the cone. "We haven't talked to him for a really long time. Probably he doesn't even know we're coming." I worried about that while Val nibbled her cone and stared out at the sky. "I wish I still lived in California," she said. "I wish I could live with my dad."

An icy finger prodded my heart. "You can't leave," I told her. "School's starting next week."

Val licked at her arm again. "Maybe we can both go there," she said. "It's way better than Chicago. It's warm all the time. We could go to the beach."

I nodded, enchanted and unsettled. I could never leave my parents, but I was, I secretly admitted, thrilled with the idea that Val would want me to, that she liked me enough to want me with her.

At the picnic table, Mrs. Adler bent down to murmur into

Chris Jeffries's ear, then rose to her feet, peering through the twilight. "Come on, girls," she called. "Time to go."

Val and I got into the car, our hands and faces butter slick and ice-cream sticky. Valerie ignored her seat belt, curled up like a kitten in the backseat, and shut her eyes. I leaned forward, eyes on the road as we drove, first east, then south, as the Cape curved in on itself and headlights—the constable's, I thought—flashed and bobbed in the rearview mirror. The wheels hummed over the pavement, and when I opened my eyes it was dark, and Mrs. Adler was shaking my shoulders, whispering, "Addie, wake up."

I stumbled out of the car. We were parked on the lawn in front of a big, dark house that seemed to start at the top of a hill and spread out in every direction: up, and out, and sideways. I could hear the suck and rumble of water nearby. Mrs. Adler pulled Valerie out of the car and propped her up beside me. "Wait here," she said. I squinted through the darkness, watching as she slipped off her shoes and trotted to the front door, then opened it and beckoned us both inside.

I saw the darkened house in snatches as Mrs. Adler padded over the wide-planked floors, leading us to the staircase: the fancy, patterned rugs, a long, oval table in what must have been a dining room, a fireplace big enough for a kid to stand in. She led us up two flights to a small white-painted room under the eaves, where there were two twin beds draped in white chenille bedspreads. "Go to sleep," she whispered. Her hair had come loose from its bun and curled in tendrils around her face. I set my backpack down, suddenly so tired that it was all I could do to wriggle out of my sneakers and crawl into bed.

"I need to go to the bathroom," Val said in a draggy, babyish voice.

"Fine," her mother snapped, "just don't flush."

I lay down, trying to make sense of that—in my house, we

always flushed. My eyes slipped shut. A few minutes later, or so it seemed, Mrs. Adler was shaking my shoulders again. "Addie," she whispered. "Wake up. The tide's going out."

I sat up, yawning. Lovely rosy light, a color I'd never seen, never even imagined, filtered through the window, and yellow-and-white gingham curtains blew in the breeze. In the bed beside mine, Val was still in her clothes, lying stiffly on top of the covers, as if she was still sulking in her sleep. At the foot of the beds was a dollhouse, and in a bookcase against the wall was an entire set of faded Bobbsey Twins and Nancy Drew books. Mrs. Adler followed my gaze. "Help yourself," she said, and pointed at a door. "The bathroom's in there. Remember: no flushing. We need to be quiet."

The bathroom floor was hexagonal black-and-white tiles, some of them cracked, and the toilet was an old-fashioned kind with a pull cord dangling from the ceiling. A tarnish-fogged mirror hung over the sink. I splashed cold water on my face and had just pulled my toothpaste out of my backpack when Valerie knocked on the door, then breezed inside.

"I can't believe we're here!" Her shorts and shirt were rumpled, her face pillow-creased, but she was smiling, closer to being the Valerie I knew.

"This is a really nice house." I suspected that this wasn't really a *house*: that it was instead a *mansion,* a thing I'd only ever read about. Through the half-moon-shaped bathroom window, I could see the bright green rectangle of a tennis court and, beyond that, grayish-gold sand and the foaming edge of the ocean. When we got back into the bedroom, Mrs. Adler, in flip-flops and the same faded pink tank top and her blue cotton running shorts, was making our beds, plumping the pillows, running her hands over the coverlets to smooth them. She looked at us, then down at the beds, and whispered, "Be as quiet as you can."

Val grabbed three of the old books from the bookcase. We picked up our backpacks and crept down the stairs. The clock hanging over the giant table said that it was five in the morning, and the sky was streaked with amazing shades of pink and gold. "Don't slam the doors," said Mrs. Adler. At the door, she murmured something to Val, who ran down the steps, reached underneath the porch, and pulled out two big mesh buckets and a short-handled rake.

I crawled into the backseat of the Bug. Val sat in front, holding the buckets in one hand and the door open with the other. Mrs. Adler got behind the wheel, put the car in neutral, and steered one-handed as we coasted down the road. I watched the house receding in the rearview mirror and saw a light go on through one of the second-floor windows. A minute later, a white-haired man in pajama bottoms and no shirt flung the front door open and stood on the porch, shouting words I couldn't hear. Mrs. Adler popped the clutch and the motor roared into life.

"Who was that?" I asked as Val and her mother closed their doors. Mrs. Adler turned on the radio, then pulled a cigarette out of the crushed pack she'd tucked into the visor. Val stuck her thumb in her mouth and started chewing, with her face set in tense lines, gazing straight ahead. "Poppy," Mrs. Adler said.

I sat back, not knowing what to make of this, and watched the road slip by. Twenty minutes later we pulled into the parking lot of a small supermarket. Mrs. Adler got out. Val sat as still as if she'd been carved, staring straight ahead with her jaw clenched, looking furious.

"Hey, Val?" I whispered.

She didn't turn around. "She wouldn't even let me say hi to him," she said in a furious whisper. "My own grandfather, and I couldn't even say . . ." She snapped her mouth shut and crossed her arms over her chest as Mrs. Adler came out of the market with two brown paper bags. I wondered how she'd paid for breakfast as she pulled out doughnuts and bananas and a giant cup of coffee. Had she taken Val's grandfather's money? I ate two bananas and a doughnut as Mrs. Adler drove down Route 6, then turned onto a narrow, sandy lane that ended in an unpaved parking lot with wooden racks of wide-bellied metal and wooden canoes along one end. The sun was shining, the air warming up. Half a dozen rowboats and motorboats bobbed in the water as gulls wheeled and cried overhead. "This is it, girls," Mrs. Adler said.

Val and I wriggled into our bathing suits in the backseat, taking turns holding a towel up over the rear window, even though the parking lot was empty. Mrs. Adler loaded her Tab cooler with bags and bottles from the market. She supervised us as we smeared our arms and legs and faces with the sunscreen she pulled from the grocery bag, and she sprayed us with bug repellent. Then she squinted at the racks of canoes, finally pointing at a metal one, which we lifted down and set on the sand. Mrs. Adler put the buckets and the rake in the center of the boat, along with the cooler, and Val and I dragged it down to the edge of the water (not a lake, Val told me, as I'd thought, but a salt marsh, which emptied out into the ocean).

Val and I sat in the middle of the canoe. Mrs. Adler pulled off her tank top to reveal a blue bikini top. She pushed us into the shallow water until the waves lapped at the hem of her shorts, then hopped into the boat and began to paddle, propelling us past sandbars thick with bright-green sawgrass and cattails, heading out to where the marsh gave way to the rippling dark-blue sea.

The sun sparkled off the water. Wavelets like tiny hands patted the metal sides of the canoe. Val scooted until she was sitting in front of me, then leaned her back against my knees. Mrs. Adler steered us toward a sandbar, and when the prow of the canoe nosed the sand, she hopped out and pulled the boat up onto the shore. "Come on, Addie," said Val.

We knelt down, and Val showed me how to look for bubbles and, when I'd found some, how to dig with the rake, then slide my fingers sideways until I felt the edges of a clamshell. It took us a few minutes to get started, and then Val squealed as she pulled her first clam out of the sand. "Here," she called, "there's tons of them!" I hurried over and knelt beside her, her bony shoulder against my round, tanned one as we worked our hands down into the sand, me in my blue one-piece, Valerie in a red-and-pink-striped bikini that kept riding up over her flat chest and drooping down her skinny hips. We dug out fistfuls of clams, laughing as they squirted us and tossing them in the mesh bucket we'd left standing in the water.

The sun climbed higher in the sky. We filled the first bucket and started in on the second, taking breaks to suck at our fingertips, which were laced with tiny cuts from the clamshells. Every few minutes, Val would pause to stand up and peer at the shore.

"What's wrong?" I asked after the third or fourth time.

"You need a permit to take clams," she said.

"Do we have one?"

"I don't know." She shook her head. "I don't think so. Probably not."

"I've still got my money," I told Val. "We'll just say we came all the way from Illinois and we don't know the rules." This earned me a thin smile, before Val plopped back down and started digging again. For lunch, Mrs. Adler gave us turkey-and-cheese sandwiches, potato chips, and warm apple juice from the cooler. We ate sitting cross-legged at the edge of the shore, slapping at the greenhead flies that landed on our arms and legs, then rinsed our hands and went back to clamming. When the second bucket was full, Valerie and I lay side by side at the edge of the shore and let the incoming tide push the water over our toes . . . then our knees . . . then our hips, our waists, our chests. Finally, we floated, our hair waving in the current, hips and hands bumping as the waves lifted us and let us down, until Mrs. Adler pushed the canoe into the water and told us it was time to go.

We clambered back into the boat and paddled back to shore. The buckets of clams floated beside us, tied to the canoe with Mrs. Adler's bandanna, our hair drying, salt-stiff, against our bug-bitten shoulders. My fingers itched for my watercolors and the pastel crayons I had at home when I looked out over the blue of the water, the green grass and silvery sand, the layered gray-blue and apricot of the sky. I held my breath as we approached the beach, worried that there would be trouble, that the family whose canoe we'd taken would be there, that our clams would be confiscated, that we'd be arrested. The parking lot was full, but the shore was empty, quiet except for the sound of the waves and the gulls. We helped Mrs. Adler wrestle the canoe back onto the struts, and watched as she wrapped the clam buckets in the paper grocery bags and set them in the backseat.

"Awesome," said Val dreamily as she climbed into the car. She said it exactly the same way the shellfish constable had.

"Vomit," I said back. *Vahhhwmit.* Val laughed and laughed.

I can remember how my nose was itchy with sunburn, the way my fingernails were ragged and torn, how my thighs were dotted with bug bites. I can remember stopping at convenience stores off the highway, buying cigarettes and Tab and black coffee for Mrs. Adler, Sprite for Val, and juice for me, garbage bags and ten-pound bags of ice for the clams.

We made it back home late Monday afternoon, after spending another night asleep in a rest stop *(Goodnight to the back! Goodnight to the front!).* My mother took one look at me and hustled me into the bathtub, pinching my dirty clothes between her fingertips before depositing them in the hamper. She made me soak, then scrub my nails with a brush she'd extracted from the depths of a vanity drawer, and wash my hair twice. After Mrs. Adler's repeated assurances that the clams could not possibly have gone bad, my mother opened her *Joy of Cooking* and made us linguine with clam sauce, with white wine and lots of garlic, flecked with fresh parsley, served with salad and crusty French bread. I remember the six of us—me and my parents and my brother, Valerie and her mom—gathered around our kitchen table, devouring plate after plate of pasta, soaking crusts of bread with the garlic-and-wine sauce. I remember the feeling of floating in the water with my best friend beside me, underneath that beautiful sky. It was the best time of my life.

EIGHT

"**H**ome sweet home," Jordan Novick announced, unlocking his front door and letting himself inside. Nobody answered. Not terribly surprising, given that he lived alone.

He tossed his coat in the direction of the closet, kicked off his boots and left them standing in the hall, then shoved a box of food into the microwave and pulled off his jacket and his tie. The TiVo had recorded a new episode of *The Nighty-Night Show*, he saw with his usual queasy mixture of shame and satisfaction. When the microwave beeped, he peeled the plastic film off his dinner, popped the top off a beer, and parked himself in a folding camp chair in front of the television set.

The food—it was some kind of pot pie—tasted terrible, the crust a sodden, gummy mess, the interior icy in sections, scalding in others, and gluey the whole way through. Jordan drained his beer, took the empty bottle back into the kitchen, and inspected the box . . . which, of course, said in very large hard-to-miss letters, MICROWAVE NOT RECOMMENDED. "Well, shit," Jordan said, and frowned at the oven, which had a heavy-duty childproof lock on its handle, a lock that only his ex-wife had ever been able to figure out how to work.

The locks had actually been one of the house's major selling points. "We're all set for a young couple," the seller had announced when they'd come through with their real estate agent, beaming as he displaying the locks on the stove's controls, the gates at the top and bottom of the staircase, and the pronged plastic caps plugged into every electrical outlet. "You'll just need to supply the baby!" He'd laughed. Patti and Jordan had laughed. The agent had chuckled, too. They'd bought the house, and when Patti had gotten pregnant for the first time in 2004, there was nothing to do and not much to buy (Patti's sister, a mother of three, had gladly handed over a crib and a changing table and a mysterious plastic pail known as a Diaper Genie). With the house prepared, Jordan and Patti had marked the occasion by programming their TiVo to record children's shows: *Blue's Clues* and *Barney & Friends, Max and Ruby* and *The Nighty-Night Show.*

The joke was on him. Now he was alone, no baby and no wife; alone in a house that defied him—how many hours had he wasted struggling with the doorknob guards or the lock the previous owners had installed over the toilet tank? He'd canceled his season passes for the children's shows, but there was no way to tell the computer chip that lived inside of the TiVo that there were no children here and never would be, so the machine continued to record scores of programs for the five-and-under set, including *The Nighty-Night Show,* which was hosted by the Nighty-Night Lady, a friendly brunette who wore V-necked ribbed sweaters while she sang lullabies and told short, sanitized versions of fairy tales. The Nighty-Night Lady was, in Jordan's opinion, smoking hot. It made no sense. He'd even considered writing a letter to the network, asking why they'd hire a babe like that to appear on a show for three-year-olds. He wondered if he was the only man who tuned in, hoping she'd bend over to pick up one of her props—the Styrofoam castle, the felt princess crown, feeling ashamed of himself even though he knew that nobody would show up to say *Hey, what are you watching,* or *Isn't that for kids?* or, simply, *Pervert!*

It didn't matter now that he was alone. He could indulge himself any way he chose, whether that meant eating a diet based on deep-fried foods, or furnishing his living room with metal-and-canvas fold-up camp chairs from the end-of-season sale at Target, or whacking off to a woman who wore a snail puppet on her hand. *Ain't nobody's business if I do.*

NINE

The Lakeview Country Club was a white clapboard building with six tennis courts off to one side, a swimming pool on the other, and a golf course stretched out behind it. At two in the morning, the club's windows were dark, the parking lot was deserted. I could hear the faint hum of a generator as I killed the Jaguar's engine.

"Over there," said Valerie, pointing. "Next to the Dumpster."

I unfastened my seat belt and opened my door. When the dome lights came on, I looked at Valerie. "Come on."

She wiped her face, then shook her head. "I can't."

"What do you mean you can't?"

"I can't," she repeated. "You know how I am with this stuff. You go. You look. I'll just wait here, with my cell phone, and if you wave at me, I'll call 911."

"We're both going," I said, but even before the word "both" had left my mouth, Valerie was shaking her head.

"I can't."

"Valerie . . ."

"I *can't*."

I exhaled, weighing my options, finally deciding that every second I spent in the car, reasoning with her, was a second in which Dan Swansea could be bleeding out onto the gravel. Behind a Dumpster. No matter what he'd done to Valerie, no matter what he'd done to me, I didn't want his blood on my hands.

"Fine." I left the keys in the ignition and Valerie frozen in her seat. The door slammed behind me with a discreet *thunk*. I cut across the parking lot, pep-talking myself along the way. *Okay, let's just get this over with, it could turn out to be nothing, maybe Val just imagined the whole thing . . .*

Then I saw something shiny and leather coiled like a snake in the shadow next to the Dumpster. My heart froze. I bent down in slow motion and saw that it was a belt, a man's black leather belt. I could see something wet and dark on the parking lot's gravel beside it. But there was no sign of Dan Swansea, living, dead, or anywhere in between.

I knelt down and touched my fingers to the wet, sticky stuff, then lifted them and sniffed. Blood. I picked up the belt, unrolled it, then rolled it up again. I reached into my pocket for my phone before remembering that I'd left it in my purse, and that I'd left my purse in Val's car. I straightened up to wave at her, then stopped, mid-wave, and stared at the car. The car was empty. Valerie was gone.

TEN

With Val as my best friend, I didn't have to depend on my brother quite as much—Val was happy to speak up for me, for both of us, for anyone, and she was full of ideas for adventures, which left Jon free to go his own way. My brother had always been a charmed child, tanned and handsome and nice to me, most of the time, even though he called me brat and gave me Indian burns and told me that I was adopted.

When I catch myself wondering if it really had been that way—if he'd been that good-looking, that graceful, that beloved—I can look at pictures for proof. There he is, a beaming, sunny baby, a towheaded toddler, a chubby-cheeked, mischievous little boy who grew into a young man with wavy hair and long, curling eyelashes and an easy grin. There he is in high school in a maroon-and-cream uniform with his name written on the back, breaking the tape of a finish line; there he is, posed on the edge of the diving board, preparing for a backflip that would send him slicing cleanly into the water with hardly a splash. Jon was everyone's buddy, everyone's friend. All the boys liked him, and lots of the girls did, too. But by the time Jon was fifteen, his kindness toward me had dwindled to the occasional pleasant word or considerate act. Mostly, he ignored me. My sense was that he was getting ready to leave our family behind.

To him, the three of us were like strangers who'd been assigned adjacent seats on a train, foreigners who talked too loudly and gesticulated with their hands and ate strange, strong-smelling foods. Jon was resigned to being polite to us for the length of the trip, knowing he'd never see us once he'd reached his destination.

Each morning, Jon and I would take turns in the bathroom and eat breakfast in the kitchen—or, rather, I'd have toast and milk and cereal while Jon would slouch against the counter, lean and graceful, gulping orange juice straight from the bottle when my mother wasn't looking, then would grab a banana or a handful of crackers and run out the door.

After school, he'd have practice. He'd made the varsity squad as a sophomore, so most of his teammates were seniors, and most of them could drive. After practice, he'd have dinner, usually at a friend's house, or the team would gather for pizza at the shop downtown. At twilight one of his teammate's cars would pull into our driveway. There'd be a burst of laughter and loud music as the door opened, a chorus of "byes" and "see yas" as Jon climbed out. By the time he'd made it up the driveway, his face would be shuttered, his smile would vanish, his shoulders would pull forward, like he was trying to protect himself from a blow. He would look at his feet, at the floor, at a schoolbook or magazine, anywhere but up at us.

When he came home, my mother would meet him at the door, barefoot in leggings and a long skirt and one of her loose cotton blouses, with a fringed shawl wrapped around her shoulders when it was cold. "Hello, honey," she'd call. "How was school?"

"Hey, champ," my dad would say, emerging from the basement and heading to the kitchen sink to wash his hands. "Good practice today?"

Jon would shrug off his backpack, let it drop to the floor, then kick it sideways into the closet. "Fine."

My mother would call questions as Jon shucked his shoes and his jacket: How was the geography test? Was he hungry? Did he think they'd win the meet this weekend, or . . .

He'd look at her, expressionless. "You don't have to come."

"I want to," she'd say. I'd be watching or listening from my seat at the kitchen table, and my heart would sink. Jon acted like he hated my mother. He flinched when she touched him, he answered her questions in as few words as possible, and he always had someplace else to be—the swimming pool, a friend's party, an extra session the coach had called, a team meeting, or, lately, a school dance. Maybe it wasn't that he hated her, I'd think as he'd hurry upstairs to his bedroom and lock the door behind him. Maybe he was ashamed of her. That, of course, was worse.

Teenagers, said my mother, unruffled, as she went back to her notebook, or the pot of whatever soup or stew she was simmering. *Teenagers are like that.* My mother never missed a race. She'd dress up in Pleasant Ridge's school colors, and she'd cheer for him from the bleachers near the finish line. I'd gone with her twice and seen that mothers did these things—they went to meets in red-and-cream sweatshirts and scarves, they whooped and hollered when their sons ran by, chests heaving, cheeks flushed, eyes narrowed to pained slits—but none of the other mothers was anywhere near as big as our mother. When she'd jump in the air, clapping and calling "Yay, Jon!" her whole body would jiggle and quiver, and continue jiggling and quivering even after she'd stopped moving. People would stare. The boys on the other team would nudge one another, laughing and pointing, and Jon would turn his back to us, talking to his coach, splashing water from a squirt bottle into his mouth and over his face. If my mother noticed him ignoring her, she never let on . . . she'd just keep clapping, cheeks flushed, cheering as each of the Pleasant Ridge runners crossed the finish line.

I tried talking to Jon about it once, in October, when the team was six weeks into its season. My mother was out on the porch, my father had gone down into his workshop. I could hear the buzz of something from down there, a saw or a drill. "Go away!" Jon called over the throbbing bass of his angry-sounding rock and roll—Tom Petty's "Refugee"—as I knocked on his door.

"I need help with math." I didn't—and if I did, Jon wouldn't have been the one to ask—but he unlocked the door and I walked inside, gingerly making my way across layers of crumpled papers and comic books, dirty sneakers, T-shirts and shorts, grease-spotted napkins and sweat-ripened socks. His comforter lay in a heap on the floor, and the blue plaid sheet was pulled halfway off his bed, leaving the mattress bare. In one corner I spotted a cardboard box containing the marionettes my father had made him, tumbled in a heap, their wooden limbs dusty, their strings tangled. "Why are you so mean to Mom?"

"What are you talking about?" He was sitting at his desk, barefoot in shorts and a sweatshirt, with a copy of *To Kill a Mockingbird* pinched between his thumb and forefinger. His room smelled like B.O. and rotting bananas, and the soles of his feet were callused and almost black.

"You're never home," I began.

"What do you care?" Jon asked. "You're home too much. You should get out more."

"This isn't about me," I said, feeling my face flush, worried that he was right. I was thirteen. My classmates were getting their ears pierced, sometimes twice; they were going to the movies at the mall with groups that included boys, but I wasn't interested in any of that. I was happy at home, with my parents, my books, my paints and paper, my best friend.

"Why'd you tell her not to come to your meet?"

Jon kicked his bare legs out in front of him, then lifted them straight into the air—some kind of runners' stretch, I thought. "I just said she doesn't need to come. She can come if she wants to. I never said she couldn't."

"Can't you just be nice to her?"

Jon set down the book, picked up his Magic 8-Ball and revolved it in his hands.

"I know she's . . . you know . . . kind of big."

"Kind of big," he repeated, with his lips tight and nostrils flaring in a way that let me know he was furious. "Sure. And the sun's kind of hot. And the ocean's kind of deep. Do you know what the rest of the guys say about her?"

I shook my head. "What do you care?"

"You don't know," he said. "You're not on a team. You don't have to deal with it."

"Why don't you just tell them to shut up?"

"Addie." He spoke with exaggerated patience. "Those guys are seniors."

"So what? You're faster than they are. Tell them to shut up. I bet they'd listen."

He shook his head and didn't answer.

"What about Dad?"

He looked at me blandly. "What about him?"

"Maybe if he came to the meets with her . . ." But Jon was shaking his head before I'd finished my thought.

"Oh, sure," he said. "That'd be great. Just have him show up at three in the afternoon in the middle of the week, so that everyone would know he doesn't have a real job."

I swallowed. A father without a real job would not cancel out a fat mother. It would only make it worse.

"No offense, but you don't know what you're talking about," Jon said. "And I've got to finish this." He turned away from me, opening his book. After a minute, I threaded my way through the rubble and out into the hall.

That night I lay awake long after I'd heard my mother's slow tread up the stairs, long after the line of light underneath Jon's bedroom door went dark. Other families weren't like this. What was wrong with the four of us? Why were we so different?

Why do you care? I heard Val asking in my head. *What does it matter?* Her family wasn't normal, and she didn't care at all . . . but her mother was beautiful, and somehow, I thought that having a father who was divorced was easier than having one who was home but didn't behave like the rest of the dads. It mattered to me that we didn't look right, that we weren't like everyone else, that Jon could pass for normal by pushing us away . . . and that maybe I'd never be able to do the same thing.

I lay there, watching the glowing numbers on my digital clock, until it was after one in the morning. Then I slipped out of bed and tiptoed down the hallway, down the stairs, to the door that led to the basement. Barely breathing, I leaned against it, pressing my ear to the grain of the wood. I could hear my father snoring. I stood there, listening for a long moment before creeping into the kitchen. My mother had given me three Oreo cookies for dessert, and the bag on the top shelf of the pantry was still almost full. I slipped six cookies into my hand and carried them up to my bedroom, where I lay in my bed and inserted an entire cookie into my mouth, underneath a David Hockney poster I'd bought at an art fair that summer—the blue of the swimming pool, the way the light moved through the water, had enchanted me. I held the cookie against my tongue until it dissolved into a slick of grainy black mush. One cookie, two cookies, three cookies, six cookies. When they were gone, I licked my teeth clean and closed my eyes and finally fell asleep.

· · ·

"Why do you think Jon's such a jerk?" I asked Valerie the next morning while we waited for the bus.

"I don't think he's a jerk. I think he's cute," said Val. It was a week away from Halloween, but it was cold already, in the forties some mornings, with an icy bite to the air. Val wore stiff blue jeans rolled into clumsy cuffs at the ankle and a too-big purple sweater. She was already taller than all of the girls and most of the boys in eighth grade, skinny and flat-chested, with sharp elbows and knobby knees that she kept hidden under layers of T-shirts and turtlenecks and sweatshirts, and, inevitably, boys' jeans. Her teeth weren't good. There was a space between her protruding front teeth big enough to hold a quarter, and her incisors pointed in different directions. "Valerie's got summer teeth," Jon had once said. "You know, some are here, some are there."

The thing was, Val didn't seem to know that she was weird-looking . . . or if she knew, she didn't care. Each year, she'd try out for Select Choir, even though she couldn't really sing in tune (although she was, in her defense, both enthusiastic and loud). In June she would audition for the leads in the summer music theater. She'd rehearse her song and her monologue for weeks, and still end up being cast as a glorified extra—a non-singing urchin in *Annie*, a nun with no lines in *The Sound of Music*, a tree in *Peter Pan*—after the kids who could sing got roles as pirates and Indians and Lost Boys. None of the rejections and refusals dented her confidence. She'd use Elmer's glue to attach felt leaves to her green leotard, or pose in front of the mirror in her wimple as if she was the star of the show, as if everyone was there to see her.

"Did Jon do something?" she asked, and flipped open the social studies book (*Exploring Our World*) that she had in her lap. "Did he do something to you?" Before I could answer, she said, "Did you finish the worksheet?"

I handed it over. Val was smart—at least that's what the results on the standardized tests we'd taken in fifth grade had indicated—but she had an attitude toward homework, and studying for quizzes and tests, that could best be described as haphazard. "He told my mom not to come to his cross-country meets. He's . . ." This part was hard to say. "He's ashamed of her."

Val pursed her lips, absorbing this. "Maybe she could go on a diet."

"I don't know," I mumbled.

"My mom does a good one," Val said. Her eyes were still on the worksheet as she copied my answers. "You eat a hard-boiled egg for breakfast, then an egg and half a grapefruit for lunch, and then you have salad for dinner, with a can of tuna fish and lemon juice instead of salad dressing. That's what my mom does every New Year's. She does it for, like, a week." She wrinkled her nose. "It makes her really gassy. But it works."

"I'm not sure," I muttered. Even though I knew by then that the world disagreed, I still clung to the idea that my mother was beautiful, a cloud come to life, and that everyone else had it wrong.

"Or how about Deal-A-Meal?" Val asked as the school bus came groaning around the corner. "You know, with the Sweatin' to the Oldies guy? I saw an infomercial for it. You get a videotape and cards to tell you what to eat for lunch or dinner."

"Maybe." The bus ground to a stop in front of us. Val handed me my homework and bent down for her backpack. We climbed aboard and took our regular seats, three rows back on the left-hand side, and that was the end of the conversation until that afternoon, when I came home from Girl Scouts and found Val sitting before our front door.

"I bet Jon's having wet dreams," she announced as we walked to the convenience store. Val didn't have a brother, but she seemed somehow to know a lot more about boys than I did. Most of what I knew came from a book my mother had given me when I'd turned twelve. It was called *What's Happening to Me?*, and it had provided me and Valerie with hours of amusement. There were cartoon drawings of a girl with breasts and a curly thatch of pubic hair, and an index in the back where you could look up "penis" and "ejaculate" and "masturbation" and "nocturnal emission," as Val had done the instant the book was in her hands.

"Gross." Ever since I'd learned about wet dreams, I'd felt a mixture of queasiness and pity whenever I'd thought of them in conjunction with my brother. How awful it must be to have everything on the outside, hanging there so obvious, to have body parts getting bigger or harder or squirting stuff on your sheets without your having any say over them.

"Does he have a girlfriend?" asked Val. She put two cans of Diet Coke and a bag of potato chips on the counter, and I dug three dollars out of my pocket, shaking my head, even though I wasn't really sure. At fifteen, Jon already had a life that was all his own, and I could only guess as to what that life included.

"I'll bet he's got a girlfriend," Val mused, cracking open her can.

"Do you think . . ." I said. Then I stopped. I knew what I wanted to ask—*do you think my family's weird?*—but I couldn't figure out how to ask it.

"We should be cheerleaders for Halloween," she said. "We can wear white sweaters and get skirts at JCPenney and buy pom-poms." For a minute we walked along in silence, past the Sheas' house at the corner, the Buccis and the Hattons, as I tried to figure out a way to ask Val what I really needed to know: *What's wrong with us? What's wrong with me?*

"Or we could be Barbies," Val said. "Or witches. Whatever you want."

. . .

We ended up going as witches, because we couldn't find pom-poms at the costume shop, but they had an abundance of pointy black hats, along with green face paint and black-and-white striped tights that we wore under our black choir robes. "I'm melt-ing!" Val screeched as I pretended to throw a bucket of water on her and my mother snapped pictures. "Oh, what a world!"

Jon wasn't trick-or-treating. "It's for kids," he'd said, coming downstairs in his jeans and team sweatshirt. A station wagon zoomed down our street, swung into our driveway, and slammed to a halt with its front bumper inches from the garage door. My mother frowned. She'd put her own witch hat on her head and wore bright-red lipstick and high-heeled red shoes.

"Gotta go," said Jon. He was going to a party at one of his teammates' houses. He'd promised my mother that there would be parents there, and no drinking. He'd even given her the phone number, muttering under his breath that she had to stop treating him like a baby. But then, on his way out the door, he surprised me by digging in his pockets and coming out with two Hershey's Kisses. "Here," he said, dropping one in my pillowcase and one in Val's. "To get you started."

"Be home by midnight!" my mother called.

"I will," Jon said. He hurried out the door and into the wait-ing car, which revved its motor and zoomed down the driveway.

Val and I went out into the chilly darkness. We spent an hour trick-or-treating, moving through the neighborhood with throngs of little kids dressed as princesses and pirates and ghosts, shivering under our choir robes, because, in spite of my mother's urging, we'd both refused to wear our winter coats. "Maybe we are too old for this," Val said, swinging her sack of candy over her shoulder and pulling off her witch hat.

"Maybe. Probably," I said. More than one of the grown-ups who'd answered our knock had made that point. "This is the last year I'll be giving you two treats," Mrs. Bass had announced before winking and dropping a handful of miniature candy bars into our bags. I was shivering, and my fingers were numb, and I thought that if I never went trick-or-treating again it would be okay.

Val grinned at me, her crooked teeth glowing against her green skin. "*Poltergeist* is on tonight. Remember that part where the meat was, like, crawling along the counter?"

"Ew," I said, recalling the scene. Val hated blood in real life, but she loved scary movies, especially the ones where, she swore, she could catch a glimpse of her father getting shot or stabbed or jumping out of a window on fire.

"Ask if you can sleep over, okay?"

I found my parents sitting in the darkened living room. My mom had a plastic salad bowl of candy in her lap, and my father was watching a rerun of *Rowan & Martin's Laugh-In* on TV, with a mug of tea in his hand. "Can I sleep at Valerie's?"

"As long as you two don't stay up too late," said my mother. For a minute, I thought about not going. I could change out of my costume and sit with my parents, hand out candy when kids rang the doorbell—but Val and *Poltergeist* were waiting. I packed pajamas and a toothbrush and went across the street, where Val had taken off her robe and was in her sweatpants popping popcorn, with her face still painted. I wished for my pastels so I could sketch a quick picture of her, standing at the stove with her green face and her witch hat perched on top of her blond hair.

"You look like you have food poisoning."

She grabbed a wad of paper towels and started wiping her cheeks. "Here. Melt this," she said, tossing me a stick of margarine, which I unwrapped and put in a plastic bowl. I stuck the bowl in the microwave as Valerie dumped popcorn into a pan on the stove and shook it briskly until the first kernels exploded. We ate popcorn and divided up our Halloween haul, first by size, then by type, then by order in which we'd be eating it. I traded my SweeTarts for M&M's, and we both agreed that Junior Mints were the worst candy ever. We made it until the part where the meat crawled across the counter, then burst open with maggots ("I'm sorry, but that is so cool!" Val chortled while I looked away from the screen with my stomach roiling), and then we fell asleep, bundled in blankets on the floor.

"Honey?" Mrs. Adler's cigarette-and-Breck smell was in my nose; her voice was in my ear. "Addie? Are you awake?" For a minute I thought I was in the car, on our way home from the ocean. *Goodnight to the front! Goodnight to the back!*

I opened my eyes. It was still morning, but very early, the sky gray, just touched with pearly light. Through the window, I saw that there was a police car in front of my house. Its flashing light painted our walls red and blue, red and blue.

"Addie," said Mrs. Adler. "Honey. Wake up. There's been an accident."

I sat up. Beside me, Val rolled onto her side, her blond hair bright against the DiMeos' dark old carpet. "What happened?"

"Your brother was in a car accident. Your dad just called to let me know."

I got to my feet and walked to the window. The front door to my house was open, and I could see my mother in her bathrobe, standing in the doorway with both hands pressed to her chest. A police officer in a blue uniform shirt and black pants was talking to her. As I watched, he took her by the arm and led her out of the house to the cruiser.

"I should go." I started looking around for my shoes.

Mrs. Adler shook her head. "Your dad said for you to stay here. They'll call as soon as they know anything."

Outside, the cruiser backed down the driveway. My father ran out of the house, his pajama top so white it seemed to glow under the gray sky. He climbed into our station wagon and followed the cruiser down the street.

Mrs. Adler put her hand on my shoulder. "Try not to worry," she said. "I'm sure everything will be okay."

I climbed on the couch and sat with my face turned toward the window and my eyes trained on my front door until the sun came up and the paperboy made his way down our street, his bicycle wobbling in front of each house as he slowed to throw a paper toward the door.

"Hey," said Val. I turned, and she was blinking up at me from the floor. "What's going on? Did someone TP the house?"

My tongue felt thick. "Jon was in an accident. My parents went to the hospital."

"Oh my God!" Val sprang to her feet and came to sit on the couch beside me. "What happened?"

I shrugged. I couldn't look at her. I had to look at the house. Maybe it was a test, and if I kept watching, if I didn't blink, if I didn't miss anything, then maybe this would be all right. Val sat next to me, and I stared at our house, fixing it in my head, turning it into a still life. My father had painted the exterior a creamy brown that August. I'd helped him, hoisting cans of paint, bringing him glasses of lemonade, holding the ladder when he climbed down.

I watched the house, the shutters, the brass knocker on the front door, the two elm trees in the front yard, trying not to cry, barely moving, barely breathing, until late that afternoon, when my parents pulled into the driveway and my mother and father crossed the street to get me.

"Your brother . . ." my mother said. Her face was pale and puffy, and her hair stuck out from her head in staticky clumps. Tissues were balled up in one of her hands; the other was curled in a fist on her knee.

"It was stupid," my father said, and rubbed the back of his hand against his red eyes. "Jon should have known better."

"What happened?"

What happened, as the whole town would eventually learn, was that there'd been three boys from the cross-country team in the car: two in front, and Jon in back. The boys weren't drunk—not legally—but they'd been drinking, and they were speeding, doing ninety miles an hour on an infamously twisty road, trying to get home in time for curfew. The boy behind the wheel had lost control of the car, which had slammed into a tree and rolled over. The driver and the boy in the passenger's seat hadn't been wearing their seat belts. They'd both died (and, the rumor that was all over school by Monday morning had it, one of them had been decapitated). Jon, who'd worn his seat belt, had sustained cuts, bruises, contusions, cracked ribs, and a concussion. And brain damage. "They don't know how much yet," my mother said, twisting a tissue in her hand. "They can't say how bad."

"But he'll be okay? He'll get better?" I looked from my mother's face to my father's, waiting for reassurance, for a verse of "don't worry, Addie," and a chorus of "everything will be fine." Instead, my mother gulped back a sob and turned her face toward the window. My father rubbed his jaw.

"Is Jon going to be okay?" I asked again.

Neither one of them answered me. That was how I knew. Jon wouldn't be okay. He wouldn't get better. The brother I'd known, the one I'd loved and resented and envied, the one who'd talked to bus drivers and store clerks and strangers on my behalf, that swift, sure boy was gone. What came home from the rehab center twelve weeks later was a pale, pudgy, moon-faced Jon-shaped lump with seizures and an unsteady gait and faulty depth perception, a Jon-shaped lump that sat in front of the television set, or at the dinner table, staring incuriously at whatever was on the plate or screen in front of him, sometimes with a finger in his nose, sometimes, especially in the first few months, with his hand down the front of his pants. *Disinhibition,* said my mother, as if giving me the technical term would make it better. *It will pass.*

Jon had to relearn everything—how to dress himself and brush his teeth, how to tie his shoes, how to cut and chew and swallow his food, how to read, how to use the bathroom (that last one they'd mostly taught him in the hospital, which was good, because it was too awful to think about my mother having to go through that again). And that was just the stuff the doctors could agree on. There was the disinhibition, the nose-picking, and the other stuff that Jon's damaged brain had forgotten was private behavior. There were fits—actual seizures, mostly little ones where he'd just stare into the distance, and fits of rage, where Jon would scream curse words, sometimes because he'd gotten frustrated tying his shoe or re-capping the milk, and sometimes for no reason at all. He'd scream "FAGGOT! FAGGOT! FAG-GOT!" at my mother, his legs flailing in front of him, bashing at the chairs and the kitchen counters until she convinced him to stop. There were also "short-term memory issues," which meant that Jon could remember the scores of soccer games he'd played when he was eight, or who'd been invited to his tenth birthday party, but not his locker combination, or his teachers' names, or where he'd put his shoes the night before.

How long would this last? Would Jon ever be himself again? The doctors said that only time would tell, but that most of his recovery would happen in the first year. "It would have been bet-ter if he was older," I overheard one of the therapists say to my mother. Her name was Sue Stumps, and she came to our house twice a week wearing scrubs printed with teddy bears, silly, baby-ish things that I hated, because Jon wasn't a baby, and if he'd been himself he would have hated them, too. "If he was older, he'd be relearning stuff that he'd done for a long time—how to shave, how to drive. For young people . . ." Her voice trailed off, but I heard what she hadn't spoken. For young people, it was worse.

My father spent more and more time in the basement, as if he couldn't stand to see what Jon had become. My mother hovered, smoothing Jon's hair, wiping his lips. I hung back, watching as Jon talked to himself, muttering words I couldn't quite hear. Sometimes, usually in front of the television set, he drooled. That, my parents explained, was a side effect of one of Jon's medications, and he wasn't doing it on purpose, and I should try to help him if I could by handing him tissues and reminding him to use them. "You'll have to take care of him," they told me over and over, when he was still in the hospital and, later, when he was still at the rehab place in Chicago. At first I couldn't imagine it—my taking care of my brother sounded about as likely, about as plausible, as my growing wings, but the Jon who came home was a different brother than the Jon who'd run lightly down the driveway on Halloween, and this brother, the new Jon, did need my help.

He spent the spring and summer at home, going to therapy, working with paints and clay and balance balls and the penmanship workbooks I remembered from first grade. At night, my parents would take turns reading out loud to him until he fell asleep, snoring. That fall, he started high school again as a freshman, in the same class as me and Valerie. Before, he'd been on the academic track, plus honors history. Now he was on the "modified" track, in class with the handful of kids who would learn a trade or go to community college or the army instead of getting a four-year degree. Three days a week he had a tutor shadow him, to make sure he took notes and paid attention and didn't doze off or start shouting in the middle of a lecture or a quiz.

At first the other kids were on their best behavior. They'd offer to help with his homework or carry his books; his former teammates would scoot over to make a place for him at the lunch table. But that didn't last. By the end of September, Jon was alone, walking by himself down the hallways, in his old-man shuffle, one hand extended, fingers brushing the wall for balance. All of his grace was gone. He sat by himself on the bus and at lunch, except on Fridays, when we shared the same lunch period and I'd sit with him. In class, it was like there was a force field surrounding him, a barrier that no one tried to cross. Passed notes flew over his head; the girls who'd once flocked around him avoided his desk and his locker. The cross-country team was an impossibility. Jon's medication had made him gain weight, and the injury had left him permanently off balance. The phone at our house stopped ringing. His friends had forgotten him. It wasn't their fault. He wasn't the same boy.

After school, Jon would sit at the kitchen table and work on thousand-piece puzzles, putting together pictures of the Milky Way, lunar landscapes, Venus and Mars, and the *Challenger* space shuttle, with his tongue wedged into the corner of his mouth and his forehead creased in concentration. My mother would clap when he finished them, and I'd wonder, listening to the sad sound of her applause, whether she remembered his races, jumping up and down and cheering for him when his chest broke the tape. Now, when she asked him questions, he answered them. He sat with us at every meal and watched TV with us after dinner. No cars came honking up the driveway to take her son away. He was hers again, all hers.

I tried to help. I made sure that his shoes were tied, that his backpack was zipped, that his belt was fastened and his pants zipped up when he came out of the bathroom. I'd stay close, hoping for those rare moments of lucidity that would come at unpredictable intervals. That spring, when the school bus was stopped at a red light, Val and I watched out the window as a car full of Jon's old friends zoomed past us, the driver honking, the girl in the passenger seat with her feet on the dashboard, laughing. Jon, who was in the seat behind us, tapped my shoulder. I'd turned, expecting him to ask me for a tissue or a cough drop or to tell me he'd forgotten his lunch or his books or both, but instead, he was looking at me sadly. "I was in a car accident, right?" he asked.

My breath caught. "That's right," I said.

He didn't answer. I watched until his eyes clouded over. "Faggot," he whispered. Val sighed. I felt tears clogging the back of my throat.

"Jon, remember? That's an inside word." This was what his therapist told us to say. "I love you," I told him. "I'm sorry you got hurt."

"Faggot," he said, almost sighing. He closed his eyes and leaned the top of his head against the window. Underneath his hair was a jagged scar. Underneath that was a metal plate: it covered the holes where they'd drilled to relieve the pressure from his swollen brain. He opened his mouth and drooled a little onto his shirt collar. A minute later, he was asleep. I made myself look away until the bus arrived at school.

ELEVEN

"Val?" I called, and spun around, my breath huffing out a white cloud in front of me. I went to the car and pulled on the handle. Locked. Of course. With everything I had—my purse, my keys, and most important, my cell phone—inside. "Stupid," I growled, and leaned against the door. I was so stupid. Why had I imagined that she'd changed? Why did I let myself think that she'd come back to me chastened, a true and loyal friend, that once she'd acknowledged the truth about what had happened back in high school she would be so grateful that she'd never leave my side? People didn't change. Not me, not Val, not Dan Swansea. I'd always be scared, she'd always be selfish, and as for Dan Swansea, he'd probably spend his whole life as a criminal and never get caught, and then I'd die of cancer and nobody would even care. Probably no one would even notice. I'd die one of those terrible single-girl deaths, my body undiscovered until someone noticed the smell, and God knew how long that would take, because Mrs. Bass had sinus issues and couldn't smell much of anything anymore.

I kicked the gravel as hard as I could, and muttered "Shit," which improved neither the situation nor my mood. What now? I walked past the Dumpster, heading for the street. The country club was a few miles from the nearest gas station—I remembered passing it on our way here. I could cover the distance in half an hour. I'd find a phone, call the police, and tell them the truth. I would tell them how Valerie had come to my house and what she'd told me she had done. I'd tell them that I'd been to the parking lot and that there was blood and a belt, but no Dan.

I pushed my hands in my pockets and hunched my shoulders against the cold when a thought hit me: What if they didn't believe me? What if they thought that I'd been the one to do something to Dan Swansea? What if Valerie lied again, took his side, defending him the way she had before? "Why are you telling these lies about me and Dan?" she'd ask, the way she had that day in the cafeteria in front of everyone, her voice cutting through the chatter until there was only silence and everyone was staring at me. I'd stood my ground, planting my feet, feeling my face turning red as I'd said, "I'm telling the truth and you know it," but my voice had come out a whisper, and Val's scornful laugh had been the loudest thing I could imagine. "Just jealous, I bet," she said, like she was talking to herself, but loud enough so that everyone could hear her. *Just jealous. Fat Addie.* That was me.

I sniffled and decided I'd just have to convince the cops that no matter what Val said, I was telling the truth. "Goddamnit," I muttered, and knelt down, thinking I could at least try to wipe my fingerprints off the belt, just as I heard Valerie calling my name.

I turned around to glare at her as she trotted out from behind a bush. "Sorry that took so long," she said.

I glared at her. "What the hell? Where did you go?"

"I had to pee."

"You had to *pee*?" I repeated.

"I had to find a good spot," she explained, smoothing her dress over her hips. "I'm wearing a bodysuit. I couldn't just go anywhere. It would have been very undignified."

When I could speak again, I said, "Didn't you once read the weather while you were riding a mechanical bull? I'm going to suggest that the dignity ship has sailed without you aboard."

Val had the nerve to look pleased. "Did you see that?"

"I read about it," I said, making the distinction clear. "I gather you have a lot of fans in the thirteen-year-old-boy demographic."

"Hey, it was sweeps week. And a viewer's a viewer. Is he dead?"

I waited long enough for her to start squirming, figuring it served her right, before I said, "I don't know if he's dead or not. He isn't here."

Valerie didn't appear to hear the news. "Well, I'm not turning myself in. Fuck that. Fuck a whole pile of that. First of all, it was an accident, and second of all, it was justice. Vigilante justice. Somebody should have stopped his clock a long time ago."

"Val, there's nobody here."

She finally shut up and stared at me, lips parted, hope dawning on her face. "Nobody?"

"There's blood," I told her. "There's a belt. But no Dan Swansea."

"Huh," she said, tilting her head sideways, giving me her profile, which, I was becoming convinced, had been surgically altered somehow: the nose a trifle thinner, the chin a tad more firm. "The blood," she finally said. "Do you think it's his?"

"Jesus Christ, Val. How should I know that?"

She frowned and walked back to the Dumpster, kneeling down to inspect the sticky gravel. When she rose up she looked relieved . . . and puzzled. "I wonder if he just went home."

"Maybe he got abducted," I suggested. "The guy I was out with earlier says there's a space shuttle that comes around."

Val lifted her head and glared at me. "Do you think joking is going to make things better?"

I jumped up and down, trying to get my blood pumping so I'd warm up. "Maybe he was Raptured. Although if that happened, his clothes would be here, too. And his clothes are still in your car, right?"

She rolled her eyes. "So you don't know whether it's his blood or not, but you know exactly what happens to clothing during the Rapture." I shrugged. Val stuck her thumbnail in her mouth and nibbled at it. "You know what we should do? We should go get the rest of them."

"Val," I said, struggling not to laugh. "You're a weathergirl. I paint greeting cards. This isn't the Wild West. We're not Thelma and Louise."

"Thelma and Louise had jobs, too," she said. "And as for me being a weathergirl, there is a long and honorable tradition of weatherpeople taking part in radical action. Perhaps you're familiar with the Weathermen?"

"Val." Giggles rose like champagne bubbles in my throat. "Those guys weren't actual meteorologists. You know that, right?"

She ignored me. "We should try to find him. Make sure he doesn't talk. Then we can go get the rest of them. Kevin, and Mark, and . . ."

"We?" I repeated. "Oh, no. You're on your own, sister. This isn't my problem."

She looked incredulous. Then, hurt . . . hurt and very young, in her high heels and red dress. "You're not going to help me?"

I shoved my hands deep into my pockets and spoke to her slowly, pronouncing each word carefully so there'd be no mistaking my meaning, remembering that day in the cafeteria, Val at one end of the room surrounded by her friends and me, alone, at the other. "Perhaps you don't remember," I began, "but the last time I tried to help you, it didn't turn out very well for me."

She bit her lip, looking abashed. "I said I was sorry."

"Yeah, well, you know what? It's a little too late for you to be . . ." I raised my hands in the frigid night air and hooked my fingers into quotation marks. " 'Sorry.' Do you have any idea what my senior year was like?" I asked, remembering the whispers that followed me everywhere I went: *Fat bitch. Fat whore. Fat narc.* Always *fat* something, as if fat was really the worst thing they could say about me, about any girl.

"Do you have any idea what my life was like?" Valerie shot back.

"Actually, I do," I said. "I was there, remember? I'm sure it was absolute hell, having to decide which guy to go to prom with."

"You have no idea."

"No, I don't. I'm sure I couldn't possibly imagine what it's like to be tall, and blond, and gorgeous, and to throw your best friend under the bus . . ."

"I hated you," Valerie said. Her voice was flat and toneless.

I stared at her. "Excuse me?"

"I hated you because you had everything." She turned away, aiming her keys at the Jaguar. There was a click as the locks popped open. "Come on. Get in. I'll take you home."

"Wait. I had everything? What are you talking about?"

She turned to face me, heels dug into the gravel, hands on her hips. "You had a mom. You had a dad. You had a brother. You had fucking food in your refrigerator, which, in case you never noticed, was something I did not have, because my mother never ate anything but Tab and fucking Wheat Thins. You had clean clothes. You had someone to sign your field-trip permission slips and give you five bucks so you could buy lunch. You had someone to show up at parent-teacher conferences. You never had to wake your mother up after she'd passed out on the couch with a lit cigarette. You had two parents who loved you . . ." Her voice caught. "You had everything." She turned away and jerked open the passenger-side door. "Get in."

"Valerie." I felt breathless, like I'd been hit in the stomach. What was she talking about? Her mother had been beautiful and fun, lively and full of adventure. Sure, she was a little scattered, but loving and good-hearted. At least that's what I'd always thought. Had I been that wrong?

"I wanted to belong somewhere," Val continued.

I stared at her, astonished. "How did selling me out help you belong?"

She lifted her narrow shoulders in a shrug, then dropped her face again. I stood in the parking lot, the night air frigid against my cheeks, not knowing what to say. Of all the times I'd imagined this scene, all the ways I'd thought about it playing out, feeling sorry for Valerie had never been a possibility. I was the victim, she was the villain; I was the ugly duckling, she was the swan. She'd escaped Pleasant Ridge, and I was stuck here, tethered to my brother, tied down by fear. In all my years of fuming and resentful imagining, all the years I'd carried my grudge like a pocketbook I was afraid to set down even for an instant, I'd never considered that there might be a different way of looking at the situation, another truth.

I took the chill of the night air into my lungs and breathed out slowly. "If Dan's not here, where do you think he went?"

Val shrugged.

"We should try to find him." I could do that at least, I told myself. I owed her that much for all the years she'd been my friend.

"Why?"

"Because . . ." I had the sense of somehow having slipped out of my regular life where logic and the normal rules applied and into some other world, a place where you could hit people with your car and escape with impunity, where you could hurt the people who'd hurt you without suffering any consequences . . . where they'd just disappear, maybe back to the real world, where the rules did apply. Everything was upside-down and backward. "Because he could be hurt."

She turned slowly, looking, now, entirely grown-up, like a

version of her mother, who could slide out of any tight spot with a pretty smile and a little judicious flirting. "Not our problem."

"But if you're the one who hit him . . ."

She rocked back and forth on her heels. "What if," said Val, "tonight is kind of a . . . kind of a get-out-of-jail-free card?"

I looked at her, wondering if she had any idea how close what she'd said was to what I'd been thinking.

"What if you could do anything you wanted?" she asked. "Get back at those boys? Get revenge?"

No, I thought. *It doesn't work that way. There's no such thing as something for nothing; the bill always comes due.* But then I thought about my life. I'd lost my mother and my father and my brother. I'd lost my best friend and my boyfriend. Worse than all that, I had lost my dreams of the life I'd imagined for myself . . . and now, if that stiffness in my belly meant what I thought it did, I was going to lose my life, too, probably quickly, and there'd be nothing left to show for the thirty-three years I'd spent on this earth except for a handful of greeting cards that sold in drugstores for a dollar ninety-nine, plus three mugs and a spoon rest, and a brother who didn't always remember that we were related and that I wasn't thirteen. I had nothing but Val . . . my best friend, who'd come back to me after all this time.

A rust-spotted sedan drove past the entrance of the parking lot. Without speaking, Val and I climbed into the Jaguar, Val behind the wheel, me beside her. The car started up with a purr and spat chunks of gravel in its wake as Val steered for the road.

"Where?" she asked as she accelerated, heading toward the highway, which could lead us back home or . . . well, anywhere, really. "Which one should we fuck up first?"

For some reason, the name that popped into my mind didn't belong to one of my classmates. Instead, I remembered the guidance counselor, one of the grown-ups, one of the people who should have been keeping me safe. Her name was Carol Demmick, and she'd kept a cruet of vinegar on her desk to sprinkle over the cut-up carrots she snacked on. The kids called her Summer's Eve, or Douche for short (I assumed she didn't know this). She'd called me into her office once in the spring of senior year, invited me to have a seat, asked me about my plans after graduation, and then asked me, gently, how my senior year had been going. It had been so long since someone at that school had looked at me with kindness, had spoken to me with anything besides indifference or contempt, that I told her. "Terrible," I choked. The details came spilling out of my mouth: the kids who tripped me and shoved me, and knocked over my lunch, the graffiti on the walls of every bathroom, how even the teachers seemed to hate me, to treat me like I had some horrible disease that might be catching. The guidance counselor had looked at me for a long minute, her big, buggy gray eyes magnified behind the green plastic frames of glasses someone had probably told her were "hip" and "cool."

"Addie," she said in her too-sweet voice, her double chins quivering gently as she studied me. "I don't mean to be unkind, but maybe, over the summer, you might think about a diet."

I'd stared at her, stone-faced. Did she think I'd never considered a diet before? That the possibility had never occurred to me? That I was not, in fact, on a diet right now, the same one I'd been on for the past six months and stuck to rigorously until nine o'clock every night? And who was she to talk to me about my weight? She was a fattie, too! "You know what they say," she continued, "you never get a second chance to make a first impression! And inside of every fat person there's a thin person dying to get out!"

I bent down and snatched my backpack off the floor. What kind of first impression did she think she was making, with her calendar of kittens thumbtacked to the wall (*Hang in there!* read the legend beneath the little white kitty clinging to a branch) and her dyed-blond Mamie Eisenhower bob that had remained unchanged in all the years she'd been at Pleasant Ridge High? "I've got math," I said.

Ms. Demmick's plump face softened. "Addie. I can see I've hurt your feelings. That wasn't my intention. I only . . ."

. . . *wanted to help,* I filled in as I walked into the crowded hall and let her door slam shut behind me. Sure. They all just wanted to help: the doctor, my mother, those boys who followed me down the halls, oinking—just trying to help! The girls I'd overheard in the bathroom—*I mean, she's got to weigh, like, two hundred pounds! That's almost two of me!* giggle, giggle—just offering their assistance! The world was just bursting with Good Samaritans, all of them dying to help out poor fat Addie Downs.

"Addie?" Val said from the driver's seat.

I pulled myself back to the present, to the heated seats of the Jaguar, to my old best friend sitting beside me. "Who'd Dan come with?" I asked.

"Chip Mason," she answered.

"First we'll check around the country club. Maybe he's on the side of the road. Then we'll go to Chip's."

"Can we stop for doughnuts first?" She looked at me, wide-eyed and hopeful.

I bit back another gust of laughter. Vehicular manslaughter, then baked goods. Sure thing! Why not? It sounded like fun, and I hadn't had any of that in a very long time.

TWELVE

"This can't be right," I said, peering through the window at the numbers on the houses as Valerie slowed the car to a crawl.

She squinted down at the class directory, open on her lap, then out at the dark street in the town of Aurora, a suburb forty-five minutes west of Pleasant Ridge. "Three-ninety-six Larchmont. This is it."

"But it's . . ." Val's headlights washed over the white sign stuck in the lawn in front of the two-story clapboard building. FIRST PRESBYTERIAN CHURCH: THANKS AND GIVING, SERVICES SUNDAY MORNING, 10 A.M., CHILD CARE AVAILABLE. "It's a church."

She cut the motor and unbuckled her seat belt. "Maybe it's been converted into condos."

I got out of the car and looked at the building, then studied the sign's small print, which advertised AA meetings Wednesday mornings at ten and read, at the very bottom, CHARLES MASON, PASTOR. "Val," I said. "When you were talking to Chip Mason at the reunion, did you happen to notice a black shirt and a white collar? Priestly garments? Rosary beads? A big wooden cross?" My father was Jewish but not observant, my mother had grown up Lutheran, and Jon and I had been raised as nothing in particular—we'd light a menorah in December and bring in a tree that we'd decorate, and there would be dyed eggs and chocolate rabbits in the springtime, without much in the way of explanation about what any of it meant—so I was a little bit vague on how you could recognize a churchgoing (or church-running) man.

Val made a face. "Oh, I'm sorry. Was I supposed to go to my high school reunion and listen to other people talk about themselves?"

"I guess not."

"Bunch of breeders passing around pictures of their kids," she grumbled, helping herself to a cruller from the wax-paper bag full of doughnuts we'd bought. "Like anybody cares." She took a big bite. "Like all babies don't look just like Ed Asner."

"Not the black ones," I pointed out.

"Funny," said Val, who knew as well as I did that of our class of 280 or so, fewer than a dozen had been black, bused in from Chicago as part of a program to give them more academic opportunities, then bused back home before they had a chance to join any teams or make any friends. The chance that one of them had felt connected enough to the class to actually show up at a reunion was slim.

I pried the Class of '92 guide out of Valerie's hands and found his name in the directory. "Reverend Charles Mason," I read. "Reverend. As in, God."

Val frowned. "Huh. Now that you mention it, he was talking about working on his service. I figured he just meant tennis or something."

"Jesus Christ," I said. Together, we walked up the flagstone path that led from the street to the church and climbed the half-dozen steps to the front door. Val cupped her hands around the pane of glass and peered through the window. "Pews," she reported. "Big cross up front." She took a step sideways to the next windowpane. "Um. Sign says Christmas organ concert on the seventeenth, but I don't see anybody there . . ."

"Excuse me!"

Val turned around. "Duck!" she hissed. I hopped off the stairs and crouched in the shadow beside, invisible as I'd wished to be back in high school, as a man in striped pajamas and a bathrobe—the elusive and now holier-than-us Chip Mason, I presumed—came from behind the church. His hair was thinning, his belly strained the waistband of his pajama bottoms, and he looked weary . . . although, in his defense, it was very late. "What are you doing here?" he demanded, then looked more closely. "Valerie?"

Val raised her hand and managed a weak wave. "Hi, Chip." She lifted the wax-paper bag. "Want a doughnut?"

"Is everything all right?" he asked, now sounding more puzzled than angry.

"I . . . came . . . for . . ."

Oh, shit, I thought, and leaned forward, ready to spring out of the shadows and defend us . . . or run.

"Salvation!" Val continued. "Just lately I've been . . . you know . . . thinking about God and stuff."

God and stuff. Kill me now. But Chip Mason actually seemed to be buying it as Val came tripping down the steps and onto the frost-crinkly lawn. "There are things in my life . . . things I've done that I'm not proud of." She stood close to him as she looked down, head bowed, then up, tossing her hair and angling her body even closer to Chip's paunch. "And it's been years and years since my last confession."

Chip frowned. "You know this isn't a Catholic church."

"Oh, of course." She gave a shrill little giggle. "Of course not. But I just thought, you know, with someone who knew me . . .

and knew God . . . it'd be, like, a setup! Blind dates are always better when there's someone who knows both people."

"Maybe we could talk about this on Sunday," he said. "Come to services. I'd be happy to speak with you after."

"Okay, but . . . well, it's just that there's something that's really been on my mind. I had . . . I guess you'd call it an epiphany last night." She led Chip to the car, and when they were directly beneath the streetlamp, she turned her head and mouthed the words *Find Dan*.

Great. I waited until she'd unlocked the car and somehow sweet-talked Chip Mason into the passenger's seat, where, presumably, they could arrange her night out with the Almighty. Then I bent over and hustled along the side of the building. The church was two stories, and behind it was a one-story brick addition that looked like living quarters—I could see a light through one of the windows, a stove with a kettle on it, a vase of red carnations on a cluttered kitchen table. I peeked through the window. No sign of Dan. Breathing deeply, I walked to the door of the rectory, or the parsonage, or whatever believers called the place where the priest lived. The door was closed but unlocked.

I turned the knob and stepped inside to a short entry hall with a coatrack and a pair of winter boots and a snow shovel at the ready, leaning against the wall. The kitchen was empty: I saw a woodcut of praying hands affixed to the wall, underneath a noisily ticking plastic clock, and a box of Entenmann's cookies on the counter. The powder room was neat and vacant. The living room had stacks of church newsletters and different religious and self-help texts on the shelves. A leather-bound Bible sat open on the wood coffee table. There was nobody on the couch or in either of the armchairs that sat across from it. I hurried down the hallway to the bedroom. Unmade double bed, vacant; closet with shirts and pants on wire hangers, ditto; bathroom with a glassed-in shower stall with a Waterpik and a tube of Rogaine next to the sink.

I pulled back the shower curtain and peered under the bed. There was nobody there. No signs of anyone, either—no kicked-off pair of shoes, no jacket draped over a chair, no droplets of blood in the sinks.

I slipped through the front door, closed it behind me, and dashed around the building, ducking back behind the hedge, then creeping forward until I could see Valerie's Jaguar. The motor was running. Plumes of white smoke rose up from the exhaust pipe. The windows were fogged. I squatted down, shivering, figuring that any minute Father Chip would conclude his spiritual counsel. He'd go back to his house, I'd get back in the car, and Val and I could figure out where to go next. The minutes crawled by. The door stayed shut. My knees creaked as I adjusted my position and held it until my thighs were shaking. Finally I approached the car, thinking that maybe I could knock on the back window as a signal to Val that it was time to go . . . but as I got closer, I could see through the window that the driver's seat was empty. Pastor Charles Mason was sitting in the passenger's seat, and Valerie had climbed on top of him. His mouth was open on her neck, and one hand groped her breast through her black lace body suit.

"Oh, for the love of God," I said, loud enough for them to hear if they'd been listening, which clearly they weren't. I waited until the car started rocking back and forth. Then I thumped twice on the window and turned my back. A minute later, the driver's-side door opened and Chip Mason climbed out into the night, smoothing the tented front of his bathrobe.

"Addie?" he said, peering at me. "Is that Addie Downs? My goodness, you got thin!"

"And you got religion!" I said.

I could see the moonlight gleaming on his bald pate as he

cleared his throat. "I was hoping to see you tonight," he said. "I wanted to apologize for my role ... in ..." He cleared his throat again and looked at me. "I've changed," he said. "I'm a different person now."

"Good for you," I said as Val came tumbling out of the driver's seat, patting her hair into place and looking like a vampire who'd just gotten a fresh infusion of blood. "We need to be going."

"Will I see you on Sunday?" asked Chip Mason.

Val gave him a silvery-sounding laugh as she slid behind the wheel. "We'll see," she said. I climbed into the car and we drove off, leaving Chip standing there in his bathrobe.

"No Dan?" asked Val, who didn't sound especially hopeful.

"No Dan," I confirmed. "Oh, and by the way, what was that all about?"

"I was creating a diversion," she said, as if this was obvious. "And it was hot. Very *Thorn Birds*."

"Val," I said, "Presbyterian priests aren't celibate. They're allowed to get married."

"Oh." She seemed disappointed to hear it. "Are you sure?"

"Positive."

Val pulled over to the curb underneath a streetlamp and grabbed the class directory from where it had gotten wedged between the seats. "You know what? Maybe we should just go see if he's home."

I felt my stomach clench, but I didn't say anything as Val pulled open the class guide, located Dan's address, plugged it into her car's GPS, and started to drive.

THIRTEEN

The New Year's Eve party was Valerie's idea, and I was surprised that my parents went for it. Maybe I shouldn't have been: Valerie, my mother used to say, could charm the bark off of trees, and she made the event sound like the most exciting thing that had ever hit Pleasant Ridge, or at least our cul-de-sac. "A New Year's Eve celebration," she'd decreed from my bedroom floor, where we'd assumed our customary positions, head to head, propped up on our elbows on the carpet, with our feet pointing toward opposite corners of the room. Val, in her usual jeans and boy's button-down shirt, was flipping through a copy of *Mademoiselle*. She hadn't changed the way she dressed now that we were in high school, but she'd started reading about clothes, and she'd show up at the bus stop with her hair puffed up with mousse or gloss painted on her lips. I was in jeans of my own and an oversized sweatshirt that fell past my hips, working through a bag of Cheez Doodles, holding each puff underneath my tongue until it dissolved. "For the neighborhood."

"Not for other kids?"

She shook her head. "A grown-up party. A dress-up party."

"Like tuxedos?" The men on our street wore suits, or at least shirts and ties to work, but on weekends they were found mostly in jeans or khakis and polo shirts.

"They can rent them if they don't have them." She flipped onto her back and gazed at the puckered plaster of my bedroom ceiling. "And the ladies should wear evening gowns. We can have a champagne toast at midnight, and we'll decorate with those little white Christmas lights." She bounced up off the floor onto her toes and clapped her hands twice, sharply, in front of her chest. This was a move I recognized from the cheerleading squad, and I wondered unhappily whether Val was planning on trying out in the spring, whether that was what the *Seventeen* subscription and the cans of TRESemmé mousse meant. "Let's ask your mom right now."

We found her on the sunporch, curled up in a pile of cushions with a legal pad half covered in looping black cursive on her lap. She'd had her most successful card yet the year before, a birthday card with a cartoon drawing of a little old lady with white curls and a cane on the front. *Think of it this way: You're not just getting older,* the front flap read . . . and then you'd open it to reveal the words *You're also getting shorter.* I wasn't sure exactly why it was funny, but it had been selling, as my mother said, like hotcakes.

"A New Year's Eve party?" my mom asked. Her hair was more silver than brown by then, her big blue eyes hammocked in a nest of fine wrinkles. I could see words on the notebook page and also, in the margin, a column of numbers. She worried about money, I knew—sometimes, late at night, I'd hear my parents whispering about the costs of Jon's therapists, credit-card bills, and insurance deductibles. My father had papered the town with his Honey-Do flyers, even venturing into other towns to put them up, and my mother was never without her notebook, not in the car or at the kitchen table, not even, I suspected, in the bathroom.

"New Year's Rockin' Eve," Val explained. "We can invite everyone on the street."

My mom propped herself up on her elbow. "Do you think your mother would like that?"

Val nodded. That summer, Mrs. Adler had had a new boyfriend, a man named Randy, who was, Val said, a stockbroker. On Sunday nights he'd sleep over, and I'd see him leaving Val's house in his suit and tie on Monday mornings, off to join the other dads at the train station. But in November, Randy disappeared, and Mrs. Adler spent even more time than normal lying prone on the couch, blowing smoke rings toward the ceiling with the silent telephone balanced on her chest.

"Were you thinking of a potluck?" my mother asked. We'd have one of those every winter. Everyone on the street brought a dish—tuna casserole with crumbled potato chips on top, ziti studded with chunks of sausage, baked beans and franks—to the Basses' house.

Val shook her head. "I think it should be a cocktail party, with champagne and fancy food. My mom makes good crab puffs."

This was true. Crab puffs were, in fact, one of the two things I'd ever known Mrs. Adler to cook. She could do crab puffs and sake-glazed duck, which was delicious, but not the kind of thing you could cook, or would want to eat, seven nights of the week.

My mother sat up, adjusting her knitted shawl, and I could see her making an effort to smile, to act like this would be fun.

"And it should be dressy," Val continued.

"Well, it is New Year's Eve," my mother said.

"Can I get something new?" I wasn't sure whether getting dressed up for the party was something I dreaded or anticipated. I was already wearing the largest sizes available in the juniors department, and I could see that unless I managed to do something, to stick to a diet, to stop the secret eating on nights when

I woke up at two a.m. and couldn't fall asleep; to actually get out of bed and go jogging when the alarm I'd set for six a.m. rang, instead of hitting the snooze button and rolling over, I'd be shopping in the big-lady specialty stores and Dan Swansea, my secret crush, would never notice me. But Val's enthusiasm was seductive. Maybe the combination of twinkling white lights and music and champagne at midnight would work some kind of magic. Maybe I'd find a dress that could transform me. Maybe my mother would let me go to Shear Elegance for an updo. Waiting for her answer, I promised myself that I'd throw out the bag of cheese curls as soon as we got back to the bedroom.

My mother looked at her legal pad. "I think it sounds like a great idea."

Valerie started listing the things they'd need: champagne and champagne flutes, serving trays for the canapés, the little lights, which would surely go on sale after Christmastime. My mother wrote a poem inviting the neighbors to come celebrate. Mrs. Bass, who did calligraphy in her spare time, wrote them out, and I painted little watercolors on each invitation, pictures of our street, each house under a dark-blue sky, with a single star visible above it. Valerie and I tied the invitations up with silver ribbons and slipped one into every mailbox on the street.

For the ten days of Christmas break, I taped songs off the radio, Whitney Houston and Simple Minds, Steve Winwood and Bon Jovi. My mother came through with an outfit for me, a long, sheer gold skirt with tiny bells sewn onto the hem and a forgiving elastic waistband, that I'd wear with a black bodysuit and black lace-trimmed leggings underneath. She even cut a length of elasticized black lace and sewed it into a headband to match the trim on the leggings.

The party started at the sophisticated hour of nine p.m., after people had had their dinners and the families with small children had welcomed the sitters and put the kids to bed. It had snowed the night before, draping the frost-burned lawns in a blanket of white. Valerie and I had twisted strands of Christmas lights into the hedges and through the bare branches of the trees, and Val had used sand and votive candles and a hundred brown-paper lunch bags to make luminarias that were set along our driveway, lighting the path to the door.

Jon stood in the entryway, waiting for the guests to arrive: first Mr. and Mrs. Bass from next door, then Mrs. Shea from the end of the street, alone and looking exhausted in green slacks and a red sweater, with an unblended blotch of rouge staining one cheek. The three of them sipped champagne and warmed up in front of the fire while Mrs. Shea told the story of how her husband had brought home a puppy for Christmas—"and just when the babies were out of diapers," I heard her say. Then the doorbell rang and people started piling into the foyer: the Carvilles and the Buccis and the Prestons. Val nudged me, grinning, as Mr. and Mrs. Kominski arrived—they were the young married couple who'd just moved to the street, and Mr. Kominski was cute, as long as he kept his baseball cap on and you couldn't see that he was already mostly bald.

Jon carried everyone's coats upstairs and piled them on our parents' bed. He was having a good night so far—he wasn't as slow or as stumbly as he normally was, he wasn't drooling or constantly wetting his lips with his tongue, and when people asked him questions, there was only a slight hitch, a barely perceptible pause, before he'd answer.

Even though my mother had tried to talk her out of it, Val had insisted that the invitations say "black tie." Most of the guests hadn't taken her literally, although people were definitely more dressed up than they were at the neighborhood barbecues or the potlucks. All of the men wore ties. Some wore suits, and a handful were in tuxedos. Most of the ladies wore wool skirts and Christmas sweaters with embroidered reindeer or jingling sleigh bells sewn on the front. Mrs. Bass was glamorous in a floor-length black velvet gown that smelled faintly of mothballs, and a few of the younger mothers wore jeans and blazers with low-cut tops underneath. Mrs. Alexander, whose kids Val and I some-times babysat, wore tight black pants and a silver halter that left her freckled shoulder blades bare. (Mrs. Alexander kept a dia-phragm and a tube of contraceptive jelly in her bedside table, and every time Val and I went over we checked on the tube to see if any gel had been squeezed.)

Valerie's mother arrived just before eleven, and when she pulled off her coat, even Jon stared. Her dress was pale pink, with a bodice that clung to her breasts and hips, and she wore high-heeled silver shoes. "That was her wedding dress," Val whispered.

I knew it was. I'd recognized it from the pictures. Valerie's parents had gotten married on the beach in Cape Cod. Mrs. Adler had described the day: the wind that had whipped their hair and the hem of her dress, blowing so hard that not even the priest could hear their vows, and he'd made them repeat them, yelling "I do!" over and over again until all the guests were laugh-ing. Their reception was at a vineyard, where they'd danced be-neath the setting sun. It had sounded so romantic. The only wedding I'd ever attended was when my mother's cousin got married three years ago. The service had been in a church, and the party had been at the Marriott. There was no salt-scented wind swallowing the vows, and the bride and groom hadn't slow-danced underneath an arbor or fed each other morsels of wed-ding cake with their fingers. There was, instead, a buffet with tired-looking lasagna set over blue-flamed tins of Sterno, and a disc jockey who played "Maneater," which, even at eleven, struck me as highly inappropriate.

"Sara / You're the poet in my heart," Stevie Nicks sang on the tape I'd made. Valerie circulated with champagne. Mrs. Adler closed her eyes, turning in dreamy circles. Her skirt spun out from around her body; her hair flared out from around her head. Val looked proud as she watched.

I played my tapes on my parents' stereo, where the songs sounded so much better than they did on my tinny little boom box. When the first tape ran out, I was ready to go with Sting's *The Dream of the Blue Turtles,* but my father intercepted me. He'd worn his tuxedo, the same one he'd been married in, but at some point he'd ditched the jacket and cummerbund and was now slim and graceful in his black pants and white shirt. "I got this, Pal," he said, setting his empty champagne glass down on the bookcase. His pale face was flushed, his hair was damp and curling over his forehead, and he looked more relaxed, happier, than I could remember seeing him. He reached into a cupboard and retrieved a stack of albums, flipping rapidly through them until he found the Rolling Stones' *Sticky Fingers,* which he put on the turntable, cranking the volume up loud. "Brown Sugar" came blasting through the speakers. By the door, Jon was so startled he jumped. Mrs. Adler threw her hands in the air, laughing. My father crossed the room and took her by the hands and spun her, and I was struck by how right they looked together, paired and partnered in a way I'd never seen my father and my mother. My heart gave an unhappy lurch as Mrs. Adler turned around, swinging her hips and smiling over her shoulder at my father.

"Whoo-hoo!" somebody shouted . . . and then another couple started dancing, and then two more. Within minutes, our living room was filled with people waving their hands, singing along, dancing. Jon leaned against the wall with his mouth half open, like a kid at a fireworks display. Val sidled up to me and cupped her hands around my ear. "Isn't this great?" she shouted. She poured more champagne into my plastic cup and clinked hers against it in a toast. As "Sway" turned into "Wild Horses," Mr. Kominski crossed the room. I held my breath as he approached, but I wasn't surprised, and I tried not to be disappointed, when he asked Val if she wanted to dance. He led her to the center of the room, where Val smiled up at him, lifting her mouth to his ear to shout answers to the questions he must have been asking, then quickly pressing her lips together, the way she'd been doing lately, to hide her teeth. I sat down on the couch that we'd pushed against the wall, letting the music pound through me. It was okay if boys liked Val better. Someone would love me someday. Even if I wasn't an obvious choice, I'd be somebody's choice, some boy's choice, the way I'd once been Valerie's. The wind was howling outside, bending the trees, rattling the windowpanes, but inside we were warm and happy, all of us safe and together.

"Here we go!" one of the husbands shouted. The music skidded into silence, and Mr. Preston snapped on the TV just in time to see the glittering ball begin its descent in Times Square. "Four . . . three . . . two . . . ONE!" The room exploded with cheers. Husbands kissed wives, and not the polite closed-lipped kisses that Val and I had seen on our babysitting jobs, when the husbands came home from work. Some of these couples were kissing like they meant it.

Suddenly Val was beside me, grabbing my hands. "Come with me," she said, pulling me off the couch.

"Where?" I asked as she led me down the hall to the kitchen. "What's going on?"

"Shh," she hissed. She stuck her head around the corner, waited, then beckoned for me. I stood on my tiptoes, craning my neck. At first what I saw hardly seemed remarkable: my father, with a bottle of champagne in his hand and his white tuxedo shirt clinging to his chest, leaning against the refrigerator, as Mrs. Adler stood in front of him, talking earnestly. Her feet were bare—she'd ditched the silver shoes somewhere—and as I watched, she tilted her head up shyly, clasping her hands behind her back. My father said something, and she nodded, breasts bouncing below her tight neckline.

"That's it, that's it exactly!" she said. "God. You really get it. To go from California to a place like this . . . it's so small-minded. Little boxes. Like the song."

I frowned. That didn't make sense. Except for college and Vietnam, my father had lived his whole life in Illinois, so how could he really "get it"? And then, as Val and I watched, Mrs. Adler wrapped her hands around his neck and kissed him.

I sucked in my breath. From far away, I could feel Val grab my hand, could hear her whisper, "Isn't this great?" I squeezed my eyes shut, but I could still hear them—Mrs. Adler (*call me Naomi!*) murmuring softly, my father's lower tones as he answered.

"I should get my mom."

Val squeezed my hand harder. "Why? This is perfect."

I made myself open my eyes. "What are you talking about?"

"Because we'll get to be sisters," she said.

"What about my mom?" As I watched, my father reached behind his head, took Mrs. Adler's hands from around his neck, and folded them on top of her chest.

"I think," he told her, "we've both had a few too many."

"Oh, no," she said, looking at him with her eyes wide, drawing her *no-o-o-o* into a little girl's whine. "I'm fine! I'm having fun!"

"Come on," said my dad, putting one hand on her waist, turning her around, and trying to steer her out of the kitchen. "Let's get you home."

She dragged her feet over the floor. "Will you walk me?"

"Addie and I will take you," said my dad. He paused by the edge of the kitchen and saw Val and me standing there. "Val, you want to grab your mother's coat?"

Val's face was unreadable as she turned and ran up the stairs.

This is perfect, I heard her say in my head. I was furious at Val if she'd meant what I thought she had, and angry at her mother and my father, too (she'd kissed him first, but he'd kissed her back). I was also, I found, consumed by a kind of guilty curiosity. What would it be like if Mrs. Adler and my father got married? What if Valerie and I were really, truly sisters? My mother could stay here with Jon and take care of him. My father and Mrs. Adler could live in the DiMeos' old house—my dad was handy, he could fix it up, scrape off the peeling paint, patch the holes in the walls, and it would be weird for a while, but people got used to all kinds of things. Val would have a father. We would finally finish her pink-and-green bedroom, and we'd get matching beds that Val had shown me in a magazine, and . . .

"Here, Mom." Val's lips were pressed into a thin line as she helped her mother slip into her coat. Then, kneeling, she slid Naomi's feet into her high-heeled silver shoes. "Come on," she said. "The party's over. Let's go home."

FOURTEEN

"So what happened to your parents?" Valerie asked as we drove east, along the wide, empty lanes of the Eisenhower Expressway, heading toward Chicago, where Dan lived in one of the high-rise buildings downtown. It was five in the morning, my first all-nighter in years, and I was exhausted, shaky from adrenaline and lack of sleep, but Val looked fresh as a flower, her skin creamy, hair falling in curls to her shoulders.

"My dad had an aneurysm the fall after we graduated." I knew from Mrs. Bass that Valerie had been in California by then—she'd been able, through her father, to establish residency and enroll in one of the state schools. Mrs. Adler was still technically our neighbor, but by then she was spending most of her time in Cleveland with a new man. I'd been in New York for ten days, had settled into my apartment and started my classes in Art Appreciation and History of Painting at Pratt. My dad had been driving home after a day of installing windows in one of the big new houses in a development that had gone up in Elm Ridge. According to the drivers who'd been on the road behind him, his car had slowed, then drifted over the yellow line and through a metal barrier and proceeded almost gracefully down a slope before coming to rest in a pool of shallow water at the bottom of a ditch. He was just forty-six, dead behind the wheel. He'd had a weak spot in an artery at the base of his brain that had probably been there for years and had finally, quietly, exploded.

I'd been numb as Mrs. Bass gave me the news on the newly activated telephone. I'd felt like one of my father's puppets, a thing made of wood and wire, as I'd told my new roommate what had happened, and called the dean of students, then a travel agent to book a flight back home. I'd stayed numb as I'd filled my suitcase and carried it to the sidewalk and caught a cab to the airport, numb as I'd boarded the plane, and then, when we were airborne, I had remembered a Saturday morning the previous spring.

I'd gotten up early and was going through what had become my weekend routine: bury the empty wrappers and ice-cream carton at the bottom of the trash can, put on a pot of coffee, pull on sweats and shoes, grab a bucket and scrub brush from the front hallway, and go outside to scrub graffiti off the drive-way. Most mornings my father would come out to help me. We'd scrub, then go inside to drink black coffee once the words were gone. But that morning, he'd said, "You know, Pal, it won't be like this forever." The older and bigger I'd gotten, the less physically affectionate he'd become, but that morning he'd pulled me close and hugged me roughly, his arms tight around my back. "I'm proud of you," he'd said. "You're going to be fine." The memory pierced me, and then I wasn't numb . . . I hurt all over, burning with an agony I didn't know I'd be able to survive. In 16D on the plane, I'd doubled over as if I'd been stabbed, sobbing, unable to catch my breath. My seatmate called the stewardess, who'd regarded me with contempt showing through her makeup. I wasn't looking pretty, crammed into the tiny seat, the seat belt cutting into my belly, my cheeks bright red and my face wet with a plaster of tears and snot. "Are you all right, miss?" she asked, and I tried to collect myself. "My father died," I blurted.

"I'm sorry," she said, and handed me a stack of napkins and a can of Diet Coke—the best she could do, I guessed, under the circumstances.

At home, my mother was sitting on the sunporch, a notebook, with both pages blank, spread open in her lap. "I can't believe he's gone," she'd said. Tears rolled steadily down her cheeks. I thought of all the condolence cards she'd written, how her job had been to find the right words for moments such as these, and how, now that it was her, she'd fallen back on that one phrase that she repeated all through the night and the following days: *I can't believe he's gone.*

The next morning, I'd been the one to take Jon to Marshall Field's for a new suit, and explained to him over and over why he needed it. He'd remember for a while, then look down at himself, frowning at the stiff white shirt, fingering his tie. "Addie?" he'd say, and I'd take him aside and tell him again.

There'd been an obituary in the paper. I waited to see if Valerie would call, or send a letter, or maybe even show up at the service or the grave, but she didn't. She was gone, her mother, too, and I guessed—at least I told myself—that it was likely neither one of them had heard the news.

My father died on a Tuesday. Though he'd been barely Jewish in life, death turned my dad into a believer. He was buried as quickly as we could arrange it, two days after his death, in accordance with the traditions of his faith—in a plain pine casket with a Star of David carved on its top, and a rabbi in a black suit with a black silk cap on his head, praying in a language I'd never heard before as the body was lowered into the ground.

On Saturday morning I woke up early, with the plan of clearing out the basement, packing up my dad's tools and whatever puppets he'd left. *Basement in the morning and his closet in the afternoon,* I thought, slipping down to the kitchen to make toast and coffee. Maybe Jon would want some of my father's clothes, cuff links or a watch to remember him by.

"Addie." I jumped, badly startled as I heard my mother's voice. She was sitting at the kitchen table in the dark. She wore her blue bathrobe, and her hair hung uncombed around her cheeks. Her hands cupped a mug I'd painted for her one of my summers at camp: a red heart with the words *I Love You* in cursive underneath. "I need to talk to you about something."

I took my customary seat at the table. I couldn't stop looking over to the stove, expecting to see my father there with his frying pan, making his famous pancakes, saying *Hey, Pal, did you have sweet dreams?*

"It's bad news," my mother began. Across the table, in the dusty shafts of light coming in through the window, she looked old, with veins bulging on the backs of her hands, and her face drawn and haggard. "In May, I found a lump in my breast," she said. "They did a biopsy and then they scheduled a mastectomy."

I sucked in my breath. "Oh, Mom."

"I was going to tell you at Thanksgiving when you came home. By Thanksgiving, I'd be through the worst of it—the surgery and then the chemo—but now . . ."

"I'll stay here." I said it instantly. "I can call the admissions office, I'm sure they'll let me defer. They'll probably even refund the tuition."

"No, honey. I don't want that." But there was no force behind her words, and she was looking down as if afraid to meet my eyes. In the silence, I understood, in a way I never had before, that as much as she'd taken care of my father and helped him navigate the world, he'd helped her do the same thing . . . and it was my job now.

I'd called the admissions office and arranged for a deferral.

My roommate shipped me the clothes I'd barely unpacked, the brilliantly colored Helen Frankenthaler prints I'd just tacked to our walls. Together, my mother and I found a halfway house for Jon, a homey, well-run place that his disability checks would pay for. "It's time," my mother said. "He should live on his own, he should have as much of a life as he can." Jon settled in, getting used to the social workers, the other men, the job they'd found him at the drugstore. Then it was just the two of us.

I drove my mother to the hospital for her surgery and then for her chemotherapy and radiation. On the way home I'd grip the wheel, watching for potholes, inching along as carefully as I could as she sat beside me, pale and silent, with Band-Aids in the bends of her elbows and a plastic basin in her lap.

I'd pick up her prescriptions and cook her meals, soft, bland things that wouldn't make her nauseous or irritate the sores in her mouth. I'd check books and videos out of the library, buy fancy lotions and skin creams when I found them marked down at Marshalls or T.J. Maxx. I taught myself to knit and made her shawls and hats—a jaunty beret in purple wool, a striped ski cap with a frothy pom-pom on top.

When she was too tired to work, we'd sit on the porch and she'd tell me stories: an Easter egg hunt where she and her sister had gotten stuck in the chimney, a trip she'd taken to Canada with her college roommates, how she'd met my father (it hadn't been in the water at all, but at the musical, when her camp had hired him to run the lights for the end-of-summer show).

On Wednesday nights we'd go to visit Jon. We'd take him to dinner at the Greek diner down the street from the Crossroads, or pick up pierogi, which he loved. If there was something playing he wanted to see, we'd go to the movies, or we'd wander around the bookstore, or the big electronics store where Jon could try out different video games. He had the tastes of the teenager he'd been when the crash had happened, a passion for starchy foods and shoot-'em-ups, comic books, and Tom Petty and Bruce Springsteen. He would be, in some ways, like a child until he died, and it was tragic, to be sure, but there was also something almost fairy-tale-ish about it. Jon would age, but he'd never grow up, never have to worry about the things grown-ups worried about.

It was on those Wednesdays, on our way back home, that my mother would try to talk to me about my future. No matter what happened, she instructed, I was to go back to college, and when I was done, I should travel as much as I could. I should spend at least a semester in Europe; I should visit Italy and Spain; I should see the Louvre and the Prado and as many Vermeers as I could. Sitting in the passenger's seat, she was hardly recognizable—she'd lost so much weight so fast that you could see the outline of her bones underneath her pale, loose sheath of skin. She'd lost her hair, her eyelashes and eyebrows. *Okay, Mom,* I would say as she instructed me on books to read, on paintings to look at, on the churches and beaches and cities to visit, a list of places I knew for a fact she'd only read about. *Okay.*

"Whatever happens to me," my mother said, her voice soft and sweet and faint as I turned off Hightower and onto Crescent Drive, past the Sheas' house. After twenty-two years and fifteen children, Mrs. Shea and her husband had gotten divorced the year before. Now Mrs. Shea lived in the house alone, with her silvery hair cut short, and could be seen each weekday morning in spandex pants, with her Bible in her hand and her yoga mat hooked over one shoulder, on her way to early-morning mass at six, then yoga class at seven. "Whatever happens, you're going to be fine."

I told her that I knew I'd be okay, even though I didn't believe it. While she'd gotten thinner with her illness, and was as flat-chested as a boy after the double mastectomy, I was getting fatter. She would sit in the chemo lounge, with classical music wafting through the air and poison dripping into her veins, and I'd take the elevator three floors up to the hospital cafeteria and gorge myself on plastic-wrapped slices of cake and pie, shoveling tasteless forkfuls of chocolate and custard and crust into my mouth and wondering whether they'd given the food a dose of radiation, too, or shot it full of chemicals that had taken away its taste. I didn't enjoy it, but I couldn't stop—not the cake and pie binges, not the cookies and candy I'd eat in my room in secret, after the lights were out and I had to concentrate on pretending not to hear my mother cry.

In between the hospital visits and the trips to the grocery store and the pharmacy and to visit with my brother, I set up an easel in the dining room, and I'd snatch an hour or two, here and there, to paint. Back in November, my mother had sent a painting I'd done to her editor. It was a watercolor of a Christmas tree with a shining star suspended above it and the words *Peace on Earth* underneath. Her editor said she loved it, and the next thing I knew I had a check for two hundred dollars and an invitation to submit more work. All through the fall and into the winter I painted, as the leaves fell and the air grew chilly, as the new gourmet grocery store in the center of town changed its display from pumpkin pie and chestnut stuffing to Bûche de Noël and, eventually, diet frozen dinners for the New Year's resolution crowd. Without any planning, I had found myself with a career. As my mother shrank and dwindled, I painted and ate, painted and ate and dreamed of New York City, which seemed farther and farther away with each day that passed, like a place I'd only dreamed.

Winter was brutal that year. The temperature rarely rose past freezing in the daytime and plummeted past zero in the night, when the wind howled down the street and battered at the walls. After a dinner of soup and pudding, I'd help my mother into the shower. We'd stand together underneath the water, and she would brace herself against the tiled wall as I washed her, trying not to notice the way her hipbones and the bumps of her spine pushed against her skin, or the bruises that bloomed on the scant, loose flesh of her arms and thighs. Once she was dry and powdered and in a fresh nightgown, I would read to her: *Pride and Prejudice, Oliver Twist, Great Expectations, A Tree Grows in Brooklyn,* her schoolgirl favorites. She was regressing, I would think. Her breasts were gone, her hips and hair were gone, and sometimes at night she would cry softly, the way I imagined a baby would.

Near the end, when there were no more surgeries or chemo and radiation, when there was only the hospice nurse and the morphine drip, I was sitting by her bed, a book in my lap and my knitting in a bag beside me, when my mother rolled onto her side and took my hand. "Addie, you have to promise me you'll go back to school. You can't just stay here."

"I know, Mom." This was a conversation we'd had many times before.

"I know you're afraid," she said. "But you have to believe me. There are good things out there. There are good people. Good men." Her bright eyes softened. "You could have a baby."

I looked down at myself, breasts spilling onto my belly, belly threatening to erase my lap. The last time I'd stepped on a scale, I'd watched the numbers roll past two hundred, then past two hundred and fifty, and I'd jumped off, shocked, before they could go any farther. Who would want to have a baby with me? "I'll be okay," I told my mother, and she sighed and closed her eyes. I thought she was done, but a minute later she said, "Have you talked to Valerie?"

I didn't answer. My mother persisted. "You two were such good friends."

"She ruined my life," I said. The words came tumbling out as if they'd been held back, dammed up. "She turned everyone against me . . ."

"Don't be so hard on her," said my mother.

"She ruined my life," I repeated.

She sighed and shook her head. "High school isn't life, Addie. Your life is not ruined." With an effortful grunt, she propped herself up on an elbow. "I think Valerie hasn't had a very easy time of it."

"Oh, sure," I said, unable to keep the bitterness out of my voice. "I'm sure it was really hard for her."

She reached for my hand. "You should call her. Promise me you will."

In the too-warm bedroom that smelled like toast and eggs and arnica gel and the lemon-scented lotion I rubbed on my mother's legs and feet, I told her that I would—another promise I had no intention of keeping.

"Addie," said my mother from the depths of her bed. "There's all kinds of love in the world, and not all of it looks like the stuff in greeting cards." She lay down, grimacing, and I glanced automatically at the clock, counting backward from her last shot of morphine, then forward to seven a.m., when the hospice nurse would arrive. "I just want you to be happy. Your father and I . . ." Her voice trailed off and her eyes filled with tears.

"I'm happy," I said. I read to her until she fell asleep. Then I sat beside her, picturing that long-ago summer morning, in the canoe with my best friend beside me. We'd paddled past half a dozen little boats riding at anchor in the shallow waters. The sky had been blue, with a few cottony pink-tinged clouds. If I concentrated, I could remember the names of each one of the skiffs: *Lovely Lu. Tall Cool One. Evangeline.*

My mother died in the middle of a warm night in September, just over a year after I'd come back from New York, as I lay beside her, listening to the spaces between her breaths grow longer and longer, until finally there was no breath, just silence. "Rest now," I said. I covered her poor skinny body, her birdy-bones and bald head, with the afghan I'd knitted from ivory-colored chenille, and kissed her cheek. "Rest." When the sun came up, I called Dr. Shoup, who said she was sorry for my loss, and the hospice nurse, who cried and said how lucky I was to have a mother who'd loved me so much. Jon and I did it all again: the long black limousine, the barely worn black suit, the neighbors over at the house, carrying cold cuts and casseroles and saying how sorry they were, my brother looking at me with muddy confusion in his eyes, tugging my sleeve to ask, "Addie, where's Mom? Why isn't Mom here?"

I was nineteen, almost twenty. I'd inherited the house on Crescent Drive, the life insurance policies my parents had both left, the small trust they'd set up to care for Jon. I could have done what my mother had wanted—sold the house, packed my bags, gone back to school, gone to Europe, gone dancing, gone to the beach—but it was as if every bit of energy and optimism I'd ever possessed had left me, and New York City was a place I'd made up, a fairy tale I'd told myself. Besides, I was so big. The world was not a place where I belonged. It was high school writ large, full of bad things waiting to happen and bad people waiting to do them. Better to stay home, to work at the easel I had set up in the dining room, to make my little circuit from the grocery store to the library, where I knew people and people knew me, where it was at least relatively safe.

My mother had insisted that I get a degree, and that was one promise I kept. I signed up for art courses at the local community college, where most of my classmates were what were euphemistically called "returning students," people in their twenties and thirties with day jobs and, in some cases, night jobs, too; with little kids and aging parents and weekend obligations. I got a bachelor's in fine arts and lived at home, where I worked painting the images I'd eventually become known for: tiny, exquisitely detailed, iconic renderings of a single thing—a heart, a flower, a gull in flight, a spray of fireworks—set against a background of white. No need for an office, no need to ever meet the people who employed me. No need for them to know how I lived or what I looked like. I'd eat oatmeal for breakfast, tuna salad or peanut butter for lunch, cookies and cakes and pudding and pie in private. I worked during the daytime; I ate, and read, at night. I didn't bother anyone, and for years, nobody bothered me.

"Addie?"

From the driver's seat, Val poked my arm with one bright-red fingertip. "You still with us?" I rubbed my eyes. We'd arrived in Chicago. The sun was up, but the street was in shadows cast by the skyscrapers on either side. I looked up at the high glass-and-concrete tower we'd parked in front of. THE MODERNE, read the marquee above the entryway. "Looks like he's done pretty well for himself," I ventured.

"I bet he's in an efficiency," said Val. "And anyhow, karma's a bitch." She unbuckled her seat belt, letting it slither over her body and smack against the door. "I'm going to go talk to the doorman. I'll tell him I gave Dan my car keys 'cause I was drinking, only now I need them back."

"And what about this car?" I asked, indicating the keys in the ignition.

"I'll tell him it's yours."

"Okay." This sounded like as good an idea as any, and I had to admit I was amused by the thought of owning a Jaguar.

"If he's there, we're fine."

"And if he's not?"

She pulled the seat belt back and forth. "Maybe we'll just go clamming."

"Clamming," I repeated. Val turned to look at me. "Hey," she said, "are you okay?" I shook my head. "What's wrong?" Val asked. I couldn't answer. She looked at me for a moment. "Sit tight, okay? I'll be right back," she said, and got out of the car and pulled open the Moderne's heavy glass doors, moving as if she had nothing more on her mind than what to cook for dinner or whether the shoes she'd seen had gone on sale.

I sat with my arms wrapped around my knees, watching the clock in the dashboard tick the minutes away. Nine of them had elapsed when Val came loping back to the car. "Not here," she reported, starting the car. "Also, no regular girlfriends, no regular guy friends, he parties a lot and . . . oh, and he might be getting fired, but he doesn't know it yet."

"You got all that from the doorman?"

"He's a viewer," she said modestly. She drove a few blocks, then pulled over to the curb.

"What are you doing?"

"We need," she said with her eyes narrowed, "to start thinking like criminals."

"What?" I asked. *We?* I thought. Valerie reached behind her and gathered an armful of men's clothing. I caught sight of a blue shirt, a pair of pants, a flash of white underwear. Then Val jumped out of the car, looked quickly over her shoulder to make sure we were alone, and shoved the clothes down a sewer grate. A minute later, she was back in the car, breathing hard and looking pleased. "I dumped everything but the wallet and his cell phone. I'm gonna leave them in a trash can. Maybe they'll think he's been the victim of identity theft." She thought as we accelerated toward the highway. "Maybe he actually will be the

victim of identity theft." I didn't answer. "It'd serve him right."
We drove for a few minutes, the wheels whispering over the road
as, behind us, the city woke up. "Let's go home. I bet you're tired,"
Val said.

"Home sounds good," I answered, and she flicked her turn
signal on.

PART TWO

Into the Woods

FIFTEEN

Dan Swansea trudged down the road toward the light of the rising sun. His legs were bare above his socks, his skin burning with the cold. The storage shed door had been unlocked, and that was lucky, but he hadn't found any clothes or blankets there, just a box of contractor-sized trash bags that he'd used to swaddle himself, poking his head and arms through one, wrapping another around his crotch like a diaper. He'd rested for a while, curled up in a drafty corner of the shack, and then he'd started down the road. He swished when he walked, and he didn't even want to think about how he looked. There was nothing he could do about it. That bitch Valerie Adler—he'd remembered her name—had taken his wallet and his phone.

There has to be something, he told himself as he walked. A convenience store or a gas station or something. He would walk until he found it. He would go home, get clothes, get warm, and then he'd find the bitch and he'd fix her wagon.

He was so lost in thought that the van was almost on top of him before he noticed, and it was too late to jump into the ditch on the side of the road, too late to hide himself. The van slowed—Dan braced himself for laughter, a hurled bottle, some kind of joke—"Time to take out the trash!" is what he personally would have gone with—but instead, he heard a woman's voice calling kindly through the grayish half-light.

"Dan Swansea? Is that you?"

Eyes dazzled by the headlights, he squinted at the van, but couldn't make the face behind the wheel.

"Are you all right? What happened to your clothes?"

"Long story," he managed. The van's door slid open without anyone touching it. For a minute, Dan thought about supernatural phenomena, about psychic forces and otherwordly visitors, about the Holy Ghost, unseen but ever-present (his mother had been big on that), before remembering that all vans these days had remote controls.

"Come on in," said the voice. "I'll take care of you."

No time to weigh his options. As he saw it, his choices were getting into the van or continuing to trudge through the frigid darkness, naked except for his shoes, his socks, and a pair of Hefty trash bags. Dan Swansea limped across the road and climbed inside.

SIXTEEN

The call came in at just after six in the morning, less than three hours after Jordan Novick had finally managed to fall asleep. Except, he acknowledged, "fall asleep" wasn't exactly accurate. "Passed out" might have been a better description of what had occurred in the folding chair in his living room after a great quantity of beer, a tumbler full of whiskey, and a fast, furtive episode of masturbation as *The Nighty-Night Show* played on the TV.

He groped for the telephone. "Novick," he grunted, noticing that his pager was spasming on the coffee table like a rodent having a seizure.

"Good morning, Chief," said Paula the dispatcher. "We've got a situation in the Lakeview Country Club parking lot. Acknowledge?"

Jordan rubbed the bridge of his nose, then his stubbled cheek. "What kind of situation?"

"That's the thing. We're not exactly sure," said Paula. "I know you're 10-10-A, but it's a possible 10-80. Or maybe a 10-81 with a 211. Or it could be . . ."

"Hey. Hey, Paula." An old line, but it was usually enough to get her to stop with the numbers. Paula Albright, the Pleasant Ridge dispatcher, was a fifty-four-year-old retired school cafeteria worker who took her work very seriously and knew the codes for everything, including "lost bicycle."

"Yes, sir?"

"How 'bout you just tell me what happened?"

"Sure, Chief. The club custodian found a man's belt and some blood in the parking lot, but no victim yet."

An actual mystery, Jordan thought, getting to his feet with the telephone pressed against his ear. That was unusual. Situations in Pleasant Ridge tended to fall into a few large and easily quantifiable categories. You had your accidentally tripped burglar alarms. Your lost dog, your cat up a tree. Your missing children, usually teenagers who hadn't bothered to tell Mom and Dad where they'd be, and neglected to keep their brand-new state-of-the-art cell phones charged. There was credit-card fraud and identity theft, car crashes and house fires and DUIs. There were, of course, husbands smacking their wives around and, occasionally but not as infrequently as most people would think, wives hitting their husbands. These incidents were unpleasant, but at least they were a kind of expected, predictable unpleasantness, and there was a protocol, honed over time, for handling them. Jordan couldn't remember anything in his ten years of service that had been along the lines of an actual mystery.

He swallowed and coughed, grimacing at the sour taste in his mouth, and tucked the phone under his chin so he could zip his pants. "10-8, acknowledge," he said to make Paula happy, and to cover the sound of the zipper. "On my way."

"You're going to the southeast corner of the parking lot, by the Dumpster."

"Got it," he said, and grabbed for his keys.

By the time he arrived at the country club, all three of the town's uniformed patrolmen (one of them was Holly Muñoz, so he supposed it was actually three patrol-people) were waiting. An investigator from the county district attorney's office with rubber gloves on her hands and a high-tech digital camera and an old-school Polaroid looped around her neck met him at his car. "What have we got?" Jordan asked the investigator, a young woman named Meghan, who wore her hair in a high ponytail and had a tiny silver stud glittering in one nostril.

"Come take a look," she said. Jordan forced himself to breathe steadily through his nose, in case during the twenty minutes it had taken him to get there, they'd discovered a body. He kept his eyes between Meghan's shoulder blades until she stopped and pointed down. "Weird, right?"

Jordan aimed his flashlight at the ground. There was something wet and rusty-red that had trickled into the gravel and splashed on the corner of the Dumpster. There was a man's black leather belt with a silver buckle coiled neatly a few feet south of the blood. That was all.

"The club custodian, George Monroe, found this stuff when he took out the trash this morning," said the tech. She pointed to a skinny guy in khaki pants sitting on the steps outside of the country club's kitchen. When the man saw Jordan looking, he raised one hand and waved.

"No body?" asked Jordan.

Meghan shook her head. "We looked: the road, the parking lot, the golf course, the ditches along the road, a mile in each direction, and we went through the Dumpster. If there is a body, it's been moved, but I gotta say, there's not a ton of blood here, so I'm not necessarily thinking corpse."

"Did the custodian see anything else?" Jordan asked without much hope. Meghan shook her head again and fingered her cameras. "We're almost done here," she said. "Then it's all yours."

"You're not staying?"

She gave him a sunny grin. "If it's a homicide, we'll be back. Obvs. But until you're sure it's not some drunk dude who fell down . . ." She drifted back to her car. "Holiday weekend, you know?"

"Got it." Jordan spoke briefly to his patrolmen, reviewing the procedure for securing a crime scene. Then he headed over to the custodian.

"Morning," he said, extending his hand. "Jordan Novick. Pleasant Ridge chief of police. You found the, uh . . ." *Effects?* he wondered. "Effects" didn't sound quite right.

"The belt," the other man said. He was in his late twenties, with brown hair and pale eyes. He had a high, rough voice, an Adam's apple that bobbed and jerked when he swallowed, old acne scars pitting his cheeks, and a fresh zit blooming on his chin. "I got here at five a.m. First tee time's at six, so I come at five. I was carrying the trash to the Dumpster when I kicked something. I thought it was a bottle or something, but then I looked down and saw the belt and the blood, and I thought, okay, this isn't right. I went back inside and called 911. Didn't touch anything. Didn't want to contaminate the crime scene." He nodded at Jordan, one professional to another. "I watch *CSI.*"

"Excellent," said Jordan.

"So what are you guys gonna do now?" asked the custodian, scratching at his chin. "DNA testing on the blood? You got that luminol?"

"I thought," said Jordan, "that we'd start by seeing if anyone who was here last night is missing a belt." The kid's zit had started to bleed. He pressed one khaki sleeve against it as he thought this over and finally grunted his approval. "Any trouble here lately?" Jordan asked. "Any ideas about what might have happened?"

The other man lowered his eyebrows and ground his teeth. "Vegans," he finally pronounced.

For a moment Jordan thought that he'd heard him wrong,

or that the man was speaking something other than English. "Vegans?"

"Because of the leather," the man said. "The belt's leather. You notice that?" He shook his head. "Vegans are fucked up. I saw some of them on the news trying to liberate the bees. I mean, vegetarians are one thing. No meat, okay, animals got feelings. I get that. But no honey?" He cleared his throat and spat onto the gravel.

"Have you had trouble with vegans here before?" *I'm still asleep*, Jordan thought. *I'm asleep and this is a dream.*

The custodian shook his head. "Nah," he said. "But I watch out for them." He tapped the side of his eye with one finger, then went back to working the pimple.

Jordan wrote the word "vegans," which made as much sense as anything else. Then he took down the custodian's contact information, his name and address, his cell phone and social security numbers, thanked him for his help, and walked over to his patrol-people. One of them, Devin Freedman, was finishing up his law degree at Loyola. The lady patrol-person, Holly, had studied sociology and trained for Olympic-distance triathlons in her spare time. The third, Gary Ryderdahl, a Pleasant Ridge native like Jordan, had worked for the department for three years and had just moved out of his parents' house and into his first apartment (Jordan had spent a Saturday helping him load, then unload, a U-Haul). None of them was older than thirty, and the three of them, plus Jordan, were all that stood between Pleasant Ridge and *le déluge*. "Gentlemen," said Jordan. "Lady. What've we got?"

Gary Ryderdahl glanced at his colleagues, pulled a notebook out of his back pocket, and stepped forward, squaring his shoulders like a batter approaching the plate. Ryderdahl had a round pink face and an unruly ruffled crest of white-blond hair that made him look like Snoopy's tweety-bird friend, Woodstock.

"It's a Kenneth Cole belt. They sell them lots of places. Department stores, and, uh . . ." He took a quick glance at his notebook. "Freestanding boutiques nationwide."

"Good work," said Jordan, straight-faced. "What was going on here last night?"

"There was a class reunion. Pleasant Ridge, class of 1992," Holly Muñoz said. "D.A.'s office is taking the blood, and they're gonna see if there's any fingerprints we can use on the belt, but Meghan said probably not. I spoke to the banquet manager. There were two hundred people here last night—a hundred and eighty-seven who'd preregistered, and thirteen walk-ins." She reached through her patrol car's open window and came out with a Dunkin' Donuts cup, which she extended to Jordan. "I got you a coffee. Light and sweet, right?"

"Thanks." Jordan looked around. Officer Freedman, the soon-to-be lawyer, was cordoning off the crime scene with yellow tape. He stuck the tape's edge onto the Dumpster, unspooled it past the belt, and then stopped, looking around with the roll of tape in his hands, realizing there was no place else to stick it unless he walked another twenty yards to the nearest tree.

Jordan made himself stop staring. "Guest list?"

"The class secretary's got it waiting for us," said Holly. Devin Freedman, meanwhile, was carefully affixing the end of the piece of tape to the ground, using a rock he'd grabbed from somewhere to hold it down. Jordan closed his eyes.

"We'll want to talk to everyone who was here last night." Holly nodded and nudged Gary, who nodded, too. "You two, go back to the station. Call all the hospitals, here and in Chicago. Ask if anyone's shown up with injuries, missing a belt." He paused, thinking. "Check out the custodian. George Monroe." He read off George's social security number and DOB. "Check with dispatch. See if any calls came in for missing persons." He thought for a minute. "Then call the body shops."

"You think this was a car accident?" asked Holly.

"Could be," said Jordan. "Worth checking."

"I hit a deer once," Gary Ryderdahl offered. "Bashed in the whole front of my car."

"Here?" asked Holly. "In Pleasant Ridge?"

"No, Wisconsin. My grandma's got a place in the Dells, and I . . ."

"Time's wasting," Jordan said. "Hospitals. Body shops." Gary marched off. Holly looked at Jordan.

"Uh, chief?" When Jordan looked at her, she asked, "What is this, exactly? When I type up my report, what do I call it?"

"For now, it's a lost belt," Jordan said. *And it's weird,* he thought but did not say.

SEVENTEEN

Class secretary Christie Keogh, perky and bright-eyed and dressed in a tight tank top and fitted running pants, met Jordan at the front door of her McMansion, with a list in her hands and a frown on her pretty face. She spoke in a whisper, explaining that her husband and kids were still sleeping upstairs. "What's this about?"

"We found a man's belt in the country club parking lot. There was also some evidence that a crime may have been committed. We need to make sure that all of your party guests are okay."

"Evidence?" Christie's frown deepened, then vanished instantly, as if someone had snuck up behind her and hissed *Wrinkles!* in her ear. "What kind of evidence?"

"Physical evidence," said Jordan. "Blood."

Christie wrapped her arms around herself and led him inside, into her vast kitchen, all gleamy stainless steel and shiny black granite, immaculate as an operating theater. "Would you like some green tea?"

"You guys vegans?" Jordan asked.

She looked at him strangely. "We do eat meat, but only organic." Christie took a seat on a rattan barstool and waited for Jordan to do the same.

"Did you see anything unusual last night?" Jordan asked her. "Arguments? Fights?"

"Unusual." She cupped her elbows in her hands. "It was a high school reunion. There were a bunch of people who hadn't seen each other in years, plus an open bar, so yeah, I'd say I saw some unusual stuff. Lots of it in the ladies' room."

Jordan raised his eyebrows, waiting. Christie tightened her grip on her elbows. "I saw Larry Kelleher and Lynne Boudreaux, being intimate. And they're married." She leaned in close enough for Jordan to smell her toothpaste. "Not to each other. Oh, and Merry Armbruster was trying to convert people in the parking lot. She's born again—she got saved the summer between junior and senior year—and I guess she wants everyone else to be."

"Any fights?"

She thought. "I heard Glenn Farber talking with his wife about which one of them was supposed to pay the sitter, but that wasn't a fight. Just kind of an intense conversation."

"If you had to guess . . ." He let his voice trail off. Christie looked at him, blinking expectantly, her eyes wide underneath the pale, unlined expanse of her forehead. *Stupid, or Botox?* Jordan wondered.

"As far as I could tell, everything was fine."

"We're going to go through the list and contact everyone. Make sure that nobody's missing a belt." *Or bleeding to death,* he thought.

Christie chewed on her bottom lip. "My God. I just can't believe it. It was a really great party."

He asked for the guest list, and she handed over five stapled sheets. "That's everyone who RSPV'd ahead of time. We had thirteen walk-ins. Judy should have their names—that's Judy Nadeau." She pointed out Judy's name and address on the sheet. "She lives about a mile away. Elm Lane, do you know where that is?"

Jordan did. "Think she's awake?" he asked.

Christie wrinkled her nose. "She had a lot of Cuervo. I'd maybe call ahead."

"Will do. You around today?" Jordan asked.

"I'll be in and out, but I always have my cell phone with me. My trainer should be here any minute. We're going joggling," she said.

Jordan figured he'd misheard her. "Jogging?"

"Nope. Joggling. You run while you juggle these little bean bags. It's an amazing upper-body workout. I'm signed up for a 10K next month."

"Amazing," Jordan repeated. He instructed Christie to keep her cell phone on, in case he had follow-up questions, and folded the list into his pocket. She walked him to the entryway and stood in front of a gold-framed mirror, tugging at the hem of her top. "I just can't believe this. I seriously cannot. I was driving home not six hours ago, thinking how well everything went."

He gave her his card. "We'll be in touch. Try not to worry," he said as she rubbed her upper arms, frowning. "This could be nothing."

Christie offered one final "I can't believe it," followed by a plaintive, murmured "There's no way they'll let me be in charge of the twentieth after this."

EIGHTEEN

J ordan had figured that Judy Nadeau would be hungover. He hadn't planned on her being actively inebriated. But when a tiny, bedraggled brunette with a crushed updo and a sheer black dress slipping off one shoulder answered the door and offered her hand through a cloud of high-proof fumes, it took him about ten seconds to realize that she was still smashed.

"A private dick!" she slurred, batting her prickly lashes and stumbling backward, giggling, as he let go of her hand. She steadied herself on the wall, blinked, and led him through a kitchen just as big as Christie's had been, but considerably less neat. "That is so noir!" Instead of granite countertops, Judy had gone for white marble and a backsplash of food-splattered tiles behind the sink. Lined up next to the jumbo food processor and an espresso machine that looked like a rocket's insides was a collection of painted ceramic roosters. Jordan tapped one, making it wobble on its yellow metal legs.

"Nice cock," said Judy, then pressed one ringed hand against her lipsticked mouth and giggled. *Oh boy,* Jordan thought as Judy pulled a container of orange juice and a bottle of champagne from the refrigerator.

"Hair of the dog," she announced, dumping juice and booze

into a coffee mug that read NUMBER ONE MOM. For the second time that morning, Jordan had to force himself not to stare.

He sat down at the cluttered kitchen table, stacking newspapers and twisting the lid onto an open jar of baby food to clear some space. "Ms. Nadeau, I need you to fill in a few details about the reunion last night."

"Sure thing," she said, and hiccuped, sliding into the seat across from him. She propped her chin in her hands and stared at him with disconcerting intensity. "Hey. You're cute."

"Thank you. Now, about last night . . ."

"My ex-husband was cute, too," said Judy. "I don't trust cute men. They're all so *entitled*."

"Last night," Jordan repeated.

"What about it?" She frowned and patted at her hair. "Oh, shit," she said. "Listen. Pete told me he was divorced."

"Ma'am, we found a belt in the parking lot."

"Almost divorced," Judy Nadeau continued. "That's what he said." She took a swallow of her drink. "And we used a condom. Let the record reflect."

"Ma'am, there was a belt and some blood in the country club parking lot. Someone might have been hurt."

"Not Pete," she said instantly. "I didn't do anything to him." She smiled slyly. "At least nothing he didn't want me to do."

"Listen," Jordan said through the thunderclouds of an incipient headache, "do you have a list of the walk-ins from last night?"

She shook her head. "But I think I remember them. I could write them down." She produced a pen and a piece of monogrammed stationery from a drawer, and after several lengthy pauses, a refill on her beverage, and a lot of tuneless humming of what Jordan eventually recognized as Michael Jackson's "Smooth Criminal," she wrote down thirteen names.

"Were there any classmates you can think of who might

cause trouble?" Jordan asked as she sat back down at the table and picked up her mug.

Judy thought for a minute before lifting her drink and sloshing mimosa onto her sleeve. "There was this one guy who graduated with us. Jonathan Downs. He had..." She paused, searching for the politically correct term. "He was in a bad accident, and he was always a little bit off after that. I'm not exactly sure what was wrong with him. But he was strange for sure. And he used to take things from other kids' lockers."

"Things?"

"Oh, just any little thing. Jackets. Notebooks. Somebody's lunch." She hiccuped against the back of her hand. "I remember once he took all the badminton shuttlecocks from the gym. It was more annoying than anything else."

Jordan wrote down *Jonathan Downs*. "Was he there last night?"

"I don't think so. If he was, I didn't see him. I kind of doubt that he'd want to come."

Jordan pulled out the class directory Christie had given him and found an entry that read *Jonathan Downs/Adelaide Downs/ 14 Crescent Drive.* "This him?"

"That's the last address we had for him. It's where he lived in high school. I'm not sure if it's current. He didn't RSVP one way or another."

Jordan tapped the name Adelaide. "His wife?"

Judy shook her head, her small face crinkling as she frowned. "Sister."

"Are they twins?"

"No, Jon was older, but he got left back after his accident."

"Was Adelaide there last night?"

Judy shook her head again.

"You're sure?"

"Believe me, I'd have remembered if Addie Downs had been

there. You couldn't miss her." She gestured with her mug. This time, mimosa spilled on the tiled floor. "She was huge."

Two kids in the same class, in the same house; one fat, one brain-damaged. Interesting. "Did Addie take things out of people's lockers?"

Judy stared at the floor. "Nah. She just . . . you know . . . moped around." She looked down into her NUMBER ONE mug and seemed surprised to find it empty, then looked up, blinking at him. "Hey, you want a drink?"

"No thank you," said Jordan.

"Wanna fool around?"

He cleared his throat. "Ma'am, I'm on duty."

"I'm *kidding*." Red lipstick had come off her upper lip and stained the skin beneath her nose crimson. "Unless you want to. I mean, if this were a porno, we'd have to, right?"

"We'll be in touch," Jordan managed, getting to his feet.

"It'd be my tax dollars at work!" Judy said.

"Take care," he said stiffly, seeing her face crumple before he turned toward the door.

"Cute guys," she said. "Screw 'em." And she slammed the door hard enough to make it rattle in its frame.

NINETEEN

Jordan Novick could read people—at least that's what they told him at work, where he'd become, at thirty-five, the youngest chief of police that his hometown had ever employed. But he'd failed to read his own wife, failed to notice the array of textbook signs: the new hairstyle, the gym membership that she was actually using instead of just paying for, the new underwear (scraps of black and nylon embellished with lace and embroidered rosebuds, items so intricate and tiny that when they'd shown up in the laundry basket, he hadn't even known at first that they were underwear). He hadn't registered any of it until Patti sat him down one Sunday night two years ago and told him that she thought they were drifting apart.

Yes, he'd said, pathetically eager. He had noticed the same thing. It wasn't surprising, after what they'd been through. Maybe they could give counseling another try or plan a trip. He had four weeks of vacation coming. They'd always talked about Paris . . .

Patti had cut him off. *No Paris,* she'd told him. He'd noticed how tired she looked, how, underneath the layers of her chemically brightened hair, the skin of her cheeks was stretched and papery and her lips were pale. *I am sorry,* she'd said. *Jordan, I'm so, so sorry. But I can't stay here anymore.*

"In the house?" he'd asked stupidly.

"In this marriage," she'd said.

Patti's mom and sister had come up the next night, and the three of them had moved Patti's things—which, per Patti and her mother, included most of the furniture and all of the wedding gifts—to Patti's sister's house. Jordan had been left with the bookcases and most of the books, the futon he'd had since college, a few IKEA chairs that wobbled if you looked at them too hard. He'd been abandoned in a house where every doorknob had a plastic baby-guard around it, where every outlet was plugged with a safety lock, where there were gates in front of the staircase, top and bottom, and a lock on the toilet tank. Patti had told him she just wanted to "be by herself" to "sort things out" until she could "see things clearly," but the truth was, not three weeks after she'd left their house and their eleven-year marriage, she'd moved out of the sham condo that she'd rented and in with Rob Fine, their dentist. Their *dentist.*

"We just got to talking," Patti told Jordan three months later in the mediator's office when, sitting across from his wife at a shiny conference table, in a voice that was too loud for the room, Jordan had recited the demand of cuckolded husbands the world over and asked his wife how all of this had started.

"Just got to talking?" he'd repeated. "With your mouth full of cotton, and that tube for the spit?"

"He listens to me," Patti had said.

"I listen to you!" said Jordan, jumping to his feet, leaning across the table, speaking right into her face. "I do your temperature charts on PowerPoint! I measure your cervical mucus! I . . ."

"Let's maintain a respectful tone," said the mediator, a smoothy in a red-and-gold silk tie that he stroked like a pet, a man who had the nerve to charge two hundred bucks an hour for his services. Jordan circled the table, heading toward Patti. The big muscles in his thighs were twitching; he had to move.

"I measure her cervical mucus," he said to the mediator, who'd pursed his lips in a prissy little line.

"I'm not sure this is a productive line of discussion," he'd said, and put his hand between Jordan's shoulders, trying to ease him back into his seat.

Jordan ignored the man. "How long?" he asked Patti.

She twisted in her chair. "Maybe six months," she muttered.

"Six MONTHS?" He leaned across the table, unable to believe what he was hearing.

"Please," said the mediator, pushing on Jordan's shoulder harder. Patti crossed her legs and stared at a spot on the wall just above Jordan's head, refusing to meet his eyes.

"Six months?" Jordan repeated. His hands clenched into fists. *I'm a detective,* he thought. *How could I not have seen this?*

"We can discuss this reasonably," said the mediator.

"She told me she had bad gums!" He turned on the mediator, who stared back at him, the gold frames of his glasses shining in the lamplight. "Advanced gingivitis!"

"*Please,*" the man said, and pointed to the chair. Reluctantly, Jordan sat down. He knew when he was beaten. He scrawled his signature on the forms they slid in front of him without looking at his wife and without reading a word.

"Good luck," he told Patti once it was over. She'd put one soft hand on his arm and said, "Be happy, Jordan. That's all I want. For both of us." He'd kissed her cheek numbly. He couldn't stop looking at her teeth, which glittered like a mouthful of pearls. Ill-gotten gains. Dr. Fine was probably giving her freebies.

He and Patti had hooked up junior year at a party, when Patti, tipsy on foamy beer pumped from a keg, had tried to climb a tree during a game of Truth or Dare. She'd been doing a pretty fair job of it, too, until someone had howled, "I can see your *bush,*" and Patti, startled, had groped for her skirt and lost her grip and would have gone tumbling ten feet to the ground if Jordan hadn't been there to catch her. Later, with the two of them sitting on the lid of the Petrillos' hot tub, he'd wiped the tears from her face and assured her that nobody had been able to see anything (even though he had been able to make out a faint shadow underneath the taut nylon of her panties, and the sight had excited him wildly).

They had gone to prom and graduation and Ohio State University together, where he'd studied criminology and she'd majored in early childhood education. He'd wanted to be a policeman since one had come to his sixth-grade class on Career Day. Jordan had been impressed by the man's uniform, by his gun, certainly, but, more than anything, by his aura of composure, the stillness at his center, the way he'd gotten the whole class to quiet down just by standing in front of them and slowly removing his tinted sunglasses (a feat Mrs. McKenna, their teacher, could manage only sporadically). Jordan craved that kind of authority, the silence that emanated from the man. At his house, his mother screamed at his father, and his father hollered at Jordan and his brother, Sam, and all four of them were given to bawling at the television set when the Bears and the Cubs disappointed.

So he'd gotten his degree, and three years after graduation, he'd married Patti and moved to a walk-up apartment in a three-story building in a Polish neighborhood in Chicago that had one bedroom, a tiny galley kitchen, and a glassed-in porch that rattled every time the El went by. They'd take long walks on Saturday mornings, go shopping in the afternoon, and spend Sunday cooking elaborate feasts from one of the ethnic cookbooks Patti had bought and invite a bunch of friends over and eat from mismatched bowls on the floor. Patti got a job as a reading specialist in the neighborhood elementary school, and Jordan worked his way up through the ranks of the Chicago police department.

When they were thirty, they'd decided that small-town life

suited them better than Chicago. Jordan had taken the job in Pleasant Ridge, and they'd moved from their apartment in the city back home, into a three-bedroom house in the same neighborhood where Patti had grown up. The house needed some updating—particularly the bathrooms, which boasted foil wallpaper in psychedelic 1970s patterns—but there was a big backyard, and a finished basement, an apple tree growing outside their window, and of course it was baby-proofed, wanting only a baby.

Patti threw out her birth control pills the month of her thirtieth birthday. At night, Jordan would pause, balanced on his elbows, to look down at his wife, flushed and breathing hard, and he would marvel, *We could be making a baby. We could be starting a whole new life.* The first month, nothing happened, but neither of them worried. By the third month, they were making anxious jokes about how they'd keep trying until they got it right. After six months with nothing to show but some rug burns from the night when they'd decided to spice things up and do it on the living room floor, Patti called her gynecologist for an appointment, but the doctor couldn't find anything wrong with either one of them. Patti's eggs were healthy and her uterus was inviting, and Jordan's sperm were plentiful and perky, but for whatever reason, nothing had taken. "Just keep trying," the man said, and so they had, every other day, except on days fourteen through eighteen of Patti's cycle, when they did it every morning, and Jordan showered and shaved while his wife lay in bed with her legs pretzeled and held in the air.

Patti's doctor put her on Clomid, which made her moody and gave her backaches and acne and caused her to gain, as she put it, ten pounds in ten minutes. Four months later, Jordan came home to find his wife weeping and waving a pregnancy test over her head like the Olympic torch. "Finally," she cried, throwing her arms around his neck, "finally!" Jordan hauled the elliptical trainer into the basement and replaced it with the crib that had held Patti's nieces and nephews. Six weeks later, she'd come out of the bathroom one night after dinner with her eyes wide and her face pale. Jordan had scooped her into his arms, the way he had when he'd carried her over the threshold of their hotel room on their wedding night, and driven her to the emergency room. Too late.

"The good news is, we know you can get pregnant," the doctor had told them as Patti lay crying on the hospital bed after the D and C. *Good news*, thought Jordan, turning away. *Yeah, right.* More hormones were added to the mix. Patti stopped eating foods that weren't organic. Then she stopped eating meat and dairy altogether, and added fistfuls of vitamins and supplements—iron and folic acid, flaxseed oil and garlic capsules—to her morning regimen. When she started smelling vaguely like shrimp scampi, Jordan knew better than to mention it. She joined an online support group. Then she joined a real-time support group that met each week at the hospital, and encouraged Jordan to attend with her, but after one night spent listening to a bunch of weepy women and their beaten-down husbands talking on and on about deteriorating follicles and poor motility, "pre-e" and "PCOS," Jordan had decided he'd had enough. "If it's meant to happen, it'll happen," he'd told Patti, parroting a line their doctor had given them. "We have to let nature take its course." She'd looked at him with big, mistrustful eyes before pointing out that she was thirty-two, almost thirty-three, that she didn't have forever. Clearly, nature needed some help.

She got pregnant again that September and miscarried November third. Their doctor told them to wait a few months before trying again, but Patti ignored him. She also neglected to pass this piece of information on to Jordan, who would have been happy to abstain. Sex with Patti had become as routinized, and every bit as pleasant, as emptying the dishwasher or taking out the trash. Instead of looking down at her in ecstasy and thinking *We could be making a baby*, the only thought going through his head as he pumped and thrust (always in the missionary position, to maximize their chances, Jordan's body slick with sweat and Patti's teeth bared in a joyless grin) was *Please, please, let it work this time*. It was God's joke on him. When he was fourteen, sex was all he thought about and all he wanted, and even the cleft of a peach in the produce section could get him going. Now that he could have all the sex he wanted—or at least all the sex he wanted during the six days when Patti was most fertile—all he wanted at night was a cold beer and a soft pillow.

By January, Patti was pregnant again. By the middle of February, they were back in the hospital, Patti crying on the bed, Jordan standing beside her, their doctor at the ultrasound monitor, saying *These things happen* and *Sometimes it's for the best* and *You're young and healthy, you just need to be patient*.

In the car, on the way home, Jordan, stumbling, had suggested that maybe they could adopt or think about a surrogate. He'd read an article somewhere, and there'd been that actress who'd given the interview on TV ... Patti had turned on him, eyes blazing, lips drawn into something just short of a snarl. "You want to just give up? After everything I've been through, you want to just quit?"

"No," he'd said, backing off clumsily. No, of course he didn't want that. He just thought that maybe they could give themselves a break. Tears spilled from his wife's eyes. "I don't want a break," she'd said, her voice cracking. "I want a baby."

They moved from the hormones to in vitro. Instead of having sex, Jordan got to masturbate into a Dixie cup every other month, with a tattered copy of *Penthouse* in his free hand and a nurse hovering on the other side of the door. Patti spent two nights a week at her infertility support group, and every spare minute online, researching homeopathic remedies and alternative medicines, or studying first-person accounts from women who'd managed to give birth to healthy babies in spite of a history of miscarriages, in spite of breast cancer or a tipped uterus or a missing fallopian tube, in spite of strokes or lupus or polycystic ovarian syndrome or, in one case Patti had shown him, in spite of having no arms and no legs.

She was pregnant again by April. She lost that baby (that was how she'd started referring to her miscarriages, as "lost babies") the third week of June. On the Fourth of July, they were supposed to attend a neighborhood picnic, then drive into Chicago and watch the fireworks over Lake Michigan. At four o'clock, Patti handed Jordan a hollowed-out watermelon filled with fruit salad and told him to have fun. "You're not coming?" he'd asked.

"I can't," she'd said, and he knew why. Larry and Cindy Bowers, who lived down the street, were hosting the party, and Cindy was pregnant with twins. Sarah and Steve Mullens from the next block, who surely would be invited, had a three-month-old, a little boy named Franklin whom Steve insisted on wearing strapped to his chest like a bomb. Steve had told the rest of the men that he had started a blog that was all about the baby— "about our adventures together," was how he'd put it—and instead of looking at him like he was crazy, the other men had nodded solemnly, had tapped at their BlackBerries, bookmarking the link.

Patti got pregnant again in September, and after she'd lost that baby the last week in October, she came home from her support group and announced that she wanted to hold a memorial service.

Puzzled, Jordan looked up from his magazine. "For what?"

She'd stared at him as if he'd grown a second head. "For our babies."

He'd folded his magazine and set it down on the side table.

"Patti," he'd said. His voice was calm, even though he could feel four years' worth of frustration and disappointment seething in his veins—the pills and the shots and the IVF cycles (none of them were covered by insurance, and their respective 401(k)s had dwindled from thousands to hundreds of dollars), the nights Patti had spent weeping at her support groups or welded to her laptop, convincing herself that this was going to happen, that she could *make* it happen by sheer force of will, the way books about pregnancy had crowded every novel and biography from their shelves, how every conversation they had—in bed, in the car, over dinner, on vacation—came back to this: sperm and egg and the empty crib in the third bedroom, so sunny in the mornings, tucked up under the dormer windows. "You can't have a service for something you flush down the toilet."

It was an awful thing to say. He'd known it was an awful thing to say almost before he'd finished saying it, even before he saw Patti's eyes narrow and her hands ball into fists. She'd taken three steps toward the kitchen. Then she'd stopped, turned, picked up the cedar box that they'd bought on their honeymoon in Mexico and heaved it, as hard as she could, at Jordan's head. The corner of the box had caught him in the corner of his left eye. The pain was instant and enormous. "Ow," he cried. "Ow, shit!" Patti had stalked to the bedroom, closed the door and locked it, leaving him sitting there with the box broken in his lap and blood running down his cheek.

He'd packed a towel full of ice, held it against his face, and driven himself to the emergency room, where he'd told the attending physician and the nurses and, later, the ophthalmologist on call that he'd walked into an open door. If a woman on his watch had given him an excuse half as lame, he'd have brought in the social workers before the lie was out of her mouth, but the eye doctor just told him to tilt his head back while she gave him drops. "You've got a bad scratch on your cornea," she proclaimed after he'd spent an eternity with his chin propped on a metal crosspiece, trying not to blink as she shone violet-tinted light into his eyes. No surprise. Every time he blinked, it felt like there were grains of sand rubbing against his eyelid.

"What do we do?" *Surgery,* he thought glumly. He'd probably need surgery, and wouldn't that be a perfect ending to the perfect day?

"Can't do much of anything but wait," the doctor said. She gave him an antibiotic cream and a prescription for Percocet, and told him he might notice his eye watering on and off as it healed.

Back home, he'd cleaned up the mess, sponging blood off the carpet, throwing the broken cedar box away. At nine o'clock at night, he'd tried knocking at the locked bedroom door.

"Patti?" he'd called. She hadn't answered. "I'm sorry," he said. Still nothing. "If you want to have a service, that's okay," he said. "Whatever you want." Silence . . . and then her voice had come, cool through the door. "What I want," she'd said, "is for you to sleep somewhere else tonight."

They'd stayed together for another year. Jordan went back with her to her support group. He'd sat beside her, holding her hand while she cried. They had done couples' therapy and had had date nights every Saturday: dinners and movies, then back to the dark house where there was no sitter to pay and dismiss. They'd slept underneath the darkened third bedroom, which was now empty—at some point after the night of the box, Patti had gone to her mother's for the weekend, and Jordan had devoted a Saturday morning to dismantling the crib and carrying it, piece by piece, down to the basement. When they made love, Jordan got used to reaching up to caress his wife's cheek and having his hand come back wet with her tears. Later, he'd decide that their marriage had died the instant she'd picked up that box, but at the time he'd managed to convince himself that they were doing okay. They'd gone to the Bahamas for their tenth anniversary, and on the plane ride back, Patti had fallen asleep with her head on his shoulder, and he'd thought, with pride swelling his chest, of the title of a poem he'd read in college: *Look! We have come through*. He thought they had.

And then had come the dentist.

Jordan shook his head and rubbed roughly at his eyes. The left one was watering again, so he wiped it with a napkin. It had healed, but it still watered three years later, and sometimes he had double vision, which, technically, he should have told the town manager about, but he never had. What was a little bit of blurriness compared to a busted marriage, and babies that never were?

He'd told the patrol-people to divide up the names on the guest lists and call them all, to stay on top of the hospitals, to make sure the dispatcher hadn't gotten any news about men wandering around with head injuries and droopy pants. Then he got in his car and called Paula the dispatcher, double-checking the database's last listing against Christie Keogh's roster. He thought he'd take a swing by Crescent Drive to see if Jonathan Downs was around.

TWENTY

"We made it," said Val as we drove up the driveway. The sun was melting the frost from my lawn, and my newspaper, in its blue plastic bag, was waiting. Val cut the engine, and I got out of the car as the Buccis' SUV backed down the driveway. Mr. Bucci stuck his arm out of the window. "Morning, Addie," he called, and I said "Good morning" back, just like nothing had changed.

At Val's instructions, I pulled her Jaguar into the garage next to my parents' old, tarp-draped station wagon and rolled the door closed behind it. "So what now?" I asked as I picked up my paper and unlocked the front door.

"I need a shower and some coffee," said Val. "After that . . ." She stretched, tilting her hips forward and her head back.

"Did you bring the class guide inside?" When Val waggled it at me, I said, "Maybe we should make a list of everyone Dan knew, or everyone he was hanging out with last night, and call them and ask if they've heard from him."

Val thought for a minute, then shook her head. "We don't want people to know we're looking for him."

That gave me pause. "Okay, what if we don't say it's us? We could pretend to be telemarketers or something, and we'll just say we're trying to reach Dan Swansea, and either they'll say, 'Wrong number,' or they'll say, 'Actually, he's right here on my couch.'"

Val nibbled on a fingernail. "I think maybe we need to get out of town."

"Oh, Val . . ." A dozen excuses rose to my mouth: my deadline on the bunch-of-flowers card, my responsibilities, my brother. The doctor's appointment I had on Thursday. My lump.

"Just think about it!" she called over her shoulder as she headed toward the stairs. "Pack a bag. It could be fun!" I heard the bathroom door open and the water turn on. "Hey, can I borrow some clothes?"

"Take whatever you need," I yelled. *Don't you always?* I thought, my old anger rising up as unavoidably as a knee jerking when the doctor's hammer hits. But it was reflexive resentment, and it didn't last long. The grudge I'd held for more than fifteen years was deflating like a pin-stuck balloon. It had been awful for me, being a teenager in Pleasant Ridge, but apparently it had been awful for Valerie, too . . . and maybe, somewhere, I'd known that all along.

In the kitchen, I sliced two bagels and put them in the toaster, and pulled out butter and cream cheese and jam. I added a few bottles of water to my tote bag and stood for a minute, breathing the smells of home: paint and Earl Grey tea and Murphy Oil Soap, the wool of the new carpets, other scents I was sure couldn't still be there except in my memory: the bay rum aftershave my father wore on special occasions, the milk of roses hand cream my mother had kept beside her bed, maple syrup heating on the stove.

I was pouring cream into a ceramic pitcher I'd painted when I heard a car door slam. I ran to the window, and there it was: a police cruiser parked in front of my house. A man with dark hair, his shoulders slumped underneath his sports coat, peered at my house, then crossed the lawn, heading for the front door.

Shit. Shitshitshit. I raced up the stairs and knocked on the bathroom door. "Val," I panted, "the cops are here."

She opened the door and stood there with a towel wrapped around her body and another one wrapped around her hair. "Oh my God. Oh my God!"

"Just stay up here. I'll deal with it." My heart was thumping and my mouth was dry, but a preternatural calm had descended on me. I didn't have a plan—didn't even have an inkling about what I'd say—but somehow, I thought that I could talk my way out of the situation, which was strange, given that, in my entire life, my mouth had gotten me into plenty of trouble and out of precisely nothing.

"Stay up here. Don't say anything. And don't come downstairs no matter what." Valerie backed into the shower, pulling the curtain shut behind her. I shut the bathroom door as the doorbell rang, then dashed down the stairs, took a deep breath, smoothed my hair, and opened the door. "Ms. Downs?" said the policeman. He was handsome—a crazy thing to notice, given the circumstances, but there it was. He had a strong jaw and a cleft in his chin. His big brown long-lashed eyes had purplish circles underneath them, and there was stubble on his cheeks. "Police Chief Jordan Novick. May I come in?"

"What's going on? Is everything all right?"

"Okay if I talk to you inside?"

"Of course," I said, and opened the door wider.

TWENTY-ONE

Jordan Novick did not believe in love at first sight. Lust, absolutely: the turn of a knee, the way a woman's hair fell against the nape of her neck, a warm smile, a nice rack—he was no more immune to those pleasures than any man. Adelaide Downs—"Call me Addie," she'd said, slipping over the floor in wool socks—wasn't a supermodel. Nor was she some four-hundred-pound behemoth, as Judy Nadeau had suggested. Addie Downs was simply a pleasant woman with a decent body in jeans and a black sweater, a nice-enough woman with a nice-enough smile, honey-colored hair and full lips and laugh lines at the corner of her eyes. Her house, though, he thought as she hung up his coat and led him into the living room, looking over her shoulder with a worried expression as he followed—her house was something special.

"What is this about?" she asked again as Jordan settled onto the couch, which was covered in some soft golden fabric and seemed to be psychically transmitting the suggestion that he slip off his shoes and put his feet up. The cherry-red blanket draped over one arm seemed like just the thing to pull up to your chin for an afternoon's nap. There were small paintings clustered in groups on the walls, some in gold frames and some in wooden ones, and they were Jordan's favorite kind of art, paintings that looked like actual things, instead of being a collection of smears and blotches called *Arcadian Sunset* or *Woman on the Verge*. Adelaide Downs had paintings of flowers that looked like flowers, and oceans that looked like oceans. There was a picture of a slice of birthday cake, with a lit candle stuck in frosting so realistic Jordan thought he could dip his finger in it for a taste, and another one of a black cat peering up, cool and green-eyed and sly, from a saucer of milk.

He looked away from the cat so he could answer. "We have a few questions about the high school reunion last night."

She looked tense as she settled into the chair beside the sofa. Then her eyes darted toward the kitchen as bluish smoke filtered in. "Oh, jeez. Hang on." She hurried out of the room, calling over her shoulder, "Hey, do you want a bagel?"

Jordan had never accepted food when he was working. Not until today. He was, he discovered, starving. He hadn't had breakfast, and he hadn't managed more than a few bites of gluey pot pie the night before, and, he realized, he wanted Adelaide Downs to bring him a bagel, and eat one with him. "If it's no trouble."

"No, no, it's fine. You okay with well-done?"

He told her that he was, and got up to study the paintings. There was one of the ocean he particularly liked, a beach scene with no people, just the water and a single brightly hued umbrella, red and orange, stuck in the sand like a flower. He stood looking until she came back, carrying a tray with toasted bagels, a pot of golden-orange jam, cream cheese and butter, a pot of coffee, a pitcher of cream, and a pair of mugs. Jordan sat down, catching a whiff of her hair as she bent over the tray, arranging plates and folding napkins. She smelled like sugar and lemons, sweet and tart, and the skin on her arms, where she'd pushed up the sleeves of her sweater, looked smooth as a magnolia petal. He bet if he touched it, it would be soft.

She was fussing with the coffee cups, still looking worried.

He wanted to take her hand and squeeze it, tell her that everything would be fine, and he couldn't figure out why. It didn't make sense. Sure, she had a decent figure, a curvy bottom, neither sinewy nor stick-thin, as so many women were these days, but she was no Holly Muñoz. Holly, with all of her running and biking, her lunges and squats, had a truly admirable ass. But that wasn't a fair comparison. Holly was twenty-six. She'd never had kids. Had Addie? With a great deal of effort, Jordan pushed himself upright, tried to shake off the pleasant torpor that the couch had induced, and pulled out his notebook. No kids, he decided—there were no telltale plastic toys, no baby playthings or big-kid paraphernalia. No husband, either—he hadn't noticed a ring, and more tellingly, there was only one remote control on the coffee table.

"So what happened at the reunion?" she asked. He was about to tell her when he noticed that Addie was looking down, blushing. "Do you want a doughnut?" she asked. She pulled a bag out of her purse and set it next to the coffeepot. "I wasn't sure if I should put them out. You know, cops, doughnuts . . ." She laughed nervously, then put her hand over her mouth.

Jordan breathed in as steam from the coffee curled in the air, and opened the bag. Raspberry jelly. God was in his heaven, and all was right with the world. "Like many clichés, the one about cops and doughnuts has endured because it is true. Are these from Ambrosia's?" he asked, naming Pleasant Ridge's best and only twenty-four-hour doughnut and coffee shop.

"They're the best, right?" Jordan nodded. He ate half of a doughnut and spooned sugar into one of the cups. Good coffee and real half-and-half, none of that skim milk or fat-free crap. Another point in her favor. "So what else?" she asked. "What other cop clichés are true?"

He sipped his coffee. She was teasing him. It felt nice. "Okay. You know how everyone thinks we've got quotas to make and we just hang around outside bar parking lots or places where we know people are speeding or driving drunk?" She nodded. "That's true. I mean, you want money, you go to the bank. You want drunks, you go to the bars. Oh, and we beat suspects."

She was smiling. "Well, why wouldn't you?"

"Not even to get them to confess," he said. "Just to have something to do with our hands. We're all trying to quit smoking, so . . . oh, and when we're on stakeout?" He lowered his voice. "We pee in empty mayonnaise jars."

"I always wondered about that. Why not mustard? Why not some other condiment? Salsa or chutney or something like that?"

"Wide mouth."

"Makes sense," she said, her lips curving, cheeks flushed. For a moment they were silent, just looking at each other. Jordan pointed at the wall. "Where'd you get all the art?"

"Those?" She looked flustered. "They're mine. I mean, obviously they're mine, I didn't steal them." She laughed a little shrilly. "I painted them." She lifted her mug. "This, too."

Jordan looked at the mug, which was heavy, cream-colored glazed ceramic. On one side was a small bouquet of flowers—daffodils, maybe?—tied in a painted ribbon. "You . . ." He groped for the terminology. "You do pottery?" That wasn't right—*throw* pottery, that was the word he'd been looking for.

Addie shook her head. "Oh, no. Not the mug. The picture on it. The flowers. I painted them."

He looked at them more closely. "Nice." Addie made a face, with the corners of her mouth lifted and her eyebrows raised. "So that's what you do?" Jordan asked. "You're an artist?" He pointed at the pictures on the walls.

She waved the word away, looking embarrassed. "I do greeting cards, mostly. The occasional mug. I did a spoon rest once. That was a real highlight."

He polished off his doughnut and tried to keep from sighing in gratitude as the carbs landed in his belly and the sugar hit his bloodstream. "This is great," he said. "You're saving my life."

"Wow," she said. She probably blushed easily when she was flustered or, Jordan bet, when she was turned on. She'd turn a pretty rosy color, pink from her throat to her chest, with her pupils dilated and her hair spread out as she tossed her head against the pillow . . . "You're easy."

"Don't tell, okay?" He looked down, remembering why he'd come here, and that it wasn't to chat up friendly single women and eat their doughnuts. "Your brother," he began. "Have you heard from him lately?"

"Thursday. I saw him Thursday, for Thanksgiving. What's wrong?" The worried look was back.

"Does he live here?"

She shook her head. "Jon's at a place called Crossroads. He moved there when he turned twenty-one. Why? Did something happen?"

"Was he at the reunion last night?"

Her hands twisted in her lap. "I can't—I mean, I wasn't there, either—but I can't imagine he'd want to go, and if I didn't take him, he wouldn't have any way of getting there." She paused, clearly deciding how much to tell him. "Jon didn't have a very easy time in high school." She looked off into the distance, fingers twining and untwining. "My brother was in a car accident when he was fifteen. The two boys in the front seat died, and Jon was hurt pretty badly. He had brain damage. Short-term memory loss, seizures—not for a while now, but he had them pretty regularly when he was a teenager—and some personality changes." She sighed. "Medication helps, but he could be—he can be—a little strange."

"Everyone's strange in high school," said Jordan.

Addie Downs seemed surprised to hear it. "You think so?"

"You should have seen me. I had such bad acne, it looked like someone taped a sausage pizza to my face."

She smiled faintly, still looking troubled. Jordan fought the urge to reach for her, to touch her hand, even as a cool, removed corner of his brain inquired *What, exactly, do you think you're doing?*

"Were you home last night?" he asked her.

"I had a date."

"How'd it go?"

She gave him her wry half-smile. "About as well as high school."

"Would you mind telling me his name?"

Addie put half a bagel on her plate. "Only if you tell me what's going on."

"We found a man's belt and some blood in the country club parking lot. We're trying to find out who they belong to and make sure no one got hurt."

Lines bracketed her mouth as she frowned. "I could call Jon and make sure he's okay."

"Was anyone in high school particularly bad to him?" Jordan asked casually. "Anyone he would have wanted to get back at?"

Addie looked surprised. Then she narrowed her eyes. "You think Jon *hurt* someone?" Her voice was rising; that pretty flush was tinting her cheeks and her neck. "Jon would never do anything like that."

He kept his own voice low. "Ma'am, we're trying to figure out who that belt belongs to and if that person is injured. We're not accusing anyone of anything." Adelaide Downs was glaring at him, cheeks pink, eyes flashing, righteously pissed.

"He used to take things out of lockers sometimes," she said. "Somebody told you that, right? That's why you're here. You think Jon did something."

"Nobody thinks Jon did anything," Jordan protested. "All we're trying to do right now is make sure everyone's okay. Jon included."

"I'm sorry," she said. Her hands were balled into fists, like she was going to sock him. It was charming, even though he was certain she didn't mean for it to be. "Have you ever been to the high school?"

"Class of 1987," Jordan volunteered.

Addie appeared not to hear him. "It's four stories high. There were boys—I never knew which ones, exactly—they'd take Jon's backpack and drop it down the stairwell. Four stories down. If it had ever hit someone, it could have really hurt them. They'd take off running, and the teachers on the first floor would find the backpack with Jon's name on it. He'd get in trouble because he wouldn't say who'd done it." She took a deep breath. "You can understand why I'm a little overprotective."

"I understand," he said. More than that, he admired it. He wondered if he'd been the one with problems, what his own brother would have had to say if the cops had come knocking. Sam probably would have thrown him to the wolves without thinking twice—would have driven the cops to his door, if it came to that. "It would help," he ventured, "if we knew where your brother was last night."

"Working." Addie snapped the lid on the tub of cream cheese and wiped off the butter knife with a napkin. A cloth napkin. Her cheeks were still pink. "He works Tuesdays through Saturdays at the Walgreens on Lower Wacker. He's been there for fifteen years. He always works on holidays so that the people with families can spend time with them."

"Sounds criminal," said Jordan. Addie didn't answer. "I'm kidding," he said. Not even a hint of a smile flickered across her face.

"You can probably talk to the manager, or check his time

cards, or something." She set the knife down. "Look, I know in the movies and on TV it's always the guy with mental problems who does it, but believe me, my brother wouldn't hurt a fly."

Jordan stood as Addie got to her feet, then bent down for the tray. "Let me help you."

"No, I've got it."

For a minute, they were face-to-face, each of them gripping one side of the tray, so close their noses were almost touching, so close he could smell her lemon-and-sugar scent, until Addie let go. "I can give you the number of the house where Jon lives, and his boss's name and number at the drugstore," she said. "They'll be able to tell you where he was last night."

"Appreciate your help." He handed her the tray. She carried it into the kitchen, and came out a minute later with a slip of paper and handed it over. "Anything else?"

"Your date last night," he said. "I'm sorry, but I need a name."

"Matthew Sharp."

"And where did you go?"

She named a restaurant downtown.

"You drink martinis? They do one there with olives stuffed with blue cheese." *Christ,* he thought, *I'm losing my mind.*

"I had wine," said Adelaide Downs.

He offered her his hand, and after a minute, Addie shook it, her palm warm against his. "I'm sorry if I offended you," he said.

"Sure," she said. Her voice was stiff. She stood there for a minute, then said, "Hang on." Jordan waited. When she came back, she was carrying the bag of doughnuts.

"Here," she said. "You can take these with you."

"Oh, no. That's okay."

"Take them. Enjoy." She gave him a little wave. "Don't beat any suspects," she said. For a minute, he thought she'd say something else—maybe "Wanna fool around?" the way Judy Nadeau had—but instead, she simply swung the door shut.

TWENTY-TWO

Up in my bedroom, Valerie listened, stone-faced, as I breathlessly recounted my conversation with Jordan Novick. "Belt," she muttered. "Fuck. We should have taken it. What if they find fingerprints?"

"I barely touched it. And I don't think it's the belt that's the problem as much as the blood. But Val, they think Jon did it!"

"Or else they think it's his belt. His blood."

I shook my head. "It's going to take the cops about five minutes to figure out that Jon's okay, and maybe ten minutes to make sure he wasn't really there, and probably another ten minutes after that to figure out who the blood and the belt belong to . . . and then five seconds for Dan to tell them what you did. What are we going to do? We have to find Dan," I said, answering my own question. "We have to find him before the police do."

"Yeah, okay, but how?" Val sat on my bed, pulled the towel off her head, and started rubbing it slowly against her hair. "I told you, we can't let anyone know that we're looking for him, because then we look suspicious."

"But we were looking for him. We already went to Chip's house! And you talked to Dan's doorman!"

"They're not going to call the doorman."

"Valerie. Of course they're going to call the doorman!"

She nibbled at a thumbnail. "Well, Chip won't say anything. He doesn't know we were there to find Dan."

"Oh, yeah. He'll just think you were suddenly overcome by uncontrollable lust, and you just had to have him."

"He probably will think that," she said. "I was extremely convincing."

"Valerie. Think. We are under suspicion. We are persons of interest. We are . . ."

"Have you ever been to Florida?"

I blinked at her. "What?"

She shook her damp hair over her shoulders. "I still think our best bet might be to get out of town for a little while."

Struggling with my temper, and with the urge to grab her tanning-bed-basted shoulders and give her a good, brisk shake, I said, "I don't think this is exactly the right moment to be taking a vacation. We're not kids. We can't just ditch everything and drive to Cape Cod."

"But what else are we supposed to do?" She got to her feet and started pacing, leaving wet footprints on my bedroom rug. "We can't look for Dan. We can't just stay here and be sitting ducks." She got to my bedroom door, turned, and walked back to the dresser. "And Dan might not even remember what happened. He could have amnesia . . ."

"Come on! This isn't *Days of Our Lives*."

"Or," she continued, "he might not want to talk about what happened. Being tricked, being naked . . . I'll bet he's just holed up somewhere trying to forget the whole thing, and hoping I don't e-mail his picture to everyone in my address book, which I totally could do. Plus, he was the one who jumped in front of my car." She paused. "I think. Now come on!" she said, bouncing on the balls of her feet and doing that old cheerleader clap. "You didn't have anything planned for the weekend, did you?"

I opened my mouth, then shut it, then shook my head. "I can't leave Jon."

"So we'll go see him." She opened my closet, stood on her tiptoes, and pulled the single suitcase I own, a small wheeled one that my mother had used for her overnight stays in the hospital, off a shelf. "Underwear?" Before I could answer, she'd opened a drawer and produced a fistful of faded cotton briefs. "Yick. Where's your good stuff?" She rummaged some more and found the pretty, lacy things I'd bought for Vijay that spring, opened the suitcase, and flung them in. "Let's see . . . swimsuit?"

"In the bathroom," I said. Maybe it was the sleeplessness, or the adrenaline rush of having to deal with the policeman (the cute policeman) in my living room, but I felt like I was nine years old again, like I'd run across the street to stuff a swimsuit in my backpack and that Val and I would soon be off somewhere wonderful.

"Makeup? Face cream?"

"I don't really wear too much, and . . ."

"Condoms? Pills? Morning-after pills?"

"What kind of vacations do you take?"

"Good ones," she said, giving me a broad wink that reminded me, with an almost dizzying sense of déjà vu, of her mother. She rifled through my closet, pulling out a pleated pink sundress, a pale-yellow cardigan, and a pair of lace-up orange espadrilles that I'd bought two summers ago for the unbelievable price of eight dollars, before realizing that they were so cheap because there was no place in my wardrobe or, really, any woman's, for lace-up orange espadrilles. Except maybe Valerie's, I realized as she held the shoes up to the light, turning them this way and that. "Cute."

I grabbed a tote bag from my closet and supplemented Val's random packing (she added a scented candle and some lotion to the suitcase, but hadn't bothered with toothpaste, or a nightgown, or bras) with workout clothes, a few pairs of cotton pants,

T-shirts, my vitamins, a sketchbook and a tin of colored pencils, and my favorite photograph of my family. We'd posed on our front steps on my first day of school: me in a navy-blue jumper, Jon in new jeans, my mother in a floaty white sundress, my father in a suit and tie, the four of us smiling into the sun.

Back in the bathroom, Val complained about the low wattage of my blow dryer, then rejected everything in my closet and wriggled back into her foundation garments and slinky red dress. I sat on the bed while she deftly applied foundation and contouring shadow, blush and gloss and eyeshadow and eyeliner and even a few fake eyelashes, all pulled from a zippered case in her giant red bag. "You know, we really should get going," I told her. "Seeing as how we're on the lam and all."

"I have an image to maintain," she said. "Do you think I want to wind up in 'Stars Without Makeup'?" Before I could answer, or point out that she wasn't a star, she stuck the end of an eyebrow pencil into her mouth and started chewing. "We need another car," she mumbled around the pencil.

"We can't take mine?"

She chewed, thinking, then shook her head. "We need a car that's not connected to either one of us."

"Why not?" It hit me as soon as I'd asked: this was real. A crime had been committed. Val had committed a crime, a crime to which I was now an accessory, and instead of doing the right, good-girl thing, instead of telling, the way I always had, I was preparing to throw caution to the wind, I was breaking the rules. I was going for it. It felt, I was surprised to find, pretty good.

"I have an idea."

In the garage, Val helped me pull the tarp off the old station wagon that hunkered down on half-flat tires like an exhausted elderly dinosaur. She wrinkled her nose as I opened the door. "Seriously? Does this thing even have a radio?"

"AM, FM, and a cassette player," I bragged, sliding behind the wheel, slipping the key into the ignition, and feeling relief flood through me when the engine started up.

Val made a face as she climbed in beside me. "This is very depressing."

"It runs. Beggars can't be choosers." I backed out of the driveway through a cloud of bluish smoke and drove gingerly down the street, plotting my course in my head: the first gas station, where I'd fill the tires and the tank, the exit onto the highway, and my brother.

TWENTY-THREE

Someone—Holly, he supposed—had decorated the police station for Christmas. There was a small tinsel tree on Paula's desk, a bowlful of green-and-red-foiled Hershey's Kisses next to the telephone, a wreath on the door, and an actual Christmas tree, smelling bracingly of the outdoors, set up next to the patrol-people's desks. The tree was decorated with red-and-gold bulbs, strands of popcorn and cranberries, and—Jordan blinked, making sure—a lacy pink bra on top, where the angel should have been.

He'd pulled off the bra, and put it in his coat pocket when Holly came up beside him. "Is it okay?" she asked, indicating the tree. "I tried to find a menorah or something . . . you know, so we don't offend anyone . . ."

"It's fine," he said. The bra—he was certain it was hers, and that Gary Ryderdahl had probably stuck it there as a joke—was a burning weight against his hip. He shifted his weight. "You making any progress with that list?"

"So far, everyone's fine. Present and accounted for." Jordan gave her a *carry on* kind of nod. Holly held her ground, looking up at him from underneath her long lashes with her soft brown eyes. "Did you have a good Thanksgiving?" she asked.

Jordan jammed his hands in his pockets—there was a bag

of doughnuts in the left one, the bra in the right. His parents, who'd retired to Scottsdale, had urged him to fly out for the weekend—his mom had turned the guest bedroom into a meditation sanctuary, but, his father said gruffly, the pullout couch wasn't that bad. Even his brother, Sam, had come through with an invitation, but Jordan had pleaded work and promised everyone he'd see them at Christmas. He'd celebrated Thanksgiving with a Hungry Man turkey dinner that he'd wedged sideways into the toaster oven (the potatoes had scorched and the turkey was half-frozen) and a marathon of prerecorded *Nighty-Night* episodes, and he'd gone to bed at ten, unable to bear his own company—his own loneliness—for another minute. "It was fine," he told Holly in a tone he hoped would forestall further discussion.

It didn't. Holly launched into the tale of her four sisters, their husbands and assorted nieces and nephews, and her father, who, each year, insisted on deep-frying a twenty-pound turkey in a stainless-steel rig he'd set up in the carport. "It's a terrible turkey," she said, her eyes wide as she described it. "So every year, the Sunday after, me and my sisters take turns hosting everyone. We make turkey in the oven, and there's lasagna . . ." Her voice trailed off. She regarded Jordan hopefully. "You could come, if you wanted. There's always too much food."

"It sounds like fun," he managed. And it did: a big round table crowded with Holly and her sisters and their husbands. And their kids. "Let's see how things go with the case." He shrugged. "Maybe it's a real crime."

She smiled at him, clearly amused at the thought. "Deep-frying an innocent turkey. That's a crime."

"Keep me posted," he said, and ducked into his office, where he yanked the bra out of his pocket and shoved it in the bottom of his desk drawer, underneath five years' worth of performance evaluations and the two boxes of Girl Scout cookies he'd bought from Paula's granddaughter the previous spring (he'd asked the girl whether the Samoas were made with real Samoans, and she'd looked puzzled, then upset, as she'd backed away slowly toward her grandmother's desk). He set the bag of doughnuts Addie had given him on his blotter and pulled out his notebook, flipping through it, considering the words that jumped out: *vegan* and *walk-ins, Matthew Sharp* and *wouldn't hurt a fly.* He ate another doughnut, feeling the sugar crystals crunch between his teeth, then googled Adelaide Downs. A handful of hits came up: her name on the Happy Hearts website, pictures of some china pieces that had been for sale three years ago. Then there were the websites where everyone, even the most misanthropic hermit, showed up these days: Did you go to high school with ADELAIDE DOWNS? Are you ADELAIDE DOWNS'S friend? He clicked through the links, plugging in her name and address, hoping for a photograph (just so he could look at it and assure himself that she was nothing special). No picture showed up: just images of her greeting cards, a set of dessert plates, the spoon rest she'd mentioned.

Jordan wiped his mouth with a paper napkin, picked up his phone, and dialed the number Addie had given him. Mr. Duncan, the Walgreens manager, put him on hold to check the time sheets and, a minute later, came back on the line, sounding apologetic. "Jon was scheduled to work last night, but it doesn't look like he showed up."

Jordan thanked the man for his help, got to his feet, waved at Holly, who was on the phone, fished a handful of chocolates from Paula's bowl, and made his way back to his car. Ten minutes later, he was on the corner of Main Street and Crescent Drive. He popped a kiss into his mouth and sat relaxed, his hands open on his legs, breathing steadily, eyes trained on the street. Five minutes later, an ancient green station wagon sagging on four half-flat tires came squealing around the corner. There was a blonde behind the wheel, another woman, with her head covered, in the passenger's seat. The car stalled, backfired once, belched a cloud of oily smoke, and puttered off toward downtown. *Jon wouldn't hurt a fly. We'll just see about that,* he thought, and started off after the station wagon.

TWENTY-FOUR

"So what have you been up to?" I asked Val as we drove west. We'd been on the road—on the lam, I corrected myself—for ten minutes, and Val had devoted most of them to complaining about the car. "This is a hooptie, isn't it?" she'd finally asked, as we'd driven past the NOW LEAVING PLEASANT RIDGE: A PLEASANT PLACE TO LIVE! sign.

"I don't know what that is."

"A beater. Crap on wheels. A death trap. A piece-of-shit car." She sniffed. "Clearly you missed our series on urban slang."

"Clearly." I had to smile. Val looked like she'd just bitten into something rotten as she twisted back and forth, peering out her window to inspect the station wagon's exterior. Finally, she gave a loud, displeased sigh. "Did something die in here?"

"My father," I said, feeling guilty at enjoying the horrified look on her pretty face. "We had it cleaned after."

She gasped. "You didn't sell it?"

"It wasn't the car's fault," I said. "It still runs fine."

Val snorted, slumping down as far as she could in the seat. "Hey," she said after a minute. "Do you watch me?"

"Sometimes." I could feel her disappointment, as if the weather in the car had dipped ten degrees. "I'm hardly ever up that late." I snuck a look sideways. Val's forehead was furrowed, arms crossed over her chest, pouting. "I get the weather online," I said. Val glared at me. I lifted my hands off the wheel and raised them, palms up, at the sky. "Everyone does! It's very convenient! They update all the time."

"That," Valerie said, "is a myth. Online weather services use the exact same meteorological models that we do, so the idea that they're giving you better information is just B.S."

"Okay, but it is more convenient."

She snorted. "Oh, like it's such an imposition on your busy lifestyle to spend two minutes watching the news. Like you've got so much else going on. We do it at the top of the hour, you know. Right at the beginning of the newscast, so you can go to beddie-bye at eleven oh three."

"Why would I watch the news when I can get the weather on my phone?" I asked.

"You know what's wrong with America?" Valerie asked. "There's no loyalty. People watched the same channels for their entire lives. For entire generations! Grandparents and parents and children, all sitting around the TV set, watching the on-air personalities. And now it's all . . ." She raised her voice to a simper. " 'Ooh, I can get the weather on my phone! I don't need the MyFox Chicago News Team anymore!' "

Her mouth was contorted. "Hey. Take it easy," I said.

Val slumped back into her seat. "It's not just you. You know what the average age of a MyFox viewer is?" She paused. "Dead. Because everyone's getting the weather on their phone or the news on their BlackBerry." She frowned. "And ever since we've gone to high def . . ." One hand rose to rub her cheek. "I mean, it shows everything. Every line, every pore . . . it's been a very stressful time for me." I considered telling her it was probably an even more stressful time for Dan Swansea, wherever he was, but kept my mouth shut as we slipped into the passing lane. "You never got married?" Valerie asked.

I never even had a boyfriend until this year, I thought of saying. Instead, I just said, "No."

"Do you want kids?"

"I don't know. Maybe." I liked the idea of being a mother, but the reality of children wasn't quite so sunny. A lot of them had pointed and laughed at me over the years. Still, sometimes I thought I'd like a baby, and the friends that came along with babies. There was a coffee shop on Main Street downtown where I'd sometimes go on my way back from the post office. On Tuesday mornings a group of mothers with tiny babies and big strollers would gather by the back door. They'd drink chai lattes and chat about their husbands or an article in the *Times* that said it was healthy for kids to eat dirt. Once, one of the women, a perky, skinny, ponytailed thing, had tried to whip up some interest in a baby sign-language class, and one of the other moms who was still wearing maternity jeans nine months later (I'd spotted the tag when she'd bent over to grab an errant teething ring) had looked at her daughter, perched in a high chair, mashing a lump of banana into her forehead, and said, "I'm not sure she's got anything to say that I'd be interested in hearing at this point in time."

"So tell me what's going on with you," Val said. I wondered what I should tell her: how, at my heaviest, I'd order frosted cookies on the Internet, and every time I'd get them in a different tin—Thanksgiving, Christmas, Happy Birthday, Fourth of July—so that whatever faceless person filling my order wouldn't guess that I was eating five pounds of dessert by myself. How, at my loneliest, I'd go to supermarkets when snowstorms were in the forecast, joining the crowds fighting their way toward the last dozen eggs or gallon of milk or roll of double-ply toilet paper, just so I could feel part of something. How, in the coffee shop, I'd watched the maternity-jeaned mother laughing at her little girl, the baby's plump little palms slapping the wooden floor as she crawled and the other mothers murmured about splinters and germs, and thought, *I could be friends with her.* Only I'd been too shy to say a word.

"Nothing much," I said.

"You've got fancy underwear for nothing much," Val observed.

I tightened my grip on the wheel. "I like nice things."

"Sure," said Val, sounding like she didn't believe me for a minute.

We stopped at a gas station to fill the tank, and the tires, then at a convenience store, where I bought chips and sodas and a tuna-fish sub for my brother, and located what I had to guess was Chicago's single remaining pay phone. I'd wanted to call the Crossroads from home, but Val had decreed that any call we made, from either our cells or a landline, could be traced. *Better safe than sorry,* I thought as Ms. Jennings gave me the news I'd been half expecting: Jon had gone wandering again.

"Bad news," I said, climbing back in the car, where Val was touching up her makeup in the rearview mirror. "Jon took off."

"So what do we do?" she asked.

I slid the key into the ignition and backed out of the parking space. "I know where to find him," I said.

Forty-five minutes later, we left my father's old car in a parking lot two blocks from the Art Institute, one of Jon's favorite non-working-hour hangouts. I pulled on my hat and scarf and mittens. Val draped the coat I'd lent her over her shoulders and adjusted the fringed shawl that she'd tied over her hair, babushka style. "There," she said, pulling on oversized sunglasses. "I'm incognito."

"Beautiful," I said, and led her toward the sidewalk.

It took us half an hour to find my brother, sitting underneath an overpass a few blocks off of Michigan Avenue, with his back against a concrete piling and his eyes on the sky. His sleeping bag, my gift to him last Christmas, was pulled up over his legs, and he'd tucked his hands inside to stay warm.

"Hi, Addie," he said when I sat down beside him.

"Hi, Jon. How are you?"

"I'm good." *Think of this as a birth,* one of the neurologists had told us after Jon had woken up from his coma, before he'd started to talk . . . and curse, and throw things. *The person you knew is gone. This is a new person.* My father had turned away, his pale face white as the doctor's lab coat, looking like he wanted to knock the horn-rimmed glasses right off the guy's smug face, and my mother had wept softly into her hands. The new Jon, the one who had been alive now for longer than the old Jon, was short-tempered and forgetful, clumsy and occasionally frustrated, with flashes of his old, childlike sweetness glinting through like sunshine on water.

I sucked in a breath of the icy air. "You were at work last night, right?"

He thought for a minute, frowning, trying to remember. "There was a meteor shower. I wanted to see."

My heart sank. No work meant no alibi. "Oh, Jon."

"But I called in! Just like I'm supposed to. I called in, and they said it was okay." His forehead furrowed. "I'm sure. Almost. I think I called."

"I'm not angry." I reached into my purse, handing him the things I'd packed: a hat and mittens, in case he'd forgotten his own (he had), a tube of ChapStick, in case his lips were chapped (they were). "Jon. I'm going to go away for a while. With Valerie. Remember my friend Valerie? We're going on a trip."

His eyes were still fixed on the sun. "Are you going someplace warm?"

"I don't know. Just . . . away for a few days. I want you to go back home. If you come with me, I'll give you a ride."

"Can I go to the movies first? I promise I'll go back for dinner. And I'll go to work tonight."

"Okay," I said. "Movie first, then home. And listen, Jon, this is important. If anyone comes to ask you questions about where you were last night, you have to tell them the truth."

His mouth hung open, and I could hear him breathe. "Addie," he said. "I always tell the truth."

"Okay."

"Always." He looked so serious. I gave him a quick hug.

"Okay."

I sat beside him for a minute, feeling the chilly concrete against my back and the sunshine on my face. "Hey," I said. "This isn't so bad." Jon tapped the back of my hand with two fingers. It was like being pecked by some small, insistent bird.

"When you get there," he said, "say hi to Mom from me, okay? Tell her I saw two total eclipses and one partial."

"Oh, Jon." It happened this way sometimes. We'd be having a perfectly normal conversation . . . or, at least, a conversation as close to normal as we could have—and then he'd say something that would remind me that nothing was normal, nothing at all. "Okay," I said, instead of explaining, for maybe the millionth time, that our mother was dead. "I'll tell her."

I helped him roll up his sleeping bag and walked him to the bus stop when he refused to let me give him a ride (Jon loved to take the El and the buses, and the social workers had told my mother and me long ago that we should let him, that the more independent he became, the better off he'd be). I wrote down the number of the bus and the name of the theater, slipped him twenty dollars and kissed his cheek. "I love you," I said. "Love you, too," said Jon. Then I made my way back to Val, who was waiting on the sidewalk, watching us from behind her sunglasses. "Everything okay?"

"Everything's fine." Back in the car, she curled up in the passenger's seat, pulling off her sweater and her scarf, making a little nest.

"Hey," I said as she yawned and slipped off her shoes. "So where are we going?"

She raised her head. "Just drive south," she said. She closed her eyes and was instantly asleep.

TWENTY-FIVE

Jordan had stayed close to the station wagon, pulling up to the curb when Addie drove in to a gas station, watching as she stopped at a convenience store, then at a pay phone, then a parking lot. He watched as the woman in the passenger's seat with her head wrapped in a scarf freshened her lipstick in the rearview mirror, and Addie, who'd been driving, got out with a plastic grocery bag in her hand. He stayed a block or two behind them as they made their way along the sidewalk until Addie approached a man bundled in a sleeping bag, leaning against a concrete post beneath an overpass. Jordan had waited while she talked to him, gave him the bag, and walked him to a bus stop. Then, when she was gone, he shouldered his way through a few homeless guys up to the man, who was leaning against the glass of the enclosure with his sleeping bag tucked under his arm, staring calmly at the sky. Jordan said hello, and when the man didn't answer, he touched his shoulder.

"Jonathan Downs?"

"Hmm?" asked the man—Jon—without meeting Jordan's eyes. Jon had Addie's fair skin and light-brown hair. There was a nick high on one cheek, and his knuckles were bruised and scabbed. Jordan looked at them and wondered whether that meant he'd been in fights.

"Jonathan, my name is Jordan Novick. I'm the chief of police in Pleasant Ridge. Can you tell me where you were last night?"

Jonathan hummed, keeping his eyes on the sky.

"I know you weren't at work. Were you here?" Jordan asked. "Outside somewhere?"

"I was watching the moon."

"Anyone see you last night?"

"Only the moon," Jonathan said, and tilted his face toward the sky again. His khakis were held up by a leather belt—brown, not black.

"You didn't go back to Pleasant Ridge? Didn't go to the country club?"

"Don't go back to Rockville," Jonathan said. "Waste another year." Jordan watched as Jon dug into his pocket and pulled out a blue nylon-and-velcro wallet, then proceeded to remove its contents: a non-driver's photo ID card and a library card, a frequent-diner's card from the Old Country Buffet, a membership card from Blockbuster video, and a paycheck stub from Walgreens. There were forty-seven dollars in cash, some change, and a laminated rectangle of paper that said IF LOST PLEASE CONTACT ADELAIDE DOWNS. Finally, with a grunt of satisfaction, Jon located a bus pass. He repacked his wallet and squinted toward the corner, looking for the bus.

"Hey, Jon," said Jordan, trying for a tone of casual camaraderie. "Anyone ever mean to you in high school?"

"Addie," Jon said instantly.

"Not your sister," Jordan said. "Other people. Other boys. Maybe the ones who dropped your backpack?"

"I didn't care about that," said Jon. "I was watching the moon. I saw two full eclipses and one partial. Have you ever seen an eclipse?"

"Who was mean to Addie?"

Jon wasn't listening. "The Perseid meteor shower can be

viewed with the naked eye beginning in the middle of August. I have a telescope, though. You can see it even better with a telescope."

"Jonathan, someone got hurt at the reunion last night. Do you have any idea who it could have been?"

Jon turned toward him, looking alarmed. "Addie? Did someone hurt Addie?"

"No, no, Addie's fine."

Jon shook his head, frowning. "Addie got hurt."

"She's fine. I just saw her." *And so did you,* thought Jordan. This must be the short-term memory stuff his sister had described.

"Not now," said Jon with exaggerated patience. "In high school. Dan Swansea and Kevin Elephant and all the rest of them. They wrote things about her on the driveway."

Writing on driveways. Kevin Elephant. It sounded like nonsense, but Jordan wrote it down anyhow.

"Do you need anything? Are you going to be all right here?"

Jonathan looked at Jordan as if he were crazy. "I'm not staying here," he said. "I'm taking a bus to the movies." He pulled a piece of paper out of his pocket. "Bus number sixty to the theater. Buy a ticket for the two-ten show. Use the bathroom before the movie starts. Take the seventy-two bus home."

"Oh. Okay." Jordan thought for a minute, then dug in his pocket and came up with ten dollars. "If you get hungry at the movies," he said. Jon opened his wallet, smoothed out the bill, and slid it inside. "Can I borrow your pen?" he asked, and when Jordan handed it over, Jon wrote the words "buy snack" in tiny letters under his reminder to buy a ticket. Jordan waved awkwardly, then walked back to his car and drove to the home where Jonathan Downs had lived for the last fifteen years.

TWENTY-SIX

"No way," said the social worker, a tall, thin black woman named Verona Jennings. She wore eyeglasses on a chain hanging down against her chest, and had her arms crossed on top of them. "Uh-uh. Not without a warrant."

"Let's back up," said Jordan. He and Ms. Jennings were in the Crossroads kitchen at a table covered in a plastic red-and-white gingham-checked cloth, with a vase of fake daisies in the middle. On the refrigerator were laminated pieces of colored construction paper with names—ROGER, DAVID, JON, PHIL—on top, and schedules—*6:15: alarm, 6:20: use toilet, brush teeth, shave, 6:30: eat breakfast, take medication*—written underneath. Only two of the residents were currently in the house. The other six had gone home for the holidays. One of the men was standing in front of the window, staring silently out at the street. "You ever know Jon to be violent?"

"He's hurt himself," Ms. Jennings said. Before she'd let Jordan through the door, she'd asked for his badge number, then made him wait while she'd called it in to the station. "I've seen him get frustrated. He smacks himself in the head if we don't stop him." Jordan couldn't keep from wincing in sympathy. "But he's never hurt anyone else. That's not to say it couldn't happen, but I've never known him to be violent toward another person."

"When did you see him last?"

"Yesterday afternoon," she said. "He came home from work that morning just before eight o'clock and went right up to his room. That's normal. He came down for lunch—we have mac and cheese on Fridays—and went out for a walk after. All normal. He goes to the library and the museum and the movies several times a week, and I'm sure Tim, who was on duty then, assumed that's where he was going. He didn't come back for dinner, though, but we didn't worry. Friday night is baked fish. Not Jon's favorite. He likes McDonald's sometimes. Tim must have figured he'd gone out for dinner and was going on to work after that." And if he didn't, it wouldn't have been unusual." Ms. Jennings explained that Jon would stick with his routine—job, and meals, and walks, and trips to the movies and the library—for three, four, even six months at a time. Then something would happen, and he'd stop taking his medication, and he'd vanish, usually just for a night or two. Addie would find him. She'd talk to him and bring him home, and if things were bad, she'd take him to doctors' appointments to try to readjust his medication—Jon, Jordan learned, took an antidepressant and a drug to prevent seizures.

He wrote it all down. "There was a high school reunion last night. Jon mention it?"

Verona Jennings gave him a sad look and shook her head. Jordan tried another tack. "What did he do for Thanksgiving?"

"His sister brought him dinner." She led Jordan to the kitchen to show him a stack of leftovers in neatly labeled Tupperware. "See? Turkey, candied yams, green-bean casserole. That's Jon's favorite. They watched some sci-fi thing up in Jon's room after. Addie went home by three, and Jon took a nap." She shut the refrigerator and gave him a level look. "Now what is this all supposed to be about?"

Jordan told her what he could: the reunion, the belt they'd

found in the parking lot, how one of Jon's classmates had remembered that Jon had taken things. Even before he'd finished, Ms. Jennings was shaking her head again. "First of all, he'd have to have gotten out to Pleasant Ridge. And Jon doesn't drive."

"No car?" Even as he asked, he remembered the non-driver's ID.

Ms. Jennings shook her head again. "Jon's never had a license, far as I know. He's got a bus pass, is all. I'd be mighty surprised to learn the bus stops in front of a country club in the suburbs, and even if it did, it'd be three or four transfers. Jon couldn't do that without someone telling him how."

Trying again, Jordan asked, "Where's his room?"

"You can't go in there. Not without a warrant."

"I don't want to search it," Jordan said. "I just want to see it." She looked at him for a long moment, possibly weighing the inconvenience and the trouble of Jordan returning with an actual warrant, before leading him up a narrow flight of stairs.

Jon's room was at the far end of the house, a small rectangle with a single bed, a dresser, and a high window with bars on the outside, overlooking the house's weedy backyard, and it looked like a wing of the world's smallest art gallery. Each wall was covered, floor to ceiling, in photographs and framed pictures, paintings and drawings like the ones on Addie Downs's walls. There were drawings of a boy—a young Jon, Jordan thought, Jon as he'd once been. In the pictures, the boy, who was slim and tanned and fair-haired, ran and jumped and swam and kicked a soccer ball. Sometimes there were other people in the pictures—a heavyset woman with blue eyes and long hair, a pale man smiling faintly with puppets dangling from his hands—but most of the pictures (some were paintings, Jordan thought, and some were drawings done with colored pencils or pastel crayons) were of the boy, doing a dozen different boylike things: dangling a fishing pole into a misty, silvery lake; riding a bike down a street

Jordan thought he recognized as Crescent Drive; waiting for the school bus with a backpack on his back. In one painting the boy and a man—his father, Jordan guessed—were standing in the darkness, peering up into the starry sky.

"They're something, aren't they?" asked Verona Jennings, and Jordan could only nod. He thought he saw what Addie had tried for, how she'd drawn and painted her brother's entire pre-accident history, how she'd given him this room, this world, where he was as he had been, young and handsome and unbroken.

He took in each of the four walls, looking at all of the pictures, finding a few of a girl he guessed was Addie, here and there, hovering behind her older brother as he held a lit candle to a candelabra (a menorah? he wondered, thinking of Holly), sitting by the side of the pool with another, skinny blond girl next to her. Their feet dangled in the water as Jon stood on the high dive, preparing to jump.

"Five minutes," said Verona Jennings. "I've got things to do." There was a thick rug on Jon's floor, cousin of the one in his sister's living room, and a pair of plump pillows in crisp dark-blue cases on the bed. A laminated schedule—a twin of the one on the fridge, although this one was decorated with gold foil stars—hung on the closet door, and a half-dozen white button-down shirts, jeans, and khakis were lined up inside, along with a red polyester Walgreens pinney with a rectangular name tag reading *I'm JON. How can I help you?* A pair of photographs in clear plastic frames stood on the dresser. Jordan stepped close to examine one and saw little Addie and little Jon in a shot that had surely been taken on the first day of school. Both children wore backpacks and brand-new clothes, and there was a yellow school bus in the background. Addie was giving a tentative smile. Jon was squinting into the sunshine, handsome and bored. Jordan reached for the picture.

"Don't touch anything!" Ms. Jennings said. He let his hands

fall to his sides and considered the second shot, this one of Jon and Addie as grown-ups. Brother and sister were posed in front of a Christmas tree. Jon wore blue jeans and a plaid shirt, and would have been handsome if it hadn't been for the dazed, vacant look in his eyes.

Addie Downs was bigger. Not enormous, but much heavier than the woman he'd met, wearing tights and a black sweater-dress that fell halfway down her calves. She had light-brown hair pulled back from her double-chinned face by a headband, thick wrists, plump hands, and she was smiling . . . the same sweet, tentative smile that made her size all the more heartbreaking, because it was the smile of a woman who hadn't given up, who still dreamed of finding something wonderful underneath the Christmas tree.

Poor thing, he thought as Ms. Jennings said, "She's lost a lot of weight." Poor things, both of them. He waited until her back was turned and she was heading down the hall before slipping quietly across the room and sliding the grown-up picture of Addie and her brother into his pocket. Jon didn't strike him as a criminal . . . but he'd been wrong about people before.

TWENTY-SEVEN

"Addie?"

I came awake with a gasp, imagining that it was Vijay's hand on my shoulder, that Vijay had come back to me. I opened my eyes to find Val sitting behind the wheel (she'd been driving for the last hour). We were in the old station wagon, in a McDonald's parking lot. I could smell hot grease and frying meat, and could see the red-and-yellow sign through the windshield. The dashboard clock claimed that it was just after two in the afternoon.

"Where are we?" My tongue felt thick. I blinked, wriggling around in the seat.

"About a hundred miles outside of St. Louis. We need money," Val said.

I tried to remember what I'd had in my purse when Val had shown up. I'd taken out a hundred dollars in preparation for my date, spent ten of them on doughnuts and coffee, twenty on gas, and given twenty more to Jon. "I have fifty dollars," I said.

She shook her head. "That's not enough. But don't worry. I have a plan." She nodded toward the entrance of the restaurant. A mother with a baby in her arms and a little curly-headed girl at her side walked through the doors.

I looked at Val. "Oh, no. Come on. You want to rob a McDonald's?"

"Maybe a liquor store," she said, a little defensively. "Or a Seven-Eleven. Don't you always read about places like that getting robbed? I bet it's easy!"

I didn't answer, thinking that I was always reading about the arrests of people who tried to rob fast-food restaurants, and liquor stores, which meant it wasn't easy at all. "We could just go to a bank," I offered.

"Of course," she said. "Because that's where the money is! Okay, here's what I'm thinking: we can buy masks at a drugstore. I'll do the talking. We'll tell them we want ten thousand dollars in unmarked bills."

"Here's what I'm thinking," I said. "It's a month after Halloween. No place is going to have masks, so we just find a TD Bank, where I have a checking and savings account, and I'll make a withdrawal."

"You can't do that," she said. "They'll find out! They'll trace it, and they'll know we were here!"

"Oh, like they're not going to catch us if we rob a bank in Halloween masks." I took a swig of warm water from the bottle in my bag. "Listen. Have you thought about what happens when this is over?"

She crossed her arms over her chest, looking sullen. "Dan will either turn up, or he won't."

"And then what? What about your job?"

"They're not expecting me back until Tuesday, and it's not a big deal if I take off for a few days," she said. "They probably just think I went to get a boob job or something."

"You don't need to tell them in advance?"

She shook her head in sorrow at the extent of my naïveté. "Addie. If you tell them in advance, then it leaks. Then all the bloggers publish before-and-after pictures of you, and everybody knows."

"But if you get plastic surgery, aren't people supposed to notice that you look different? Isn't people noticing kind of the point?"

She rolled her eyes. "You just say you got some sun."

"Fantastic. Look, just drop me off at TD Bank, and I'll get us all the money we need."

Of course, it wasn't as easy as that. The bank was packed and overheated, and I had to wait by the automated change-counter for a spot at the back of the line. Filling out the withdrawal slip, trying to guess just how much cash we'd need to finance an unspecified length of time at an undisclosed location, I told myself it was unlikely that Jordan Novick had already faxed my name and photograph to every bank in the chain. He was thinking of me only as the relative of a potential suspect, if he was thinking of me at all.

He'd been nice, though, I thought as I joined the throng of upstanding citizens. It figured that the first nice, non-crazy guy I'd meet would be investigating a crime, a crime in which I was now implicated. Even if Dan Swansea did turn up and clear Val's good name, Jordan probably wouldn't be interested in me. "I'd like to make a withdrawal, please," I said when the teller beckoned me forward, and I slid my slip and driver's license across the counter. An instant later, Valerie, with the fringed scarf wrapped burka-style over her head and most of her face, sidled up beside me and snatched the withdrawal slip back.

"This is a robbery," she told the teller.

"Oh, for God's sake, Val, it is not. It's not," I said to the teller. She had a round face and red lipstick and a felt and fake-fur Santa hat on her head. She looked from my face to Val's and back again. "I've got a gun," Val whispered. "Give me whatever's in the drawer." She pulled a plastic shopping bag out of her purse and held it open in front of the teller's startled face. "Put it in here. Nobody moves, nobody gets hurt. Come with me if you want to live." And then, apparently having run out of movie lines to quote, she waved the empty bag for emphasis.

"Ignore her," I said to the teller, whose name tag read TIARA.

I tried to give her my license and the withdrawal slip again. Val clamped her hand down over mine.

"We need ten Gs in unmarked, nonsequential bills," she said through lips that barely moved. "No dye packets. No alarms. Be cool, sister, and we'll all make it out of here just fine."

Tiara finally opened her mouth, revealing a wad of grape-scented gum the size of a golf ball and a silver stud through the meat of her tongue. "Ohmygod."

"Ignore her," I repeated. "She doesn't have a gun."

"Do so." Val reached into her purse and pulled out a slim rectangle of what looked like sterling silver. "Now get busy livin' or get busy dyin'."

"Valerie," I said. "That's a tampon case."

"Yeah, well. I've got a gun. It's in here. Somewhere." Val unloaded mints and makeup and leather luggage tags onto the narrow granite ledge of the counter. Meanwhile, Tiara had unlocked her drawer and was sliding banded stacks of money at me. I was pushing them back at her as Val pulled something out of her handbag.

"Here!"

"That's an eyelash curler."

"This?"

"iPod."

"Listen." Tiara was whispering to us. "Just leave two stacks of fifties in the green Saturn parked in the corner out back, and we're all good. I won't pull the alarm until you leave."

Val's eyes lit up. "Seriously?" she asked in her normal newscastery voice. "You are so cool!"

"Jesus," I said. "Listen. Tiara. We aren't doing this. We're not . . ."

"Here you go," said Tiara. She'd gone pale, but her hands were working smoothly. Packets of bills tumbled into the bag. I looked around to see if anyone in the bustling bank was noticing the robbery in progress. It didn't look that way. At the station next to me, a small, bald man was arguing with the teller about when his out-of-state check would clear, and there was a commotion over by the change-counter that seemed to have resulted from someone's purse-dog pooping on the floor.

"That's ten thousand dollars," said Tiara. "You're gonna take care of me, right?" With one long pink-glossed acrylic nail she pointed at a picture she had Scotch-taped to the side of her computer. A little boy in corduroys was sitting on Santa's knee. "That's my baby."

"We got you," Val promised. She looped the bag's handles around her wrists. "Thanks."

I waited until Val was out the door, then took my withdrawal slip back, crossed out the $2,000 I'd planned on taking out, and wrote in $10,000. "Just take it out of my account, okay?" I said to Tiara, who nodded, continuing to work at her gum, as placid as if she got robbed every day of the week. "As long as you take care of me," she said, and I nodded—what choice did I have?

"Merry Christmas!" she called, and I wished her the same.

Out in the parking lot behind the bank, we found Tiara's Saturn. The doors were locked, but the passenger's-side window was open wide enough for us to slip two of the wrapped money packets through. "Ho ho ho," said Val. She stared at the bank's backside for a minute. "Wow. She was cool."

"Okay, just for the record? You are insane. And we need to get out of here."

"You don't want to rob the McDonald's?"

I thought about it. Strange as it seemed, part of me actually did. "We should go," I said again.

"How about you drive for a while?" she said, and tossed me the keys.

TWENTY-EIGHT

*H*e was in heaven. That explained everything. On his way along the road, he'd been hit by a car, and he'd died, or maybe he'd frozen to death on the road somewhere, and now he was in heaven, and heaven was a white bed with a white lace canopy on top and a cross made of scalloped white wood nailed to the wall above it, across from a doily-topped dresser covered with painted plaster dolls in elaborate gowns, the kinds of things he thought lonely women who lived alone with their cats bought late at night on QVC. "A new . . . day . . . has . . . come," a sweet soprano sang. In heaven, thought Dan, Céline Dion provided the sound track.

He sat up, groaning at the tsunami of pain that rolled through his head, as a woman came into the room. She carried a tray in her hands—there was a steaming mug of something, a bowl of what smelled like oatmeal, a small glass of orange juice so bright it looked almost psychedelic, and a larger glass of milk.

"You're awake," she said as Dan hastily rearranged the blankets over his morning erection. He wasn't sure if the woman in the pink velour bathrobe was an angel—she looked kind of grumpy and also kind of familiar—but he wasn't taking any chances or risking causing any offense.

"Here," she said, and set the tray on his lap. Not gently, either. Hot tea slopped over the edge of the mug and trickled through the *blankets. Dan looked at her, really looked at her, and the pieces fell into place.*

"Holy Mary?" he blurted. That wasn't really her name. Her real name was Meredith Armbruster, but to Dan and his friends, she'd been Holy Mary, who'd joined that weird culty church that convened in a renovated gas station in Pleasant Ridge's crummiest neighborhood; Holy Mary, who'd gotten herself excused from gym class (her faith forbade her from letting the other girls see her underpants) and biology class (no evolution) and health class (no fornication). They'd called her Holy Mary, and Carrie, after the girl from the movie who'd gotten doused in pigs' blood and then burned down the prom.

She blinked, then frowned. "Take your aspirin," she said. "Drink your milk."

Dan lifted the cup. "What happened?" He could remember how she'd found him on the side of the road and driven him to her house. She'd helped him into the bathroom, out of his trash bags, and then, when he was naked and shivering before her, dabbed the blood away from the wound on the side of his head. Then she'd shooed him into the shower and washed him, head to toe, kneeling to soap and rinse his feet as he huddled, shivering and sick and aching and still, he realized, very very drunk, against the pink-tiled walls.

"What happened?" he asked again, hearing the silence that surrounded them, guessing that the rest of the house was empty, that this was Merry's parents' house and that he was in what had been her high school bedroom. Where other girls might have had posters or pictures, she had that cross, draped with a set of rosary beads. Tucked into the edge of the mirror, where other girls might have kept a picture of their boyfriend or their best friend, was a mass card. Jesus had his hands clasped in prayer and his eyes tilted toward the heavens.

"What happened," said Merry, "is between you and Our Father." She clasped her hands and looked heavenward, just like Jesus on her mirror.

"Last night," Dan said. "You found me . . ."

"You were walking along the road. You were wearing garbage bags. I helped you—that was just Christian charity; any decent person would have done the same thing. I brought you back here. I cleaned you up and I let you sleep."

Dan gave a dry and rueful chuckle. "I guess I was pretty wasted."

Merry pursed her lips. " 'Do not gaze at wine when it is red, when it sparkles in the cup, when it goes down smoothly. In the end, it bites like a snake and poisons like a viper.' "

He nodded, grimacing as his stomach roiled and the world wobbled in front of him. "True that."

She closed her mouth, looking at him sternly. "You ruined those girls' lives," she said after a moment.

Dan put the cup down. "What are you talking about?"

"Valerie and Adelaide."

"I didn't . . ." The words echoed in his head, rolling around like bowling balls on a dance floor.

" 'And the devil that deceived them was cast into the lake of fire and brimstone, where the beast and the false prophet are, and shall be tormented day and night for ever and ever.' "

Dan shook his head, which made it ache even worse. He hadn't done anything wrong. He and Val had been kids, fooling around. Val had cried afterward—he'd remembered that—but that was because it had been her first time. At least that was what he'd thought, what he'd told himself for years, and when Addie had accused him, Val had said no. She'd backed him up. She'd sat with him at lunch for the rest of the year, for Chrissake, and was that the behavior of a girl who'd been harmed, who'd been violated? No. No, it was not.

Except, Dan thought as Merry continued to look at him. If that was true, why had Val been so angry at the reunion? You ruined my life, she'd hissed at him, her pretty face contorted. Dan lifted one hand to his head and rubbed at the sore spot there that felt disturbingly mushy, like a bruise on an apple.

"Repent," said Holy Mary. Her face was flushed, her eyes were *alight. She fell to her knees beside the bed with a wall-rattling thump. "Repent," she said, and reached for his hands and gripped them, pulling him out from under the covers (he was indeed naked, he saw) and onto his knees. Milk and juice and tea sloshed over the edges of their cups and soaked the quilt. Dan Swansea knelt next to Holy Mary and squeezed his eyes shut.*

TWENTY-NINE

Back at the station, Jordan's patrol-people were hunched over their desks, fingers clattering over the keyboards, telephones tucked under their ears. They'd made progress, he learned as he hung up his coat and went to his office, with the three of them in their blue uniforms (Holly, he was sure, had hers specially tailored to make the most of her admirable ass) following him like something out of *Make Way for Ducklings*, which the Nighty-Night Lady had read two nights before. Of the one hundred and eighty-seven registered attendees and thirteen walk-ins at the previous night's reunion, ninety-six of them were men, either members of the class or spouses of women who were. Of those ninety-six, eighty-four had been accounted for—they'd answered their home phones, or their cell phones, or the phones at their parents' houses to say that they were fine and well and were not missing their belts or a significant amount of blood.

That left an even dozen. Of those, Christie Keogh, reached at her home, post-workout, pre-pedicure, told him that eight were out-of-towners, most likely on Saturday-morning flights taking them back to California and Connecticut and an army base in Stuttgart, Germany. Which brought them to four.

Jordan stood in front of his desk as Holly Muñoz fumbled with a folder. "Oops!" she cried as a folder of paper-clipped pages slipped between her fingers. Jordan crouched down, plucked the pages out of the air before they hit the ground, and handed them to Holly.

"Wow," she said, taking pains to make sure that their fingers touched as she took the folder. "Fast." If this kept up, Jordan thought, she'd show up at work one morning with I LOVE YOU written on her eyelids, like that girl in the Indiana Jones movies. She was adorable, but she was also significantly younger than he was, and his subordinate. She deserved someone better, someone who hadn't already fucked up a marriage and did not have a fantasy life starring an icon of the non-potty-trained.

He sat as Holly read the list. "Scott Erhlich. Lives in Chicago. Unmarried, no kids, not answering his home or his cell phone. Eric Ramos. Lives in Cincinnati, married to Kelly Granville—she's the Pleasant Ridge grad. They've got three kids. No answer at home, and neither one of them has a cell phone. We're in the process of trying to reach the wife's family. We figure they might have gone there after the reunion. Kevin Oliphant . . ."

Jordan interrupted, remembering what Jon had said: *Kevin Elephant.* "Wait. Who was that last one?"

Holly repeated the name, then spelled it. "He lives in Pleasant Ridge."

"He got a record?" Jordan asked.

Holly flipped a page. "DUI times three, drunk and disorderly, disturbing the peace. Bar fights, it looks like, and one assault. Looks like he pushed his ex-wife down a flight of stairs, after she alleged that he'd hit her son with . . ." She paused, peering at the notebook. "A cast-iron frying pan?"

"My mother had one. You use them to fry chicken," said Gary.

"Or bake cornbread," offered Devin Freedman. "They're heavy."

"They sell them at Williams-Sonoma," Gary said.

"I know what they are," Holly said. "I just can't see someone using one as a weapon."

Jordan pressed his hand against his forehead. "Who's number four?"

"Daniel Swansea," said Holly. "He's not answering his cell or his home number. Single guy, lives downtown in a high-rise. His parents say he doesn't really keep in touch. Day doorman hasn't seen him; we left messages for the night guy. He works at a Toyota dealership, but nobody there was expecting him until Sunday."

Jordan wrote the names down, then studied them. "Daniel Swansea," he muttered, and flipped through his notebook to confirm that Jon had mentioned that name, too. "Field trip." He pointed to Holly. "You take the first guy, Scott Ehrlich." He pointed to Gary. "You find Daniel Swansea. Go to his place, and if he's not there yet, talk to the neighbors and the people at the dealership. Figure out who his friends are, where he might be crashing. Both of you, bring a picture of the belt. Maybe one of them'll recognize it." He gave Eric Ramos to Devin and got Kevin Oliphant's information from the computer. An assault charge, a bunch of DUIs and bar fights, pushing a lady, hitting a little kid. That sounded to him like a guy who could end his high school reunion minus his belt and some blood.

THIRTY

Kevin Oliphant lived in a crappy apartment in a subdivided three-story vinyl-sided house behind the Discount Food-mart on the very edge of Pleasant Ridge. Jordan checked the name on the mailbox and located unit 1-C at the end of a dark hallway that smelled like garlic and wet wood. He banged on the flimsy wooden door and called "Police!" and eventually, Oliphant exited, chest-first. The chest in question was bare, covered by a few sparse, dark curls. Oliphant's belly was slack and white, bulging above a pair of brown sweatpants. His bare feet were pale and surprisingly dainty, and he smelled not unlike the homeless men hanging around Jonathan Downs's bus stop: same signature scent of *eau de* Pabst and puke.

"Yeah?" he grunted, blinking at Jordan's face.

"You weren't answering your phone," Jordan said.

"Is that against the law?" He belched. Delightful fellow.

"Were you at the reunion last night?"

"So what if I was?"

"We found some stuff in the parking lot. You missing anything?"

Kevin Oliphant scratched his head. "If you've got papers, just go ahead and serve me."

"Why would you think I'm here to serve you?"

Kevin cleared his throat, a wet, rumbling sound. "Fuck do you care?" It happened in an instant. One second Jordan was standing six feet away from Kevin Oliphant, and the next he had the man backed up against the rattling living room wall of the shitbox apartment that smelled like fried food and stale farts.

"How about you answer my questions?"

Kevin struggled, wild-eyed. Jordan shook him. "If I run your name," Jordan rasped, "what'll I find? Couple of restraining orders? Parking tickets? Your child support all paid up, Kevin?" He shook him hard enough to make his head bounce on his neck, but Kevin said nothing. "Belt," Jordan said, letting him loose.

The other man stared at him. "Huh?"

"Show me the belt you wore last night," Jordan said.

Kevin stared at him for a moment, then skulked down the shitbox's hallway. A minute later, he came out with a black leather belt in his hands. "Okay? Are we cool?"

"We are not." Jordan peered around the apartment. The living room had scratchy gray wall-to-wall carpeting, a single stained recliner, and a stack of yellowed newspapers beside it. There was a pair of crumpled pizza boxes in the corner, and a thirty-gallon garbage can overflowing with empty beer cans and Popov vodka bottles beside it.

Kevin Oliphant followed Jordan's gaze. "What?" he asked. "I recycle."

Jordan walked down the hall. The grimy kitchen's sink was piled high with dirty dishes, the counter crammed with Chinese take-out containers and an eight-pack of paper towel rolls (from the look of it, Oliphant used paper towels as plates, napkins, and probably toilet paper, too). The bathroom was exactly what Jordan expected, the toilet seat up, the floor in front of it showered in piss droplets, a scroungy blue rug in front of the tub, which looked like it hadn't seen a sponge or a scrub brush in months, if ever. There was a coat closet off the hallway, empty except for a winter coat on a wire hanger, and some dirty T-shirts kicked into a pile. The bedroom closet was a tumbled mess of clothing. The bed was a mattress on the floor. It would have been depressing even if it didn't remind Jordan of his own place, which was cleaner and marginally better furnished but, for all that, still the place of a man who lived alone, a man who'd had a woman once, then fucked it all up.

Kevin trailed behind him as Jordan made his way through the apartment. "What are you doing? Hey, don't you need a warrant?"

Jordan stopped in the living room and glared at the guy. There was a pair of photographs in cheap wooden frames perched on top of the television set. Two kids, a little boy and a baby, wearing swimsuits (the baby's swimsuit bottom was swollen with diapers underneath), and just the thought that this foulmouthed, shitbox-dwelling, kid-hitting asshole had children, and that Jordan didn't and probably never would, was enough to make him want to grab Oliphant and shake him so hard that he'd need a construction-paper chart to remind him to wipe his ass after he took a dump. "Where's the basement?"

Kevin's mouth hung open. He shut it in a sneer. "Why? You think I'm hiding something down there?"

"Are you?" Jordan asked.

"Are you shitting me? I don't even have a basement."

"Storage unit?"

Oliphant worked at one of his back teeth with his tongue. "They wanted thirty bucks a month extra."

"Show me."

Oliphant shrugged and led Jordan to a door next to the laundry room. The door led down a flight of wobbly wooden stairs that led to a coin-op washer and dryer and a half-dozen chicken-wire cubicles packed with people's stuff: rolls of Christmas wrapping paper, tricycles and baby swings, cardboard boxes full of old

clothes and books, mildewed plastic lawn chairs, bundled magazines tied with twine. Jordan pulled out his flashlight and looked
around, shining the light into each cubicle as Kevin stood, shivering and barefoot, at the top of the stairs.

"Where's your car?" Jordan knew that Oliphant had one, or
that at least there was a ten-year-old Ford Explorer registered in
his name.

"Out front." Kevin cocked a thumb. Jordan walked outside,
looked the vehicle over, and saw a number of crushed coffee cups
and empty soda bottles strewn around the front seat, but no
blood, no dents, no body.

He marched back inside. Kevin Oliphant had pulled on a
T-shirt reading CERTIFIED PUSSY INSPECTOR and a pair of grayish socks. His big toe poked through a hole in the right one. This
guy just got better and better. "Who were you with last night?"
Jordan asked.

"Chip Mason. We went to our high school reunion together."

"Just the two of you?"

"And Dan Swansea."

"What time did you get to the country club?"

"Around ten."

"Who'd you talk to?"

"My buddies."

"They have names?"

"Phil Tressler. Russ Henderson. Jamie Wertz. We played
football." Kevin flexed his shoulders. "Won the conference junior
year."

"Congratulations. You leave by yourself?"

"Chip took me home. Dan said for us to go ahead. He was
talking to a bunch of girls. Probably figured he'd get a ride with
one of them, if you know what I mean." He leered.

"Do you know where he is?"

"Probably hooked up."

"Hooked up with who?"

"Shit, I don't know. Kara Tait, maybe. She was always a good time."

"Did you see Jonathan Downs last night?"

"Jonathan Downs?" Confusion flickered across Kevin's face. "No way. No way he'd show up. Not him or his fat freak of a sister."

"You know Adelaide Downs?"

"Know her?" Kevin's voice acquired a nasty edge. "That bitch ruined our senior year."

"What are you talking about?"

Kevin squinted at Jordan mistrustfully. "You know what? I don't have to tell you shit." He lifted his chin and then, with more dignity than a man wearing a PUSSY INSPECTOR T-shirt should have been able to muster, said, "I think you should leave now," and pointed at the door.

THIRTY-ONE

Kevin Oliphant didn't have to tell him shit. But Christie Keogh was more than happy to oblige. She met him at the door, face drawn and worried, with her son and daughter huddled behind her. Jordan crouched down, smiling. He thought he remembered hearing that it was important to get down to kids' level when addressing them, but once he'd gotten in position, he thought maybe that was dogs. The little girl shrank back with her hands over her eyes, peeking at him from between her slitted fingers. The boy, who appeared to be seven or eight, looked him up and down. "Are you a policeman?" he asked. "Do you have a gun? Can I hold it?"

"Oh, God," Christie murmured. She hustled the kids into the family room, put a program on the TV (Jordan was relieved it wasn't *The Nighty-Night Show*), and walked him back to the kitchen.

This time she was barefoot, with Styrofoam toe-spreaders on her feet. She'd changed out of her workout wear and was dressed for the day in dark jeans and a gray cardigan with a silver zipper she kept tugging as she explained what Addie Downs had done to ruin Kevin Oliphant's life. "It was when we were seniors," she began. "Right after homecoming, there was a party at this guy Pete Preston's house. He was the quarterback on the football team." She looked up, stealing a glance at Jordan's face. "Anyhow. Valerie Adler hooked up with Dan Swansea, and they went off into the woods, and ..." She peeked at the TV room, making sure the door was shut. "They had sex, I guess. I wasn't there. This is just what I heard." She pulled the zipper up, then down. "Anyhow. Addie and Val were best friends. They lived on the same street. They'd been best friends forever. They were both at the party, and what happened was, Addie told her parents that Dan had raped Valerie. Addie's parents—her mom, I think—told the guidance counselor at school. But Val said that nothing had happened. She told the guidance counselor nothing happened—that it had been, you know, consensual—and she told her friends that Addie was jealous. That Addie had been the one with the crush on Dan and that she didn't like it when Dan hooked up with Valerie. And the boys ..." She dropped her eyes. "People were pretty hard on Addie until we graduated."

"How do you mean?"

She tugged her zipper, looking unhappy. "Well. Addie had never been really popular anyhow—she'd been heavy and Val was really her only friend. After the party, after what happened, they weren't friends anymore, and everyone at school ..." She paused. "Dan and his friends kind of ganged up on Addie. People would say stuff. They'd call her a narc or trip her in the halls. Write stuff about her in the girls' room. High school stuff. Her locker was vandalized a few times, and some of those boys got in trouble for painting things on her driveway."

"What things?"

Christie shrugged, with her eyes trained on her immaculate kitchen floor. "Nasty things. I don't really know. They got arrested—Dan and Kevin Oliphant, Russ Henderson and Terry Zdrocki. They got suspended from school for three days, and they couldn't go to graduation."

Jordan considered this. "Were any of them at the reunion last night?"

The zipper went up, the zipper came down. "Terry died in an accident after graduation. I think he climbed on top of a trolley—he was drunk—and he tried to grab the wires. He was electrocuted." She swallowed. "The rest of them were there."

"We've been able to locate almost every man from the party except for Dan Swansea," Jordan said.

Christie looked up at him. "You think something happened to Dan?"

"We don't think anything yet, ma'am. We'd just like to find Mr. Swansea. Do you know who he left the party with?"

Eyes wide, Christie shook her head.

"Okay. Let's back up. What time did Mr. Swansea arrive?"

"I'm really not sure. I think he came with Chip Mason, and I remember seeing him at the bar with his friends, but I don't know when he came."

"Which friends?" Jordan asked.

"The football guys. Russ and Kevin Oliphant . . ." Her face went into a brief spasm of distaste. "He let himself go. Big-time."

"Did Mr. Swansea talk to anybody? Dance with anyone?"

She tapped her fingers against the countertop. "Different girls."

"Which girls?" asked Jordan.

More tapping. "I was running around a lot last night, so I can't really swear to any of this. Kara Tait, I think. Um. Lisa Schecter. That's her maiden name, I'm not sure what her married name is. She hyphenated. Oh, and I thought I saw him talking to Valerie." She raised her shoulders in a shrug. "So maybe I'm wrong. Maybe everything's fine with the two of them. Val's a meteorologist now. She's on TV."

"On TV," Jordan repeated as his cell phone started buzzing.

He excused himself, stepped into the foyer, and lifted the phone to his ear. "Yeah?"

"Chief? You told me to call you if we got any 10-57s," said Paula. She paused. "Missing person reports."

"Right. Did someone call one in?"

"Yes," said Paula. Jordan braced himself for the words "Daniel Swansea," but Paula said, "It's Adelaide Downs. Her next-door neighbor's reported her missing."

Jordan pulled his coat out of the closet where Christie had hung it, pointed at the door, then waved at her before telling Paula, "I'm on my way."

THIRTY-TWO

By the time Jordan rolled up to Crescent Drive, it was just after six and already dark. The sky was dotted with stars; a brisk wind rattled the tree branches as Addie's next-door neighbor, Cecilia Bass, came thumping down her front steps to meet him. She was an aged party with a wrinkled neck, a hawklike profile, and stringy gray hair pulled into a knot at the nape of her neck. She frowned at his badge, her bony, veined hands protruding from the cuffs of her floor-length down coat. Her legs were bare, traced with bulgy blue veins. Her feet were jammed into fur-lined boots, and she had a four-pronged metal cane in one hand.

"I understand there's a problem?" Jordan said once she'd handed his badge back.

"My neighbor is missing." Mrs. Bass raised her cane and swung it toward Addie's darkened house, narrowly missing Jordan's nose. "Adelaide Downs of Fourteen Crescent Drive."

"For how long?"

"Since four o'clock this afternoon. Perhaps earlier. Four o'clock was when I called and got no answer on either her home phone or her cell." Mrs. Bass swung open her door and led Jordan into a warm, cluttered, book-lined living room that looked oddly familiar. It took him a minute to place it, but finally, he realized that he'd seen the room—the red-and-white fleur-de-lis wallpaper, the heavy wood furniture—in the framed photograph in Jon Downs's bedroom. This was where Addie and Jon had once posed in front of the Christmas tree.

Mrs. Bass settled herself into a recliner bracketed by teetering stacks of Agatha Christie paperbacks and *National Geographic*s, raised the footrest with a whoosh, and waved her cane at a loveseat covered in slippery-looking cat-scratched beige satin. Jordan perched on its edge, swiped at his watering eye, and pulled out his notebook. "Normally, the department requires an adult be missing for at least forty-eight hours before we can file a report."

"These are special circumstances. Addie is definitely missing."

"How do you know?"

"Because," she answered, "Addie is always home. I have been her next-door neighbor since her birth, and Addie is always home."

"She never takes vacations?" Jordan asked. "Never travels? No boyfriends?"

Mrs. Bass shook her head. "Her brother is unwell," she said. "She stays here in case he needs her. She goes out in the afternoons for a few hours—swimming or shopping. And she always answers her phone."

Jordan nodded. With a brother in Jon's condition, he could see why she'd be attentive to her telephone ringing. "No boyfriends?" he asked again, assuring himself that he was asking out of professional curiosity. Mrs. Bass paused before she said, "None that I've met." She hesitated again. "Addie was very heavy for a number of years. I always believed it would take a special man to see past that. Men of your generation are dismayingly superficial. But I always hoped . . ." Her voice trailed off. "She's missing," she finally said. "And I am concerned."

"Had Addie had trouble with anyone?" Jordan asked.

Mrs. Bass frowned. "Not for years. Not since high school. There was a situation involving Addie's friend Valerie . . ."

He took notes while she gave him a version of the same story Christie Keogh had told him: a wild party senior year, Val and Dan Swansea off in the woods, Addie's accusation, Val's denial, and the months of harassment that had followed. Addie had gone off to college and come home weeks later, after her father died. She had stayed to take care of her mother and had been in Pleasant Ridge ever since. Addie worked from home, had no boyfriends that Mrs. Bass mentioned and no friends that Mrs. Bass was aware of, although she allowed that "perhaps Addie does her socializing online." Either way, Addie Downs was always available to sign for a package or help shovel a driveway or unlock a frozen computer, which was why Mrs. Bass had called her in the first place.

"I spoke to Ms. Downs this morning," Jordan said. Mrs. Bass's bushy gray eyebrows lifted.

"And she seemed well?"

"There was a high school reunion last night," he said.

"I doubt," said Mrs. Bass, "that Addie would have any interest in attending."

"We found blood and a belt in the country club parking lot."

The eyebrows shot up even higher. "You can't possibly believe that Addie was involved in a crime."

"We have to investigate every lead. And this morning, I saw Addie leaving Crescent Drive, in a green station wagon."

"Her father's car," Mrs. Bass murmured.

"She was with someone. Another woman," said Jordan, "A blonde."

Mrs. Bass looked thoughtful. "I wonder if it could have been Valerie," she said in a low, musing voice. Then she surprised

Jordan by lifting her big, spotted hands and clapping them together in a noisy volley of applause. "Well, good for her! Good for both of them!"

"Except," said Jordan, "I have a crime to solve."

Mrs. Bass gave a definitive shake of her head. "Addie's a good girl."

"Gets the mail when you're away," he said. "Signs for packages. Shovels your driveway."

"Addie would never . . ."

". . . hurt a fly?" he said.

She snapped the recliner's bottom down and pushed herself to her feet. "Young man," she said, "you may be an officer of the law. But, may I humbly suggest, you have a great deal to learn about human nature."

THIRTY-THREE

Jordan ended up fixing Mrs. Bass's computer—it turned out to be a simple matter of hitting "restart"—then made his way through the darkness, over the frost-crunchy lawn, to Adelaide Downs's front door. It was locked. No one answered his knock or the doorbell. He walked around to the back of the house, where he stood on his tiptoes and shone his flashlight through the windows. Laundry room: unremarkable. Dining room: ditto. There was a light on in the kitchen, shining over the sink, and he could see the kitchen table, with a teacup and what looked like a water glass on top. A woman's coat was draped over one chair, and on the refrigerator, stuck in the middle of what looked like coupons and shopping lists, was a laser-printed piece of paper. He squinted to make out the words: I WENT TO MEET MATTHEW SHARP ON FRIDAY, NOVEMBER 23. IF ANYTHING HAPPENED TO ME, IT'S PROBABLY HIS FAULT. There was a Pleasant Ridge address and telephone number, and a postscript: I WOULD LIKE A MILITARY FUNERAL.

Jordan pulled out his cell phone and called the station as he walked around the house. "Hey, Holly, did we get anything on that Matthew Sharp?"

"Didn't you get my text?" Jordan gave a vague kind of grunt, a noise that could have meant "yes" and could have meant "no" and could have just meant "my lunch didn't agree with me." "He's the one who calls the station every time there's a full moon to complain about the alien spaceship outside his window," Holly said. "He said he and Addie Downs left the restaurant at nine-thirty, and then he went home and was online in some psychic phenomenon chat room. There are date-stamped messages that prove it."

"Good work," he said, and peered into the garage, where a silver Jaguar sat like it was preening. Addie drove a Jag? "Hey, Holly, run a plate for me, okay?" He recited the number, then waited until Holly came back on the line.

"Car is registered to Valerie Violet Adler," she said.

Bingo, he thought.

"And guess what?" said Holly, her normally alto voice high and squeaky with excitement. "She's got a gun."

"What?"

"Well, at least she's got a permit to carry one. To carry, concealed. She got assaulted in the TV station's parking garage . . . or at least she said she did, but she never called the cops, so there's no report, but the station did a series about it last February. 'I Walk in Fear.' There was theme music and everything. You can get it on YouTube."

"How'd you find that out?"

Holly paused minutely. "I did a Google," she finally said. Jordan winced. One little mistake, one tiny screwup, one single reference to "doing a Google" when everyone knew you were just supposed to say you'd googled so-and-so, and his patrol-people would spend the rest of their careers treating him like he was an old dog, good for nothing but lying on a mat by the door, farting and licking the place where his balls used to be.

"Thanks," he said to Holly, and flipped his phone shut. Old Mrs. Bass had nailed it. Val had been here. Val was probably the other woman in the car; Val and Addie were together, and Val had a gun. And theme music to go with it. So now what?

Pocketing his phone, he walked to the back door. He was going in. He had to. "Official business," he said out loud. "Reasonable expectation." That was what he'd tell the D.A. if the admissibility of the fruits of this search ever came up in court. Addie was not answering her door or her telephone. Her neighbor had reported her missing. The note on the refrigerator suggested that she might have been harmed, and Valerie Adler had a gun. It was his duty, his sworn obligation, to make sure that Addie was safe. Then he reached under the welcome mat and pulled out a key. He shook his head as he unlocked the door—he always told the women who came to his Safe Home seminars that a key under the welcome mat was as good as just leaving the door open—and stepped inside. First, he trotted up the stairs, calling Addie's name, moving quickly from room to room, opening doors and shower curtains, sticking his head into the crawl space above the closet, working his way down to the first floor. On a table just inside the front door was a painted clay bowl with pocketbook detritus—he poked around and found a nail file and a half-empty packet of cinnamon gum. He could hear the furnace rumbling in the basement, and he could smell the ghost of woodsmoke from the living room fireplace.

The living room was to the left, the dining room to the right, a staircase straight ahead of him with the kitchen beyond that. Addie's house was warm and cozy, just as nice as he'd remembered. It looked like it had come out of one of those decorating magazines that Patti used to read when she still read things that weren't baby-related. She'd stick Post-its to pages about retiled bathrooms or overhauled kitchens. *Maybe someday,* Jordan would tell her.

Jordan sat down on the couch and surveyed the living room again: the paintings and drawings on the walls, the flat-screen

TV, the brass tub full of split wood next to the fireplace, a pile of heavy, oversized art books centered on the coffee table. He leaned back with a sigh. It was a place where a man could watch the game, have a beer, relax by the fire. It was . . .

He shook his head. So Addie Downs had good taste in couches and pretty paintings on her walls. That didn't mean anything. *Get a grip,* he told himself, and proceeded to the dining room. Addie had filled the windowsill with plants and set up a wooden easel in front of the window, and a tilted architect's desk next to that. Arranged on the dining room table were a stack of creamy paper, palettes of watercolors, and three empty coffee cans stuffed full of brushes and sharpened colored pencils. A Macintosh computer with an oversized screen occupied the far end of the table. Next to it was a watercolor painting of a small white bird flying over a blue ocean against a pale-blue sky.

He pulled on a pair of thin plastic gloves and tapped the Mac's mousepad. The screen flared to life, and hallelujah, finally some good luck. Addie had left her e-mail in-box open. He scrolled through a month's worth of e-mails, looking for something from Matthew Sharp or Dan Swansea, or Valerie Adler, or anyone connected with Pleasant Ridge's class of 1992. He didn't find anything. There was a note from an editor at Happy Hearts Greeting Cards thanking Addie for turning in something called a page proof before the holidays ("We can always count on you!") and a solicitation from the Crossroads, asking for Addie's continued support of the important work they did on behalf of clients living with brain damage and mental illness. Other than that, zip. No dirty jokes (Jordan could count on at least one of those in his own in-box every day, courtesy of his brother, Sam, who communicated primarily through blow-job jokes, probably because he had two kids and a functional marriage and didn't know what to say to Jordan anymore). No all-caps e-mails about how Barack Obama was a Muslim or how your cell phone would give you cancer if the fluoride in your toothpaste didn't give it to you first (Jordan received those on a weekly basis from his grandmother in Miami, who'd discovered the Internet at the age of ninety-two and had become a devoted conspiracy theorist).

He walked back to the kitchen. There was a copper teapot on the stove, a blue-and-white sugar dish beside it, paintings of different flowers on the walls—he recognized irises and lilacs and couldn't name the rest. In the sink he saw the dishes he and Addie had used, one with a few doughnut crumbs still clinging to it. On the table he found a mug of tea, half-full, ice-cold, and, across from it, an empty water glass. Jordan lifted it in a gloved hand and sniffed. Vodka. He went methodically through the cupboards, examining boxes of pasta and crackers, plates and glasses and mugs, many of them hand-painted, decorated with flowers or birds. The fridge and freezer were the inverse of his own: instead of being filled with single-guy food (Swanson and Stouffer's frozen meals, beer, whole milk, and red meat), Addie's were heavy into single-lady stuff, low-fat this and whole-grain that, the groceries of a person who lived alone and didn't have to worry about anyone else's tastes or preferences . . . although there was also real cheese and real butter and a six-pack of beer with two beers missing (was Addie a beer drinker? Did she have a boyfriend? Had Mrs. Bass gotten it wrong?). Hanging over the back of one of the chairs was a trench coat, Burberry, size two. Jordan squatted, knees popping, and used his pen to lift the sleeve of the garment, which was stiff with a tacky dark-brown substance that had the unmistakable look and smell of dried blood.

He poked at the stain, then stared at it, trying to imagine the scenario: Addie is sitting at the kitchen table when Val drives up in her silver Jag, asks for a drink, and says, *Guess who showed his face at the reunion,* and Addie says, *Let's go get him.* Or: Val arrives, shaken and bloody, and says, *Guess who I just hit, or shot, or stabbed, or drove over,* and Addie puts down her tea, pours her best friend a shot of vodka, and says, *You'll need some help getting rid of the body.* Or: Addie can't sleep, makes herself some tea, upgrades to vodka, cuts her leg while shaving, tries to stop the bleeding with the itty-bitty trench coat she'd bought on sale in hopes of squeezing herself into it someday (every March, Patti used to tape her bikini to the fridge as inspiration), then gets in her dad's old car and drives off on the spur of the moment to visit Disney World or Dollywood or some fucking place he'd never think of in a million years.

Jordan stomped back up the stairs to take a closer look, now that he was fairly certain there wasn't a dead body in the house. There were three bedrooms. One was set up like a guest room, with a half-dozen uselessly small pillows on top of a bed that didn't look as if it had been slept on recently, if ever. A second bedroom had been converted into a gym. There was a fold-up treadmill, and one of those ab rollers you could buy on TV sat beside it on the floor, along with a yoga mat. Hot-pink hand weights, stretchy resistance bands, and a stack of DVDs: *Gentle Yoga for Beginners, Pilates for Weight Loss,* and *Skip Your Way to Fitness!* At the end of the hall was the third bedroom. Addie's bedroom.

Here, for the first time, was the appearance of disorder. The king-size bed was rumpled, as if someone had lain on top of it, and one of the pillows had fallen onto the floor. Jordan picked up the pillow in its crisp cotton case. It was surprisingly heavy, dense with feathers. He set it on top of the bed. White sheets, a tan comforter, a scrolled, painted metal headboard (Brass? Iron? It was the kind of thing his ex-wife would have known). There was a table on either side of the bed, both with reading lamps, one of them stacked high with books, the other with a glass of water and a tube of hand cream (Vaseline, $7.49, from Walgreens; Jordan approved). He slid open the drawer of the nightstand closest to the unmade portion of the bed. There was a box of condoms, half of them gone, and he found himself suddenly, ridiculously, hotly jealous.

At the foot of the bed was a padded bench, covered in the same soft fabric as the couch downstairs. A pair of flannel pajamas was tossed on top of the bench. Jordan lifted the top in his hands, then, without planning it, he lifted the fabric to his nose, inhaling the fragrance of perfume and shampoo. Jesus. There was something wrong with him. If one of the patrol-people could see him, standing in a suspect's bedroom, sniffing her clothes, for God's sake, with half a hard-on . . . Jordan dropped the offending garment back where he'd found it and turned away from the bed. More bookshelves against a wall that was lined with windows and overlooked the backyard. More paintings on the walls, wise-eyed dogs and sly, clever kittens. A bathroom with a deep jetted tub, big enough for two. Heated tiles on the floor. Heated towel racks on the walls. Heavy, fluffy towels, pristine white, and an oversized shower stall with no fewer than half a dozen jets embedded in the glass-tiled wall. "It's like a whorehouse in here," he said out loud, but he thought that that wasn't right. It wasn't like a whorehouse, it was a place made for pleasure. He wondered whom Addie had been entertaining, who'd been enjoying the condoms in the drawer and the beer in the fridge.

He closed the closet door and walked downstairs, turning off lights, locking the door. He bent down and tucked the key back under the welcome mat, where he'd found it, and cut back across the crackling lawn to his car.

THIRTY-FOUR

I was never sure who started the graffiti. On the third day of my sophomore year, almost two years after Jon's accident, I'd gone to use the bathroom and found it carved into the paint in a bathroom stall. *Addie Downs stinks.* My heart started thundering in my chest, and I felt nauseous, like invisible hands were squeezing my guts. I looked around, which was silly—I was obviously alone. The door was locked, and besides, there wasn't room in here for anyone but me. Tentatively, I lifted one arm over my head and sniffed. Nothing but Secret spring fresh deodorant, which I'd applied that morning. I swallowed hard, then bent my head and sniffed between my legs. At first I didn't smell anything besides the Downy my mother used to wash our clothes, but when I inhaled as deeply as I could, I smelled—or thought I did—a faint whiff of something dank and fleshy.

Oh, God. I held my breath, stuck my head out of the door to make sure that I was alone, hurried over to the sinks, grabbed a wad of rough brown paper towels, covered them with foamy soap, dunked them under the cold water, hustled back into my stall, slammed the door, yanked down my blue sweatpants, and started scrubbing. Another peek out the door, another dash to the sinks, another wad of paper towels, this time minus the soap. Finally, I pulled a Bic out of my backpack and painstakingly scribbled over each letter of what someone had written about me.

It didn't matter. The next day, in study hall, I saw the same words on a desk, this time in black ink. *ADDIE DOWNS STINKS*. And underneath it, someone writing in blue had added *she has big tits tho*. I propped my math book in front of me, licked my fingertips, and started rubbing, managing to smear the letters but not erase them. I licked some more, rubbed some more, and looked up to find Mrs. Norita standing over me and frowning.

"Miss Downs? Would you mind telling me what you're doing? Because it's clearly not your math assignment."

From the seat beside me, Kevin Oliphant snickered.

"Let me see," said Mrs. Norita. I knew it was hopeless. I slid my math book aside. She looked at the words, then looked at me. "We'll have the janitor take care of that" was all she said. "Okay," I whispered, and slumped down as far as I could in my seat, my belly pushing against the elastic waist of my skirt, my chest straining at the fabric of my top, wishing I could sink all the way down to the floor and then through it.

I didn't understand what I'd said, what I'd done, that had turned me into a target. I hurried to class in a head-down shuffle, clinging to the left edge of the corridor, with an eye on the open doors, the bathrooms I could duck into when I heard the hissed whispers that trailed in my wake. *Hey, fattie. Hey, stinky. Fat ass. Lard butt. Wide load. Yo, Hindenburg* (this was after we'd covered the *Hindenburg* disaster in history class).

"You should smile more!" Valerie counseled on the bus home from school. She bared her own teeth in a tinselly grin. That summer, she had finally gotten her wish and spent six weeks in California with her father. I had counted the days until she came back and had accompanied Mrs. Adler to the airport to meet her. Waiting by the gate, I'd felt my heart shrivel painfully when Val came down the walkway, tanned and taller, with brand-new breasts pushing against the front of her brand-new Izod shirt, and her hair hanging in a heavy gold curtain down her back. Beside me, Mrs. Adler had given a little yelp, her expression the strangest mixture of pride and sorrow, as Val pulled off her sunglasses and flashed her braces in a smile. In the car, she'd babbled excitedly about the amazing time she'd had, showing me pictures of herself posing in front of the HOLLYWOOD sign, telling stories about visiting her father "on set" and having lunch at "craft services" with Tom Cruise's stunt double. She'd come back with a suitcase full of new clothes, even more confidence than she'd had already, and a seemingly inexhaustible supply of advice about how I should behave. "Say hi to people," she told me, as the bus labored up the hill toward home. "Be friendly!"

"They hate me," I said. Saying hi and being friendly would never work for me, but it had worked for Val. That fall she'd made the JV cheerleading squad, where her enthusiasm and volume made up for whatever she lacked in rhythm and grace. She wasn't the best-looking girl, or the most coordinated, and she was off-key as ever when the squad attempted to sing, but she was the one you'd watch anyhow, the one your eyes would follow as she cartwheeled on the sidelines or jumped in the air to celebrate a touchdown. She had a whole crew of new friends, fellow cheerleaders, giggling, ponytailed girls.

As for me, I had Val, and that was it. Everyone else seemed to hate me, and I didn't know why. I wasn't even the fattest girl in our class. There were three girls bigger than I was (there'd been four once, before Andi Moskowitz had gotten shipped off to fat camp in the Berkshires). Yes, I was heavy, and yes, I was plain—I'd spent enough time studying myself in my bedroom mirror to know that even with makeup and my hair done just right, no one would ever be tempted to call me beautiful, nobody from the cheerleading squad would be slipping a note in my locker inviting me to tryouts, the way they had with Val, not even if they needed a large, stable base for their pyramids—but I wasn't out-rageously heavy or ridiculously ugly. So why were they picking on me?

I wondered sometimes whether it had to do with Jon. Maybe they hated me because they couldn't hate him. My brother was living, vacant-eyed, occasionally drooling proof that everything they were could be taken away. Just one bad decision, one wrong turn, a car's wheels that went off the road instead of staying on it, and they could end up like he was. They couldn't hate him, though; he was a victim, a survivor . . . but they could hate me, just by virtue of proximity.

I stayed as close to Val as I could, tagging along with her new friends, trailing in her perfume-and-mousse-scented wake, be-cause nobody was mean to me when she was around. I also started carrying a bar of Dial soap in a plastic case, and a wash-cloth and a hand towel around in my backpack, plus fresh under-wear and even an extra pair of sweatpants. I'd shower in the mornings for ten, fifteen, twenty minutes, standing underneath the scalding water until my skin was bright red and my mother banged on the door and told me for the third time to come out. After lunch, I'd duck into the bathroom and change my under-wear, just in case . . . and when I had my period, I'd change my napkin between every class and change my underwear, too. I went through cans of what the drugstore coyly called "personal hygiene spray" at the rate of one a week. Val and I were in differ-ent classes except for science and English, and three days a week we didn't even have the same lunch. I sat by myself at assemblies and in chorus, and two days a week, I'd be all by myself at lunch-time, at a table in the cafeteria corner. Sometimes Merry Arm-bruster would plop down for a few minutes. She'd bow her head in prayer, lips moving rapidly while I ate the carrot sticks and rice cakes that I'd packed. Merry belonged to some weird church. She didn't cut her hair or wear pants or talk to boys, and she got sent to the office almost as much as Dan Swansea, because of her propensity for hissing things like "hellbound Sodomite" at girls who French-kissed their boyfriends in the halls. She'd sit with me and talk to me, but I didn't think she liked me very much. Merry viewed me as a lost cause, the closest thing Pleasant Ridge High had to a leper whose feet she could wash.

After school, Val had cheerleading practice. I would walk the two miles home (I'd quit taking the bus by myself after we'd had to back down a blocked-off street and the meep-meep-meep noise had prompted some wit to shout, "Hey, that's how Addie Downs sounds when she's getting on the toilet"). The yellow-and-black bus would labor past me, up the hill just beyond the high school parking lot, and usually, someone would stick his head out the window and yell "Burn it off, fattie!" as I climbed. I kept my head down, biting my lip, feeling my thighs rubbing together, feeling myself start to sweat, start to chafe, start to stink.

At home, I'd take another shower, and then I'd go to my job, babysitting Mrs. Shea's youngest children, a set of three-year-old twins. I'd stay until seven, sometimes later. I would take the twins to the park, pulling them in their Radio Flyer wagon, and at din-nertime, we'd play restaurant, where I'd take their order in a little notebook, then bring them their mac and cheese or cut-up hot dogs, rice or chicken noodle soup. I'd bathe them, read to them, supervise teeth-brushing and pajama selection, and leave them on their beds, waiting for their mother to come home and tuck them in.

The Sheas lived at the end of our street. Most days, I'd go straight home, but once or twice a week, I'd cross the busy road and walk to the convenience store on the corner of Main and Maple, or the drugstore down the street, and wander through the aisles slowly, sometimes murmuring "milk" or "bread" or "butter" to myself, to make it sound like I had a legitimate reason

for being there. Meanwhile, I'd fill my basket with bags of cookies and chips, family-sized Cadbury candy bars wrapped in crisp
blue-and-white paper and gold foil, boxes of Sno-Caps, plastic
cups of butterscotch pudding so loaded with artificial colors and
flavors and preservatives that they didn't require refrigeration,
chocolate-iced cupcakes, raspberry-filled doughnuts, and lemon
pies. I'd shove my money across the counter without meeting the
clerk's eyes ("Having a party?" an older lady in a dark-blue apron
had asked me once, and I'd been forced to mumble my assent),
cram the treats into my backpack, and hurry out the door.

At home, my mother would have dinner waiting: broiled
chicken breasts, sweet potatoes with a sprinkling of cinnamon
and Butter Buds, a bowl full of chopped iceberg lettuce doused
with fat-free vinaigrette. The four of us would sit at the kitchen
table, cutting and pouring and moving food into our mouths and
answering questions about our days. Jon would work on word
searches, or read *Omni* magazine at the table, his cheek propped
up in one hand, his mouth hanging open.

When we were done with our meal, I'd wash the dishes, wipe
off the table, and sweep the floor. My father would head to the
basement. Jon would drift toward the television set. He liked
sitcoms with laugh tracks, shows that told him what was funny.
I'd hear his own hoots of laughter, a scant second after the taped
audience started laughing. My mother would change into sweatpants, and we'd take our evening constitutional, ten laps around
the block. I'd take another shower, my third of the day. "Goodnight," I'd call before locking myself into my bedroom.

Every night I'd promise myself I wouldn't do it, that I'd just
finish my homework and go to sleep like a normal person. Some
nights I'd last until eight-thirty or even nine. I'd rinse my mouth
with mouthwash so astringent it would make my eyes water. I
would brush my teeth until my gums bled. I'd chew sugar-free
gum and gulp mint tea. I'd sketch frantically, using charcoal and

colored pencils to capture a scene from the day—the twins in the sandbox, their round faces crinkling when they laughed; the sun coming up over the cherry tree in our backyard; my mother's hands on Jon's shoulders. I'd replay the day's taunts in my head. I would review what I'd eaten, and think about how well I had done, how I hadn't had as much as a spoonful of the twins' mac and cheese or a single cookie from their box. None of it did any good. Eventually I'd think, *Just a taste. Just a little taste of something sweet.* And then, almost before I knew it, I would find myself with my hand down deep in one of the plastic bags, the stiff waxed paper and foil wrappers crinkling as I tore the packages open. I'd turn off all the lights except the small one by the side of my bed, and I'd lie on my side, curled around my sketchpad, or one of the heavy art books I'd take out of the library, looking at paintings and photographs from museums in Italy and Paris, places I'd never been and would probably never visit. And I'd eat, ferrying the sweets from the box to my mouth in an unbroken chain, chewing and swallowing and chewing and swallowing, feeling the pillow cool against my cheek, the chocolate coating my mouth and my tongue, the syrupy caramel melting deep in the back of my throat, my left hand dipping and rising into the bags and boxes as my right hand turned the pages.

The Saturday after Valentine's Day all of those heart-shaped boxes of candy that hadn't been bought were 75 percent off. I'd buy half a dozen boxes and stack them in my closet. At night, I'd start off with cookies, move on to something salty, like cheese curls or potato chips, and finish my evening with nougats and caramel chews, buttercreams and cherry cordials. I would flip the pages, looking at the pictures with my fingers scrabbling through the fluted brown paper cups in a box with the words *To My Sweetheart* twining across the cover in gold script, and I'd fall asleep without brushing my teeth, with all of that sweetness

gilding my mouth. I would dream about love, about being magi-
cally lifted out of my house, out of my town, even out of my body,
and deposited someplace better, where I'd be a thin beautiful
laughing girl in a two-piece swimsuit or a short cheerleader's
skirt. Sometimes I would let my mind wander to Dan Swansea,
how he'd looked at the swimming pool in the summer, beads of
water flashing on his smooth brown back, more water slicking
the dark hairs against his calves. *Hey, pretty,* I'd imagine him saying as we passed in the hall. In my dreams, he reached for my
hands, he tugged me into the secret vestibule outside the gym
teacher's office to steal a kiss before class. None of this would
ever happen, but my dreams, carefully embroidered and unfolded
each night, were as sweet as candy.

"I don't understand it," my mother said after my checkup.
My pediatrician had shaken his head, frowning, while I stood
on the scale, and then, bald head gleaming, he'd bent over his
prescription pad and written the words "Weight Watchers" and
"exercise," before tearing it off and ceremoniously handing it to
me. She'd add another lap to our evening walk, or subtract half
a sweet potato from my dinner, and I'd promise myself that
I was going to stop with the chips and the cookies and the
To My Sweetheart candy. I'd wake up full of resolve, thinking
that this would be the day that things would change: I'd stick to
my diet, I'd smile, I'd be friendly, I'd do whatever Val told me,
because clearly she'd figured out the secret to being liked by
everyone.

"Just don't worry so much," Val lectured one spring morning.
She wore a pink tank top that left her arms and the top of her
chest bare, and a khaki skirt—since she'd started with the cheerleaders, she wore skirts almost all the time. A few she'd bought
herself, over her California summer, and a few I recognized as
Mrs. Adler's, the long, lacy cotton ones that swept the ground
like a bridal train. Val's braces had come off, her teeth were white

and straight and shiny, and her figure had filled out—she wasn't very big on top, but her small breasts looked right with her tight hips and long legs. To look at her you'd never believe that she'd once been geeky or gawky, that her clothes had been weird, that she and I had once belonged together. The balance had shifted. In high school the things that I was (smart, neat, polite, artistic) mattered far less than the things Valerie was (blond, cheerleader). "You smell fine."

"I know," I said, and pulled at the hem of my sweater. It was too hot for sweaters, but mine came from Benetton and was exactly the same as the ones the other, thinner girls wore, only bigger. I had the same designer jeans, too, special-ordered from Marshall Field's, where they didn't normally stock my size. My mother had bought them for me, and I didn't have the heart to tell her that I could wear exactly the same things as the other girls and they would still look wrong, because I was wrong, and nothing I wore could change that.

"You're too self-conscious," Val scolded, shading her eyes and peering down the street. "It's like you're already thinking of every bad thing someone could think about you before they even think it. If people know they're getting to you, they're just going to keep doing it."

I ducked my head. She was right.

"You're fine," she said as a white Civic zipped around the corner and squealed to a stop in front of us. Mindy Gibbons, one of Val's fellow cheerleaders, was in the driver's seat.

"Hey, Val!" she singsonged. There was a momentary pause. "Hi, Addie." Another pause. "Hi, Jon."

I raised my hand as Jon raised his head from his word search, looked at me before raising his own hand in a wave. Val picked up her backpack and put her hand on the car door. "Do you want to ride with us?" she asked.

My throat felt dry. Mindy was a senior and a cheerleader, and I was sure she didn't want me in her car. "That's okay," I said.

"What?" Val asked impatiently. "I can't hear you."

"Go ahead," I said.

"Come on," Mindy said over the blare of Mariah Carey. "We're gonna be late."

Val gave me a look I couldn't read before climbing in next to Mindy and slamming the door. I watched them drive off, feeling furious and bewildered and sad. When had Val and Mindy made this arrangement? When had they gone from being squadmates to being friends?

I picked up my own backpack as the school bus lumbered around the corner and, bracing for the stares and the whispers, pushed Jon onto the bus and climbed on board behind him.

THIRTY-FIVE

Pleasant Ridge town manager Sasha Devine was a handsome, dark-eyed woman five years older than Jordan, who did not look happy to see him on her doorstep late Saturday night.

"I assume this isn't a social call," she said, leaning against her door. Blue light from the television flickered behind her, making her short, curvy body glow like she was radioactive.

Jordan kept quiet. Sleeping with the town manager, technically his boss, had been a huge mistake. Sleeping with his boss and then not calling her afterward had been an even worse one. "Can I come in?" he asked.

Sasha tilted her face up and looked at Jordan like he was going to try to sell her something she didn't want. "How about you just say what you need to say?"

"Okay." He should have called her. He'd *meant* to call her. He'd had every intention of calling her, but by the next night, the task of lifting his telephone, punching in her numbers, actually speaking to her, had seemed insurmountable. *I'll call her tomorrow,* he'd told himself, but on Sunday he'd just . . . what? Gotten busy. There was a *Sports Illustrated* he hadn't read, and when he'd turned on the water to make coffee, the faucet was dripping. He'd set about fixing it, only his socket wrenches were under the sink, with the cleaning supplies, and the cabinet was shut with one of the childproof locks he couldn't remember how to open, and rather than try to figure it out, he'd made a trip to Home Depot to buy more.

Home Depot was right by the movie theater, and there was a showing of that movie he'd wanted to see, and by the time he got home, it was seven o'clock and he'd figured that Sasha was giving her kids dinner. She had two daughters, eight and ten, and a husband who'd done a runner for reasons she hadn't divulged. Back in his camouflage camp chair Jordan drank one beer while watching a TiVo'ed episode of *SportsCenter,* and another beer watching the news. Beers three, four, and five had followed, and then the Nighty-Night Lady came on and he'd gotten involved in the episode, and afterward, zipping his pants and disposing of the Kleenex, he was too embarrassed to speak to anyone. Then it was Monday, but he had Mondays off, and on Tuesday he'd figured he'd see her at some point during the week, and he had, but it had been awkward, and the week after that, when he'd finally decided to ask if she wanted to have dinner, she'd snarled, "Don't do me any favors," and that had been the end of their romance. He'd never gotten to apologize. Certainly, he'd never gotten to tell her the truth, which was that after they'd had sex (and that part had gone well, all things considered—out of her suit and hose and heels, with her thick hair loosed from its pins, Sasha was an old-fashioned beauty), he'd gone to her bathroom and seen, amid the cosmetics on the countertop, a tube of Dora the Explorer toothpaste, bright-red gel in a red-and-white container sized for little kids' hands. And really, what could he say? *I can't see you again because I'm afraid of your toothpaste? I can't see you again because you have kids and I don't and I kind of hate you for that? I can't see you again because, before things fell apart, my wife used to get tipsy on white wine and sing "I Loves You Porgy" to me, and she never will again, and it hurts so much I can't even think about it?*

He stared down at Sasha, thinking that he was supposed to have his life by now: his wife, his family, the house they would live in together. Instead, he had nothing. Nothing at all.

"Dan Swansea," he began. His breath formed white clouds with every word. "We think the belt and the blood belong to a man named Dan Swansea."

Sasha sighed and nudged the door open with her hip. "C'mon." She kept an office on the first floor, just off the kitchen, with a tiny antique desk and two upholstered armchairs, and it was there that she led him, sweeping a half-dozen stuffed bears and bunnies off one chair and sitting down in another.

Jordan took a seat and made his case. "Fifteen years ago, when Dan Swansea was a senior at Pleasant Ridge High, he was accused of raping one of his classmates, a woman named Valerie Adler. He and some of his friends got in trouble for harassing the woman who'd accused them. Valerie denied anything had happened. The woman who accused Dan was Valerie's best friend, Adelaide Downs."

"Go on," said Sasha, pulling out a pen and a piece of paper.

"Three of the boys who got in trouble were at the reunion last night. Swansea's missing. He's not answering his phone. Nobody's seen or heard from him since the reunion."

Sasha regarded him with her fine brown eyes. "So what happened?"

"We're looking at the woman who made the accusation. Adelaide Downs."

She raised her eyebrows. "Not the victim? The one he allegedly raped?"

"We think that Ms. Adler and Ms. Downs are together," Jordan said. "We think maybe whatever happened to Dan, the two of them are responsible."

The wheels of Sasha's chair squeaked against the floor. "So

what happened? The two of them waited fifteen years, then snuck up on Dan in the parking lot, took off his belt, and did what, exactly?"

Stiffly Jordan said, "We're working on that."

"Have you questioned them?"

"I was at Ms. Downs's house this morning," he said. Never mind that he'd been there to ask about her brother. "She's missing now. Her neighbor reported her missing. Her house is locked. Valerie Adler's car is in the garage, and Ms. Adler has a permit to carry a weapon, concealed. I want permission to get a warrant to search their houses," he said, leaving out the fact that he'd been through Addie's house already, that he'd found a coat with blood that he thought would match what they'd found in the parking lot.

But even before he'd finished pronouncing the word "warrant," Sasha was shaking her head. "No can do, Chief. There's no physical evidence connecting them to the crime, right?"

"Right." They looked at each other for a moment, Sasha with her eyes narrowed, Jordan with his hands on his thighs. He guessed that he could get her to authorize his request for a warrant if he could get her into bed again, but given his past behavior, that probably wouldn't be happening.

"I can't let you go after a warrant based on circumstantial evidence," Sasha finally said. Jordan nodded and got to his feet. This was the answer he'd expected, even though it had been worth a shot. Sasha's expression softened. "You look awful. Go home. Get some sleep," she said.

Back in the car, Jordan called his team and sent them home, telling Holly and Gary to be back at the station at seven a.m. sharp ("I'll bring you coffee," Holly told him, and Jordan didn't have the heart to tell her no). At home, there was a new episode of *The Nighty-Night Show*. Jordan showered, stuffed his clothes in the hamper, and pulled on pajama bottoms and a T-shirt. He cracked open a beer, shoved a frozen pizza in the toaster oven (he had to fold it in half to get it to fit), and settled into his camp chair. But he couldn't relax. He kept thinking about Adelaide Downs, whom no one had believed, and Valerie Adler, the best friend who'd betrayed her and then come back. *The ladies,* he thought . . . and by the time the Nighty-Night Lady came on, with her V-neck exposing a wedge of creamy cleavage, Jordan was asleep.

THIRTY-SIX

The next morning, Jordan huddled with Holly and Gary as the two of them led him through the intricacies of Wikipedia and explained, in painstaking detail, what Twitter was. When he was up to speed on everything the Internet could tell him about Valerie Adler, Girl Reporter, from her feuds to her Facebook fan page, he took a pocketful of Holly's frosted Christmas sugar cookies, cut in the shapes of bells and stars and candy canes and decorated with seasonal sprinkles, and drove to Chicago.

There was no answer when he buzzed Val's high-rise condo on Lakeshore Drive. The doorman out front was resplendent in a uniform of red wool and gold braid, like he was planning on marching off to fight for the British as soon as his shift ended. His name was Carl, and he hadn't seen Ms. Adler since Thanksgiving Day. "Her mother was in town," he said, and lowered his voice to a conspiratorial murmur. "You know the term 'cougar'?"

Jordan nodded. The other man's teeth gleamed as he grinned. "Man, I'da hit that with stuffing!"

"So you haven't seen Valerie Adler?"

"I'da hit that with candied yams on the side!"

"Got it. Now, can you tell me—"

"I'da hit that," the man said, shoulders heaving with laughter, "and then three hours later, when the football game was over, I'da gone back to the kitchen for a hit-that sandwich with cranberry sauce!"

"*Okay,*" said Jordan.

"Funny?" asked the doorman, smoothing the braid on his shoulders. "I'm doing open-mic night at the Laugh Hut next week. Anyhow, the hot mama left Thursday night, and I haven't seen Miss Valerie since then."

"You got a key?"

Carl shook his head. "I'm sorry, man, but Ms. Adler would kill me. She would literally end my life as I know it. So unless you got a warrant . . . look, fella, I'd help you out, but comedy's not paying yet, and I got kids, you know?" Sure, Jordan thought, thanking the man. Didn't everyone?

Valerie's parking spot underneath the building was empty. Her cell phone went straight to voice mail. That left work.

Jordan pulled up in front of the Fox studios on North Michigan Avenue just after eight-thirty in the morning and consulted the printout in his lap. Ten minutes later, the man he was waiting for approached the building. Station manager Charles Carstairs was tall and rangy, with a tartan scarf around his neck and a tweed cap shading his eyes. He carried a slim leather attaché case in one hand and one of those brand-new smartphones in the other. Beneath his overcoat, he wore a navy-blue suit that appeared to be more expensive by a factor of five than the best thing Jordan owned.

"Mr. Carstairs?" Jordan jumped out of the car and crossed the sidewalk fast, with his badge in his hand. "Jordan Novick from the Pleasant Ridge police department."

Carstairs scowled down at his telephone's screen, then up at Jordan. "What can I do for you, sir?" Another glance at the screen. "Whatever it is, it'll have to be quick. We're on live at nine."

"This shouldn't take long," Jordan promised. Carstairs frowned and started tapping at his telephone again. Jordan gave him a minute and then, in a voice that was loud enough to carry, he said, "Mr. Carstairs, I need to speak to Valerie Adler, your employee, with regard to an ongoing investigation. I need your assistance, sir."

Carstairs put his telephone away. "Fine. C'mon up."

In his office on the thirty-seventh floor, Carstairs sprawled in his seat, legs spread, arms stretched above his head behind a desk filled with framed family pictures. Jordan checked out a handsome Irish setter, two little boys with their father's sharp features, and a woman whose auburn hair was significantly less glossy and whose expression was marginally less intelligent than the dog's. He wondered which one was better behaved. On a wall to the right of the desk, six flat-screen TVs broadcast local and national news; on a wall to the left, three clocks kept time in Chicago, New York, and Los Angeles. Through the windows that looked out on the mostly empty horseshoe-shaped newsroom, Jordan could see a few people tapping at computer keyboards. At one desk, a man draped in a barber's cape was getting his hair trimmed.

"What is this about?" Charlie Carstairs asked, rocking forward and planting his forearms on the desk. "What do you want with Valerie?"

"Right now," said Jordan, "we just need to find her. She isn't at her condo, she isn't answering her cell phone."

Carstairs turned to his computer, tapped a few keys, and peered at the screen. "She worked Thanksgiving, and she's scheduled off until Tuesday. Her high school reunion was Friday night, and she called in puffy."

"Excuse me?"

"Well, not called in. She asked for the time off weeks ago. She said she'd be drinking, and she didn't want to be on the air with carb face."

"Carb face," Jordan repeated.

"Vanity." Carstairs allowed himself a small smile. "Par for the course with on-air talent. Wish I could help, but I really couldn't tell you where she is . . . and like I said, we're live at nine."

I think you can tell me, thought Jordan. *You can, but you don't want to.* He stood up and inspected the family pictures. One of Carstairs's boys was missing his front teeth. "Did Valerie ever mention any places she liked? Vacations she'd taken? Any friends or relatives in other cities?"

Carstairs twitched in his seat. "None that I recall."

"Okay," said Jordan. He lifted a photograph of Charlie Carstairs in a Hawaiian shirt with a garish print, posing in front of a statue of a dolphin as big as a city bus. "Where is this, Florida?"

The other man's voice was waspish. "Why do you ask?"

"Just wondering." Jordan set the picture down. "Were you the one who hired Valerie?"

Carstairs shoved his chair away from his desk. "Look, I've really got to get out there."

"What is she like?"

The other man hesitated, his hand on the doorknob. "What do you mean?"

"What's she like?" Jordan said. "We're trying to find her. We need to make sure she's safe. The more we know about her, the better."

The appeal to Carstairs's better nature, the mention of Val's safety, seemed to work. He stepped away from the door and sat down behind his desk again. "Let's see. She runs," Carstairs said. "Or at least she dresses like she does. She likes sushi. And nice clothes. Her wardrobe budget . . ." His face softened as he re-membered something . . . something personal, something tender, Jordan bet. He recognized the look. He was pretty sure he'd felt it on his own face when he'd told stories about Patti—how he'd proposed, for example, by hiding the ring in a box of chocolates, only Patti had been on a diet. She'd thanked him sweetly and set the box by the door to bring to school the next morning, and he'd had to tell her that she might want to take a cruise through the caramels before she dropped it off in the teachers' lounge with a HELP YOURSELF sign on top.

He pulled himself back to the present. "Did you ever see Ms. Adler lose her temper?"

Carstairs shrugged. "She gets annoyed, just like the rest of us."

"What does she do when she gets angry?" Jordan asked. "Does she throw stuff? Curse? Sulk?"

"She . . . plots, I guess," Carstairs said, surprising Jordan, who'd been expecting more typically diva-esque behavior—curs-ing, or ranting, or throwing cell phones and wire hangers at an assistant. "She doesn't raise her voice or curse, but the thing about Val, if you cross her once, she never forgets it."

Cross her once, Jordan wrote. "Did she ever get in any trouble?"

Carstairs sighed and looked longingly out his office window. Through the studio's open double doors, Jordan could see men pushing cameras on wheeled dollies, quick-stepping over the cables that trailed behind. The anchor desk sat empty, looking smaller and somehow less solid than it did on TV. "Well, there was that thing in the dog park."

"What was that?" Jordan asked.

"A few years back. What Val said was that she was walking her dog and some lady with a German shepherd came along and let her dog off the leash, and the German shepherd attacked Val's dog. This little yappy thing. Val was screaming at the woman, and the woman was yelling back, and they were both trying to pull the German shepherd off of Val's dog, and then Val . . ."

Jordan continued to stare at Charlie Carstairs, remembering the headline in the *Tribune:* THE SH*T HIT THE FAN. As it turned out, the German shepherd's owner, a lady of seventy-eight, had been a longtime Fox Chicago viewer, and she was none too pleased when its star meteorologist had beaned her with a plastic bag full of dog poop. She'd filed assault charges. The papers and blogs had feasted on the mess for weeks; Val had taken what the station insisted was two weeks' worth of previously scheduled vacation, and then the whole thing had blown over, with the only lasting consequence being that Val never reported on stories involving dogs for that channel again.

"And the peanuts," said Carstairs. Jordan remembered that one: how, at the very end of a sweeps week story about area schools going nut-free to accommodate the increasing number of children suffering from allergies, Valerie, apparently not realizing that her microphone was on, had referred to the afflicted kids as "God's mistakes." She'd delivered an apology at the top of the next night's five o'clock newscast ("I was inappropriately flippant about what I realize is a most serious subject, particularly to the families living with nut allergies and nut sensitivities"), but that hadn't kept pissed-off allergy-awareness activists from pelting her with Styrofoam packing peanuts when she'd shown up at a White Sox game that weekend . . . a move, of course, that had enraged the green freaks, who'd spent the next two weeks waving recycled-paper signs outside the station's windows.

"Do you like her?"

Carstairs paused before giving a stiff, grudging nod. "We had a good working relationship."

Jordan looked at the man innocently. When Carstairs didn't

blink, Jordan pulled a frosted Christmas cookie out of his pocket and started to eat it.

The news director's jaw tightened. "Are you implying something?"

"Nothing." Jordan wiped his mouth and returned his gaze to the photographs: husband and wife and kids and Irish setter. "Nice dog. Did you ever hear Valerie mention Dan Swansea?"

Carstairs shook his head no.

"Adelaide Downs? Ever hear that name?"

Another headshake.

"But you knew Val was going to her reunion Friday night."

"Oh, I knew all about *that*." Charlie Carstairs gave him a humorless smile. "She did the Master Cleanse. Cayenne pepper and maple syrup for a week. Good times." He narrowed his eyes at Jordan. "What's this about? What happened?"

"At this point, we just need to find Ms. Adler."

Jordan noticed Carstairs's right hand creeping toward the pocket where he'd stashed his fancy phone. "Valerie's due in Tuesday afternoon. I can have her call you when she gets here. But until then . . ." He opened the door. "I've got a show," he muttered, and hurried out of his office across the newsroom and through the swinging doors. As Jordan watched, a sign above the door lit up. ON THE AIR, it read. Jordan stared at it, marveling. It was just like on TV.

He ambled out of Carstairs's office and took a tour of the newsroom. It didn't take him long to locate Valerie Adler's desk, which had photographs of its tenant thumbtacked all over its particleboard walls and a sliver of a view of the lake.

Jordan sat in Valerie's seat, took a deep breath of what he guessed was Valerie's scent, and tapped the touch pad of the computer. The screen bloomed to life. The in-box was closed and password-coded. Jordan didn't even try. Instead, he sat at her chair, inhaled hairspray and perfume, and inspected her desk. There was a blue glass cup filled with pens, a calendar filled with cursive notations for *Hair* and *Facial* and *Trainer* and *News meeting*. Beside the computer was a makeup mirror surrounded by miniature lightbulbs and a rolling caddy filled with more photographs, each one sheathed in plastic. Jordan twirled the wheel slowly. There were pictures of Val shaking hands with the mayor and Val dancing with the governor, before he'd been removed from office, at what looked like a black-tie fund-raiser (the governor wore a tuxedo, Val wore a dress that seemed to be missing its back). Finally, there was a shot of Valerie in shorts and a bikini top, posed in front of the very same dolphin sculpture from the snapshot on her boss's shelf. On the back of the picture was written *Key West/Valentine's Day/2007*. Sometimes, Jordan thought, slipping the picture in his pocket, being a detective didn't require much actual detection at all.

THIRTY-SEVEN

By the time I was a senior, I'd spent hours thinking about Dan Swansea, but I'd never actually spoken to him. In real life, as opposed to my daydreams, Dan was part of the larger, amorphous pack of guys who ignored me. Maybe he'd made meep-meep-meep backing-up noises at me in the hallway. Maybe he'd written *Addie Downs stinks* on a desk or a wall, but he'd never been mean to my face (or directly behind my back, where I could hear it). He'd existed on a different plane, the one reserved for handsome athletes, or beautiful girls like Valerie, and even though in my head we had lengthy, sparkling conversations that were frequently interrupted by torrid make-out sessions, in real life, I don't think we'd ever even said hi.

One Friday afternoon in October, Val bounced over to our workstation in chemistry class. It was a game-day weekend, so she wore her cheerleader uniform: a short, pleated maroon-and-cream skirt, a matching sweater-vest. Her legs were still tan from summer, set off by white socks and white sneakers. "Hey, Addie. Want to hang out tonight?"

I stared at her from my seat, which I'd jammed against the wall, trying to make myself as small as I could be in my leggings and loose knitted vest. I didn't want to say yes too eagerly, and

I wondered what had motivated this request. Val and I still sat together at lunch a few days a week—or, rather, I sat next to her silently at the cheerleaders' table while Val chattered and giggled and sipped her Diet Coke. We still waited for our rides together in the morning (I'd take the bus, even though Val insisted that her friends would be happy to drive me), but she had another life by now, one where she stayed out late on the weekends and got dropped off by cars with music blaring and laughter drifting from the windows—I knew this because sometimes I'd watch her from my bedroom. Before I could ask why she wanted to spend her Friday night with me, Valerie leaned close enough that I could smell her shampoo and Certs. "Listen," she whispered. "There's a party at Pete Preston's house tonight. I'm grounded, but I know my mom will let me go over to your house. We'll tell your parents we're going to the movies, and we can both go to the party!"

My heart sank, knowing that I was just a convenience. It sank even farther when I realized that I wouldn't say no, that I'd take whatever I could get of my best friend's time, no matter what the circumstances.

"We'll have so much fun!" she said, all cheerleader-bouncy.

"Okay," I said as Mr. Newsome slammed the door, set his briefcase on his desk, and bellowed, "Attention!" which was how he typically began class. Val zipped back to her desk. I opened up my backpack, sighing. In my darkest moments—usually the ones in the middle of the night, when I'd wake up sick to my stomach and queasy with regret about what I'd eaten—I would think that Val bothered with me only because she liked the idea of herself as a good person. *You're so loyal,* the cheerleaders would say, and Val would tell them, *Well, I've known Addie for a long time. I can't just turn my back on her. Poor thing.*

On Friday night, I came home from babysitting to find Val sitting on our front step with a zippered nylon case full of makeup in her lap instead of an Encyclopedia Brown book, and a jelly jar full of vodka tucked into her pocket where her red rubber bouncy ball used to be. I had let her paint my face, let her dress me in black tights and a black, ruffly skirt that fell to the tops of my knees, with a scoop-necked black bodysuit underneath and a denim jacket on top. "You've got the best boobs," she'd said, pinning one of her rhinestone pins to the jacket's lapel, and I'd blushed and said, "They're big, anyhow," and Val had said, "Big is good!"

We'd said goodbye to my parents, and I'd followed Val out into the mild, smoky-smelling autumn night and walked with her to Pete Preston's street ... but once we were there, I lingered at the curb, my mouth dry, my hands sweating.

"Come *on*," said Val. She took my arm and tried to pull me across the street, but I was bigger than she was, and I wasn't moving. The Prestons' front door was open, and kids were streaming inside. All of the lights were on, and I could hear a Will Smith rap song blaring through the open windows. Val's eyes were bright as she shook her shoulders to the beat.

"I don't think this is a good idea."

"Of course it's a good idea. We're going to have so much fun!"

I shook my head again. Pete was the football team's captain. His parents had gone to London for the week and decided that Pete was old enough to be left home alone, with the car keys and forty dollars for food and incidentals. Pete, delighted, had invited all of his friends to a party, and now it looked as though more than half the school was there. "I don't know anyone," I said as a pack of girls in lace-up Chuck Taylors and pouffy hair bounded through the front door.

"Yes you do." Val pointed at a group of boys in varsity jackets standing in the front yard, laughing. "See?" I watched as Dan Swansea high-fived one of his teammates and walked through the door. "It'll be fine."

Reluctantly, I let her lead me across the street into Pete Preston's house, into the heat and the noise of the crowded kitchen. A battered metal keg stood on the kitchen table, next to a stack of blue plastic cups. At the counter, four red-faced boys were hooting and laughing as they tried to flip quarters into their cups. Girls stood behind them, chattering and clapping when one of the quarters found its mark. We went upstairs to dump our coats on a bed, then came back to the kitchen, where I edged into a corner.

"Here." Val handed me a cup of beer. She wore a short pink skirt, white tights, and a striped rugby shirt. Her hair was in a French braid. Dainty gold hoops hung from her earlobes. She was so pretty. It gave me a pang that was both pride and regret.

I took a sip and winced. I'd never had beer before, and it was terrible—watery and sour. "Now go say hi to Dan," Val said.

I shook my head. I wasn't going to say hi to anyone. I wasn't going to talk to anyone, I wasn't going to look at anyone, I wasn't going to do anything but stand in a corner, next to a shelf filled with Mrs. Preston's collection of dusty Hummel figurines, and drink my beer and wait. Making the first move was not part of my fantasy. In my dreams. Dan noticed me first. That could still happen. Maybe he'd see me, standing in the corner. Maybe he'd get sick, or get in a fight, and I'd help him. I'd put an ice pack on his nose or something, and he'd look at me with his groggy eyes (groggy was good, I'd determined, dizzy was excellent, and passing out, then waking up with his head in my lap would be best of all). He'd look at me, blinking, and slur, *You're beautiful.*

"I'm okay. You go."

"Fine." She pumped herself another beer and marched away. I put my cup down next to a china shepherdess and shoved my hands in my pockets. Time passed. The boys tossing change into their cups got louder. As I watched, one of them pulled one of the girls into his lap. "Ry-an! I swear," she said, before he closed her mouth with a kiss. I picked up my beer and sipped it slowly, just to have something to do with my hands. When it was gone I spent twenty minutes edging my way through the five feet to the keg, and pumped myself a refill. "Ry-an, I swear!" I whispered to myself, and went back to my corner. When my cup was empty, I went looking for Valerie.

She wasn't in the dining room, where more boys sat around the table, playing a drinking game that involved singing in a language that might have been French and moving their cups and bottles back and forth, faster and faster. She wasn't in the TV room, which was thick with loud conversation and with cigarette smoke. Nobody was in the living room. Pete stood at the door with a hockey stick. "Don't even think about it," he growled as I tried to peek past him, and I murmured, "Sorry," and hurried away before he could ask what fat Addie was doing at his party.

I walked through the laundry room, then the kitchen, then past the powder room, where, from the sounds coming through the door, someone was throwing up. I pulled the biggest book I could find—a collection of Ray Bradbury short stories—off the bookcase in the TV room, went to the screened-in porch that was a twin of the one at my house, and checked the Swatch I'd bought with my babysitting money. It was ten-fifteen. I was giving Valerie until eleven, and then, with or without her, I was going home.

At eleven, I stomped through the house, glaring into each of the rooms. No Val. I went outside, letting the door slam shut behind me, when I heard familiar laughter and saw a flash of blond.

In the backyard, four boys stood in a semicircle around a tree with their hands stuck in their jacket pockets or holding bottles of beer. Valerie was sitting on the ground, her back against the tree trunk, giggling. A cup of beer had spilled next to her, soaking the ground, and there was a lit cigarette burning between her fingers.

I pushed through the boys and looked down at my friend. "Val? What's going on?"

"We're playing spin the bottle," said one of the boys.

"Let her play, too," said Val. There was something funny about her voice. She sounded like a tape being played on a Walkman when the batteries were dying.

One of the boys looked me up and down, then shook his head. "We don't need her."

I swallowed hard. Valerie was trying to push herself upright. Her rugby shirt was rolled up, exposing a crescent of pale belly. Dan Swansea leaned down beside her, and I felt my heart twist. Were they together now? Was he her boyfriend? Val giggled, shaking her head as Dan leaned close, whispering something in her ear. I felt like I was going to throw up. Val knew how I felt about Dan; she was the only one who knew.

As I watched, Val reached down the front of her shirt, pulled her lacy pink bra out from underneath her shirt, and stuffed it in her pocket. "Oops." She giggled, then burped against the back of her hand and tugged the hem of her shirt down.

"Val," I said. "I want to go home."

"I'm having fun," she said. "Aren't you having a good time?"

I looked down at her. She was drunk, I decided. "Actually, no."

"Look, just go inside and wait for me. I'll come get you when we're done."

"Okay." My face was burning, my head echoing with the words *We don't need her.* Of course they didn't need me. I wasn't what boys wanted. Valerie was.

"Give me twenty minutes!" Val called. I didn't answer. I went upstairs for our coats, then sat on the porch, holding my book tightly, reading the same page over and over until the words quit making sense. It was twenty-seven minutes, according to the glow-in-the-dark hands of my Swatch, before I felt my friend's hand on my shoulder.

"Let's go."

I jumped to my feet and pulled on my coat. As soon as we got out of the house, I was going to ask why she'd even bothered bringing me. I was going to tell her that she'd used me for the very last time. I was . . . I turned and got my first look at Val by the light of the moon. Half of her hair hung in tendrils around her cheeks. Her eyes were red and puffy, and there were pine needles stuck in her braid. "Are you okay?"

"I'm fine," she said, her voice cracking. It took her two tries to put her hands in the right sleeves and get her coat zipped. She yanked a knitted hat over her hair. "Let's go."

"Where were you?"

She paused for so long that I'd given up on getting an answer when she said, "In the woods."

We were halfway down the street before I got up the nerve to ask another question. "Did something happen?"

She gave a short laugh, then wiped underneath her nose with the back of her hand. I followed her through the Biancos' backyard and climbed over the low rock wall of the field that ran behind Main Street. We were walking home. "Are you . . ." I had to proceed carefully or she'd forget who she was really mad at and be mad at me instead. "Are you okay?"

"I told you, I'm fine." She kept her head down and kept walking.

I thought of what else I should ask her, thinking back to health class, to the *What's Happening to Me?* book my mother had bought me. "Did you and Dan . . ." I swallowed. "Did he use something? A condom or something?"

"I told him no," she said. Her voice was thin and bleak. I looked at my friend and saw that she was crying. "He said not to be a prick tease. He said I showed him my . . ." She wiped her

eyes, then waved her hand in front of her chest. "We were playing Four Minutes in Heaven. We were just fooling around, and
that part was okay, but then he . . . he . . ."

I swallowed hard. "Was it your first time?"

Valerie made an unpleasant sound, half snort, half sob. "Are
you kidding me? You thought I was a virgin?" She gave the word
a nasty, sarcastic spin.

"Guess not," I said softly. She gave another choked sob and
wiped her eyes again, and I wondered if it occurred to her that I
was a virgin.

I felt the balance shifting, the fulcrum tipping, as if she were
the hurt child and I the capable grown-up, the one who would
take care of things. "We have to tell someone," I said.

Her head jerked up. "No! No we don't!"

"Yes, we do, Val. He raped you."

She bent her head. "It wasn't like that."

"If you told him no, and he didn't stop? That's exactly what
it's like!"

"It wasn't like that," she repeated, her voice a whisper.

"How much beer did you drink?" I asked. "Did you take anything else? Did he give you something?

"I just had beer. Not that much. A few cups. Addie, listen, it's
okay. It's fine. What happened . . . it was no big deal, and if we
tell someone, then everyone's going to know."

"But he raped you," I said.

"It was my fault," she said. "I shouldn't have gone with him. I
shouldn't have played . . . Addie, please," she said, and grabbed
my hand. "Don't tell anyone. It's okay. It's no big deal. Really."

"He can't just get away with this," I said. At that moment,
I could feel the cloak of responsible adulthood falling over
my shoulders, making me brave in a way I never had been before.
"I'll tell my parents. They'll know what to—"

"Don't say anything. I mean it. Don't." We walked through

Mrs. Bass's backyard, Val half running, me struggling to keep up. When we reached Crescent Drive, Val stood at the base of my driveway, as I walked to the front door, into my warm, lit living room. My mother was out on the porch with her note-book and her tea. My father was in the basement—I could hear the hum of something, a drill or a sander. Jon sat at the kitchen table, working on a puzzle. I waited, breathing in the smells of home, until my mother came into the living room and saw me. "Addie? Are you all right?"

I looked through the window and saw Valerie standing at the base of the driveway.

"Something happened to Valerie," I said. *I'm doing this for her,* I thought as my mother looked at me, waiting for me to say more. *I know better than she does. I know what she needs.*

THIRTY-EIGHT

Valerie and I spent Saturday night at the Four Seasons in St. Louis. On Sunday we stayed at the Ritz-Carlton in Atlanta's Buckhead neighborhood. My friend, I discovered, had developed a taste for five-star hotels in the years since I'd known her. "Let me do the talking," she said in Atlanta after we'd handed off the car to the valet guys (they'd had the good manners not to wince at the sight of it) and gone inside. I stood back, awaiting a repeat of the previous night's performance, wondering what the clerk would make of her, with her head swaddled in a fringed scarf, her eyes hidden behind enormous sunglasses, and half a dozen shopping bags from Saks and Neiman Marcus in her hands. Probably he'd think that she was a rich lady who'd had a face-lift, I decided. I probably looked like her nurse.

I caught a word here and there as Val leaned close, her hand on the clerk's forearm: "public figure" and "discretion" and "pay in cash" were a few of them. A moment later, after the exchange of a significant stack of bills, she had the room keys in her hands. "Do you need to be validated?" the clerk called after her, and Val grinned and said, "You could tell me I look pretty."

I rolled my eyes as Val approached. "I got them to give us a room without a credit card. I registered as Betty Rubble," she said, heels clicking over the marble floor.

"Wow," I said. "Nice improvement." In St. Louis she'd been Tinker Bell.

She gave me an indulgent look, carried her bags into the elevator, and hit the button for the sixth floor. On the way down the hall, she swiped a handful of chocolates and two extra bottles of conditioner from the maid's cart. Once we were inside, she kicked off her shoes, dropped her bags, and flopped down on one of the double beds, closing her eyes and sighing.

We'd driven all the way to St. Louis on Saturday and spent the afternoon at a fancy mall with a fancy name: Plaza Frontenac. Val, who'd elected herself custodian of our cash, had purchased "a few necessities," including but not limited to a beaded Tory Burch tunic, a La Perla bra, a pair of two-hundred-dollar jeans, and Chanel eye cream that she swore she couldn't go even a single night without, while I spent thirty dollars on deodorant and dental floss and a pair of nightshirts from the Gap's clearance rack.

We'd gone for dinner at a restaurant in the mall, a big, bustling steak place full of men in suits, with booming voices and, I presumed, expense accounts to cover the forty-dollar hunks of meat. I'd had my usual salad and grilled fish, to make up for the early-morning doughnuts. I hadn't expected much, but the sea bass was delicious, seared crisp on top and tasting of ginger and lemongrass. Val had ordered a thirty-six-ounce Delmonico, bloody rare, with a baked potato and a side of creamed spinach, and then, working steadily with a fork and a heavy German steel knife, proceeded to devour every morsel. I watched in awe and made a mental note to buy Tums as she walked me through her employment history: the small TV station outside of L.A. where she'd worked right out of college as an intern, gofer, girl Friday, and eventually, substitute weekend anchor; then the medium-sized station in Lexington, Kentucky, where she'd done the weather and, it emerged, her coanchor. She'd made stops in Dallas and Boston before she'd landed back in Chicago.

"How do you eat like this?" I finally asked after she'd pushed her empty plate away and then, unable to decide between the cheesecake and the crème brûlée, ordered both.

"Oh, well, normally I don't."

"Normally you don't eat like this?"

"No, normally I don't really eat. At all," she explained. "I have protein shakes, and soup sometimes. Oh, and sushi."

"That's it?"

"Oatmeal." She sighed. "With almond milk and blueberries. And salmon."

"On the oatmeal?"

"No, no, I have that for lunch. There's this service I use that delivers my meals . . ."

"I didn't hear anything in there that sounds like a meal."

"This is the life I have chosen," she said, and looked up, beaming, as the waiter brought her desserts.

"Yeah, about that," I said. "Weather? I never remember you caring that much."

"News flash," she said, forking cheesecake into her mouth. "Nobody really cares that much about the weather. It's a means to an end. What I care about is the anchor's job."

I snagged a spoonful of her crème brûlée. "You want Austen Severson's job?"

"Old," she said, still eating. "He's old and in my way."

I winced. Austen Severson was a Chicago institution, a trim, silver-haired grandfatherly type with twinkly blue eyes and a reassuring manner who'd been reading the news since the 1970s. "Is he going to retire?"

She smiled sweetly, patting her lips with her napkin. "Yes indeed," she said. "He just doesn't know it yet."

Back in the hotel room, I pulled the nightshirts out of the

shopping bag, handed one to Valerie, and went to the bathroom to wash my face, brush my teeth, and change. When I came back she was still lying on the bed, barefoot in her new jeans and silk halter top, staring at the ceiling.

"Are you all right?" I ventured. She gave a tiny nod. "Want your eye cream?" She shrugged. "Pillow chocolate?" I threw her one. She batted it away.

"We should get some pot," she said to the ceiling. "Maybe I'll see if one of the valet guys can hook us up."

I sat cross-legged on my bed, sinking into the down-filled duvet. "I think that we should maybe try not to break any more laws."

Valerie ignored me. "Did I ever tell you about my mother's don't-do-drugs speech?"

I shook my head.

"Naomi sat me down one night—I think we were, like, in seventh grade—and looked at me very seriously and said, and I quote, 'Valerie, you shouldn't do drugs. It's not like it was in my day, when you knew what you were getting. They lace that shit now.'"

"That's what she told you?"

"Good old Naomi." Val unwrapped her pillow chocolate and popped it in her mouth. "Mother of the year."

"Where is she these days, anyhow?"

"Remarried. Her current husband is twice my age and exactly half as interesting. She's still in Cleveland." She shook her head in disgust—at Naomi, or at her new stepfather, or at Cleveland, I couldn't tell—and rolled onto her side. "This is fun," she said. "Like a slumber party. Hey, wanna raid the minibar?"

I shook my head. I'd fantasized about going out of town with Vijay—he traveled often, for conferences and drug-company-sponsored retreats, usually held at some fancy golf resort or at a beach. We could go out to dinner, in a town where nobody knew either one of us. We could hold hands at the table and spend a whole night together in some plush hotel room. "I had a boyfriend," I told Val, who was crouched down in front of the minibar, inspecting the options.

She looked up and waved a fistful of miniature bottles at me. "You did?" She sounded so proud. "Ha. I knew that lingerie was for something. Good for you!"

"He was married," I said.

"Oh." Val considered this. "Well, did you have fun?"

"So much fun," I said. "At first. And then for a while. I liked being with someone. You know. Watching TV. Holding hands."

"Sweet," Val said. She patted my arm and poured me a shot.

"I felt sorry for his wife," I said, and drained my glass.

"Wives," said Val. "So problematic." She dumped another tiny bottle of vodka into a cup filled with ice and sat on her bed, sipping.

"Hey, Val." My tongue felt like a sock stuffed full of quarters. Wine with dinner plus vodka after equaled more than I'd had to drink in a long time. Carefully, I set my glass aside. "What happened that summer you went to California?"

"Ah yes," she said. She pulled a mirrored compact out of her purse, dug around for a cotton ball and a bottle of face cream, and started removing her makeup. "Old Naomi had a new boyfriend that spring. He used to hang around the house when I came home from school, and Naomi thought it would be a good idea if I went away for a while."

I thought this over, not liking the way it sounded. "Did he do something to you? The boyfriend?"

"Not exactly." Her eyes were trained on the tiny mirror in her hand. "Not really. He bought me dresses. He wanted me to wear them. Try this one, try that one; try the white, try the pink. Come sit with me. Pretty girl. You know. That kind of shit."

"Oh, Val." I thought that I should try to touch her—her arm, her hand—but she was too far away.

"Anyhow." She flicked the mirror shut and stuffed her equipment back in her bag. "I don't think Naomi wanted the in-house competition. So she scored a ticket somehow and put me on a plane, and then she called my dad to tell him I was coming."

My throat clicked as I swallowed. "Was your father glad to see you?"

"Thrilled," she said drily. "What forty-year-old down-on-his-luck stuntman turned craft service manager wouldn't want a sixteen-year-old showing up for the summer? He had a girl-friend, though. Shannon. She was nice. Do you remember how bad my teeth were?"

I spoke carefully. "They were pretty crooked."

"Oh, it wasn't just that. I'd never been to a dentist. Not since we left California."

"Naomi never took you?" I was shocked.

Val shrugged. "Shannon fixed me up. I got my teeth cleaned, got my cavities filled, got braces, got a haircut, got some new clothes. Shannon ran a tight ship. She had two kids of her own. Little girls. I wanted to stay with them."

"Why didn't you?"

She shrugged again. "No room at the inn. They had a two-bedroom apartment, and Shannon's girls were eight and six. I tried all summer long to be . . . what's the word? Indispensable." She pronounced it slowly, then said it again, "Indispensable. I'd wake up early, do all the dishes, unload the dishwasher, sweep the floors, get the girls dressed, braid their hair, make their lunches . . . everything." She tucked her hair behind her ears. "Turns out I was completely dispensable. They had me on the first plane back home the week the girls started school. Naomi took me to the orthodontist a few times. Then she started dating the orthodontist. Then they broke up, and she got drunk one night and told me she was gonna pull my braces off herself. She had pliers and everything."

I shuddered, wondering why I'd never known about any of this, why I'd never even guessed. Val reached across the space between the beds and patted my arm. "But never mind. It's ancient history. Let's talk about you! I bet your parents would be proud of you. All responsible, and thin and stuff."

"Hah." It was revoltingly superficial, I knew, but it made me sad to think that neither one of my parents had lived long enough to see me thin. Or thin-ish. Neither one of them would know about my career, or how beautiful the house was, neither would ever look at my cards, my mugs, the spoon rest I'd done, and think, *Hey, she turned out okay.* "We should get some rest," I said, and got under the covers, pulling them up to my chin. I rolled onto my back and shut my eyes. Then I opened them to see Val, still seated on her bed. Her knees were drawn up to her chest, and her chin rested on top of them as she gazed at the gold-striped wallpaper.

"What's wrong?" I asked.

"Dan."

Oh. That. "Listen," I said. "Maybe he'll turn up. You said you didn't hit him that hard, right? Maybe he was just stunned."

"Not what I did to him," she said impatiently. "What he did. What he did to me." She yanked back her covers and flicked off the light, plunging the room into darkness.

"Did you ever tell anyone?" I asked after a minute. "Your mom?"

She snorted. "Naomi. Hah. She would have probably been mad that I didn't get him to buy me dinner afterward." She sniffled. "She was dating his father for a while."

"Your mother was dating Dan Swansea's father?" Another

thing I hadn't known. I thought back to what my mother had said about Val not having it easy, and wondered what she'd known; if she'd had more of a sense than I did about what kind of mother Naomi Adler had been, if she'd seen behind the beauty and the glamour and the spur-of-the-moment road trips and been a lot less enamored than I was.

Valerie's voice was muffled, so faint it could have been coming from the far end of a tunnel. "The Swanseas split up for a while freshman year. He had car dealerships. Naomi drove me by their house once. This great big place with a three-car garage. I think she'd had her eye on him for a long time."

"Oh, Val."

The room was quiet for so long I figured Val had fallen asleep until she said, "I told my dad, though. I called him up. Woke him up. It was the middle of the night. I thought . . ." I heard her take a wavering breath. "I don't know what I thought, really. That he'd get on the next plane and fly to Illinois and beat the shit out of Daniel Swansea. Tell him, 'That's what you get for hurting my little girl.'"

"I take it that didn't happen?" I asked, even though I knew the answer.

"He told me he'd call me in the morning, after I'd had a chance to calm down. I waited by the phone all day. He never called." She pulled in a breath, and I heard the sheets rustle. "For the longest time, I just never let myself think about it. It was nothing. That's what I'd tell myself. It was nothing. But it wasn't . . ." Her voice cracked. I thought that she was crying, and I didn't know what to do. Should I try to hug her? Say something consoling? It had been so long since someone had told me a secret, so long since someone besides Jon had needed me.

Before I could decide on a course of action, Val got off the bed and padded to the bathroom. There was a brief flash of light as the door opened, then shut. Poor Val. If it had been me, if I'd told my father, I was sure that he would have done exactly what Val had wanted her father to do. He would have found a way to make the boy who'd hurt me sorry.

A few minutes later, Val stepped out of the bathroom and flicked on the light. Her face was scrubbed, her hair pulled back, and she was wearing her new nightshirt, a long-sleeved navy-blue cotton number. "Hey," she said, climbing under the covers, "we're twins!" She fished a discarded chocolate off the floor and popped it in her mouth, and as she chewed, I thought of what I could tell her; of how I could help.

"I missed you, you know," I said.

Slowly, she unwrapped another piece of chocolate and spoke without meeting my eyes. "Even though I was such a bitch? Even though I lied about you?"

"It wasn't all lies," I confessed. "I did have a crush on Dan."

She gave a short, bitter laugh. "Big mistake."

"And I did think that there'd be consequences. If you wound up accusing Dan, some of the cheerleaders would probably drop you."

She gave another unhappy snort. "Try all of them."

My throat tightened. "I thought they'd dump you, and then you'd need me again."

She was quiet for a minute. When she rolled over, I thought she was going to turn off the light, but instead, she stretched her hand across the space between the beds.

"I always needed you," she said, and grabbed my hand. "Friends?" she asked.

I felt the warmth of her palm against mine, the comfort of another body in the room, someone to laugh with, to drive with, to be with . . . until the end, if that was what was coming. "Friends," I replied.

PART THREE

Best Friends Forever

THIRTY-NINE

" '*He that covereth his sins shall not prosper: but whoso confesseth and forsaketh them shall have mercy,*' " said Merry. "*Proverbs 28:13.*" Her voice was hoarse. Outside the windows, the sun was coming up, which made it, by Dan's fuzzy reckoning, Sunday morning. They'd been at it for hours, kneeling bare-kneed on the wooden floor, with only a cup of chicken broth for sustenance, a few hours' sleep, and only one bathroom break (when Dan had worked up the courage to ask for another, she'd merely looked at him narrowly and launched into another prayer).

He pressed his hand against his head, feeling faint. When Merry looked at him, when she spoke to him about his sins, about the harm he had done to Addie and to Val, she didn't look angry, she looked . . . He shook his head. Never mind how she looked. He had to get out of here. "Listen," he said in a voice as raspy as hers. "Merry. I have a friend."

She stared at him impassively.

"Chip Mason. Remember him?"

She shook her head. "*Another idolator. 'He that shall blaspheme against the Holy Ghost hath never forgiveness, but is in danger of eternal damnation.' Mark 3:29.*"

"He's changed," said Dan, hearing the edge of desperation creeping into his voice, but unable to stop it. "If I did something wrong—and I'm not saying I did . . ."

" 'And it shall come to pass,' " Merry continued, raising her voice, " 'in that day, that the Lord shall punish the host of the high ones that are on high, and the kings of the earth upon the earth.' "

"I want to talk to Chip," Dan said, keeping his head down, his voice low. "He's a minister now. I want to make amends."

That shut her up. She stared at him, lips clamped together, finally quiet, watching him.

"I want to go to my church. Chip's church," he said, and held his breath as time stretched out until, finally, she gave one brief nod. She handed him clothes he guessed belonged to her father—baggy old khakis, a mothbally plaid shirt, a pair of cracked old rubber boots that pinched his toes—and led him out into the twilight, to a minivan festooned with HONK IF YOU LOVE THE LORD bumper stickers. She waited until he'd fastened his seat belt, then drove into the sunrise.

FORTY

By the time I turned thirty, my weight hovered somewhere south of three hundred and fifty pounds. That was just my best guess. I didn't ever weigh myself, and I didn't go to doctors—in fact, I rarely left my house. By 2004, you could get almost anything you wanted: your clothes, your groceries, new toothbrushes and dental floss, fancy chocolates, art supplies—over the Internet. Supplement that with the pizza and Chinese food and the dry cleaner's that did pickup and delivery, and weeks could pass without my venturing beyond the end of my driveway unless I was on my way to visit Jon.

Mostly, I was happy at home, filling my days with books and work, my online Scrabble games and the little black cat that sometimes came by my door, but every once in a while, I'd get an itch. I'd want to go to a department store and spray a new perfume on my wrists, to browse in a bookshop, holding the hardcovers in my hands, cracking their spines, smelling the paper. I'd want to go to Pearl Art Supply and touch the bristles of the paintbrushes, or sit in a coffee shop or a restaurant, eavesdrop on strangers' conversations, look at different faces; be part of the ebb and flow of a normal day.

One winter morning I'd found myself at the post office. I could order my stamps online and arrange for FedEx pickups for my art, but I liked one of the clerks—she remembered my name, and I'd ask her about her grandchildren or her vacations. Walking back to my car, picking my way along the slushy sidewalks of what passed for Pleasant Ridge's downtown, I'd paused in front of a diner with a neon sign in the window reading HOT APPLE PIE. Transfixed, I stood there, watching the words light up, one at a time: HOT ... APPLE ... PIE. A piece of hot apple pie, maybe with ice cream on top and a cup of coffee, sounded like just the thing for this chilly, overcast day.

The hostess looked at me dubiously before leading me to a booth. Booths, I saw, were all they had, unless you counted the spinning seats bolted in front of the long, curving counter, and I knew for sure that I wouldn't fit on one of them.

I took a deep breath, sucked it in, and slid into the seat. The hostess dropped a menu in front of me and fled. This was a mistake, I thought, even before the little kid in the booth in front of mine turned around and stared at me. I tried a wave. Ignoring my overture, the kid turned to his mother and whispered loudly, "Why is that lady so fat?"

"Probably because she eats large portions of foods that aren't healthy," the mother responded without bothering to lower her voice. I felt my face heat up. What ever happened to a simple *Shh!* or *I'll explain it to you later?*

By the time my waitress arrived, I'd given up on the pie—I was too ashamed to order or eat it in front of judge-y Mommy, and the edge of the table was digging painfully into my belly. I asked for a cup of soup, slurped it down as fast as I could, scalding my mouth in the process, slapped a ten-dollar bill on the table, and was poised to make my getaway ... except I couldn't. I was stuck.

I pushed my hands on top of the table, inhaled hugely, and pushed as hard as I could, wriggling my ass as I shoved. Nothing

Best Friends Forever   271

was happening. I tried again, a little squeak escaping me. Still nothing. "Mommy," said the kid through a mouthful of half-chewed French fries (the little brat had turned around and propped himself up on his knees, so as not to miss a minute of the show), "is the fat lady stuck?"

My waitress wandered over. "Everything all right?"

"I'm fine," I managed. I was sweating—I could feel it trick-ling down my back and my sides in hot rivulets—and I was sure my face was red as a stop sign. "I'm fine," I repeated, and sucked, and pushed, and as I finally, thank you God, felt myself move incrementally to the left, toward freedom, a single word rose up in my mind, and that word, which might as well have been writ-ten in ten-foot-high neon letters that had been doused in gaso-line and lit on fire, was ENOUGH. I had had ENOUGH.

Head down, I hurried out of the restaurant and back to my car. I drove home. I unlocked the door, turned on the lights, pulled a trash bag out of a kitchen cupboard, and then, before I could lose my nerve or change my mind, I swept every piece of junk food in the house into that bag, the chips and cakes and candies, the cups of pudding and frozen pies, the boxes of muffin and brownie mix, the Valentine's Day chocolates, the canisters of heat-and-eat biscuits and cinnamon rolls. I filled the first bag, then another, then loaded them both into the trunk of my car, drove them to the dump, and tossed them. Then I drove to Dr. Shoup, the oncologist who'd treated my mother twelve years be-fore, the only doctor I knew.

I gave my name to her secretary, explaining that I didn't have an appointment but that I needed to see the doctor as soon as she could manage. Then I sat in her waiting room, holding *Good Housekeeping* open in front of my face, trying not to let any of the other patients, the ladies in wigs and scarves, see that I was cry-ing, because if they saw, they'd probably think that I was sick, like they were, that there was something wrong with me besides too much dessert.

Dr. Shoup was wonderfully calm. Her eyes did not widen as she saw me for the first time in over a decade, and her hands, when she took my blood pressure and listened to my heart, were steady and gentle.

"There's no big secret to weight loss," she told me. "Burn more calories than you're taking in, and you can expect to lose a pound or two a week."

Dr. Shoup handed me a sheet with a twelve-hundred-calorie-a-day diet, a prescription for a diet pill that, she said, might take the edge off my appetite, and, after I'd told her that I was having trouble sleeping, a prescription for pills that would help with that. "Good luck," she said, and sent me home.

My diet, which was a mash-up of every weight-loss plan I'd read in any women's magazine, started the next morning. For breakfast, I'd have two poached eggs, a slice of multigrain toast, and water. For lunch, I'd have a big salad with sprouts and beans, a drizzle of olive oil, and four ounces of salmon or chicken. For a snack, I'd have blueberries and almonds and a stick of string cheese. For dinner, I'd have another four ounces of chicken or fish and a bowlful of broccoli or spinach, plus half a cup of brown rice or half of a potato. For dessert, I'd have sleeping pills, enough to knock me out until the next morning. I had twelve hours' worth of willpower. I couldn't let my days go any longer than that.

It was brutal. There were nights when I'd lie awake practically crying until the sleeping pills took hold, thinking about warm corn muffins with melted butter and honey, crisp-skinned fried chicken and biscuits soaked in sausage gravy, chili with a dollop of sour cream and chopped onions on top. Pound cake, shortcake, blackout chocolate mousse cake, gelato, biscotti, biscuits and popovers, caramel popcorn and warm apple pie, which I knew I'd probably never be able to eat again.

In eight months' time, I'd made my way from scary-fat into the neighborhood of regular-fat, where I could fit into the clothes at the plus-size shop at the mall, instead of having to order everything on the Internet, where I could walk down a street and not feel like everyone was staring at me and I was going to collapse from the effort. I could tie my shoes without sweating, I could wear pants with snaps and zippers. "You look fantastic," said people I'd never spoken to before, people I'd never noticed noticing me. "What did you do?"

"Nothing special," I would say. "Just cutting back." Meanwhile, I would think, *suffer*. What I did was *suffer*.

"Nice work," said Dr. Shoup when I came for a checkup. "We can do a tummy tuck when you've hit your goal weight and stayed there for a while." She looked me over dispassionately. "You should get some exercise. Tone up a bit. Find something you like."

I looked at her. If there'd been an exercise I'd liked, would I have gotten this big in the first place?

She noticed my expression. "Find something you can tolerate," she amended. "And do it for at least thirty minutes, five times a week."

"Does sex count?" I asked. Ha—like I was having any of that.

"Anything that gets your heart working at its aerobic threshold," she said. Trust Dr. Shoup not to get a joke. "Maybe start with something low-impact. Walking or swimming."

I drove home thinking about my mother, the way I'd always pictured her as a teenager, swimming through the lake at summer camp with my father's arrow in her hand. I got online and ordered a swimsuit, a one-piece in dark purple from a company that specialized in "the active lives of larger women."

The morning it arrived, I bundled the swimsuit and a beach towel into a tote bag and drove myself to a fancy health club I'd passed on my way to see my brother. There I allowed myself to be bullied into a one-year membership by a woman who was maybe twenty-two years old and approximately the size of my right thigh. My gold-level membership, she recited, while keeping her eyes carefully trained on the wall above my shoulder, came complete with one session with a personal trainer, free towel service, and a half-off coupon for the juice bar.

"We also offer complimentary body analysis," she said. In addition to being tiny, she was deeply, alarmingly tanned. She looked like a tangerine with a ponytail.

"What is that?" I asked.

"Height, weight, body-fat percentage . . ."

"I'll skip it," I said hastily.

". . . Then you run on the treadmill for twelve minutes . . ." She looked at me. "Or walk. Whatever. Then there's a sit-up test, and a flexibility test, and we enter all the data into the computer . . ."

"Skip! Skip! Skip!" I was positive that I couldn't do a sit-up to save my life, and what would the computer tell me after they'd sent it my data? Probably that I owed the treadmill an apology. I glanced through the wall of windows, toward the Olympic-sized pool. There were three swimmers, a man and two women, all of them in swim caps and goggles. I didn't have a swim cap or goggles. "Do you sell swim stuff?" I asked the tiny tangerine.

"Oh. Um. No." She giggled. I guessed that she'd never seen anyone as big as I was. People my size were, most likely, infrequent and unwelcome visitors to the land of free weights and stairclimbers and Yogalates stretch classes. I felt like telling her that she didn't have to worry, that I wouldn't break anything or eat anyone, but I decided that calling attention to her discomfort would only increase it.

I struggled out of the little foam-and-wire armchair across from her desk. "When is the pool the busiest?"

"Mornings," she said. "It's real crowded right when we open, which is at six, and it stays busy until eight. Then it's busy at lunchtime, and then it kind of empties out, and it gets real busy after four or five."

"So how are things at ten in the morning?"

"Ten's pretty empty."

I thanked her and made my way to the locker room. In my purple skirted suit, in the unforgiving three-way mirrors at the end of the locker room, with wobbly white flesh fore and aft, even with the weight I'd lost I bore a disconcerting resemblance to Barney. *Ah well,* I thought, and dunked underneath the shower and made my way into the steamy, chemical-scented air of the pool.

The two women swimmers were gone by then. There was just one man with silvery hair and black goggles doing the crawl, plowing up and down the lap lane closest to the windows. I stuck a toe into the water, which was as warm as a bath, then eased myself, inch by inch, down the steps and into the shallow end, all the while maintaining a death grip on the metal handrail, terrified that I would slip and fall and hit my head and drown, and that my death would be written up in *News of the Weird:* TITANIC-SIZED WOMAN DROWNS ON MAIDEN VOYAGE.

I walked toward the deep end, letting my feet drift up and back behind me, until I was floating. Then I put my face in the water, the way I'd been taught at my swimming lessons long ago. I blew a gentle stream of bubbles out of my mouth and stretched my arms in front of me, parting the water as if it were a curtain. I hadn't been swimming in years, but I had to hope that it was like riding a bike, that it would come back to me once I got started.

I put my face back in the water, set my feet against the concrete wall, pushed gently, and did a tentative breaststroke toward the opposite end of the pool, twenty-five yards away. I figured I'd try two laps—one out, one back—and then call it a day, but I felt okay. Before I knew it, my fingers were brushing the lip of the deep end. I turned around, pushed off again, and stroked gingerly to the other side. I looked at the clock. The entire enterprise had taken me less than three minutes. I started off again. My eyes were starting to sting from the chlorine, so this time I kept my face above the water. I fanned my hands out in front of me and fluttered my legs behind. Every four laps, I checked the clock, and before I knew it, twenty minutes had gone by.

I didn't realize how hard I'd been working until I pulled myself up the steps in the shallow end and felt the muscles of my thighs and calves trembling.

"Harder than it looks, isn't it?"

The man in the other lap lane had gotten out of the water and was toweling off. He was thick-shouldered, barrel-chested, with brown skin and a thatch of silvery hair on his chest that matched his close-cropped silvery hair. I nodded, breathless, certain that my cheeks were red and that I was sweating as well as dripping. I dabbed at my face with the tiny towel I'd picked up on my way to the pool, wishing I hadn't left my bigger one back in the locker, wishing that I wasn't panting like an elderly asthmatic dog.

"Have a good day," the man said, and I managed, "You, too," before wobbling back to the locker room and collapsing on the bench in front of my locker, where I stayed until I could breathe normally and trust my legs to support me.

I went back to the pool every day, Monday through Friday. I

would have gone on weekends, too, except then the pool was usually filled with kids, or the members of a water aerobics class made up of women age seventy and up, their swim-capped heads bobbing genteelly in the deep end. Each session, I'd alternate between trying to go a little longer or swim a little faster.

After eight weeks of swimming five times a week, my Barney swimsuit was flapping around my hips. I ordered a smaller one, this time in black, figuring I'd be Orca, a killer whale, instead of a friendly dinosaur.

"A new suit!" the man from the next lane said, and smiled his approval with teeth that were slightly stained and a bit crooked. "You are shrinking." His accent clipped each of his words precisely. I watched as he shook beads of water from his hair, unselfconsciously rubbing his towel over his arms and his legs. I nodded and picked up my own towel. "Will you join me for some juice?" he asked. I was so startled that I couldn't think of how to tell him no, or that I had somewhere else to be, which would have been a lie.

Twenty minutes later, I sat in the juice bar with my smoothie, and the silvery-haired man from the pool sat across from me. His name was Vijay, he said, and he slid a business card across the table: Vijay Kapoor, M.D.

"You're a doctor?"

"Retired." He rolled his *r*'s. I imagined his tongue, curled against the roof of his mouth, trilling lightly. "Now I do a bit of consulting for the drug companies. I fill in, here and there, to keep busy. And you?"

It had been so long since I'd had a conversation like this with someone who wasn't, in some way, paid to talk to me, to take my medical history or my credit information, to give me my prescriptions or my latte or my stamps. "I do illustrations for greeting cards," I said.

He smiled kindly. "And may I have your name, my dear?"

I felt my blush intensify. "Addie Downs."

We lingered with our drinks as he coaxed the particulars from me. I told him where I lived, a little more about what I did, and how I'd started swimming. "I lost some weight," I said. "I'm just trying to tone up a little." He raised his eyebrows and said nothing. I felt my face getting hot, wondering if he was trying to figure out exactly how big I'd been before the weight loss began.

"You look well," he said, making me blush again.

"What about you?" I asked. He said that he was fifty-nine, which was older than I would have guessed, and he was married, the father of two grown sons. He and his wife lived in a big house in Evanston. She volunteered for charities and as a docent at the Art Institute. He kept busy with part-time work, with the consulting he did for drug companies, the occasional lecture he delivered to medical students. "It is not a bad life," he said, and he looked at his watch, a gold disc that glowed against his burnished skin. "Until next time?" he asked, and I agreed, bobbed my head shyly, an oversized schoolgirl in a sweatsuit. We were friends. That was all. He was old enough to be my father, and he was married, so what else could we be?

Vijay was always in the pool by the time I arrived, and he'd lift his sleek, dripping head out of the water and raise one hand. "Halloo, Addie!" he'd call as I waded, as gracefully as I could, into the shallow end, and took the lane next to his. At first he was always faster, but eventually I found myself able to keep up with him. Our fingertips would touch the edge of the pool at the same time. We'd raise our heads, inhale, duck back under the water, and start swimming again.

Afterward, he'd help me out of the water, extending one square hand, handing me my towel. I'd take my shower, change my clothes, and we'd sit at what I'd come to think of as our table in the juice bar, talking about everything: the election, the weather, a prime-time medical drama we were both addicted to, even though he said the technical mistakes they made were cringe-inducing, and that the show would be responsible for "an influx of idiots" into medical school. He inquired about my family. I told him about Jon, and he'd listened, asking thoughtful questions about the location of Jon's injury and the length of his rehabilitation, what seizure medication he was on and whether it was adequate.

"And Mommy and Daddy?"

I blinked, caught off guard by the diminutives, thinking for an instant that he was talking about *his* parents. "Oh, they died when I was a teenager. My father had an aneurysm, and my mother had breast cancer."

"So you are an orphan." I almost laughed—the word sounded so strange, like something out of Dickens, or a song I'd heard Emmylou Harris sing about being an orphan girl. Vijay clicked his tongue against his teeth. "I am sorry," he said, and briefly placed his hand on top of mine.

At night, in bed, I could call up every detail about him: the shape of his bare feet on the pool's tiled deck, the tilt of his head when he asked me a question, the aggressive jut of his nose, his endearingly crooked teeth. I knew that I was being silly, that he didn't like me as anything more than a friend, a person he saw in the pool, a fellow swimmer he barely recognized as female.

Except I knew that wasn't true. My black tank suit started bagging around my hips, so I ordered a new one. The smaller I got, the more cuts and colors were available. Now, if I wanted, I could buy a tankini, or a magical patented Slimsuit in an exotic tiger print designed to whittle inches off my waist and keep spectators' eyes from resting too long on what the tag coyly called my "trouble zones." I went for a variation of my comfortable, familiar black tank suit ... only I bought it in a color the catalogue called "bright raspberry," imagining how Vijay's eyes might light up when he saw me, picturing his smile.

I wasn't wrong. "Addie," he crooned when he saw me, "how nice!" I smiled at him, did a modest, mocking half-turn before hurrying into the water, tugging my swim cap over my ears. An hour later, we sat across from each other in the juice bar and, unprompted, he started talking about his sons. "American boys," he said, his voice half proud, half rueful. One of them had an MBA, and the other was in medical school. The one with the MBA lived in Texas and was married with a baby, the other was engaged. Then he started telling me about his wife, whose name, I'd learned, was Chitra. It had been an arranged marriage in London. Vijay had met her the day before their wedding, and they'd been married for forty-two years. "The two of us rattle around in that house like the last two peas in a can," he said. "There is no passion left, no connection. We are like roommates; just two people living together." Even as I made eye contact and sympathetic noises, I recognized this as a variation of the song that every married man who'd strayed had ever sung to another woman: *My wife doesn't understand me, but oh, you, kid.* Still, I couldn't keep my heart from lifting, couldn't ignore the way his touch thrilled me when he pressed his hand on mine and then, as I held my breath, reached across the table to stroke my cheek with one blunt fingertip. "Addie," he murmured. "Do you know how lovely you are?"

He took me to a hotel downtown, not too expensive but not cheap, either. As I sat on the bed and watched him slip off his belt, then his shoes, then his wedding ring, the thought crossed my mind that I was no better than Valerie's mother, no better than any woman who thought it was okay to help a man break his wedding vows. *He has children,* I thought as he embraced me, smelling faintly of the pool's water. I could see our reflection in the mirror above the dresser, his middle-aged body, with the slight paunch that the laps hadn't eradicated, the purplish discs of his nipples, the silvery tangle of his chest hair. His hands looked tiny on the vast white field of my back, his short, compact body dwarfed next to mine. I felt the old self-loathing rise up inside me, and I squeezed my eyes shut, willing myself not to think, not to see, only to feel, telling myself that I deserved this, I deserved a little happiness; after everything I'd been through, I deserved some sweetness, even if it was only for an afternoon, in a rented room that smelled of cigarette smoke and bleach, even if it was with someone else's man.

His lips brushed my forehead, then my cheek. I shivered, closing my eyes. I kept my legs pressed tightly together as he caressed me, whispering in my ear, swirling his fingertips against my breasts and my belly. "Imagine that we are in the water," he whispered, twining his fingers in the tangle of my pubic hair. I felt my hips lifting, as if they were borne upward on a wave, my thighs locked and trembling as he bent his head over my breasts. It hurt a little bit when he slid inside of me, but I didn't bleed, and Vijay didn't seem to notice my sudden, shocked inhalation, or that I'd started to cry, from the pain of it and from the joy that was just as intense, the feeling of being fused with someone else, being entirely connected, of not being alone anymore.

I thought of him when I woke up in the morning. At night, I'd remember something he'd said, the way he'd wrapped his hand around mine, showing me how to touch him. I was giddy, giggly, girlish, lighter than air. For the first time in my life, I found myself forgetting to eat. When we were together, I would take in every detail of how he looked and moved, of what he said, and replay them at my leisure when I was alone and he was with Chitra. I let myself imagine a life together, the two of us coming back from the pool to my house, eating lunch together in the kitchen, walking together in the cool of a summer's evening.

Vijay had never lied to me or led me on, never once suggested that such things were possible. Still, I couldn't shake the feeling that grew into certainty every time we swam that he was falling in love with me, that he would leave his wife for me, that we would have a life together.

If this was going to happen, I knew that some changes were in order. My house would look shabby and small compared to the eight-bedroom mansion that he and Chitra had bought twelve years before (how did the lovelorn manage before the Internet? I'd wondered as I'd looked up street maps and the purchase price and, eventually, downloaded satellite pictures of his house on Google Earth). I considered the rooms in which I'd spent almost my entire life and saw all the ways they were wanting: the linoleum that was thin and graying, the carpet worn down to the fibrous backing in spots, the dingy paint and scratched-up toilet bowl, the scraggly rhododendron beside the front door.

I started slowly, with a pile of renovation magazines: *Kitchen & Bath, Cottage Style, Metropolitan Home,* and *Country Living,* figuring that I'd pick from the best of all worlds. After a few weeks' consideration, I ordered new tile for the kitchen floor, big hand-glazed squares imported from Mexico, the color of butterscotch, and a tiled backsplash in a pattern of azure and gold and plum.

Every day I fixed something, bought something, did some small bit of rearranging, imagining with each change Vijay's reaction to coming home to such a sweet, cozy little place. (He'd complained to me often about the extravagant size of his current home, the trophy house Chitra had pushed for, with the two-story foyer and the his-and-hers bathrooms, and rooms Vijay claimed he didn't even understand. ("A mudroom? Are we pigs?")

Outside my little house, the landscapers I hired planted rose-bushes and morning glory and trumpet vines that bloomed pro-fusely and twined around new wrought-iron railings and the latticed frame I'd built around the front door. Working from a picture I'd seen in a magazine, I hung new shutters in dove-gray and had the house painted a warm, soft white the catalogue called buttermilk. I pulled up the worn old carpet and had the oak floors underneath refinished, and I painted the walls in shades named after foods I no longer ate: bisque and cream, va-nilla and honey. I drew up plans to redo the kitchen, combining the dining room and living room into one big "great room," with one of the new flat-screen TVs anchoring one wall, new couches and a red-and-gold wool rug. Bigger windows, sliding doors, a brand-new master bathroom with a Jacuzzi tub big enough for two, a shower that converted to a steam stall . . . nothing was too grand for me to imagine, and to imagine sharing with Vijay.

Besides, I could afford it. The house was paid for; disability paid for Jon's room at the Crossroads. The only expenses I had were health insurance and my car payments, and there'd been years when I hadn't bought much besides groceries and the oc-casional new bra or cotton panties or socks. The small savings account my parents had left me for going to college and caring for Jon had been quietly increasing in a money-market fund, and I'd added to it every time I got paid, holding on to just what I'd need to pay my bills, socking the rest away. I'd never been ac-quisitive, never traveled, never wanted fancy cars or clothes (even if they'd fit me) . . . but now it felt as if I couldn't get rid of the money fast enough. Sometimes I imagined it whispering to me at night: *Spend me, spend me, spend me.*

So I pored over my plans and painted walls and ripped up carpet and tilled a patch out back for a garden. On Saturday afternoons, I took the free classes at the local home-improvement store and learned how to strip paint from furniture, how to install a new sink and hang wallpaper (I felt such a pang at that, remembering the pink-and-green stripes that Val had yearned for, hearing her voice in my head: *All I wanted was a nice pretty room with pink and green. A nice pretty room like Addie has*). I suffered through blisters and splinters and hot-glue-gun burns, throwing out my back, ripping out a fingernail, not minding any of it as I imagined Vijay's delight.

I finished my bedroom first, splurging on a king-size mattress and a headboard, because Vijay had once told me how he loved to read in bed once the day was done. I tossed the percale sheets that dated from my parents' marriage and replaced them with the most sumptuous, silky-soft, outrageously expensive Egyptian cotton I could find. I ordered a fringed cashmere throw that spilled over the foot of the bed like a pool of caramel, and set up a wooden table against one wall that I stocked with a coffeepot, a grinder, and a little refrigerator underneath for juices and cream. I pictured the two of us in bed on a lazy Sunday morning, swapping sections of the newspaper before we got out of bed and went swimming.

I wasn't his first. Vijay had told me that early on, one rainy morning when we lingered at the juice bar, waiting for the skies to clear before attempting the dash to our cars. "Over the years, I have had friends," he said. "Friends?" I'd repeated. And he'd shrugged, cocking his head at me in a gesture that made it easy to imagine the little boy he'd once been, stuffing his pockets with sweets, then turning his charming smile on whatever woman caught him. His friends were nurses, a psychologist who worked down the hall, one of his son's teachers. There was a mutual understanding about these adventures, he explained: he was looking for companionship, not to leave his marriage.

"And your friends?" I asked. "What were they looking for?"

He lifted his shoulders again. "Who can say?"

"That would be you," I said. "The one who was there."

He smiled at me, touching my cheek. "Funny girl." He paused, thinking. "Perhaps they wanted excitement. Something new."

"A treat."

His eyes crinkled in the corners when he smiled at me. "A treat. I like that."

I knew without asking that all of his "friends" had been white. I could guess that they'd see him as exotic, with his accent and his dark skin, and even his arranged marriage. He would have been a kind of diversion, something new on the menu—strange spices, a different taste, a rich dessert they could savor but wouldn't want every night. I guessed that none of them had ever fallen in love with him: these were probably experienced women, sophisticated ladies who'd made places for themselves in the world, who'd never been stuck at home, or behind the edge of a table at a diner, or anywhere at all.

It was snowing the first time he came to my house. We'd been swimming and had our drinks, and then Vijay had asked if I wanted to go with him—to the hotel, I assumed; this was where we'd gone each time we'd been together. "Come home with me," I said.

"Addie," he said, and I could tell from his tone, from his eyes, that he was getting ready to deliver a speech that he'd given before, one that would tell me not to get my hopes up, one that would let me down easy.

"Please," I said. I could hear the rawness in my voice, and I made myself pause and start over. "Please," I said softly. "I'd just like you to see where I live. It would mean a lot to me."

He shrugged, that sheepish, charming shrug, and held my

car door open for me, then got into his own car and followed me home to Pleasant Ridge. I could imagine his lips tightening as he turned down my street—its jumble of forty-year-old ranch houses and smallish lawns must have been a shock after his palatial neighborhood—but once we were through my front door, it was just the way I'd imagined it: the house warm and snug, scented with the green chili I'd been simmering since the night before. Vijay made his way along the newly finished floors, exclaiming over each little touch: the vibrant tiles in the kitchen, a bouquet of roses I'd set in a ceramic vase I'd painted myself, the sumptuousness of the bedroom, how soft things were, how sweet, how warm.

At some point after we'd made love, I lay beside him, half asleep, and watched as he collected his cell phone from the table next to the bed, the one I'd painted with half a dozen coats of cherry-colored lacquer. Icy rain pattered on the ceiling. I listened as Vijay spread his hand against my belly and made excuses to his wife.

After that, he came over every Wednesday afternoon, once we were done swimming, and sometimes on Saturdays. I'd installed a pair of bedside lamps with bubble-glass shades, tinted pale-green and turquoise, that cast the room in a cool underwater glow. I would keep my eyes open for as long as I could—I was still so shy of my own body that it was almost painful to look at it—but always I would open my eyes and watch his face at the moment of orgasm. He would squeeze his eyes shut, press his lips tightly together, and I would feel him shudder against me and think, *I made him feel this way; I did this to him.*

Afterward, he'd roll toward me. He'd kiss my ear and my neck, pulling the sheets out of my clenched fists, easing them down my body. "You see, Addie? You're lovely. Lovely," he would say, sliding his fingers against me in a steady rhythm that sped up gradually and made me arch my back and, finally, curl against him, panting and spent.

He had never lied to me. But still, I let myself hope. One afternoon in July, with sunshine pouring gold through the skylight, I said, "Do you ever think that we could be . . ." I let my voice trail off, hoping he'd start where I'd stopped.

Instead, he sat up and swung his legs off the edge of the bed. "Addie," he said. "I have always been honest with you."

I felt like I had swallowed a stone. I closed my eyes, dreading what was coming, unable to prepare myself for it, to thicken my skin or harden my heart for the blow. I wasn't like his other ladies. I had no defenses.

"I am sorry, my dear," he said in his accented speech. "But you must know that I will never leave my wife. And I think . . ." This time, his voice trailed off. "Perhaps it would be best if we were to spend some time apart."

"You don't want to see me anymore?" I asked, hating the pathetic way I sounded but unable to keep from asking.

"Of course we will see each other," he said, pulling on his underwear (white cotton boxers that looked as if they'd been ironed. For the first time, I wondered by whom). "We will swim."

I felt numb, ill, miserable, lost. But I made myself move, get to my feet, pull my robe around me, walk him to the door. I said that I understood. I told him I would be all right, that I had enjoyed him. "My treat," I'd said, and I even managed a smile. None of the things I said were true. I didn't understand: If we were happy together, and if he was unhappy in his marriage, why not end the marriage and be with me? I wouldn't be all right: I would be lonely again, trying to fill all of those empty hours and empty rooms with something, an unnamed and unknown something, because I didn't have food to do the trick anymore. I'd be even worse off than I'd been before, because now I knew exactly what

I was missing: the feel of the water moving over my body, the warmth of his body beside mine in a car or on a couch; his crooked teeth, his charming, head-cocked grin, his thick fingers moving against me.

"Addie," he said at the door, with his hands on my shoulders. "Do not look so sad. All is well. You will find someone."

I bent my head, then raised it, staring at his face, his liquid brown eyes, his crooked teeth, trying to memorize it, because I knew I would never see it again. I would never find anyone else. I didn't see how I could put myself through it: the lift and plummet of hope and rejection. I didn't have a thick skin, I didn't have the practice or the skills. I wasn't strong.

"I understand," I made myself say. "But could you do one thing for me? Just one thing first?"

Vijay frowned when I told him what it was. "It is not possible," he said curtly (and in that curtness, in his tensed shoulders and stiffened neck, I imagined that I was seeing a part of him that Chitra was privy to on a daily basis, a part that his "friends" never imagined).

"Please," I said. "I won't bother you, and I won't ask for anything else. I just want this one thing."

So on the Friday night before Labor Day weekend, in a little town between Milwaukee and Chicago, Vijay Kapoor took Addie Downs to the fair. The bright colored lights of the midway that blazed against the indigo sky. The air was scented with fried dough and grilled sausage, and the moon hung heavy and orange as a pumpkin. He paid twenty dollars for a roll of tickets, bought me a lemonade, and, after six tries, won me a teddy bear at a game using high-powered water guns to inflate balloons.

We played Skee-Ball. We pitched Ping-Pong balls into goldfish bowls, and slid dimes across a scarred sheet of Plexiglas, trying to get them to land on our lucky numbers. We rode the rickety Ferris wheel (a man with vacant eyes and tattooed hands slammed the metal safety bar down across our carriage, and I wondered what he'd say if I'd told him that a year ago that bar wouldn't have closed at all). Vijay wouldn't look at me, but he did take my hand as our car rose to the top of the wheel and hung there, rocking, suspended in the sky. "Buy a flower for the pretty lady?" asked a woman with an armful of roses, and Vijay did.

Outside the fortune-teller's patched tent, a pack of laughing teenagers passed by. One of the girls had the same pink teddy bear that I did. She swung it loosely by one of its arms. Her jeans dipped low enough to show the pink elastic edge of her panties, and as she ran by, laughing, I felt enormous, and ancient, and exquisitely out of place.

I left my bear sitting on a bench. I sat quietly with my hands in my lap as Vijay's big car purred along the highway. When he pulled into my driveway, I said, "Thank you for a lovely evening," the way I'd imagined saying when I was a teenager, coming home from the dates I never had.

His face looked troubled in the glow from the dashboard. "Addie," he said, "are you sure you'll be all right?"

"I am sure," I said. "Sure I'm sure. I'm fine."

"You are crying," he observed, and ran his finger along my cheek to prove it.

"I'm fine. Thank you again," I said, and hurried out of the car. For a minute, I thought he'd come after me, racing across the lawn and up the steps and saying, *Addie, I have been a fool. Don't leave me. Never leave me.* When I turned, I could see him in the car, behind the wheel, but couldn't make out his expression. I unlocked the door and walked inside, and after a minute, his car slid out of the driveway. He flashed his lights, blipped the horn once. I barely slept that night, sitting up with the telephone, which, of course, didn't ring. On Monday morning I went to the pool as usual. "Where's your friend?" asked the tangerine, waiting to hand me a towel from behind the check-in desk.

"I don't know," I said. I guessed that Vijay had found another pool. After that night in my driveway, I never saw him again.

FORTY-ONE

"Oh, no," said Greg Levitson. "No, no, no." He was shaking his big bald head back and forth in time with his nos. It was Sunday morning at the TD Bank branch in downtown Pleasant Ridge, and it looked as if everyone who wasn't in church or at the mall was waiting in line for the tellers.

"Take you ten seconds," Jordan wheedled.

Greg Levitson stopped shaking his head and glared at Jordan. "I could *lose my job.*"

"Sure you could," Jordan said. "You could also lose your job if certain other facts came to light."

Greg pursed his lips, closed his eyes, and exhaled a stream of stale coffee breath in Jordan's direction. "You're blackmailing me?"

"I'm doing no such thing."

"This is unfair."

"Nobody said life was fair," said Jordan. He crossed his legs, ate a candy cane, and stared up at the ceiling as if he had all the time in the world.

Greg Levitson had been in Jordan's class in high school. Back then Greg had been a slope-shouldered, pink-faced boy with a sunken chest and wide, almost womanish hips, whose brown hair was starting to recede by senior year. He'd gone to Pennsylvania for college, had put in a few obligatory years in the big city (in his case, Philadelphia) before returning to Pleasant Ridge with a wife and baby in tow. Greg's and Jordan's paths would cross occasionally—they'd nod "hellos" in the supermarket, exchange "how've you beens" at the Exxon station, and that might have been the end of it, except one night Jordan had pulled over a blue Chevrolet doing seventy-five in a fifty-five zone, and found his former classmate trembling behind the wheel.

"Please," Greg had whispered after handing his license and registration through the window. "Please don't make me get out of the car."

Jordan looked down and saw that Greg Levitson was wearing a dark-blue gown that left one of his meaty pink shoulders bare, high-heeled shoes and sheer black hose. His cheeks were rouged, and his fingernails were fire-engine red.

"You know the speed limit, right?" Jordan asked.

Greg's chins were quivering as he spoke. "It was a dare," he said in a raspy voice. "I don't do this normally."

"I'm going to give you a warning," said Jordan. "No ticket this time. Just slow down." He handed the papers back through the window, with Greg practically weeping in gratitude, promising that if Jordan ever needed *anything* . . . if he could *ever* be of service to the department . . .

Jordan had called on him twice in the last three years, in cases where he needed financial information and didn't have—or couldn't get—a warrant. The first time Greg had been eager to help. The second time, he'd pursed his lips until they looked like the knot at the bottom of a big white balloon. Now it looked like he was prepared to dig in his heels—his *high* heels, Jordan thought, and smiled to himself. "You look good," Jordan offered, helping himself to a second miniature candy cane from the bowl on the desk. "You lose a few pounds?"

Greg puffed out his lips. "Look, it's not that I don't appreciate what you did for me, but this . . . I just can't . . ."

"Or maybe it's your shirt," said Jordan, eyeing the other man's button-down. "I think blue is your color."

"Fine." Greg leaned forward and worked his thick fingers over the keyboard. "Valerie Adler. I got nothing. She must bank somewhere else." Jordan sat back, silent, waiting. "Adelaide Downs, Fourteen Crescent Drive. Recent activity: we've got an eighty-seven dollar payment to FreshDirect. Nineteen dollars to Netflix." Greg waved his fingers, jazz-hands style. "Ooh, suspicious."

"Keep going," Jordan said.

"Visa, three hundred and nineteen dollars. Lakeshore Athletic Club, a hundred and ninety-nine. That's a recurring payment. Um." Greg leaned forward and closed his mouth. "She took out ten thousand dollars in cash yesterday."

"Ten thousand dollars," Jordan repeated.

"Not here, though. Branch number 1119 . . ." He leaned closer to his computer, tapping away. "That's in St. Louis."

"She just went in and took out ten thousand dollars in cash?"

"She had plenty in her account. She's got, like, sixty thousand bucks in checking, another forty in savings . . ." Greg shut his mouth, perhaps realizing he'd said too much.

"Ten thousand dollars," Jordan repeated.

"And there's one more charge. A gas station in . . ." He paused, squinting. "Nashville."

Heading south, thought Jordan, writing it down. "You should go now," said Greg.

"I'm gone," Jordan said, getting to his feet. "You have the thanks of a grateful nation."

Greg looked surprised. "This is a national matter?"

"International," said Jordan. "Extremely important. Very hush-hush."

"You're welcome. Oh, and congratulations," Greg said.

Jordan paused, his hand on the door. "What's that?"

"Your little girl. I saw your wife at the Whole Foods . . ." He must have also seen something in Jordan's expression, because he shut his mouth fast.

"We've been divorced for a year and a half," Jordan said. "Patti's remarried."

"Oh," said Greg. "Oh, I'm sorry."

Little girl? "Stay safe," said Jordan, pushing the new information to the back of his mind.

"Will do," said Greg. "Hey, I'm sorry . . ."

"It's fine," said Jordan, and then repeated the words, as if he was trying to convince himself. "It's fine."

FORTY-TWO

Jordan drove back to the station, fighting the impulse to call Patti, or her mother, or her sister, or Rob Fine, DDS, or just turn the car around and drive to their house and get to the bottom of this. Had Patti finally had a baby? Had they adopted? Hired a surrogate?

Never mind, he thought, swinging into his parking spot, feeling the new knowledge settling in like an infection. *Focus.* Gary Ryderdahl was at his desk. "What've you got, chief?" Gary called.

"Maybe something." Jordan sat down in Holly's chair and wheeled it to the room's far wall, where he paused, pulling himself back and forth with his toes.

Gary's face lit up. "Do it," he said.

"You're a bad influence," said Jordan.

"Aw, c'mon, Chief, nobody's gonna see."

Jordan shrugged. Maybe it would cheer him up. He looked left, then right, then pushed off from the wall and spun down the length of the room, rolling to a neat stop in front of Gary's desk.

Gary high-fived him. "How do you do it? Every time I try I hit the wall."

"Years of practice," Jordan said, forcing himself to sound casual. "Listen. Adelaide Downs took out ten thousand dollars in cash in St. Louis. There was a gas station charge in Nashville. What does that tell you?"

Gary rubbed his hair. "Um. She's gone country?"

Jordan waited patiently. When Gary looked blank, he said, "Tell me what we know for sure."

"That she has money. That she was in St. Louis and Nashville."

"She had money," Jordan corrected. "It could be gone, and she could be anywhere by now. Why don't you start calling hotels in Nashville? See if any of them have two women registered as Valerie Adler and Addie Downs, or two women who sound like they fit the description."

Gary thought this over and finally asked, "What's the description?"

"Early thirties," said Jordan. "Blond hair. No southern accents. Maybe driving an old station wagon with Illinois plates. You can find Val's picture on her station's website."

Gary nodded. "One more thing," he said. "Holly and I were doing a . . ." Jordan looked at him sternly. Gary flinched and swallowed. "We were searching on the Internet, and every year, Addie Downs donates a painting to this auction that raises money for cancer research."

Jordan shrugged. That didn't mean much, other than that his suspect was charity-minded.

"I had a hunch," Gary continued. "Holly called the doctor who runs the auction. Dr. Elizabeth Shoup. She's an oncologist. Holly said she was Adelaide Downs's assistant and that she was calling to confirm her next appointment." Gary was so flushed with pleasure that he was practically glowing. "And guess what?"

"She's got an appointment?"

Gary's face fell. "Next Thursday. How'd you know?"

"Lucky guess," said Jordan, and patted the other man's shoulder.

"I'll get started on the hotels."

"Sounds good," said Jordan. He walked into his office and closed the door behind him, savoring the quiet. Holly was off interviewing the half-dozen salespeople and suppliers Dan had tangled with during his tenure at Swansea Toyota, including the garbageman whose throat Dan had threatened to slit with a box cutter if his crew kept leaving empty soda cans on the curb, and the Parts and Repairs receptionist who'd told Holly confidentially that Dan had gotten fresh with her at the dealership's Christmas party last year. The police station, which occupied the ground floor of Pleasant Ridge's municipal building (Parks and Rec had the second floor) was too warm, as usual, and filled with the smell of coffee and the ghost of a departed meatball sub. Through his window, Jordan could see Gary hunched over his desk, poking at his keyboard as if it were the corpse of an animal he wasn't entirely sure was dead.

Jordan checked his notes, lifted his phone, dialed information, and was eventually connected with the Lakeshore Athletic Club, which, a mellow recorded voice informed him, was the Midwest's premiere facility for fitness, relaxation, and rejuvenation. *Jesus.* Jordan hit zero until he was connected to a human being, then suffered through five minutes of wind chimes and gongs that he supposed were someone's idea of music until he was finally put through to a manager.

"Good after*noon*," said a man with a high, enthusiastic voice. "This is *Max*, how can I help you?"

"Hi," Jordan said to the man. "My name's Sam Novick." Sam, whose name Jordan borrowed occasionally, worked as an engineer specializing in adhesives, an occupation that caused follow-up questions to wither and die on the inquisitor's lips. "I just moved to the area. My sister-in-law Addie Downs is a member of your gym."

No hesitation at all. "Oh, Addie! How *is* she?"

"She's great."

"She looks fan*tas*tic," the manager said. "She's one of our biggest success stories, you know."

"She is something," said Jordan. "Listen, I wanted to set up an appointment, see if I could come and maybe take a tour or something."

"Of *course*," said the man, with visions of commissions probably dancing in his head. "Are you familiar with the facility? We have a state-of-the-art track, an Olympic-sized swimming pool, a hot-yoga studio, two aerobic rooms, a basketball court, a rock-climbing wall, and a five-thousand-foot spa with three wet rooms. We offer a variety of group classes as well as individual training, in addition to yoga, Pilates, Yogalates, spinning, suspension training, coached treadmill workouts, salsa dance, strip aerobics . . ."

"Any joggling?" Jordan asked.

"Of *course*," the man said again. "Have you tried it? A*ma*zing upper-body workout."

"Did Addie do that?"

"Oh, no. Addie swims. That's all I've ever seen her do. I tell her she should be cross-training, you know, mixing it up a bit. But we just can't get her out of the water. She's here five days a week, like clockwork."

"Wow." Jordan chuckled. "I don't know if I'm going to be quite as dedicated as that."

"Tell you what, Sam. I can give you a week to try the club out for free. Come on down, take a few classes, see how you like it."

"Good deal." Jordan thanked the man, hung up the phone, and slipped out of his office, past the little Christmas tree that Holly had bought and trimmed, and unlocked the door at the

back of the room that connected the officers' workspace to Pleasant Ridge's three-cell jail. Two of the cells were just normal,
nine-by-nine, with a metal bunk and a sink and a seatless metal
toilet. The third cell was bigger, with a wider door and a lower
sink. Handicapped-accessible, per federal regulations, in case any
of Pleasant Ridge's badasses used wheelchairs. Jordan unlocked
the door and sat down cross-legged on the flimsy mattress,
pushed the question of his ex-wife's new daughter out of his
mind, and considered Adelaide Downs.

He thought of the photograph he'd seen in her brother's
room, a woman for whom the words "ordinary" and "regular"
must once have seemed like a dream. But Addie had reinvented
herself. She was normal now, a woman you wouldn't necessarily
notice or look at twice. She wasn't huge. She wasn't even brunette. She was possibly sick . . . or maybe she'd been sick and was
going in for a checkup. Maybe she'd faced her own mortality and
decided to change her life. Which made her capable of what,
exactly?

Jordan sat on the bunk bed, perfectly still. *Addie, Addie,
Addie,* he thought, remembering the shape of her face, her smell
of sugar and lemons, her full lips curving into a smile, her blond
hair brushing her cheeks. He leaned back against the concrete
wall, trying to find the place he went to in his mind, a place he
thought of as a small storage shed, like the one where he and
Sam had kept their bikes and sleds and skateboards when they
were kids. In his mind, he entered the shed and locked the door
behind him, sat down in the darkness, and conjured Adelaide
Downs.

Addie, he thought as her face floated before his eyes. What
was Addie like? *Fat,* except she wasn't anymore. *Shy,* he thought
. . . but that wasn't quite right. *Sick?* Possibly . . . which could
mean that she'd decided she had nothing to lose. *Scared,* maybe.
She'd been hurt when she was a teenager, picked on, laughed at,

ostracized . . . and then, as an adult, she probably spent years unable to walk out the door without people staring or whispering. Now she had a new body; now she was a blonde, not a brunette, now she could slip into the tide of regular people and swim there, unremarkable and unremarked-upon.

And she swam. He pictured Addie in a swimsuit—a modest black one-piece, because she would never be the bikini type, no matter how much weight she'd lost. He added a white bathing cap, a bottle of drugstore suntan lotion, and a towel. He imagined Valerie Adler by her side. Val would definitely be the bikini type, the smaller the better, with maybe those big black sunglasses that made perfectly attractive women look like giant bugs. Two girls in swimsuits. Where would they go to escape the miserable Chicago winter, where the wind blew off Lake Michigan and slipped, knife-edged, under your coat?

"Key West," he said out loud, remembering the inscription on the back of Valerie's photograph. Through the wall, he heard Gary Ryderdahl let loose with a juicy string of expletives and slam his phone down. Jordan went back to his desk, turned on his computer, and called up a map of the United States, noting that St. Louis and Nashville were both on the way to Florida. Maybe they were there already, Addie and Val, the country mouse and the city mouse, sitting on the beach, each holding a frozen drink, something frothy and sweet with a wedge of pineapple perched on the rim, listening to the waves, feeling the breeze in their hair. Maybe it was a dying woman's final wish, or maybe they'd done something terrible and decided to run. It made no difference to him. Either way, he'd do his job. He got to his feet, pulled on his heavy coat, waved goodbye to Gary, and climbed back in his car.

FORTY-THREE

"Key West?" said Sasha. Her eyebrows arched skeptically. Behind the open door, the house was quiet. Jordan wondered where her daughters were. Maybe at their father's. Sasha's hair was pulled into its usual tidy knot, but her cheeks and forehead were shiny with some kind of face cream that she wiped at with her sleeve before leading him back to her office. "You think they're in Key West?"

Jordan kept quiet. He'd decided, going in, that the less he said, the better. Besides, he didn't trust his voice entirely. He worried that if he opened his mouth, what would come out would not be the right questions and answers but, instead, the words *My wife and the dentist have a baby now.*

"You're basing this on what, exactly?"

"They went to Chicago together to find Addie's brother. Addie took out a bunch of money in St. Louis. There was a charge at a gas station in Nashville, and I think the two of them are still together, so it . . ."

"Cell phone records?" Sasha Devine interrupted, as if she hadn't heard him. "Airline tickets? Hotel reservations? Anything?" She wiped her sleeve against her cheek again and looked at Jordan.

"I . . ." said Jordan, and shut his mouth.

"Did she speak to you?" Sasha asked. "Adelaide Downs? Did she find you in the small storage shed in your mind? Or did you go sit in the handicapped cell to think it over?"

He swallowed hard, thinking he'd have to be a lot less chatty with any future one-night stands. This shit was embarrassing. "I know she's down there."

"You're guessing," she shot back.

"Look," said Jordan, trying to sound reasonable. "I know she likes to swim. I think she went to the beach."

Sasha raised her eyebrows, which were the same glossy brown as her hair. "So why Florida?" she asked. "Why not Nantucket? Why not Maine?"

"Because it's freezing there."

"So?" Sasha said, shrugging. "Some people like to go to the beach when it's cold. You bundle up, sit by the fire. Watch the waves." The subtext was clear: *If you hadn't been such an asshole, all this could have been yours,* the blanket and the fire and Sasha herself, warm and naked under the covers.

"She's heading south, and she likes to swim," he repeated. Sasha was looking at him with that expression women have, like they can see exactly what you're thinking, as if it's a movie showing on the screen of your forehead, like she knew that the real mystery on his mind had nothing to do with Daniel Swansea's disappearance and everything to do with his ex-wife and a baby.

"Not a pool?" Sasha finally asked, hands on her hips, eyebrows cocked.

"I think she wants to see the ocean." This, too, was purest conjecture, but somehow it felt right. "And she might be sick."

"Might be?" Her eyebrows edged even higher. Jordan shut his mouth and waited. Sasha stared at him, then sighed. "I'd send you if I could, but on this . . . I mean, it's nothing, really. Just taking out money in one city and buying gas somewhere else doesn't add up to Florida."

"It's fine," he forced himself to say. "I understand." He drove back to the station. Holly was still off at Dan's Toyota dealership. Devin was still home. Gary was still on the telephone, working his way through a list of every hotel in Nashville. It took Jordan fifteen minutes online to book a place in Key West, an efficiency with the word "Budget" in its name and a kitchenette attached. He spent another ten minutes booking a flight for the next morning. He composed an e-mail that he'd send from the airport and drove home to pack shirts and sports coats and an ancient, half-used bottle of sunblock that he suspected had been bought on his honeymoon. *I am coming for you, Addie,* he thought. Then he said it out loud, not a threat, more like a simple statement of his intentions. "I am coming to bring you home."

FORTY-FOUR

I climbed out of the car, blinking in the sticky sunshine on Monday afternoon. White shells crunched underneath my feet. Palm fronds rustled above my head. I smelled salt in the humid air and could hear—or imagined I could—waves lapping at a nearby shore. In front of us, tucked behind a tidy garden of clipped hedges and spiky palms, was a white wooden cottage with a broad front porch and louvered windows, like an illustration from a fairy tale. SHELL COTTAGES read a plaque beside the doorbell.

"Check it out," Val said, and led me through the French doors. There was a living room with a tiled floor and a ceiling fan paddling at the humid air. Two bedrooms down a short hall, a bathroom in between them. A bowl of mangoes and papayas and limes sat next to the kitchen sink. In the back was a small brick patio that was thick with the scents of jasmine and jacaranda and filled with spiky-leaved palms and orchids.

Val led me to the screened-in porch and reached for a glass pitcher full of pale-green liquid. "Key limeade. The landlady leaves it for new tenants," Val said, and poured us each a glass. I sipped mine, tentatively at first, then more deeply: I was thirsty, and this was delicious, the perfect balance between tart and sweet.

"Isn't that good?" Val looked pleased.

"Have you been here before?"

"Twice." She slipped off her shoes and settled into a chaise longue, stretching and sighing with pleasure. "With a friend." She fanned her hair out against the cushions and looked at me sideways. I recognized my cue.

"Anyone I know?"

"Charlie Carstairs." The name was pronounced reverently. Clearly, I was supposed to know who he was. Sadly, I didn't.

"Isn't he . . ."

"My station manager."

"Ah." I rummaged around in my brain for Val-iana. "Wait a minute. He's the one who's married to——"

"It's a marriage in name only," she said quickly.

"Ah." Charles Carstairs's wife, Bonnie, was herself a former newscaster turned full-time fund-raiser for breast cancer research. You'd see her picture in the paper a few times a year, her head swathed in a hot-pink bandanna, beaming at the finish line of some bike event or swim or marathon. After my mother's sickness, I'd started contributing to breast cancer research and advocacy groups, and I'd ended up on her mailing list, which meant I got her hot-pink bandanna'ed face smiling up from my mailbox at least once a month, exhorting me to race for the cure, or dance for the cure, or shop or garden or dine out for the cure.

"You know her hair grew back," Val said. "She's been in remission since 1993. She just wears that bandanna for show."

"Well, in that case, you go on and take her husband. If she's got hair, she can get a new one."

Val frowned faintly. I took a sip of my limeade. "You know," I offered, "they don't actually leave their wives. Even if they say they want to . . ."

She shook her head, ice tinkling in her glass. "Oh, God, like I'd ever want him to leave his wife," she said. "Please. Six a.m. tee times and stinky cigars after dinner! Once a week's about all I'd want of Charlie." She stretched back in her chair, reaching her arms up over her head. Her eyes were hidden under the dark glasses she'd bought in St. Louis, her arms and shoulders bared in the red halter top she'd picked up in Atlanta. I wondered if Val missed her old clothes—the boys' jeans and T-shirts, the laceless sneakers she'd wear until the soles peeled away from the uppers. Maybe she pined for the days when she would cut her bangs with the craft scissors she'd swiped from school and ride a too-big boy's bike, helmetless, through town. Now there wasn't an inch of her that hadn't been worked on, improved somehow, from the tips of her polished toes to her tanned legs, lasered hairless and painted brown in the privacy of a spray-tan booth. Her belly was prairie-flat. There were acrylic fingernails glued to her fingertips, and hair extensions (for volume, not length, she'd taken pains to tell me) cleverly braided and knotted onto her scalp. She had, she confessed, done some "fine-tuning" on her nose and chin out in California, where she'd gotten her first job on-air. Still, I could catch glimpses of my old friend underneath the polished facade; like a coin or a shell glimmering underneath shallow water. She still bit her nails when she was nervous, still tucked her hair behind her ears as a conversational placeholder, still preferred snack foods to actual meals, and was, as ever, still full of plans, adventures I would never dream of, up to and including running from the law for a tropical vacation.

I went inside to use the bathroom. "Don't take a bath!" she called. "There's an outdoor shower!" Val led me to the backyard, where, sure enough, a showerhead sprouted from the wall. It curved over a square of wooden planks with a drain set in the middle. A white fence surrounded it and there was a built-in shelf with an oversized bar of creamy pink soap, bottles of shampoo and conditioner and body wash made of raspberry and avocado oil. "It's really just so you can rinse off after the beach," Val said. "But I use it all the time." She gave me a slanting smile. "A couple of times, Charlie and I used it together."

"Just tell me you cleaned it after."

"Addie. It's a shower. Showers are clean by definition." She tossed me a towel. "We can go shopping later, pick up some more clothes."

"And then what?"

"Shower first. Then we'll talk."

It felt strange, taking my clothes off outside, in the middle of the day, exposing my poor imperfect body to the sunshine. But after a few minutes under the warm spray, I started enjoying myself. I could feel the breeze, scented with salt and jasmine, moving across my skin. When I tilted my head back to rinse my hair, I opened my eyes and saw the blue sky above me.

Finally, the water turned cold. Inside the bedroom closet, I found a white robe, plush and thick as a comforter. I tied the sash around my waist and walked barefoot back to the porch and sat on the chaise longue opposite Val's. I thought she was sleeping—her eyes were closed—but as soon as I sat down, she started to talk.

"Have you ever been in love?"

"I . . ." I stared at the bumps of my knees and pressed the heel of my palm gently against the bump in my belly. Tell her more about Vijay? Keep the details my secret? Before I could decide, Val plunged ahead.

"Listen, all I'm saying is that we're going to have to go home eventually, and while we're here, you should take advantage. Do everything you always wanted! Get drunk! Get high! Have sex with the pool boy!"

I looked around. "There's a pool?"

"Out back," said Val, pointing. "Behind the hedges. We share with the other cottages." She leaned back, eyes narrowed at the horizon. "I bet I could get you a guy."

"I appreciate the thought, but I'm okay. How about this," I said. "We rent bikes and pack a picnic and go to the beach?"

She frowned. "That's not very exciting." Reaching underneath her chair, she pulled out a blue-and-white plastic bag. "Pork rind?" She waved one at me. "Low carb!" I shook my head. She shrugged and popped one in her mouth. I listened to the crunch, frowning. Something was teasing at the edge of my mind, and when I finally figured out what it was, I gasped.

Val looked up at me, mouth full, blue eyes wide, freckles dotting her cheeks. "What?"

"Val," I said, struggling to keep my voice even. "Where'd you get those?"

She popped another pork rind in her mouth. "Nashville? Wherever we stopped for gas yesterday morning." I remembered. I'd gone to use the bathroom, and when I'd come back to the car, she'd had a plastic bag of snack food at her feet and a jumbo-sized fountain drink in her hand, and was complaining about the car's lack of cup holders, and I hadn't thought anything about it at the time, but now . . .

"How'd you pay?" The gas station where we'd stopped had abutted a six-stall car wash. Shirtless guys in droopy jeans had been standing there, waiting with rags in their hands. As the wet cars had come through, they'd toweled them off. A radio had been blasting reggaeton. I remembered the guys smiling at Val as she'd twitched her shoulders to the beat before I'd gone to the restroom, leaving my purse in the car beside her. I'd reclaimed custody of our cash, and that had been tucked into the front pocket of my jeans, but my purse held my wallet . . . and all of my credit cards. Now I held my breath, hoping that I was wrong. Maybe Val had tucked a twenty into her bra—a Naomi-style trick.

"I used a . . ." Her face got pale, and her voice, when she spoke, was tiny. "Oh. Oh, shit."

"You used your credit card?"

"Um." She folded up the bag of pork rinds and tucked it back under her chair. "No. Yours."

"Valerie!"

"Well, I'm sorry!" she said, jumping to her feet. "I left mine at home, and I figured you wouldn't mind, and I forgot we weren't supposed to be using them."

"How could you forget?"

"I've got a lot on my mind right now! You know, this whole mess with Dan, and remember how I told you that the station went high-def? I'm already getting laser resurfacing once a month, and even that . . ."

"Pork rinds," I said, grabbing the bag and waving it at her. "Pork rinds! I can't believe this. We're going to go to jail because you had to have your freakin' pork rinds!"

"It's not that I had to have them," she said sullenly. "They're just a relatively healthy snack option." She swung her legs off her lounge chair and started pacing. "Okay," she said. "Let's not panic. Maybe they'll think we're in Nashville."

I started talking, thinking out loud. "We got the money in St. Louis. We spent the night in Atlanta . . ."

"But they won't know about that," she said patiently. "We paid cash at the hotels, and we used fake names."

I made myself take a deep breath and let it out slowly. "Val. This isn't going to work. Not for very much longer."

"It's not my fault," she said. Her face set in a pout.

I waited until she picked up the bag and shoved another pork rind into her mouth. Then I said, "We need to talk about what comes next." I paused, watching her face, reading the weather in her eyes. "If they find Dan."

She crunched her snack thoughtfully. "We'll tell them it was an accident," she said. "Tomorrow. I'll call the police tomorrow and tell them what happened."

"Will you tell them what Dan did to you?"

A crease appeared between her eyes. "I don't know. It'd be all over the papers. And the blogs. Everyone would be all up in my business."

"There's worse things than that."

Val didn't seem to hear me. "And I left the scene of the crime. I never reported it."

True. "Maybe say you had post-traumatic stress disorder? That you saw him and you flipped out?"

She was shaking her head, the crease deepening as she frowned. "I'm never going to get my job back. I'm in a position of public trust, you know."

I made myself breathe in, then out. "Val. You know I love you, but you're not exactly Walter Cronkite."

"People will laugh at me," she said darkly, and tugged at a strand of her hair.

"Walter Cronkite never rode a mechanical bull . . ."

"Oh, would you let that go?" she snapped.

"Having people laugh at you is not the worst thing in the world." I remembered the little boy in the booth in the HOT . . . APPLE . . . PIE restaurant. I remembered his mother. I remembered the guidance counselor and her fistful of platitudes, a football player with his face hanging out of the bus window, mouth open, hollering "Burn it off, fattie!"

I touched her shoulder. "Maybe Dan's okay."

"I hit him with my car." She had her chin tucked against her chest, her eyes on her knees. "You're generally not okay after that happens." She lowered her eyes some more. "Probably dead in a ditch."

"We checked the ditches," I said.

"We're going to get in trouble." Her voice was flat. "I mean, we did rob a bank."

"We'll just say it was a misunderstanding," I said. Let her think we'd actually robbed the bank, I decided. She'd been so pleased at the time.

She scrunched her eyes shut. "Maybe they'd buy that," she said. "I could say we just wanted to make a withdrawal, but the girl saw my gun and got scared." She picked some polish off her nails, letting the scarlet flecks drift down around her. The sun was setting, a glowing orange ball dipping majestically toward the water to the cheers and applause of the crowd in Mallory Square, where, I knew, the tourists gathered each night to sip frozen drinks and watch the sunset and the street performers—guys who juggled chainsaws, dogs who swallowed fire.

"Screw it," Val muttered. "Who needs it, anyhow? Stupid weather. Like I care. I'll just stay down here. Be a waitress. Whatever." She looked at me. "You could stay, too. I'll bet it's great for painting. The light, you know. And Jon could come. We could take him to the beach . . ."

I closed my eyes. That was Val, always running. To California, to Kentucky, to Dallas and Boston and wherever else her glamorous job would take her. She could run, and I was stuck in place, and I would be until I died.

"You could sell your house," she said. "And I'll sell my condo. We could work at a bar. I'll bet half these places are hiring . . ."

"I need to tell you something," I said.

She looked unsurprised as she settled into her chair and waved the bag in my direction. "Pork rind?"

I shook my head. "I think I might be sick."

"Huh?" She blinked. "What are you talking about? You didn't even eat any."

"I found a lump."

Val sat up fast. "You did? When? Where?"

"About a week before the reunion. I think ..." I gulped. I wasn't sure I could say the words out loud, wasn't sure if speaking them would somehow make them real. "I think it's what my mother had."

"Oh my God." She stared at me. "What are you going to do?"

"I'm supposed to see a doctor on Thursday. My mom's doctor. Her oncologist. That was the soonest they could take me. Thursday morning."

"We'll go home," Val promised. "First thing tomorrow, so you can go see the doctor. We'll go to the police, and I'll tell them what I did." She thought for another minute. "But I'm totally going with that post-traumatic stress thing." She chewed on her thumb. "Maybe I should get a book about it. Or look it up on Wikipedia."

"Okay."

"Can I stay with you?" Before I could answer, she nodded as if she'd made up her mind. "Yeah. If I don't go to jail, I'll stay with you."

My throat was tight, my eyes were stinging. Nobody had ever stayed with me. Vijay had never spent the night. It had just been me in the house since my mother had died. "For how long, do you think?"

Val took my hand and I felt her fingers, thin and strong, lacing through mine. "For as long as you need me," she said.

FORTY-FIVE

Even through his sorrow, through the tape loop playing the words "little girl" over and over in his head, Jordan Novick managed to be impressed when his Monday morning flight, on an airline he'd never heard of, pulled away from the gate on time and touched down a mere fifteen minutes behind schedule. In the noisy Miami airport, he waited in line behind a family chattering in a language he didn't recognize for thirty minutes before the rental-car line inched forward enough to deposit him in front of an agent (there were puddle-jumper flights from Miami to Key West, but driving was cheaper and he hated little planes).

By the time he'd picked up his car and made his way onto I-95 South it was after two o'clock. He got off the highway long enough to grab a burger and fries, and drove until the road dwindled to two lanes, a ribbon of blacktop draped like a necklace over astonishing blue-green water. His rented car had satellite radio with an all Bruce Springsteen, all the time station, which was a nice surprise. When he drove past the Dolphin Research Center in Marathon (SWIM WITH THE DOLPHINS! invited a billboard out front), he gave the school-bus-sized concrete dolphin leaping in the parking lot a thumbs-up and sang along to "Badlands" in a voice that was, to his own ears, credibly Bruce-like.

He passed Key Largo and Islamorada, Lower Matecumbe and Conch Key, Little Duck Key and Little Torch Key, heading toward the sunset with the windows rolled down.

By six o'clock, he'd arrived in Key West. Making his way through the outskirts of town, Jordan thought it could have been any medium-sized city in America, with its big box stores and fast-food chains ... but as a series of turns took him closer to the water, the streets narrowed, and the palm trees got more plentiful, and pedestrians and cats outnumbered the cars. The sky was pink from the sunset. The air smelled like salt and liquor, and everyone seemed cheerful (although, to be fair, many of them also seemed drunk). After a few wrong turns, he found his motel and checked into his room, a cheerless, boxy bedroom on the second floor of a two-story cinderblock building, with a mattress that sagged in the center and the scent of mildew and Pine-Sol in the air. He hung his jackets in the closet and put his shirts and underwear in one of the bureau drawers, and looked at the telephone for a long moment before making himself look away.

At seven, he turned up the rattling air conditioner as high as it would go, made sure he had his wallet and his room key (this place was so budget that it still had actual keys attached to a diamond of aqua plastic with the room number printed in white), and made his way to Duval Street, which the brochure he'd grabbed informed him was Key West's main drag. Before he'd left Pleasant Ridge, he'd printed a list of the rental agencies and was pleased to find one of them still open. But his good luck ended there: the clerk behind the counter hadn't ever rented a cottage to Charlie Carstairs or Valerie Adler or Adelaide Downs, and he didn't recognize their pictures (Jordan had downloaded Valerie's from the TV station's website, and Addie's he'd pocketed at the Crossroads). "It could've been a private rental," one young man told him. "You know, they could have set it up over the Internet with someone who owned their own place and not gone through an agency at all."

Great. Jordan marched up one side of the street and down the other, ducking into scooter-rental shops and souvenir stores, galleries and boutiques and bars, plodding through packs of drunks and rowdies and sweating parents who pushed tank-sized strollers and glared at pedestrians who didn't get out of the way fast enough, flashing Addie's and Val's photographs, asking over and over *Have you seen them,* unsurprised when, over and over, the answer was no.

By ten o'clock he was lightheaded. A beer and a burger seemed like a good idea. (*Two burgers in one day?* Patti asked in his head, and Jordan told her to shut up, because what did she care what he ate anymore? She had a new husband and probably a baby now, unless the cross-dressing banker had gotten it wrong, so what did she care about anything?) He stopped into the first place he saw, not realizing until he'd taken a seat at the bar and been handed his laminated plastic menu that he wasn't in a restaurant as much as a Jimmy Buffett theme park, with a gift shop up front and a menu filled with Buffett-inspired fare.

If you can't beat 'em, join 'em, he thought, and ordered a Cheeseburger in Paradise and a Red Stripe. One beer became two, two turned into three, and then the guy next to Jordan at the bar bought everyone a round of Coronas and paid the bartender fifty bucks to put "Fins" on repeat, which necessitated more beer, plus a shot of tequila to dull the din of a hundred sunburned middle-aged Parrotheads waving their hands in the air and singing.

"You okay?" asked his ponytailed waitress as she dropped the check in front of him. She had a steel bar through the top of her ear, through her pinna, which was a useful Scrabble word. Jordan and Patti had once been Scrabble buffs. They'd had a travel set and taken it everywhere they might have been stuck with time to kill. They'd played on the beach on that last trip to the Bahamas and, before that, in the doctor's waiting room, and in the hospital, where Patti lay, pale and wan, an IV needle in the back of her hand, ultrasound gel on her belly, trying not to let him see her cry.

"Can I ask you a question?" He fumbled in his pocket with the waitress staring at him, and wondered how many times she'd been propositioned by vacationing Midwesterners who were old enough to be, if not her father, then her much older brother. "Have you seen either of these two ladies?"

She gave the pictures a cursory glance, then shook her head. "Did you lose someone?" she asked.

Oh yes, he thought.

"Hey, good luck," said the waitress. He left her a big tip and dragged himself back out into the sticky, thumping night. A group of three guys in khaki shorts and baseball caps were standing underneath a streetlamp, consulting a map. Jordan tapped the smallest one on the shoulder and flashed the photograph. "Have you guys seen . . ." He swallowed, struggling to remember the rest of the sentence, and the small guy patted his shoulder.

"Dude," he said not unkindly. "You are wrecked."

Jordan licked his lips. "What are you drinking?" Each of the boys had a plastic pail—the things were too enormous to be called cups—full of something pale-brown and eye-wateringly potent.

"Voodoo Bucket," said one of the guys. He lifted his pail in a toast as his friends whooped, and used his elbow to point toward an open-air bar on the opposite corner. The place had walls papered with autographed dollar bills. A tanned man wearing nothing but a Speedo and a cowboy hat sat alone at the bar, his elbows propped on the polished wood. Somewhere nearby, a steel drum band was playing "Oye Como Va." Jordan crossed the street and caught the bartender's eye.

"One Voodoo Bucket, please." A Voodoo Bucket, Jordan thought as he carefully carried his beverage back to his car and then up to his room, was festive. It was the kind of drink you'd enjoy on the deck of a cruise ship, or in a lounge chair overlooking the pool. It tasted like rum and fruit juice. Possibly grain alcohol. Maybe antifreeze. Jordan wasn't sure. Up in his room, stripped to his boxer shorts, he sat as close to the rattling air conditioner as he could, sipped his drink, and dialed the station to check in. Things were fine, Holly assured him. They were following up. Tracking down leads. Watching the phones. Everything was completely under control.

Jordan made all the right noises, offered all the right praise and words of encouragement, saying "nice work" and "good job" and "I'll check in tomorrow morning," and cut Holly off before her voice could soften as she asked how he was doing. And then, as the hands of the clock slipped past midnight, he did the thing he'd resisted doing for the more than twenty-four hours since he'd heard the news: he dialed Patti's number, her cell phone number, which was still the same as it had been in the days when they'd lived together.

She answered on the third ring. "Jordan?"

Hang up, he told himself. *Hang up right now.* Instead, he asked, "Remember when we used to play Scrabble?"

From two thousand miles away, he heard his ex-wife sigh. "Oh, Jordan."

"Remember? In the hospital that last time? You spelled '*fromage*,' and I challenged you because it was a foreign word, and then they came to give you that shot . . ."

"Epidural," said Patti. She sounded unhappy. He'd made her unhappy. As usual.

"I was right, you know," he said. "You can't use French." He squeezed his eyes shut. His face was wet. Sweat, he figured, or maybe he'd spilled some voodoo. "Guess where I am."

"Wherever you are, I hope someone else has your car keys," said Patti.

"Key West," he said, pronouncing each word carefully. "I am in Key West conducting an investigation." Shit. He'd been doing all right until "investigation," but that hadn't come out so well.

"Jordan," said Patti. "Are you seeing someone?"

"A woman?" he asked stupidly. "No, Patti. I don't want that." *Only you,* he thought. *Only my wife.*

"Not a woman, a therapist," said Patti.

"Oh. Yes," he lied.

"No, you're not," Patti said. Before he could try to insist that he was, she continued. "Do you know what I think you should do? Get yourself some Tylenol, and a big bottle of water, and take the Tylenol, and drink the water, and go to sleep."

"I can't," he said querulously. "I'm investigating, remember?"

"Your investigation can wait until morning," she said.

"Maybe I'll move down here," he said, and gulped a mouthful of his drink. "It's very warm." He set his bucket down and wiped his face with the washcloth he'd brought from the bathroom. "There's palm trees. Jimmy Buffett's got a restaurant."

"That sounds nice," she said. She was humoring him. It was the same tone he imagined she used with her remedial reading students. *That's excellent work! Good job sounding that out!*

"Come here," he said. "There's an airport. You fly to Miami, then connect. Or I'll drive back up and meet you. Just bring a bathing suit. I can buy you whatever you need."

"Oh, Jordan," she said. She made a noise into the telephone, and he thought he'd made her cry.

"I miss you," he said, and that was true, but it wasn't the biggest part of the truth, which was that he missed being a husband, having a home to come back to at the end of the day, having a wife across the table, next to him on an airplane or in a car; a wife who knew his whole history: how he'd gotten stung by a jellyfish in the Bahamas and tried to pee on himself to make the stinging stop, how he hated beets and little airplanes and the smell of gasoline; a wife who would sing "I Loves You Porgy" in the original politically incorrect dialect when she was drunk.

"Water," said Patti, from her warm bed in Chicago. Undoubtedly, Rob Fine, DDS, was at her side, maybe curled up and snoring, or maybe glaring at her, squinting and pissed, knowing it was only a handful of hours before the alarm clock rang, sending them out of their beds. "Tylenol."

"I heard you had a baby." For a moment, there was silence, and he thought that she wasn't going to answer, or that maybe she'd hung up.

Patti's voice, when she finally started talking, was proud and shy and embarrassed. "Rob and I adopted a little girl from Guatemala. We brought her home three weeks ago. Her name's Lily, for my grandmother."

Lily. Lily had been their girl's name. He rubbed his palm over his wet cheek, thinking he wouldn't be able to force his voice around the lump in his throat. "I'm sorry about '*fromage,*'" he said. "I should have let you have the points." But he was talking to a dial tone, which eventually became an unpleasant beeping, which turned into a mechanical voice. *If you'd like to make a call, please hang up and try again. If you need help, press zero for an operator.*

I need help, Jordan thought. He gulped from his bucket, then lay on the bed and closed his eyes and pictured Patti, Patti in heels and a tight black skirt he'd liked, walking briskly down a hallway, towing a wheeled suitcase behind her, maybe holding a little girl's hand; Patti steering a rental car through the streets that led toward the ocean, driving along with a cup of coffee in the cup holder, trying to find him.

After forty-five minutes of lying there, he decided that if he couldn't sleep, he might as well work. He picked up his car keys and his Voodoo Bucket, and went out to continue the hunt.

FORTY-SIX

"**D**an?" It was morning, Monday morning, and Chip Mason was shaking his shoulder. Dan groaned, squinting in the light. Merry had dropped him off at Chip's on Sunday morning. He'd hurried to the door, almost running, desperate for Chip to answer and shoving his mouth close to his friend's ear when he did. "Don't you go all Holy Joe on me," he'd hissed. "This woman is batshit insane, and you've got to let me in." Startled, Chip had looked past him, at Merry's minivan, then opened the door.

"You got any beer?" Dan had asked, making his way to the kitchen and hoping that Chip wouldn't ask what had happened and how he'd come to be driving around in Holy Merry Armbruster's minivan.

"It's nine in the morning," Chip had said.

"Don't be an old woman." Dan opened the refrigerator, where of course there was no beer. There was milk, and apple juice (apple juice? What kind of grown man drank that?), but nothing stronger than Sprite.

"What happened?" Chip asked as Dan lifted the green plastic bottle to his mouth and commenced chugging. And there must have been something in his voice, a familiar tone somewhere between skepticism and indulgence—oh, Danny, what did you do now?—that reminded Dan, bruisingly, of his mother. That was what it had been, he realized, feeling stunned and sick, back at Merry's . . . the way *she'd looked at him, not in anger but in disappointment. In sorrow. His mother had been the one who would pick him up when he'd get suspended, the one who'd drive him home when he got benched from the football games, and each time she'd ask him that question, then sigh and say,* You'll be the death of me.

He put the soda down on the table. When he and his friends had gotten in trouble for painting shit on Addie Downs's driveway (Downs Syndrome, they'd called her, a name he'd thought of himself that never failed to crack him up), he'd given his mother the bare minimum of information. They'd painted some graffiti, just a prank, no big deal, the freakin' vice principal had it in for him, he'd said. He'd reminded her that Addie had been the one to accuse him—falsely, he took pains to point out—of messing with Valerie Adler. He didn't say that Addie had it coming, but he let the implication hang in the air and linger. Only that time, his mother hadn't sighed, hadn't indulged him. She'd sat him down at the kitchen table—he was a foot taller than she was by that point, a hundred pounds heavier, but she could still scare him—and had looked at him steadily before dropping her eyes and starting to cry.

"What?" he'd asked. "What, Ma?"

She'd wiped her face and looked at him, eyes blazing, looking . . . It took him a minute to sort out, and when he did, he had felt that same sick, stunned feeling that came over him in Chip's kitchen. His mother had looked ashamed. Do you know what it's like, *she asked him,* to raise a son who's no good? Do you have any idea how it feels?

He'd started to protest, to launch into his litany of excuses—no big deal, it was just paint, it would wash right off—only, midway through his recitation, she'd gotten to her feet and turned her back on him. I'm done with you, *she'd said.* I'm done trying. And even though she'd cooked his meals and washed his clothes, had dropped him off for the first day of college and made Thanksgivings and Christmases for years, what she'd said that day was true. In some way that was undefinable but undeniable, apparent mostly in the absences and omissions, in the things she didn't ask him about (girlfriends, future plans), she'd given up on her only son. He had disappointed her. He had broken her heart.

Slowly, he sank down in a chair at Chip's kitchen table. "What happened?" his old friend asked again. Dan shook his head. Then he'd lowered it into his hands and sat there with his eyes shut until Chip told him that services were starting soon, and Dan surprised both of them by saying, "I'll come."

That had been his first time inside a church since he'd left his parents' house. When Chip, looking all official up in front of the altar, had said "Let us pray," Dan had dropped his head so fast he heard his neck crack. He'd spent the afternoon on his knees again, still not talking, not answering when Chip asked what was on his mind or if he wanted to talk about it. Instead of thinking, he washed Chip's floors with a brush and bucket he'd found underneath the sink, then worked over the bathroom grout with an old toothbrush. Even with all of the cleaning, even with the praying and the fasting (which was mostly inadvertent, since it turned out he was so hungover he couldn't actually keep solid food down), he couldn't get Valerie Adler out of his mind, Valerie's face in the country club parking lot, twisting as she told him he'd ruined her life, and a younger Valerie, her face blurred with tears, her hands pushing at his shoulders, saying, Please. Saying No. Valerie's pleas getting mixed up with his mother's voice, quietly asking if he knew what it was like to raise a son that was no good.

Chip had made them dinner—spaghetti with jarred sauce, a salad from a bag. Dan couldn't eat. "What's wrong?" his friend asked for the third time . . . and that time he'd told.

"She said she'd tell her father," he'd groaned to Chip by the end of it. "And you know what I said? I said, 'You don't even have a father.'"
He'd squeezed his eyes shut, hating the stupid teenager he'd been, drunk on cheap beer, taking what he wanted, breaking his mother's heart. Chip had listened while Dan told the story, bringing it up like

a hunk of rotten meat, talking until his throat was hoarse and Chip spread a sheet on the couch and told him to get some rest.

Now it was morning. Dan got up from the couch, still dressed in the clothes Merry had given him, the too-short pants, the shirt that smelled like someone had died inside of it, probably while smoking an entire carton of unfiltered cigarettes. He jammed his feet into the tight rubber boots and looked at the doorway, where Chip was waiting.

"Can you take me somewhere?"

He waited for Chip's nod, then went to the kitchen, where he found a glass and drank two glasses of warm, mineral-tasting tap water. It occurred to him that this might very well be the last thing he'd drink, the last thing he'd taste as a free man, and the thought made him gag and sent him reeling over to the kitchen table. He collapsed into a chair. Chip watched him for a moment, then crossed the kitchen and gave Dan's shoulders a squeeze. Dan got to his feet.

"Where are we going?" Chip asked.

"I'll tell you," said Dan. He got to his feet, bracing himself, getting ready for what he knew was coming. "Get in the car and I'll tell you."

Chip nodded, picked up his keys, and led Dan out the door.

FORTY-SEVEN

Don't drive, Patti had said. But Jordan didn't have to listen to Patti anymore. "Bad gums," she'd said, and he'd believed her. Dentist-fucking Patti and her new little girl. Jordan unlocked the rental car's doors, got behind the wheel, and started driving, up one street and down the other. Key West wasn't that big. He bet he could hit every house in the place by sunrise.

He made his way to a neighborhood called the East End, a series of narrow streets, each one lined with trim wooden cottages set on postage-stamp lawns. He drove slowly, seeing whose lights were on, looking at the license plates of the cars in the driveways. After an hour or so of this, he slowed and then stopped in front of an ancient green station wagon with Illinois plates that he'd last seen speeding away from Crescent Drive.

He sat back behind the wheel and stared past the car at the dark windows of the little white cottage, snug behind a yard full of red-and-pink blossoms and the spiky leaves of palm trees. *Gotcha,* he thought, and waited for the feeling of triumph to flare in his veins. Nothing happened. He just felt lonely, and sad, and sick.

Hair of the dog, he decided, remembering Judy Nadeau grinning at him drunkenly, asking if he wanted to fool around, and took a sip from the Voodoo Bucket, which he'd brought with him and belted into the passenger seat. Patti's voice said *Her name is Lily* in his head. It was just after three in the morning. *Let them sleep,* he decided. He'd confirm that Val and Addie were in there as soon as they walked out the door, which they would have to do eventually. He'd corner them, talk to them, convince them to confess. He would take them to the Key West police station where they'd turn themselves in. Then he would call Sasha and tell her that he'd solved the crime.

Jordan leaned his head against the window, and his eyes must have slipped shut. When he opened them, the sun was rising, turning the sky an unnatural flamingo pink. He could hear the wind moving through the trees and, faintly, the sound of the ocean . . . and the sound of someone tapping on the window. He straightened, bracing himself for a pissed-off neighbor or, worse, a fellow officer of the law, asking him his business, telling him to move along. Instead—he blinked, wiping at his watery eye—he saw the Nighty-Night Lady. No snail puppet, but he recognized her anyhow. She'd gotten a tan, and with the pink sky behind her, she was even more beautiful in person than she was on TV.

"Jordan?" she said. She looked puzzled . . . maybe even afraid. "Jordan Novick?"

He blinked again, and the Nighty-Night Lady's features resolved themselves into Addie Downs's face. He got out of the car, stiff-legged and achy, waiting for that hit of adrenaline to come roaring through his veins.

"What are you doing here?" she asked.

"What are *you* doing here?" he countered.

She looked sideways at a gumbo-limbo tree. "Vacation." Her voice was so quiet he could barely hear her. "I'm on vacation."

He cleared his throat, hoping his own voice sounded authoritative, no-nonsense, but even as the oxygen reached his brain, he realized that he was much, much drunker than he'd planned on being.

He spoke slowly, keeping each word distinct, each syllable precise. "Where is Dan Swansea?"

"I don't know," she answered. He didn't think she was lying—there was no hesitation, no flinchy look away, no hand raised to the hair or fingers to the mouth.

"Why'd you run?"

"I didn't run," she said. "I just decided to take a little vacation."

Jordan took a step forward—to do what, to say what, he wasn't sure. The toe of his foot caught a tree root, and he stumbled, astonished at the speed with which the ground rose up to meet his face. He heard Addie say, "Hey!" and felt her fingers brush his sleeve as he fell . . . and then his forehead bounced off the sidewalk and he groaned, thinking, before the world went black, that this wasn't going well at all.

FORTY-EIGHT

"The police chief?" Valerie stared down at Jordan Novick's driver's license and then up at me. "What's he doing here?

"I assume he came here to find us. He had our pictures in his pocket."

Valerie considered this. "Was it a good picture? God. I hope it's not the one from Wikipedia. Some asshole who's, like, obsessed with me keeps posting this terrible shot, and it looks like I have three chins ..."

"Valerie. Focus."

She sat down cross-legged in an armchair. "Well, shoot," she finally said. "What are we going to do now?"

I wasn't sure. I'd gone out to watch the sunrise, thinking that I'd snap some pictures with the cheapie camera I'd bought, maybe do a few quick sketches of the sky. We'd been walking on the beach the day before, and the setting sun, the play of that strange fiery light on the water, enchanted me. I wanted to paint it, and not one of my miniatures, either. For this, I'd want a big canvas, maybe one as wide as a whole wall, and maybe something other than my usual watercolors. Maybe I'd do it in encaustic. The colored wax gave you a rich, layered look, the illusion of depth. It was wonderful for water, and I bet it would be great for the sky here, too.

So I'd gone out barefoot, in my nightshirt, with my camera in one hand and a house key in the other, and noticed the car parked in front of our driveway, with Jordan Novick asleep behind the wheel. After he'd fallen, I'd thought about calling 911, telling whoever answered that a man had passed out in front of our cottage, then just hanging up and leaving him there, but when I'd bent down to see if he had a phone in his pocket, Jordan had moaned and grabbed the hem of my nightshirt. *Please,* he whispered. I'd helped him inside, half walked, half dragged him into the bedroom, and left him on my bed, on his side, so that he wouldn't choke on his own vomit. Then I'd woken up Val, who'd been on her way to the bathroom. She'd peeked into the bedroom long enough to see his passed-out, prone figure, and said, "Oh, hey! You met someone!"

I'd told her what had happened. Together, we'd taken off Jordan's shoes and cleaned off his face. Then we'd adjourned to the living room to try to come up with a plan.

"How about this?" said Val. "We'll put him in a shopping cart, and we'll leave him in front of the emergency room. Like they did with that girl in *Animal House.*"

Oh, Lord. "Okay, first of all, I don't think *Animal House* was supposed to be instructional. He might have really hurt himself. And where are we going to get a shopping cart?"

Val thought it over. "Excellent points. Okay. We call a cab . . ."

"I think we'd better just take him to the police station." I paused. "And confess."

"I don't know," said Val, frowning. "He doesn't seem to be exactly in an official capacity at the moment." She picked at a cuticle. "Especially since I took his pants off."

I stared at her. "You did?"

"Yup," she said, looking pleased with herself.

"Why?"

"They were dirty." She nibbled at her thumbnail. "Also, you know, if he tried to escape or something. It's very hard to escape when you don't have any pants." She worried at her nail some more. "Not that I know this from personal experience."

"Valerie." I struggled for patience. "Have you ever considered that there might be something wrong with your brain?"

She gave me a sweet, guileless smile. "Oh, I think that maybe there's something wrong with everyone else's."

I picked up the telephone. "Maybe we should just call the cops."

"Let's wait until he wakes up," she said, standing and stretching. "Why rush?"

"I should make sure he's okay."

"You do that," said Val. "Go on with your bad self." She drifted toward her bedroom, and, after a minute, I walked into mine.

Jordan Novick lay underneath the light down comforter, his face already starting to swell where he'd struck it. I brushed the hair off his forehead, feeling its thickness against my fingers. I was just looking, I told myself. My interest was purely professional. I had to make sure he wasn't bleeding. He sighed in his sleep and burrowed his head into the pillow, looking like a little boy. I went to the kitchen, wrapped ice in a dishtowel and pressed it against his cheek. He groaned and rolled over.

"Patti," he said.

"Shh." I let myself stroke his hair again, very gently, just once, and touched his cheek. This was what I'd wanted, maybe all I'd ever wanted: a man to lie beside at night, a man who knew me, and who'd say my name. Or who'd lie beside me and say someone's name. At this point, I'd take what I could get.

"Nighty-night," said Jordan.

This was weird. What if he had a concussion? What if his brain was bleeding? I thought for a minute, trying to remember the dialogue I'd read in medical mysteries or remembered from TV. *Pupils fixed and dilated* were bad. *Reactive* pupils were good. A patient who was *oriented to place and time* was also good. I knelt on the bed beside him, took the shade off the lamp by the side of the bed, and brought the bulb down close to his face.

"Jordan," I whispered.

He opened his eyes. His pupils shrank to slits. He squinted, then covered his eyes with his hand. "Ow." I flicked the light off.

"Do you know where you are?" I whispered.

"Bed," he said. There was a pause. "Florida."

"Can I call someone?" I asked. "Your wife or ... someone?"

"No ... wife." He was struggling to push himself upright. The covers and sheets slipped as he did it, exposing white boxer-briefs. "Divorced." He rubbed his head, wincing. "She married our dentist. They adopted a girl."

"Oh." I wasn't sure what I was supposed to say to that.

"You sure you don't know where Dan Swansea is?"

I sighed. "Valerie—my friend Valerie Adler—thinks maybe she hit him with her car in the country club parking lot after the reunion."

"She thinks?" I couldn't see his expression in the dark—couldn't see anything more than the outline of his face and body—but I could imagine the skeptical look. "Isn't that the kind of thing you'd remember one way or the other?"

"For most of us, yes," I agreed. "My friend is an exception to many rules." I gave Jordan a minute to take that in, then continued. "She came to my house all upset because she thought she'd hit him ..." I paused. "In her defense, though, she said he jumped in front of her car. And he was naked. Val made him take his clothes off." I waited for Jordan to ask me why, but he didn't. Then I remembered that Val had taken off his pants. Maybe he remembered that, too, and figured that, with Valerie Adler, de-pantsing was standard procedure. "We drove back to the country club . . ."

"You didn't call the police?"

I pulled my knees up toward my chin. "We were going to see if he was okay."

"It was November, and he was naked, and he'd been hit by a car." Jordan sounded skeptical.

"Well, Val wasn't sure she'd actually hit him. We just wanted to see . . ."

I heard Jordan take a slow, deliberate breath, the kind I'd heard the mommies in the coffee shop take when their kids dumped their lattes on the floor. "Okay," he said. "Val shows up, you go back . . ."

"And Dan was gone! We found his belt . . . and then we went to look for him . . ."

"In Key West?"

I bit my lip. "Well, no. We actually started our search in Pleasant Ridge. The Key West part was only after we couldn't find him. We thought maybe we'd get out of town until he showed up again."

The bed creaked as Jordan shifted. "He hasn't. Shown up."

I wrapped my arms around my knees. Jordan sighed again, and when he spoke, his voice was a raspy growl. "I liked you," he said.

"You . . . you did?"

"I liked your house."

I gulped, thinking I was going to start crying. "Oh."

"And your bedroom."

My skin bristled with goose bumps. "Wait. You were in my bedroom?"

"Looking for you. Only because I was looking for you. Your neighbor's worried."

I sighed. Mrs. Bass. Lord love her. But still. How long had I been waiting for a man to say that he liked my house, that he'd been looking for me? Under different circumstances, of course, with the words meaning something else entirely. Jordan reached for my face, cupped my cheek in his palm and turned me toward him.

"I liked you," he said again, his voice cracking as he pulled me close. His lips were warm against mine, his hands moving in my hair, his body easing mine down into the bed. I felt like I was slipping under the water, as if the warm air, the heavy smell of flowers, the sunshine outside were all conspiring to make me behave in ways I never would in sober, cold Chicago. Jordan's whiskers rasped against my cheeks.

"Addie." We kissed and kissed. The bed rocked like a boat on the sea, and I could feel myself glowing, every inch of my skin lit from the inside, and somewhere nearby, something was buzzing, louder and louder.

It took everything I had to pull myself away from him, to recognize the sound, to form the words. "Phone," I said, and reached across him to turn the light back on.

He sat up, bruised and blinking. "Huh?"

"Phone," I whispered, and pointed toward the chair where Val had left his pants.

Jordan crossed the room in three long steps, pulled out his cell phone and looked at the screen.

"Novick," I heard him say. "Gary, is that you?" He listened for a minute, rubbing his head, frowning in the faint light, his body—stocky, but graceful—turned to the side. "He's here?" he said after a minute. His voice had gotten louder, and he sounded confused. "Turned himself in for what?"

I couldn't keep quiet, couldn't hold still. "Is it Dan Swansea?

Is he all right?" The words had barely left my mouth when Valerie burst through the door. She was wearing her Gap nightshirt, and there was a small silver gun in her hand.

"Hands up. Drop your weapon."

Jordan looked at her and let the cell phone slip to the floor, where it landed with a thunk. "Chief?" said a tinny voice. "Chief, you there?"

Valerie kicked the phone into the corner of the room without taking her eyes, or the barrel of her gun, off of Jordan, who had raised his hands in the air. "Now listen to me, you son of a bitch," she hissed. "My friend and I are walking out of here. Doesn't make any difference to me whether we do it with you dead or alive."

"Val," I said.

"Chief?" said the voice from the phone. "Chief, can you hear me?"

"She's sick," said Val, pointing her chin at me. "She needs to go home. She needs to see her doctor, and . . ."

"CHIEF! WHAT DO YOU WANT ME TO DO ABOUT SWANSEA?" shouted the voice on the telephone. For a minute, there was silence. Then Jordan looked at Valerie, eyebrows lifted.

"May I?" he asked.

She waited a moment, then nodded and lowered her gun. Jordan crossed the floor, keeping his hands in the air, and waited for Val's okay before he picked up the phone and pressed it against his ear. "Gary? What's going on?"

Val came to sit on the bed beside me, gripping my right hand in her left one. Her own right hand was aiming the gun at Jordan's head. "You might want to put that down," I whispered.

"Not a chance," she whispered back as Jordan said, "I'm on my way. I'll give you a call from the airport," and flipped the phone shut.

For a moment there was silence. The three of us were as still as if we'd been frozen—Val and I on the bed, Jordan standing in his blood-spattered button-down shirt and boxers, Val still pointing the gun toward his head.

"Swansea turned up," he said, and Val exhaled in a gush and quickly made the gun disappear. Shakily, I rose to my feet and looked at Jordan. His face was closed up tight as the phone as he grabbed his pants. "We'll be in touch," he said, pulling his pants on, pocketing the phone, and walking without a backward glance through the front door.

FORTY-NINE

Jordan had to give Daniel Swansea credit—the man had his story, and he was sticking to it.

"Just one more time," Jordan said for the fourth time that night. He was exhausted—the two-hour drive back to the Miami airport, the delays waiting for the rental-car shuttle, the special security screening that buying a last-minute one-way ticket guaranteed you had all taken their toll. "You left your belt in the country club parking lot?"

"If you found it in the parking lot, then that's where I left it." Seated across from Jordan at the conference table, with his hands folded in front of him, Dan Swansea was, as Christie had said, a good-looking guy, but he was wearing old man's pants that left a good three inches of his hairy shins bare, and a shirt that smelled like it had been exhumed from an attic, if not a coffin. Dan was tall and rangy, square-jawed and well built, with a full head of dark-brown hair and a dazed look in his eyes. He did not look like a man who'd trashed lockers and vandalized driveways, who'd raped a high school classmate. Sitting there, pale-faced and clean-shaven, he looked like a man who'd had all the fight taken right out of him.

"Do you remember leaving the party with Valerie Adler?"

Swansea rubbed at his head, saying nothing.

"Do you remember being struck by a car?"

Dan looked puzzled. Then he shook his head. "No, sir," he said. "I don't remember anything like that. I think maybe I fell in the parking lot." He rubbed his forehead and gave Jordan what was meant to be a rueful smile, except it looked like he'd learned how to smile only a few hours before and hadn't gotten good at it yet. "I was kind of wasted. They had an open bar. At the reunion."

"And you went home with a woman."

An odd look passed over Swansea's face. "Yes," he said. "That's right."

"You won't tell us her name?"

Swansea shook his head. "A gentleman never kisses and tells."

Jordan bit back a frustrated sigh and looked down at his notes. "You spent Sunday and Monday with your friend Reverend Charles Mason."

"Chip. He's a minister," Dan said.

"And you said that you wanted to confess to something?"

Dan balled his hands into fists, set them in front of him on the table, and stared straight ahead as he said, "When I was in high school, I was at a party with Valerie Adler. We'd both been drinking, and we were fooling around, and we went into the woods, and we . . ." He rubbed his head, swallowing again. "She told me no," he said, his voice barely audible. "I didn't listen. I raped her. I want to confess to that."

"This happened when?"

"Senior year," said Dan. "Fall of 1991. October, I think."

Jordan slid a pad of paper and a pen across the table. "Write it down," he said. Dan bent his head over the paper, holding the pen between his fingers for a minute before he started to write. Jordan slipped out of the room, easing the door shut behind him, and went to his office. It took him a few minutes to get the county's district attorney on the phone.

"One more time: He wants to what?" Glen Hammond asked.

"Confess," Jordan said.

"Jesus, did he hear a really inspiring grace at Thanksgiving?"

"Not sure," said Jordan.

"And he says this happened when?"

"October of 1991."

"Ancient history," said Glenn Hammond, laughing to himself. "Look, I hate to be the bearer of bad tidings, Chief, but your guy's shit out of luck. Statute of limitation's ten years. Even if he took a Betamax of himself and his buddies screwing third graders and their little dogs, too, the state of Illinois officially no longer cares."

Jordan hung up the phone and sat at his desk, thinking. It was what Grandpa Sam would have called a boondoggle, in his thick New England accent ("A boon-dawgull, Jordy!" he'd cackle, steering his Cadillac one-handed through downtown New London, "that's what this is!"). He couldn't arrest Addie or Valerie. Without a victim willing to press charges, without witnesses, without any evidence of a crime, there wasn't a case. Nor could he charge Daniel Swansea with Valerie's rape. Which left him with a hot, steamy bucketful of nothing, as his grandfather also used to say.

Back in the interview room, Dan lifted his head from the pad when Jordan came through the door. "I'm sorry," Jordan said, feeling awkward. "We can't prosecute you. The statute of limitation has expired."

Dan pressed his hand against his forehead, then stared up at Jordan. "What does that mean?"

"It means that even if there's evidence, even if you confess, we can't prosecute. Too much time has gone by."

Dan was shaking his head. "I did a terrible thing. I know that now. I want to make it right."

"Well . . ." Shit. Jordan was good at many things: solving crimes, punishing wrongdoers, finding lost cars, lost cats, lost keys. Lost ladies, down in Florida. He was not equipped to handle a perpetrator's plea for justice that the courts and the system couldn't deliver. "You could do good things, I guess. Good deeds."

"Good deeds," Daniel repeated, looking unhappy. He got to his feet and, after a moment, stuck his hand out at Jordan. "I'm sorry for any trouble I caused," he said. "If people were looking for me over the holiday weekend. I'm sorry."

Jordan shook his hand. "You can see where we'd be concerned."

"I'm sorry," Daniel said again. He stared at Jordan intently for a moment, clasping his hand. "If I was guilty . . . if I got arrested . . . where would you put me?"

Jordan frowned. "In one of the cells here, until your arraignment."

"Can I see?"

Figuring there was no harm in it, Jordan led Dan past the narrow metal bench with three sets of handcuffs attached, unlocked the heavy door, and pointed out the department's three cells, including his favorite. Dan sighed. It was the sound of a starving man seeing a feast, the sound of a man dying in the desert glimpsing water . . . a sound Jordan thought he recognized. Hadn't he heard similar sighs coming from his own mouth as he settled into his camp chair with his beer and his remote, hoping for a twenty-two-minute respite from thoughts of Patti and the dentist, of all the things he'd hoped for that had eluded him?

Dan extended one hand to the metal door and let his hand touch the bars. "Could I . . ."

"No," said Jordan. "You can't."

"Please," said Dan. "You don't have to lock the door. You don't have to tell anyone I'm here. I won't cause any trouble, I just . . . I can't . . ." He was trembling all over. "Please," he said, and Jordan, puzzled, unlocked the first cell and watched as Daniel Swansea walked inside. He spread the thin blue plastic-sheathed mattress on the metal bunk and curled on his side, with his shoes on and his back to the hallway and his cheek pillowed under his hands. Jordan watched him for a minute. Then he slid the door shut and left him there.

Something had happened to Daniel Swansea whether the man wanted to admit it or not. Something had, as the kids said, gone down, and Jordan Novick, chief of police, was going to find out what.

FIFTY

"How was your Thanksgiving?" Dr. Shoup asked from the sink, where she was scrubbing her hands.

"Fine." I couldn't believe how little time had passed. It felt as if I'd lived a year since Valerie had shown up at my door. It was Thursday now; not even a week had gone by. The morning was unseasonably warm, the sky a mild blue, with a soft breeze stirring the remaining few leaves on the trees. I lay on the examining table in a gown and socks and panties, keeping the appointment I'd made a lifetime ago, while Valerie sat in the waiting room outside. "I was in Key West. Have you ever been there?" Dr. Shoup shook her head. "How was your Thanksgiving?" I asked.

"Uneventful." Dr. Shoup was not what you'd call talkative. Then again, I hadn't picked her for her scintillating conversation. "Let's take a look."

I stared up at the lights. This afternoon, unless I had to go right to the hospital, I'd go swimming. My bag was in the back of the car, packed with my swimsuit and goggles and towel. Maybe Val would come in the water with me. Maybe, after, I'd take her to the juice bar, point to the table where Vijay and I used to sit before he'd decamped for bluer waters and other adventures. Dr. Shoup's cool fingers skimmed the contours of the bump, pressing lightly on one side, then the other.

"It isn't my hipbone, is it?" I asked, knowing the answer.

Dr. Shoup didn't reply. "That hurt?" she asked, pressing harder.

"Not really."

"How about here?"

I shook my head. "Is it my liver?"

Ominously, she didn't answer. "How have you been feeling?" she asked me instead.

My heart sank. "Fine." I paused. "Worried."

Her fingers ran along my belly, pressing and prodding. Finally she wheeled her little stool away from me, snapping off her rubber gloves. "Follow me."

"Where are we going?"

"Ultrasound."

Holding my gown closed behind me, I followed her down a long hall, so scared I could barely breathe. It must be bad if she was doing an ultrasound without scheduling it ahead of time, without asking for a referral, without billing Blue Cross. I lay on a little cot with my gown pulled up and bunched underneath my breasts, afraid to say anything, afraid to even breathe.

She squirted gel on my belly and pressed the transceiver against it. "Any nausea? Weight gain? Weight loss?"

I shook my head. "No. Nothing I've noticed. Just the lump."

"What have you been using for birth control?"

"Huh? Oh." I felt my face getting hotter. "Condoms. Mostly." The truth was *condoms, occasionally*. Vijay hadn't liked them, and I'd figured we were safe. He'd been tested, he assured me . . . and I, of course, had been a virgin, so if I had AIDS or something, I'd be the first person in the world to get it off a toilet seat, and as for pregnancy . . . "I never really had regular periods, you know, when I was heavy, and then they were kind of random when I was losing weight." Great. Now, in addition to late-stage liver cancer, I probably had a nasty STD, too.

She tilted the screen so that I could see ... what? Something bean-shaped and gray, flickering like a tiny strobe light. "I'd say you're four months along."

For a moment, I thought she was telling me I'd had cancer for four months. When I realized what she meant, I couldn't speak, couldn't breathe. I could only stare at the flickering gray bean that wasn't a tumor, that was the furthest thing away from a tumor that anything could be. "I thought," I said. I swallowed, licked my lips, and tried again. "I never thought ..."

She looked at me briefly, and her expression was not unkind, before she shifted the transceiver on my belly and turned her eyes back to the screen. "I take it this comes as a surprise?"

"Surprise," I repeated. "Well, given that I thought it was cancer, yeah, I'd say that I'm surprised."

I thought I saw the flicker of a smile. "It's an understandable mistake." Which was, of course, what she'd said about my hip-bone diagnosis. Pulling off her gloves, she turned her back to me and stepped on a lever that opened a metal trash can. "Do you want some time to think about your options?"

"No. No." I shook my head and laid my hands on top of the lump. The bump. The baby. Later, there would be the familiar embrace of the water, and the house I'd made my home. I would go out into the sunshine with my best friend and tell her my news, and we'd celebrate together. My time with Vijay, the kisses with Jordan, those would be memories to be cherished and polished and eventually tucked away, like I'd once put away my old, sweet daydreams about Dan Swansea. I would turn my face toward the future and not look back. "Thank you," I said, and if Dr. Shoup was surprised when I hugged her and kissed her cheek, she hid it well.

Valerie was sitting in the waiting room, hair swept up in the same messy ponytail she'd worn since Florida, floating in a pair of my sweatpants and a long-sleeved T-shirt, working her Black-

Berry with her thumbs. At the Key West airport, as the porter loaded our bags in exchange for a tip of my father's old car keys, Val found a pay phone and had a long, murmured conversation with Charlie Carstairs, who'd agreed with, Val said, surprisingly little fuss to give her a month-long leave of absence, which she'd promised to spend with me. She tucked her BlackBerry into her purse and got to her feet as I walked past the receptionist's desk with my hands full of slips of paper: the telephone number of an obstetrician, a prescription for prenatal vitamins, pamphlets about prenatal diet and fetal development. "Is it okay?" she asked, her face tense and forehead furrowed. "Do we need to go to the hospital?"

I shook my head.

"So what, then?" I grabbed her hand and pulled her out the door, down the stairs, out into the daylight. "What's going on?"

I looked at her, smiling so widely it felt like my face would split. "I'm pregnant."

"You're . . . Wait. What? From the married guy? The doctor?"

"It doesn't matter." I bounced up and down, so full of joy that I had to move. "It doesn't matter. It's my baby."

"Oh my God," said Valerie. She leaned against the side of her Jaguar, which she'd liberated from my garage as soon as we were back in Pleasant Ridge. "Oh my God," she said again, and grinned at me. "A baby! Can I have it?"

I stared at her incredulously. "Can you have it?"

"Kidding! Kidding! Come on," she said, and grabbed my hands. "Let's go buy baby stuff and drink champagne!"

"I can't drink . . ." I looked at the pamphlets in my hands. I didn't know anything about having babies, or raising them. I'd have to get books. I'd have to check Wikipedia.

"We'll pretend you don't know. Or you can have sparkling apple juice or some lame shit like that. Come on," she said, "this place gives me the creeps." She was still holding my hands, and she looked at me, her face suddenly serious. "I didn't really want your baby."

"I know, Val."

"I want you to have everything you want. You're my best friend," said Val. The wind lifted her hair, and for a moment I imagined us as girls again, floating in the water, with our hair trailing like ribbons behind us. She held the car door open, and once again, as always, I was powerless to resist her. "Now come on. Get in. There are small, expensive pieces of clothing waiting for us to buy them."

FIFTY-ONE

"She's on the move," said Holly, leaning forward, practically quivering, like a dog on point. Her eyes were trained on the living room window; her breasts strained against the seat belt. Jordan barely noticed. His own eyes were focused on Merry Armbruster's front door. Merry Armbruster, Class of '92, the one Christie Keogh said had spent her fifteenth reunion trying to convert her classmates in the parking lot . . . the one who, Jordan suspected, had been Daniel Swansea's mystery lady. Glen Hammond, the D.A., had gotten the wheels turning when he'd asked whether Dan had heard a really moving grace . . . and when Jordan had called Chip Mason, Chip had told him that Merry Armbruster had dropped Dan off at his place on Sunday morning, which meant, he figured, that Dan and Merry had spent the night together.

When the front door swung open, he braced himself for that lady from *Misery*, Kathy Bates with fire in her eyes and an ax in her hands. But the woman who walked out to her mailbox was barely five feet tall, ax-free, and not even remotely menacing. She wore a zippered down coat that brushed the toes of her thick, insulated purple boots, the kind they'd called moon boots back when Jordan was a kid.

He got out of the car with Holly bounding behind him. "Ms. Armbruster?"

She squinted at them. "Yes?"

"We'd like to ask you a few questions about the high school reunion," said Jordan.

She tugged her hat against her hair. "Come inside," she said, and led them into the living room. Jordan and Holly sat side by side on a sleek leather couch in front of a flat-screen TV that spanned most of the wall.

"That's a big one," Holly said, pointing at the set.

Merry's lips thinned. "It's my parents'. This is their house."

"Are they home?" asked Holly.

She shook her head. "They are in Las Vegas." She raised her chin. " 'Wealth gotten by vanity shall be diminished: but he that gathereth by labour shall increase.' Proverbs 13:11."

"So they're at a casino?" Holly asked.

"What can I help you with?" Merry asked.

Jordan leaned forward. "Did you happen to run into Daniel Swansea on Friday night?"

For a minute, he thought that she wasn't going to say anything—that she was going to press those thin lips together even more tightly, lift her pointy chin even higher, and refuse to answer, or tell him that she wasn't talking without a lawyer. Instead, after a minute, she said, "We prayed together."

"Prayed for what?" asked Holly.

Merry looked at them proudly. "He had a great sin upon his heart. But now he has repented of his wickedness. Now he walks in the light of the Lord and forgiveness. Now he sees . . ."

Jordan cut her off. "Ma'am, was he hurt the night you found him?"

"He was lost," Merry said gently, a schoolteacher correcting a very young child. "He was lost, but now is found. Was blind, but now he sees."

Holly looked at Jordan helplessly. Jordan thought for a minute, then got to his feet, pulling a card out of his wallet and handing it to Merry. "Thank you for your help," he said, imagining the expression that went along with Holly's gasp. "You'll be in touch if you need us?"

Merry tucked the card into her pocket. "Take care," said Jordan, and Merry replied, "God bless," and then locked her parents' door behind them.

"So what now?" Holly asked once the heater was on and their seat belts were fastened. She squinted through the windshield, staring at the Armbrusters' house. "We can't do a search?" Holly's face suggested that she knew the answer to the question even before she'd asked it. "She did something to him. I just know she did."

Jordan nodded. "I agree. But I'm not sure that what she did to him was wrong." He paused, struggling for the words. "Maybe it was a corrective." He thought of Dan Swansea, huddled in the handicapped cell, Dan Swansea saying *I did a terrible thing. I know that now.* "And there's nothing else we can do. We've got no warrant, no grounds for an interview."

"So that's it?" Holly cried. "She just gets away with it?"

"We'll keep an eye on her," he promised. "On both of them. If they ever slip again, we'll be ready."

FIFTY-TWO

"You met someone," said Sasha Devine. She looked Jordan up and down. "Is it that Adelaide person?"

He stared at her, open-mouthed. She met his look with a smile. "Maybe you're not the only one with a small, quiet place in your mind."

He could only look at her, speechless.

"Fell for the suspect?" Sasha seemed amused. "Is she a good person?"

"I think so."

"She's back home, right?"

"I guess." He shrugged. "I don't know if she wants to see me."

"Stop by," Sasha suggested. "Bring her flowers or something. Ladies love the flowers."

"I was going to arrest her," Jordan said. "Won't that make things weird?" He left out the part about how he'd already been in her house; how he'd fallen down in front of her; how they'd kissed, which would, of course, only make things weirder and would not bode well for his next performance evaluation.

Sasha shrugged. "I took one of my old boyfriends back after he cheated on me with my sister," she said. "And gave us both chlamydia." She made a face. "Bad example. Anyhow, I bet she'd be glad to see you." Jordan wasn't sure he agreed. "So what do you think, really?" Sasha asked. He knew what she was asking him: What happened to Daniel Swansea that night? Had Addie and Val gotten away with a crime?

"I think," he said after a minute, "that Dan Swansea has mended his ways." He thought some more. "I think that he was a guy whose ways needed mending."

"Fair enough," said Sasha.

Jordan got back into his car. Downtown, the foofy little candle-and-potpourri shop had gone out of business, replaced by a place called In Bloom. There, he bought flowers, a bouquet of hot-pink tulips wrapped in pale-green crepe paper, out of season and insanely expensive. He filled his tank and washed his windows, and when he couldn't stall any longer, he drove to Crescent Drive.

FIFTY-THREE

Addie didn't answer his knocks. She didn't respond when he rang the bell. When he punched in her number on his cell phone, her phone rang and rang until it went to voice mail, where a computerized voice invited him to leave a message, not sounding as if it cared much one way or another whether he did. Jordan hung up the phone, waited for five minutes, then started knocking again, calling "Police!" Finally he heard her voice, coming from the upstairs bedroom window.

"Jordan?" On her face, he saw what he'd seen in the photograph on her brother's wall—hope. Faint, but still there. Then she turned away.

"Addie. Hey. I just want to talk."

Her voice floated out the window. "There's really not much to talk about."

"There's everything to talk about. Come on, Addie. Please?"

For a minute, he was sure that she wouldn't come down, that she'd leave him standing there with his tulips. Then the front door opened, and she was standing in front of him in black pants and a loose red top, with a towel in her hand and her hair—light brown, not blond—still damp from the shower.

He stared at her. "Your hair's different."

She touched it shyly. "I decided I wasn't meant to live life as a blonde." She smoothed one hand over her shirt. "Valerie's the blonde."

He cleared his throat. "Did you guys have a safe trip home?"

"It was fine."

"Are you . . ." He cleared his throat. "In Florida, your friend said you were sick."

She smiled, then ducked her head. "I'm not sick. It was a misunderstanding. I'm fine. I'm . . ."

From the top of the stairs, he heard someone call "Addie?" As he watched, Val came down the stairs, barefoot in sweatpants, with a book in her hands. "Did you read this one yet? You're supposed to be eating kale. Like, crates of it. Or else your kid could have . . ." She bounded to the bottom of the staircase. Jordan recognized the book she was carrying from Patti's shelf: *What to Expect When You're Expecting.* "A neural-tube defect? What the hell is that?"

Jordan looked at Valerie, then back at Addie. "You're pregnant?"

She blushed. "A little bit, yeah."

Jordan's head was spinning. "You . . ." He stared, remembering the condoms, and also Mrs. Bass's insistence that she didn't have a boyfriend. "Did you go to a sperm bank?"

"Something like that," she said.

He made himself stop staring and tried to remember why he was there, what he'd meant to tell her. "I wanted to tell you I'm sorry. About . . ." His voice trailed off. He had no idea what to call what had happened between them, no certainty of what he was sorry for except that he was indeed sorry.

"I appreciate that. Dan's okay, right?"

Depends how you define "okay," thought Jordan, remembering

Dan curled on his side in the jail cell and Meredith Armbruster's calm assertion that they had prayed together. "He's fine. But that's the other reason I came. I wanted to make sure he hasn't been bothering either one of you."

Val's face darkened. Addie's hand crept back to her belly. "No," she said. "Should I be expecting him?"

"I don't think so. I think he's turned over a new leaf, or he's trying to."

Val snorted. Addie said nothing. The wind gusted, making the bare branches of the trees in her front yard shake. He saw Addie shiver, and he wished he could hold her, open up his jacket and tuck her tight against him. "Go inside," Jordan said gruffly. "It's cold out here." He remembered the flowers and held them out to her. "These are for you."

"Oh." She took them and held them awkwardly in one hand, barely noticing as Val drifted discreetly back up the stairs. "Thanks, they're beautiful."

"Addie, listen," he said. "Do you think we could get together sometime? For a drink, or dinner, or something?" His heartbeat thundered in his ears, and his palms and armpits started to sweat.

She looked at him, her smile fading. "You've been in my house," she said. He didn't answer. "You met my brother, I bet." He waited. "You chased me all the way down to Florida ..."

" 'Chased' is a little bit strong. It was pursuit." He looked at her, straight-faced. "Official police business."

She narrowed her eyes. "You were showing people my picture. And it wasn't even a good one. And we ..." She ducked her head. That pretty flush was back, coloring her cheeks and her neck.

"Well, that's just standard police procedure. Didn't I mention it the last time I was here? We do that with all our suspects. First the kissing, then the arresting. The kissing calms them down."

Her laughter had a lovely, musical sound. He went on. "I'm sorry about being in your house. But we did have some pretty compelling circumstantial evidence. And your door was unlocked."

"Was not."

"Was too."

"You had a key under your welcome mat."

"That's not the same thing."

"Have dinner with me."

She leaned against the side of the doorway and sighed, with one hand on her belly. "It won't work."

"Is it because of the baby?" She didn't answer. Jordan wiped his palms on the sides of his pants and plunged on. "My wife and I, my ex-wife, we couldn't have kids. I always wanted them—she did, too—but . . ." He shut his mouth.

Addie shook her head again, looking as if she might cry. "I wish things were different. But I'm not brave."

"You are." He looked into her eyes, making her believe it. He was sweating everywhere, hands and armpits and behind his knees, knowing just how important this was and certain that he was going to screw it up somehow, the way he'd screwed everything up lately. "We're good together. You know we are."

She didn't answer. She didn't say yes, but she didn't say no either. Jordan kept talking. He wasn't sure he could have stopped even if he'd wanted to. "Just a chance," he said. "That's all I want."

Addie shook her head. "The baby . . ." She paused, regrouped, and tried again. "The, um, father . . ."

She seemed about to say more when Jordan interrupted. "I don't care about that. As long as it's over."

"Oh, it is so over."

"Then that's fine."

She looked at him, standing there in the cold. For a long moment he was sure she was going to shake her head and shut the door. Instead, she exhaled slowly and looked at him, her face alight, smiling. "Would you like to come inside?" she asked. She held the door open, and Jordan followed her into the warmth and the light.

FIFTY-FOUR

"Can I just say how much I love this?" Valerie asked. It was a ripe June afternoon. We were in the backyard, barefoot in shorts and T-shirts and canvas gloves, digging up a patch of grass in the backyard, where my mother had once had her garden.

"What, weeding?"

"No. Your whole setup." She beamed at me. She'd tied her hair back in a bandanna. "You. Jordan. The baby. It's so *South Pacific*!"

"People are going to think it's weird." I sank my spade into the dirt, then got up, setting my hands in the small of my back and stretching. My due date was ten days away, and I was just starting to think through the logistics: how, in all probability, my daughter's skin would be darker than mine and Jordan's. Maybe they'd think she was adopted . . . or that I was the nanny. That would be interesting, I guessed.

I rubbed my back again, then scratched my belly, which itched all the time. In the wake of our adventure—and that was consistently how she referred to it, as "our adventure"—I'd seen a lot of my best friend. After her month off, Val had gone back to work, and back to her condo in Chicago, but she'd signed up for improv classes—in case, she said, she decided to leave the glamorous life of a meteorologist for the even more glamorous life of a thirtysomething wannabe actress. Every weekend she came to Pleasant Ridge, taking over the guest bedroom where no guests had ever slept, filling the house with her music, her chatter, her self-help books and baby books, the bags of designer maternity clothes and crates of kale, her running shoes, unlaced and stuffed with her socks, by the door. Once in a while, she'd join me and Jon for Wednesday-night pierogi. Jon was delighted that he was going to be an uncle—he'd made a sign with the baby's due date for his room, and one for the refrigerator, and a reminder card for his wallet—and he'd used his employee discount at Walgreens to buy a NUMBER ONE BABY onesie, a state-of-the-art wipe warmer, and more diapers than I'd need for a year.

"Who cares what people think?" Val asked impatiently. "Jeez. You can't worry about that. You should see what they say about me on the Internet."

I grinned at her new-and-improved, post–Key West attitude. The truth was, Jordan and I had talked about it. He'd told me I was worrying too much—"buying trouble" was how he put it. There were kids who didn't look like their parents all over the place now, and nontraditional arrangements were normal—"practically normal," I thought he'd said. He knew of kids with single moms, with two moms, with two dads, which meant that nobody would look at us strangely, or comment on how the two of us and the baby didn't match. "If anyone asks, tell them you got her at Target," he'd said. I figured at some point I'd have to come up with an explanation: for the world, for my daughter, maybe even for Vijay, whom I hadn't been in touch with—but that could wait. For now, I was painting the bedroom, assembling the stroller and the crib, installing the car seat, taking classes in infant first aid and CPR . . . and being with Jordan, who came by every night after work.

Val stood up, groaning dramatically (she'd been weeding for all of seven minutes). Then, shading her eyes, she looked out across the street. "Check it out," she said, pointing across the street. "New neighbors."

"Really?" The DiMeos' house—for that was how I would always think of it, no matter how many times it changed hands—had gone on the market in April. The FOR SALE sign had come down six weeks later, but in the euphoric blur of my pregnancy and being with Jordan, I hadn't spared the new homeowners a thought. Now I watched as a moving van pulled up to the curb, and two men got out of the cab. One of them had a braided goatee and an iPod strapped to his arm. The other had rubber plugs the size of wine corks in his earlobes. They walked around to the back of the truck and pulled open its gated door.

A hybrid car whispered to a stop behind the moving van, and a man and a woman got out. She looked to be about our age—in her early thirties—and she was pregnant.

Valerie squealed and gave me a little shove. "Oh my God, it's perfect! Go say hi!"

I shook my head, feeling my little-girl shyness rushing back. The woman was staring at the DiMeos' house—her house now. Then she turned, said something to the movers, and turned again and looked at us.

"Go on," Val said. I took a deep breath and crossed the street to the DiMeos' front yard, where our new neighbor was waiting. "Hi," I said. "I'm Addie Downs. Welcome to the neighborhood."

The woman's face lit up. "Hey, you too!" she said.

I patted my belly. "Me too."

"Do you know what you're having?"

"A girl," I said, and her smile widened.

"Me too!" Her name was Pam Rollins, wife of Sean, twenty-two weeks along. "It's so pretty here. I didn't think I'd like it. Sean and I lived in a high-rise, so this ..." She looked around and made a wry, funny face. "Big change. We're not used to all this green. But, you know, the city . . ." Her voice trailed off. "We wanted to start our family somewhere safe."

I nodded. I could have told her that places that look safe sometimes aren't. I could have said that pretty houses and neatly kept lawns didn't mean that bad things didn't happen in the basements or the backyards or the woods . . . but I kept my mouth shut. Maybe someday she'd learn for herself. Or maybe she'd be lucky and she would never find out.

Valerie, who'd pulled off her gloves and stuck them in her back pocket, crossed the street to join us. "Valerie, this is Pam Rollins."

"You're living in my old house," said Val.

Pam nodded . . . then, shyly, she said, "You're on Fox News, right?"

"I am," said Val, and turned to me. "See, not everyone gets the weather on their cell phone."

"Right," I said, and smiled at my friend before turning back to Pam. "Do you need anything? Directions to the grocery store? Pediatricians' names?"

"We're all set," she said. "This is just so perfect!"

"Perfect," Val agreed. "Maybe your girls will be friends."

ACKNOWLEDGMENTS

As always, I am grateful for the hard work and stewardship of my agent, Joanna Pulcini, who is dedicated, enthusiastic, and given to writing "make this more poetic!" in my margins (which, it turns out, does not mean that the passage in question should rhyme). Joanna believed in me six books ago and believes in me still, and I'm so happy that we've built our careers together. And that I can stop trying to gratuitously insert the word "Nantucket" into my novels.

My amazing editor, Greer Hendricks, has been with me for every book I've written. Greer is a shining star for her good judgment, humor, generosity, kindness, and endless reservoirs of calm.

My thanks to Joanna's assistant, Molly Ahrens; Greer's assistant, Sarah Walsh; and my assistant, the funny, friendly, and altogether fabulous Meghan Burnett.

I am grateful to work with everyone at Atria Books, the most enthusiastic, attentive, and hardworking publishers in the business. My thanks to my publishers, Judith Curr at Atria and Carolyn Reidy at Simon & Schuster; to Nancy Inglis, who has the unfortunate job of copyediting my manuscripts; and to Deb Darrock, Natalie White, Kathleen Schmidt, Lisa Keim, Christine Duplessis, Craig Dean, and Jeanne Lee. Across the pond, I am very lucky to work with Suzanne Baboneau, Julie Wright, Ian Chapman, Jessica Leeke, and Nigel Stoneman at Simon & Schuster UK.

Lucky is the writer who has publicist Marcy Engelman and her girls, Dana Gidney Fetaya and Emily Gambir, on her team, and who gets the fabulous Jessica Fee to arrange her speaking gigs.

For technical expertise, my thanks to Detective Sergeant Gary Pierce of the Haddonfield, New Jersey, Police Department and Detective Sergeant John Stillwagon of the Lower Merion Police Department; to Sara Jacobson for explaining the legalities of fictitious hit-and-runs at high school reunions; and to Sue Serio of Fox 29 Philadelphia for details on the secret lives of on-air personalities.

Curtis Sittenfeld and Elizabeth LaBan were generous and perceptive first readers.

I am lucky to have wonderful friends and family, near, far, and on Facebook, who supply me with laughs, companionship, and raw material (a special shout-out to Jeff Greenstein for being hilarious and helpful and loving Harry Crews's *Body* as much as I did). Jake and Joe Weiner are not only my little brothers, they also take care of me out on the coast, and my sister Molly is an endless font of inspiration and amusement. I'm grateful to my Nanna, Faye Frumin; to my mom, Fran; and to my mother's partner, Clair Kaplan, for laughing with me and at me. Thanks also to Terri Gottlieb, who takes care of my girls while I'm working.

Last but never least, all my love to my husband, Adam, and our girls, Phoebe and Lucy, who make everything else worthwhile . . . and to all of my readers, who've come with me this far.